THE WITCH'S CANDY

Matilda allowed him to place a small piece of candy she'd made on her tongue. The ginger in it gave her a jolt as the sweet began to melt in her mouth.

"You next," she said. Taking another piece between two fingers, she offered it to him. He ate right from her hand, closing his lips over her fingers and sucking the sweet into his mouth. His lips barely touched her flesh, but still she shivered.

Something extraordinary was already happening. The tingle that had started on her tongue spread through her body like wildfire. She felt, so clearly and warmly, the place on her fingers where Declan's mouth had briefly touched her skin. She still felt the brush of his fingers against her mouth.

She looked up at him, meeting his stare. His eyes burned the way her soul did, with dark fire. Her fingers itched to reach out and touch his harsh face, to trace the line of his jaw and the outline of his lips. She wanted to push back the strand of hair that had fallen over his forehead, then trail her fingers over his face.

"It works fast," Declan said softly.

"Yes, it does," Matilda agreed in a whisper. Why deny what she felt? Why pretend she didn't look at him and feel something wonderful? Something powerful, and knee-weakening, and truly magical. Under the candy's spell, there was no reason to pretend. No reason to hold back.

Into The Woods

Linda Jones

LOVE SPELL   NEW YORK CITY

For Ginny

A LOVE SPELL BOOK®

February 2001

Published by

Dorchester Publishing Co., Inc.
276 Fifth Avenue
New York, NY 10001

Cover art by John Ennis.
www.ennisart.com.

ISBN 0-505-52428-7

Printed in the United States of America.

Visit us on the web at www.dorchesterpub.com.

Into The Woods

Chapter One

Tanglewood, Mississippi, 1875

"Everyone knows witches make the best sweets," Gretchen said softly as she followed the narrow path through the woods. Hanson, her twin brother, walked close behind her. Even though he was only a few minutes younger than she, he sometimes acted more like a baby than a nine-year-old.

"What if she wants my spit again?" he asked warily.

"Then you'll give it to her," Gretchen snapped. "You have plenty to spare."

It was full-blown summer, and the low branches of leafy trees and straggling bushes grew over the path that wound through the woods between their farm and Matilda Candy's cottage. Gretchen pushed supple branches out of the way and continued on, determined. It was Wednesday, and the witch always made sweets on Wednesday.

"Mother will miss us," Hanson protested.

Gretchen stopped in the middle of the overgrown path and spun to face her brother. They stood nose-to-nose. "She is *not* our mother!"

"She said we were to call her—."

"She is our father's wife, but that does not make her our mother," Gretchen interrupted. She had her suspicions about Stella Hazelrig, the woman who had been her stepmother for the past three months. "And she certainly won't miss us," she added softly. "Even if we never come home, she won't miss us." She turned her nose up in the air. "She'd probably be *glad* if we never came home."

Hanson looked like he wanted to argue. But he didn't.

Soon enough they reached the end of the path, and there before them stood the Candy house. Made of stone and cypress, with an arched doorway and many windows, it was very different from Gretchen's own family's simple home. Matilda Candy's cottage looked much older and sturdier, as if it had been standing in this clearing forever and would continue to stand, unchanged, for countless years to come.

All the fun took place behind the cottage, Gretchen knew. There, Miss Matilda's large separate kitchen stood, her huge garden bloomed all year round, and a gigantic greenhouse held all kinds of exotic plants. Sometimes the witch worked in the courtyard between the kitchen and the greenhouse, grinding up plants or simmering some evil brew in her huge, black cauldron.

Gretchen closed her eyes and took a deep breath. "Do you smell that?" she whispered.

"Yep," Hanson answered softly. "What do you think she's made this time? Caramels? Spiced nuts?" Those were his favorites.

Gretchen took a deep breath. "A sweet bread, I think," she announced as she breathed out again. "And maybe . . . something else."

No longer worried about the outcome of their adventure, Hanson stepped past his sister. He rubbed his palms together. "If she's in the greenhouse, we can swipe whatever we want."

Sometimes they were lucky, and Matilda Candy was busy in her greenhouse while the sweets cooled. Staying close together, Gretchen and Hanson ran on light feet to the corner of the house. Hugging the wall, they rounded the corner, keeping an eye out at all times for the witch. Luck was not with them today, though. They could see her through the open window of her kitchen. She stood before the huge brick oven that formed one wall of the building, peeking in at something, squinting as if she were not quite happy with what she saw. Bread cooled on the windowsill.

"Until we met Miss Matilda," Hanson confided in a whisper, "I thought all witches were ugly."

Matilda Candy was not ugly, not at all. She had fair hair, a blonde not quite as pale as the twins' own curls, and strange eyes that were not blue or green—but both. Gretchen had looked into those eyes many times. They were pale green on the inside, but were rimmed with a darker blue. It was hard not to stare, when those witch's eyes landed on you.

"Perhaps she used to be ugly, but cast a spell to make herself beautiful," Gretchen answered, her voice low. "Maybe at night she turns into an ugly old hag."

They watched as the witch used a long wooden paddle to shut the heavy iron door of her stove. She disappeared from view for a moment, and then the door to the kitchen opened wide and she stepped outside and took a deep breath.

She never wore shoes, except when she walked to town to sell her bread and sweets to Mr. Fox at the general store. For that long walk she put on a pair of high-top leather boots that looked as old as the house she lived in. But for now she was barefooted, as usual. Her pale green skirt was a few inches shorter than was proper, revealing her ankles, and the sleeves of her white blouse had been rolled up to her elbows. Her fair hair had been fashioned into two long, braided pigtails that fell over her shoulders.

Gretchen held her breath. Hanson cowered behind her. And then the witch looked directly at them.

"Well?" she said in a voice that sounded deceptively sweet. "Why are you two skulking about?"

Matilda watched as first one golden head and then another appeared around the corner. From the kitchen window she'd seen the Hazelrig twins run from the woods to the front of the house, and then she'd heard them whispering as they crept closer and closer.

"Good afternoon," she said, smiling. "What brings you to my house today?"

As always, Gretchen was in the lead and her brother, Hanson, followed close behind. The little girl stepped boldly forward, her big blue eyes calm yet sad. "We're so sorry to disturb you," she said, her voice nearly forlorn. "You see, our stepmother took us into the forest and left us there with no food. She hates us, and she wanted us to get lost and starve to death so she won't have to bother with us anymore." Gretchen's lower lip trembled.

Matilda withheld a laugh. The child was putting on quite an act. Her poor brother simply looked confused; as always.

"We did get lost," Gretchen continued. "For a terribly long time. We wandered around in circles, holding hands, afraid we'd never find our way out of the forest."

"I see," Matilda said calmly.

"We're frightfully hungry," Gretchen finished, and then she turned to her brother. "Aren't we, Hanson?"

Hanson nodded his head quickly. "Frightfully," he reiterated in a soft voice.

"Well, then," Matilda said. "I suppose I must feed you."

Hanson grinned widely. Gretchen gave in to a small, secret smile.

"There is a price, however," Matilda added softly. Immediately, the twins' expressions changed from happy to suspicious. "Hanson, have you eaten onions in the past three days?"

The young man sighed. "No." Then he gave his sister a poke in the shoulder. "I told you she'd want my spit again!" he hissed.

"Not today," Matilda said as she turned toward the kitchen. "Come back tomorrow. I'll need it then."

She filled a plate with fresh-made bread and a few slices of cheese. When she stepped outside and handed the plate to the children, they looked more than a little disappointed. "Eat this," Matilda said. "When you're finished, I'll give you sweets for dessert. She set her eyes on the shy Hanson. "I have caramels. Your favorite."

The boy's pale blue eyes went wide as Gretchen took the plate of bread and cheese. "How does she know caramels are my favorite?" he whispered to his sister, his voice no doubt much louder than he intended.

"Because she's a witch, stupid," Gretchen snapped as she turned away from Matilda. "She knows *everything*."

Matilda watched as the children sat on a grassy spot and ate their bread and cheese. A witch, indeed. As if any magic powers were the source of her knowledge. She knew caramels were Hanson's favorites because every time he spied a plate his eyes lit up and he licked his lips. She smiled.

Matilda didn't mind that some of the people of Tanglewood, Mississippi, thought her to be a witch. There were only a few who hissed and whispered when she saw them in town, or who stared at her as if they *really* believed. Those were enough to keep the rumors circulating, however, especially since Matilda lived alone and had no time for socializing or making certain the people of Tanglewood knew the rumors were untrue.

Matilda enjoyed the reputation, though. It gave her some measure of privacy and, like her grandmother before her, it kept unwanted visitors at bay. She only saw people when she went to town to sell her goods, or when they came to her for a cure or a beauty cream. Making bread, sweets, rose water and other rose-based goods kept Matilda busy, and she did a very good business in pomades and beauty creams, as well. She knew herbs and their uses almost as well as her grandmother, the first Matilda Candy, had. Matilda used her granny's recipes for almost everything, of course, relying on the books and notes from the shelves that lined the wall of the main room in her cottage.

If people believed her to be a witch, who was Matilda to tell them differently? Who knew, maybe it was true. Granny had always sworn that all the women on her side of the family had hidden powers and unearthly gifts. Matilda had no unearthly gifts that she knew of, though Granny had always told her to be patient. *"The time will come, Matilda,"* she'd said on more than one occasion, *"when your gift will be revealed to you. When you need it."*

Granny had been gone two years now, and Matilda missed her as much today as she had the day of the funeral.

When the bread and cheese were gone, Gretchen and Hanson came to her for their treats. The caramels were the real reason for their bold trip to her house, she knew, and for the lie they'd told about their father's new wife.

Matilda fetched a few caramels from the kitchen. She'd made the sweets early this morning, and a few of them were still warm. The children offered their hands, palms upward, and Matilda placed two pieces on each palm.

"Did you know," she said, her eyes on Gretchen, "that

if you lie often enough you might forget how to tell the truth? If you tell too many tales, no one will ever believe you, not even when you swear something to be true."

"I *never* lie," Gretchen said, pulling back her hand.

Matilda smiled. "Of course not. I just wanted to warn you against future falsehoods. Too many tales and one's tongue gets so tied in knots the words become entangled."

Sweets in hand, the twins ran away.

"Tomorrow, Hanson," Matilda called after them. "Don't forget. I know where you live," she added as they disappeared into the forest. She was certain she heard the young man squeal in response.

Declan Harper shook his head at the poor selection of cigars. As soon as the remodeling of his new house was finished and he'd hired a foreman to see to the running of the plantation, he'd buy this general store and see that it was properly run. He had no patience for ineptitude, and everywhere he turned he was confronted with the crudeness and ignorance of Tanglewood.

One thought calmed him: In a few years time he'd own the whole damn town. The inept would be replaced, one by one. His town would run smoothly and efficiently.

A woman entered the general store, hauling two chattering youngsters with her. They were a matching set, except that one was a pretty little girl in a faded blue dress and the other was a boy in a battered hat and worn denim trousers and a homespun shirt. "You're staying with me today," the woman said sharply. "I'll need help carrying the supplies, and when we get home the house needs a good cleaning from top to bottom."

"But I have to go see the witch today," the young man wailed. "She said that if I don't, she'll . . . she'll . . ."

He seemed unable to continue, but his sister finished for him. "If Hanson doesn't fulfill Miss Matilda's request," the girl said calmly, "she'll shove him in her big

15

oven, cook him until he's crispy, and eat him for dinner.
Witches *do* eat children for dinner, you know."

"Gretchen Hazelrig," the woman snapped. "I will listen to no more of your tales. There are no witches in
Mississippi."

Declan smiled. How could he have forgotten Matilda
Candy? Years ago, as a young man no bigger than the
poor lad who was presently being led around by the ear,
he'd lived on his father's farm just outside Tanglewood.
Matilda Candy, a widow who lived alone just south of
town, had been called a witch even then. The stories told
about her were outrageous and sometimes frightening,
but Declan had never been afraid.

In his youthful wanderings, he'd stumbled upon the
witch's cottage and found a kind of refuge there. More
than once he'd made strange exchanges with her; candy
for spittle. He'd spit in some concoction she was grinding
in an earthenware bowl, and she'd make him a whole
plate of hard molasses candy.

Yes, many strange stories had circulated about Matilda
Candy, and he suspected that as a child he'd only heard
a few of them; and he'd understood even fewer. All he
knew, all he'd cared about, was that she was kind to him
when no one else was, that she never made fun of his
mother's Irish brogue or his father's tendency to get and
remain drunk, like many others had. She didn't care that
he was poor, that he never had any good clothes, that his
boots had holes in them. She'd smiled, and given him
sweets, and told him he was a fine boy who would grow
into a fine man.

And on the day he left, his father dead, his mother a
widow, his sisters so afraid of what awaited them out
West that they cried all the time, Matilda Candy had
given him a sack of candy and sweet bread and assured
him, with a smile, that he was going to be all right. That
one day he would be a very rich man. That one day he

would return to Tanglewood and all his dreams would come true.

And she'd been right. He was doing well. He was a very rich man. And as soon as Vanessa Arrington agreed to be his wife, all his dreams would come true.

Matilda Candy had been an old woman then, when he'd been a boy. She was surely ancient by now!

As he left the general store, cigars forgotten, it occurred to Declan that the "witch" might have an answer to his current problem.

Matilda used the wooden pestle to grind the carefully measured ingredients into the marble mortar. Working at the bench in her courtyard, as she had been all afternoon, she already had the ingredients worked into the fine powder necessary for this potion. Where was Hanson?

Rose water alone would do in a pinch, but Granny always swore that the spit of a young man made this formula extra special.

She'd just about given up on the young man when she heard him running through the woods. He broke free of the trees but did not slow his step. In fact, he ran harder as he approached.

"I meant to be here sooner," he said breathlessly as he slowed his step and approached her warily. "But my mother . . . I mean, my father's new wife wouldn't let me come."

"But you're here now," Matilda said calmly.

"I'm supposed to be cleaning the barn, so I'm going to have to spit and run."

She smiled and continued to grind. "And where's your sister?"

Hanson grinned as he took a long, deep breath. He still hadn't recovered from his run. "Gretchen's learning to cook."

"That's lovely," Matilda said.

Hanson shook his head. "I don't think it's so lovely. I'm going to have to eat her cooking!"

Matilda laughed, and her laughter seemed to do something magical to the boy. He was less afraid of her, now. More relaxed.

"She'll never be as good a cook as you," he said, sincerity in his young voice.

"Well, thank you, Hanson," she said as she held the mortar in both hands, lifted it from the bench, and held it close to his face. "Now, spit."

He did as she asked. Matilda glanced into the mortar and held it out once more. "Again."

Hanson complied, and Matilda was satisfied.

"Wait right here," she said, setting the mortar aside and hurrying to the kitchen where a plate of treats waited. Sweet bread, caramels, hard candy, sugared pecans. All of Hanson's favorites.

When she stepped outside she saw the young man leaning over the mortar, studying the mess inside with a grimace on his face.

"Here you go. A small thank-you for your contribution."

Hanson took the plate, eyeing the goodies there with a new suspicion. "Can I ask . . ." he began shyly.

"Anything," Matilda said, returning her attentions to the old mortar and pestle.

Balancing the plate in one hand, Hanson pointed at the mortar. "What *is* that?"

"This is a very old recipe for beauty cream," Matilda said as she worked the contents into a paste. "*Very* old. There are herbs and roots and many other components to this particular formula, but the secret ingredient is the spit of a fine young man."

"You don't use that nasty stuff on your face, do you?"

Matilda laughed. "By the time I'm finished, it won't be nasty stuff. But no," she added. "I don't use it."

"You don't need any beauty cream," he said, holding

his head high. "You're already beautiful, even if you are a witch." All at once his face turned beet-red. Matilda was unable to tell if he was embarrassed because he'd said she was beautiful or because he'd called her a witch to her face.

"That's a very sweet thing for you to say, Hanson," she said.

He glanced down at the goodies on his plate. "Nobody spit in any of the candy, did they?"

"Of course not."

Hanson grinned widely as he backed away. "That's good."

"Share with your sister," Matilda said without looking up from her work.

"I will," he said as he turned and took off at a slow jog. "I have to get home!"

Matilda worked the beauty cream for a while longer, before setting it in the afternoon sun to settle for a while. Most of her chores were done for the day, but if she hurried she'd be able to put together one more batch of candied pecans. Tomorrow she'd carry bread and sweets to the general store, as she always did on Friday, and the pecans always sold especially well.

As the sun went down she brought the mortar in and set it on the table in her work area. Tomorrow morning, early, she'd add the last few ingredients and then the rose water, mixing until she had a wonderful beauty cream that fetched a good price from a special customer.

It was completely dark when a firm knock sounded at her door. She wasn't surprised. When people wanted a cure, a special tea, or just advice, they almost always came to her under cover of darkness. It wouldn't do for their neighbors to know they'd consulted a witch, even though many of their neighbors were frequent visitors to Matilda's cottage as well.

She opened the door expecting to see a familiar face, someone who came to her on a regular basis for a healing ointment, or a cure for a baby's rash, or an herb tea to prevent another baby from coming too soon.

The door swung open on a very tall man she had never seen before. He was dressed in a finely cut dark suit that should have made him look civilized, but somehow . . . didn't. Well-groomed, with a clean-shaven jaw and very dark brown hair cut in a precise short style, at first glance he almost looked like a gentleman. Almost. But his shoulders were too wide; this man had done physical labor and done it often. His features were handsome but sharp, tense, as if he were never at peace. His hands were large and lightly calloused, and his eyes . . . his dark brown eyes were much too passionate and fierce to be gentlemanly.

"Yes?" she prompted.

"I must have the wrong place," he said, taking a step back to glance at the cottage, and then looking past her into her home. "I'm looking for the Candy house."

"This is the Candy house," she said softly.

He shook his head. "No, I'm looking for Mrs. Matilda Candy." Annoyance crept into his voice. Matilda found herself thinking that a gentleman would have more patience than this man possessed.

"*I'm* Matilda Candy."

His fierce eyes narrowed suspiciously. His clean-shaven jaw clenched. "Impossible."

Matilda smiled at his obvious confusion, as she realized his mistake. "You must be looking for my grandmother."

He sighed, almost in relief. "Your grandmother. Yes, of course. Is she here?"

Her smile faded. "She passed away two years ago."

The tall man in the doorway looked saddened, but not devastated. Still, she was warmed to see the flash of true dismay in his eyes. Ah, she thought, a true gentleman didn't reveal his feelings so easily.

"I'm sorry to hear that." His warm eyes roamed her

face. "Your grandmother was a wonderful lady. I haven't seen her in years, obviously, but I was rather hoping she might help me with a . . . small problem. I'm sorry to have bothered you."

Her heart softened when he called Granny a "wonderful lady," and she couldn't help but wonder what "small problem" had brought this man to her. A rash? A persistent stomachache? Trouble sleeping, perhaps. She wanted to know, so she spoke before he could turn to leave.

"My grandmother taught me much of her craft in the years I lived with her. Perhaps I can help you."

Once again the man looked past her, and she knew what he saw. Tables and shelves heavily laden with books and jars of precious oils. Earthenware pots and wooden spoons. Glass jars of herbs and roots. It was a room for working, not visiting. A laboratory of sorts. There was no traditional parlor for entertaining in the Candy house, no vases of flowers or useless knick-knacks on the tables. Matilda *worked* at her tables.

She had long ago accepted who she was, and she apologized to no one. Not ever. She fearlessly looked this almost-civilized man directly in the eye when he returned his full and somehow unnerving attention to her.

"Perhaps you can," he said, determination in his voice. "Miss Candy, I need a love potion."

Chapter Two

For a moment, a split second perhaps, Declan had actually believed in magic. The woman who'd come to the door was enough like the Matilda Candy he remembered to give him pause, if only for a minute, when she'd said that she was the woman for whom he'd asked.

Her small stature was the same; neither Matilda Candy stood taller than five foot two. The pigtails were the same, though he remembered gray braids instead of golden. He'd never seen the old Miz Candy wear shoes, and this one's small feet were bare against the smooth wooden floor. The eyes were . . . similar, a green he remembered from years ago. But as he looked closer he realized that this Matilda Candy's eyes were rimmed in darker blue.

And those eyes laughed at him now. "A love potion," she repeated. "Really, Mr. . . ."

"Harper," he said. "Declan Harper."

"Mr. Harper," she said, her eyes dancing with an amusement she could not, or would not, hide. "While it's

true that my grandmother passed on quite a bit of knowledge to me, I must confess there were no love potions
included. I'm sorry." She looked as if she were about to
gently close the door in his face.

To prevent that from happening, he reached out and
grabbed the edge of the door in one hand. "Can I come
in?" he asked. "Just for a minute."

With a barely disguised sigh, she moved back and invited him to enter. He stepped into a room he remembered well; not much had changed. The rug at the center
was a bit more worn than he remembered, and there were
more books on the crowded shelves, but all in all it was
very much the same. The room was magical, interesting,
different, as was the woman in it.

"I used to visit your grandmother," he began, looking
around the familiar room. He'd never felt such a warm
fondness for any place he'd called home. He smiled at
the colored jars filled with God-knew-what, and at the
books so old the spines were falling apart. "I'd spit in
her potions and she'd give me hard molasses candy."

"Really?" There was a touch of genuine interest in the
woman's voice, a new lilt. "Why, just today . . ."
Abruptly she stopped speaking, and when he turned to
look at her she pursed her lips. "It's not important."

"Mrs. Candy was always very kind to me," Declan
said softly.

"She was a kind woman."

Intrigued, Declan studied the young Matilda Candy,
looking her up and down. She wasn't what one might
call beautiful, but she was very pretty, in an odd sort of
way. Already he'd discovered that she had an expressive
face. She smiled, she wrinkled her nose, her eyes told
too much. Her manner of dress was unconventional, but
the skirt and plain blouse she wore showed off a shapely,
uncorseted figure. Her hairstyle, those golden braids,
while definitely not the height of fashion, suited her. She
had a face like a pixie, and pigtails to match. Yes, she

belonged in this strange room as much as her grandmother had, was an integral part of its charm.

"Miss Candy," he said in answer to a question he felt
was unspoken between them, his voice stern. "I do not
believe in witchcraft."

She lifted her eyebrows again, pinning glittering,
amused green and blue eyes on him. He was surprised
she didn't out-and-out laugh.

"Then why are you here?"

"Because I believe your grandmother had a gift." He
reached within himself for patience, which was never
easy. When he wanted something he wanted it done without unnecessary explanations!

Her smile faded, and he wondered if he'd said something wrong.

"Call it a talent or a skill, if you like," he said tersely.
"Whatever you call it, the fact remains that she knew
more about herbs and natural cures than anyone I've ever
met or even heard of. If there was a way to make a
woman turn her attentions to a particular man, a powder
or a pill or a . . ."

"Potion," she finished as he faltered.

"Yes. Perhaps there are notes in one of these books."
He pointed to the nearest shelf, wagging one impatient
finger.

"I don't have time to . . ."

"I'll pay you well for your time," he said before she
could refuse him again. He had money to spare, and any
knowledge that the old Matilda Candy might have
gleaned would surely be worth having as an ace in the
hole. "Whether you find what I'm looking for or not, I'll
make it worth your while, I promise."

Her strange and beautiful eyes no longer twinkled with
amusement. They were dead serious as she stared up at
him, studying him as blatantly as he had studied her earlier. She scrutinized him as if she expected to find answers on his face.

"Mr. Harper," she finally said, her voice low and calm. "There's no such thing as a love potion. There's no magical recipe I can concoct that will affect the workings of the heart. My granny taught me that much."

His little bit of patience fled. "But . . ."

She held up a small hand to silence his protests. "However, I might be able to find something in the way of an aphrodisiac that will meet your particular needs."

"An aphrodisiac."

"A tonic that will—"

"I know what an aphrodisiac is, Miss Candy."

She smiled again, but without the withheld amusement. "A lust potion. Will that work?"

He considered the possibility. In truth he didn't care why Vanessa Arrington agreed to marry him, only that she did. He had no qualms about doing whatever was necessary to achieve his goals.

"How can I be sure this potion will be, ummm, guided in the proper direction?"

"You want to make sure this woman's attentions turn to you and not to just any man, is that it?"

"Yes."

He could see curiosity light Matilda Candy's eyes, the way she fought back the urge to smile and ask him outright who his intended victim—recipient was a better word, he decided quickly—would be.

"Be present when she takes it," Matilda said sensibly. "Stay with her until the aphrodisiac takes effect." She glanced at the books on a far shelf. "This is, of course, assuming I can find something that will work properly."

Declan felt a rush of great relief, as if he'd handed his problem of how to deal with Vanessa to someone else. Of course, he'd always found it wise to delegate those chores he found distasteful.

"When do you think you might have this aphrodisiac ready for me?"

"Come back on Monday." Matilda walked to the door

and opened it for him, signaling, without question, that their visit was over. "After dark," she added in a low voice as he passed. "I'm much too busy during the day to devote much time to your . . . special project."

"Thank you," he said as he stepped through the door. "I really appreciate—"

She closed the door before he could finish his thanks. He scowled at the closed door. The old Matilda Candy had never been so rude!

Matilda leaned against the door and closed her eyes. What an impossible man! He couldn't simply take no for an answer, and now she had another chore to accomplish. A love potion! How ridiculous.

She heard his horse galloping away. Even though she did not care for Mr. Harper or his demanding, persistent type, he didn't look like the kind of man who would have trouble attracting women. What on earth did he need a love potion for?

A love potion. Ha. If she were smart, she'd concoct an *un*-love formula, a tea or powder or pill to make someone afflicted return to a sane state of mind. Love? As far as Matilda could see, no good had ever come from the affliction.

Her grandfather had sworn to love Granny, or so she'd said, but in reality he'd found he couldn't live with her special talents. He certainly hadn't loved her enough to dismiss the rumors of her witchcraft or the uncanny moments when she claimed to know something she should not have known. One day, when their only child—Matilda's father—was eight years old, Granny's husband had climbed on his old horse and ridden away. He'd never returned.

Some, of course, had whispered that the old witch had done away with her husband, or turned him into a toad. Those nasty rumors had followed Granny all her life.

Matilda's father had left home years later, certain he

could not build a normal life in this place where he was known as the witch's son. He'd become a doctor, married a woman he loved very much . . . and a few years later that horrible war had taken his life. Matilda had watched her mother grieve until she'd died of a broken heart.

Yes, an *un*-love potion made much more sense. If only Matilda had had such a medicine to give her mother. . . .

She knew most of Granny's books well, but there were some that were so old and dusty they looked as if they hadn't been touched in a hundred years. Matilda pulled a chair to the shelf where those books were stored, stepped onto a chair, and stood on her tiptoes to reach the top shelf. She carefully grabbed the largest book by the cracked spine and drew it from its place. Dust tickled her nose and made her sneeze viciously. The chair she stood upon rocked slightly, teetering on one slightly short leg. When that episode had passed, she stepped down, moved her chair to the nearest table, and sat with the book before her. Very carefully, she opened the book and leafed through the brittle, yellow pages.

Some of these recipes called for ingredients she'd never heard of, and some she knew she could not obtain, such as ground silver and crushed pearls, ash of oleander leaf and burned nasturtium. Fascinated, she almost forgot what she was looking for as she perused the cures. In this old book there were potions for barren women, cures for diseases she'd never heard of, elixirs for eternal youth.

And, more than halfway through the book, she came upon a precious lotion for "a man impotent in the ways of love."

As she turned the page, she saw a piece of newer paper, stark white against the old yellowed pages, folded and stuck into the crease. *Matilda*, in Granny's hand, was written on the outside of the note.

She hesitated before lifting the note from the book. Granny's special gift, or so she'd said, was the knowing of things to come. Matilda had humored her beloved grandmother, but she'd never really *believed*. And why should she? Granny had said revealing her visions did no good; whatever was to be was to be, so why distress oneself and everyone else with the sharing of the knowledge? Matilda had always smiled and agreed, but dismissed her granny's claims as a sweet but strange old woman's eccentricities.

Granny had been dead two years. How long had this note been here, waiting?

Matilda plucked the sheet between two reluctant fingers and let it fall open.

Be careful, the familiar handwriting said. *It is dangerous to trifle with the ways of the heart.*

Matilda fiddled with the note, quickly dismissing the flutter of uneasiness in her chest. The warning might have been placed there at any time since she'd come to live with her grandmother, just in case she should ever run across these old potions. That explanation made perfect sense. Still, a strange tingle worked its way through her body.

She herself had no special gift, no hint of the alleged blessings or curses of the women in Granny's branch of the family tree—a lack Granny had explained in many different ways. Matilda's father had been the first boy child born in many generations. Perhaps that had weakened his daughter's gifts. Too, Matilda had been fourteen when she'd come to live with her grandmother, and Granny had supposed the fact that she'd lived so many years without knowledge of her heritage had also suppressed her gift.

But Granny had always said that one day Matilda's power would manifest itself; when the time was right, when Matilda was ready. Granny claimed to have the power of knowing what was to come. Her mother, she'd said, had possessed a great healing touch, and her grandmother had been able to make objects move, simply by concentrating and calling on her gift. There was even an ancestor, Granny said, who had been able to make it snow in the middle of summer.

The healing touch might be nice to have, Matilda thought skeptically, but she saw no practical use for the other so-called gifts.

She replaced the note where she had found it and slammed the old book shut.

It looked to be another clear, blue-skied summer day. Declan never took the time to slow down and enjoy such observations, but he did make them on occasion, in an off-hand sort of way.

Less than a day had passed, but already he was anxious to know if the witch had found a formula suitable for his particular situation. He was not a patient man, and when something or someone stood in the way of his well-laid plans he was not particularly agreeable.

He needed to marry Vanessa Arrington for a multitude of reasons. First of all, she was the belle of Tanglewood, of this entire county, and perhaps even of the state of Mississippi. She was, by far, the most beautiful woman in these parts. And she was a real and true lady, genteel and refined. If he were to become the man he wanted to become and accomplish all his goals, he needed a *lady* as his wife. It didn't hurt matters any that Vanessa was an only child and her father's plantation bordered Declan's own newly purchased land.

It was only icing on the cake that her father had been one of the worst of the upstanding citizens who'd made Declan's life hell, years ago. He'd openly disdained the ragged son of a drunken farmer and his Irish wife. He'd sneered and turned up his nose, and called Declan and his sisters poor white trash—both behind their backs and to their faces.

Fortunately for Declan, Warren Arrington had always referred to him as *that Harper boy*, and he hadn't yet recognized the wealthy man who'd come to town and started buying up everything he could get his hands on. If Declan were lucky, Arrington wouldn't make the connection until after the wedding. Declan wanted to share the news with the old man himself, *after* he was a part of the family. Perhaps after the old man asked Declan to call him Dad. That thought brought a wry smile to his face.

Grand plans, considering that he had not actually met Vanessa Arrington yet.

Declan's mother had not wanted him to return to Tanglewood, had in fact begged him not to. She insisted on regular letters from him, and he did his best to comply. Now, short note to her dutifully posted, he stopped to peer into the one saloon in Tanglewood. What a dump. No self-respecting man would go into that place even if he were dying of thirst. The ratty establishment would be one of his next purchases, and, once it was his, major changes would be made. The place needed to be gutted or completely rebuilt. New floors, new walls, a long walnut bar, and new tables, to start. Barmaids in pretty dresses and a bartender who knew what he was doing would be nice. Maybe a few tables for gaming in the back. He began to work an almost unconscious equation in his head, calculating the cost of the remodeling and the increased business that would follow.

A small smile crept across his face. This was what he was good at, how he'd made his money.

After leaving Tanglewood, all those years ago, his mother had found employment in Texas as a housekeeper, and after a few years there she'd moved on to the same type of job in Colorado, working for a man who'd made a fortune mining. While men desperate for money had busted their asses digging for gold and silver, Declan had settled in town. He'd worked at the general store for a while, and then one night he'd won a ratty old saloon in a poker game. It was the luckiest night of his life.

He'd turned a dump much like this one in Tanglewood into a fine establishment, and people had come. They'd bought whiskey and lost money at the gaming tables. Hell, in his saloon he'd touched more gold than if he'd struck a vein himself. But once the place was up and running, he'd quickly gotten bored. The general store was next. He bought it from his old employer and made vast improvements. Within months he was raking in money from that enterprise as well. And he'd been bored again.

In the following five years he'd opened saloons and general stores in several other mining towns. He'd gotten the businesses running smoothly, hired the best men he could find to run them, then he'd moved on to something else. He'd arranged fine marriages for his sisters, and had set up his mother in a nice house.

And now that that was all done, he had only one other objective: He wanted to own Tanglewood, Mississippi, and everyone who had the misfortune to live here. He didn't just *want* to own Tanglewood, he needed it. Craved it. Dreamed about it. His life would not be complete until this mission was accomplished.

The wheels of a slow-moving conveyance caught his attention, and he turned about to watch the distinctive Arrington carriage coming his way. It stopped in front of the dress shop, and the driver jumped down and opened the door.

Watching Vanessa step from the carriage and onto the street was like watching poetry come alive. Graceful and elegant, she all but floated from the carriage. He caught sight of a delicate foot encased in a lavender slipper, then her lavender silk skirt, then slender gloved fingers that took the steady hand offered by the driver. Before he could get a good look at her exquisite face, she opened the parasol that matched her gown, protecting her delicate skin from the summer sun.

She was the perfect woman; she'd make the perfect wife. Unfortunately, she very much enjoyed being the most sought-after woman in the county. Practically every man for a hundred miles either was courting or had courted her. And though he wanted her, Declan was not one to stand in line, not for anything or anyone. Still, until she tired of stringing along suitor after suitor, he didn't have a chance of marrying her.

Unless the witch's granddaughter came through.

As Vanessa stepped toward the dress shop, she turned her head in his direction, and Declan caught a glimpse of her perfect face. Even from this distance he could see that her eyes were an extraordinary shade of violet-blue. Her hair was dark and fine as silk. Her skin was like the finest cream.

As her driver, a finely dressed man with a head of black curls, opened the dressmaker's door, she smiled at Declan. It was a small, almost invisible smile, but it encouraged him all the same.

When the door to the dress shop had closed behind her, Declan headed across the street to the general store. The cigars he'd looked at yesterday were not the quality he would've liked, but he needed a smoke. He forgot about them as soon as he stepped through the open door of the general store, for Matilda Candy stood at the counter. With her hair still in long braids, and attired in a plain brown dress that was a couple of inches too short, and wearing worn leather boots that laced up her ankles, she was still somehow charming. She laughed at something Charles Fox said in a lowered voice, and handed the shopkeeper a small jar he quickly scooped up and deposited under the counter.

She placed a large wicker basket on the counter, and Fox rifled gently through the contents. Several loaves of bread were visible on the top of the basket, but the contents beneath were hidden. They seemed to delight Fox, though.

"Oh, those wonderful caramels," Fox said. "And sugared pecans. And candied lemon peels." He shook his head. "You're a marvel, Miss Matilda."

Declan remained silent and still, but as he stood there watching, the young woman turned her head to look directly at him. She did not smile or say a single word, but Fox must have noticed something, for he lifted his eyes from the goodies in the basket.

"Mr. Harper," he said enthusiastically, a fitting greeting for a good customer. "What can I get for you today?"

"Cigars," Declan said, entering the store and walking toward its lackluster tobacco section.

"You must try some of Miss Matilda's sweets," Fox said as Declan grabbed a handful of cigars.

"Sweets?" Declan asked as he approached the counter.

Fox nodded. "Mr. Harper, this is Miss Matilda Candy. Every Friday morning she brings me sweets and breads to sell. You *must* try her caramels."

The woman remained silent, waiting for him to respond. It would be a bad idea, he imagined, to let on that he already knew her. "It's a pleasure to meet you, Miss Candy," he said with a small, curt nod.

"Oh, the pleasure is all mine, Mr. Harper."

Was he the only one who heard the humor in her voice? The air practically dripped with it.

Fox handed over several coins and an empty basket he'd had stored beneath the counter, and with a smile the woman left the other basket and bid them both goodbye.

As she reached the door, something unexpected overcame Declan. A compulsion, a yearning, a need to make this moment last. "Miss Candy," he said calmly, "do you, perhaps, make hard molasses candy?"

She turned. With the sun behind her he couldn't see her face. Just as well. She was probably grinning, flashing that knowing, witchy smile his way. "Not normally, Mr. Harper, but I believe my grandmother had that recipe. Perhaps I can find it and try my hand at something new."

Declan left his cigars on the counter and stepped toward her. "It was a childhood favorite of mine. I'd like to purchase some from you, if you find the recipe and have success with it."

She turned away from him. "I must start for home, Mr. Harper, since I have a long way to go and much work to do today. But if you'd like to walk with me for a few minutes we can make arrangements for your order."

"Splendid," he said, feeling strangely light-headed as he joined her in the doorway. "Splendid."

Chapter Three

Matilda was accustomed to people pretending not to know her, pretending that they didn't come to her for cures under darkness of night, so she shouldn't be upset. But she was. Why had she expected more of Declan Harper? Why were her feelings just a teeny bit hurt when back in Fox's General Store he'd acted as if he'd never seen her before? She did not quicken her step to accommodate his longer stride, but stubbornly walked slower than usual.

He lowered his head slightly as they walked down the street. "Have you had any luck?"

"Finding the formula for your love potion?" she asked, not bothering to lower her voice. "No, not yet."

Again he looked almost the gentleman, in his fine gray suit. He did try, she had to give him that, to appear civilized and ordinary, but he couldn't quite pull it off. There was a restlessness about him, an intensity in his eyes and the set of his jaw that placed him apart from the gentility. He rolled one shoulder nervously as he glanced around to see if anyone was listening. There was no one close enough to hear their words, of course.

"It hasn't even been a full day since you came to me with your request. Patience, Mr. Harper."

He muttered something unintelligible.

"I do wonder if Vanessa Arrington will be susceptible to something so common as a love potion," she said casually, glancing out of the corner of her eye to gauge Harper's reaction.

He stared sharply at her. "How do you know she's the one?"

She really shouldn't tell him. She should keep her mouth shut and let him believe that she had unearthly powers. With a sigh, she told the truth, instead. "When I walked into town you were staring into the saloon as if you were very, very thirsty, and then when Miss Arrington appeared, you forgot all about your craving for a drink and stood there all moony eyed with your tongue hanging out and drool running down your chin."

"I am never moony eyed," he said calmly, regaining his composure with little apparent effort. In fact, he seemed to hold his head higher and his spine straighter. Proud. Self-assured. Haughty. "My tongue was not hanging out. And I do not drool."

"There was definitely drool," she countered with a touch of humor in her voice.

Amazingly enough, a moment later Declan Harper smiled and shook his head. His hard face softened as he broke into an unabashed grin, his dark eyes twinkling mischievously, and she could see a hint of the boy her grandmother had known. In that moment Matilda decided she liked him. A man who could laugh at himself was rare indeed.

"I will need several days, Mr. Harper."

She expected him to make a quick escape, his question answered, but he stayed beside her. "Fair enough, Miss Candy. You can call me Declan, if you like." He made the offer in a rather offhand manner, but she sensed it was an important gesture.

"All right. Declan." She liked the way the name rolled off her tongue, different and foreign and somehow tasty. "And you may call me Matilda."

He barely withheld a smile. "So tell me, Matilda. Do you think you can find that recipe for hard molasses candy?"

"You really want it?" she asked, genuinely surprised. "I thought that request was just a ruse to get me alone so you could ply me for information about love potions for your Miss Arrington."

He glanced at her sharply, studying, scrutinizing. Then he softened. "No. That candy was one of my few good childhood memories of this place. Hard molasses candy and your grandmother."

They walked a bit further, and still he didn't leave her side. He seemed quite content to walk with her, and she decided she didn't mind the company.

"If you have no other pleasant memories of Tanglewood," she asked, "then why are you here?"

He didn't answer the question. "All in good time, Matilda. All in good time," he said softly. "You're the only one I've told about my previous residence here. I hope you'll keep my secret."

"Mr.—Declan," she said, "I am the keeper of all of Tanglewood's secrets. I can surely keep yours."

He glanced at her and gave her a small smile. His eyes were so dark and deep, she had a feeling she'd never know all of his secrets. "Somehow I knew I could trust you."

As they reached the edge of town, he stopped. She stopped with him. "You have such a long way to walk. Can I give you a ride? I don't have a buggy, yet, but my horse can easily carry two."

She shook her head. "No, thank you. I don't care for horses, and they care for me even less."

He didn't believe her. She saw the skepticism and the question in his eyes, the subtle tightening of his lips. Did he think her refusal was a rejection of some sort? Yes, he did, she saw.

"Horses throw me," she explained, for some reason wanting Declan to know that she was not spurning him, knowing it was important. "Always. They simply don't like me, and therefore I don't like them. My refusal to ride seems perfectly reasonable to me," she added somewhat snippily, then turned toward home, presenting her back to Declan Harper. "But you can walk with me a while longer, if you'd like."

To her surprise, he did.

Declan couldn't remember the last time he'd talked to someone, anyone, this way. As they walked down the dirt road, he and Matilda discussed the recent lack of rainfall, her grandmother, and candy. His favorites and hers. He told her of his remodeling plans for the plantation house he'd bought, and when she asked, he told her about the first saloon he'd won and how his venture into the business world had begun. She seemed truly interested in it all.

They weren't far from town when he slipped out of his jacket and flung it over his shoulder. A moment later he loosened the top button of his confining shirt. He felt like he was breathing deep and clean for the first time in days. Weeks. Years, maybe.

"I can't believe you have five sisters," Matilda said, swinging her empty basket. A sly smile crept across her elfin face. "I wish I'd had five sisters. Or six. Or a dozen."

He laughed. "No, you don't. It's very daunting to live in a household with that many women. My life with five sisters and a widowed mother was a constant turmoil, and there was never enough money. For some reason women have a need to go from one disaster to another."

"Depends on the woman, I suppose," she argued.

Perhaps she was right. "So, you are an only child? Or are there brothers out there somewhere?"

Her smile faded. "I'm an only child. My mother wanted more children, but . . . it never happened."

She looked to be lost in thought, contemplative but not terribly sad. He didn't know what to say.

She shook off her brief bout of sober reflection and turned her attention to him again. "I can guess, from the tales of the way you built your fortune, what you have in mind for Tanglewood."

Was he ready to tell her everything? No. Not yet. "I have nothing in mind for Tanglewood," he said in a tone of reassurance. "It's simply time I settled down, and this town is as good a place as any."

She laughed at him, a bright, summery sound that seemed to seep through him. "You're much too young to retire, and much too impatient to think about settling down." She locked her eyes to his, briefly. "You don't want anyone to know you once lived here, which means you don't want them to know who you really are." Her smile faded, but her eyes still sparkled. "Why not?" she asked softly, as if she were questioning herself. He saw the answer on her face as it quickly came to her. "Declan Harper, what are you trying to prove?"

"I'm not trying to prove anything."

She shook her head. "Of course you are. You bought your big house and all that land, and I imagine soon you'll want the saloon and the general store and anything else you can get your hands on." She looked at him boldly and smiled. "Declan Harper, king of Tanglewood. And Vanessa Arrington is to be queen. Would you care to tell me why?"

Why argue with her? She'd seen right through him, with those witchy eyes. "Not really," he answered nonchalantly.

She narrowed her eyes and swung her basket as she

continued to walk toward home. Her full brown skirt swished about her legs, as she took the longest strides of which she was capable. "That's all right, I can guess. You were an outcast, I suppose. Only an outcast would be so determined to come back and make himself . . . one of *them*. Not only to *be* one of them, but to lead them. And then to rub their noses in it, I imagine."

His heart lurched, just a little, but he didn't allow her words to disturb him for more than that single heartbeat. "You don't know—"

"Please don't tell me I don't know what it's like to be an outcast," she interrupted, her voice sharp. "Even before I was told that my grandmother was a witch, when I was living with my mother and father in Georgia and leading a fairly ordinary life, I knew I was different. Always on the outside looking in, wondering what the rest of you were thinking. Wondering why I always felt . . . strange. I was fourteen when I came here to live with my grandmother, ten tears ago, and I hadn't been here three days before I knew what had been missing from my life."

"Witchcraft?" he asked, almost afraid to say the word aloud.

She wasn't offended. In fact, she smiled. "Purpose, Mr. Harper," she said. "Purpose."

Purpose, he understood.

The tree-lined road was silent and deserted, but for the two of them. Here there were no plans to be executed, no calculations to be made as they passed in and out of the shade.

"Don't you mind that people call you a witch?"

She shrugged her shoulders. "No. Who knows? Maybe they're right."

"But . . ." He paused as he looked around him, at the deserted road and the deep woods on either side. "Don't you ever get lonely?"

"No," she answered quickly, her voice as light as the breeze through the trees. "I like my life. I enjoy living alone. I am free, I answer to no one." She cast a quick glance in his direction. "And if I ever get tired of living alone, I'll marry Ezra Cotter and have a dozen babies."

She said it with a smile, as if it were a joke, but Declan sensed there was some truth to her statement. "Who's Ezra Cotter?"

She swung her basket twice and contemplated a moment before answering. "Ezra has a general store in Jackson. Several times a year he visits to buy beauty creams and special oils and rose water for his store, and he always asks me to marry him while he's here."

Declan felt a strange sense of relief. He'd known dozens of merchants in his lifetime. He'd worked for them, bought them out, and competed with them. They were, for the most part, dull men. Every one he'd ever known had been middle-aged or older. Declan didn't count himself in the group, of course. He wasn't a mere shopkeeper; he was a shrewd businessman. Ezra Cotter was probably a quaint old man, charmed by Matilda's youth and smile and eyes. The frequent proposals were probably a kind of joke between them, a lighthearted jest.

"And one day you might say yes?" he teased.

She smiled again. "Maybe." And then she confirmed his suspicions about Cotter. "There is the age difference to consider, though."

He didn't especially like her smile; it spoke of a hundred secrets. He wanted to ask more about this shopkeeper, but couldn't think of a way to do so without sounding as if he were interrogating Matilda the way he used to do to his sisters when they took up with someone unsuitable.

"Well, thank you for walking me home," Matilda said. "I'd invite you in, but I'm afraid I have so much to do I'll be working straight through lunch."

Declan was more than a little startled to find himself standing before Matilda's cottage. He'd had no intention of coming this far, had no idea he'd been talking and walking for so long. He'd lost all track of time.

"I have to get back, anyway."

"Let me get you a glass of water, before you go," Matilda said, opening the door to her cottage wide. "There's a spring just over the hill, and I always keep a jar or two of fresh water on hand. It's better than any well water, I can promise you that."

He stood in the entrance to her house, not stepping inside, since he hadn't been invited. Matilda placed her empty basket on a table in the main room, and continued on to the small kitchen at the rear of the house. How could a petite woman in a plain brown dress look so tempting? Why did the way her hips moved as she walked away from him make his teeth ache?

Perhaps Matilda Candy *was* oddly attractive and even tempting, in her own surprising way, but nothing ever got in the way of Declan Harper's plans. Nothing and no one. All his adult life he'd planned for this return to Tanglewood. He'd made money because he needed it for this moment. He'd saved it, spending only on his mother and his sisters, so he'd be well funded. He'd worked too long and too hard to get here and allow one woman to muddy the waters.

She came toward him with a jar of water in her hands, and he reminded himself: he only wanted her love potion. Nothing else.

Declan quickly drank the water Matilda brought him. It was, indeed, quite good. He'd worked up quite a thirst, walking and talking with her. Still, it was a pleasure he should not plan on indulging in again.

He handed her the empty jar with a soft thanks, added, "I'll see you Monday," and turned to make the trip back to town. He had a feeling this second half of the journey, without Matilda's uplifting company, was going to be much longer than the first.

*   *   *

Two days later, Matilda placed yet another ancient book on the table, adding it to the musty pile. Declan would be here tomorrow, looking for answers. Tomorrow!

She had gathered more information than she'd ever thought to find out of these old books. Some of what she found was unusable but interesting. Some intrigued her but had at least one unavailable ingredient. And then there were the recipes for oils and lotions meant, obviously, for those already married. Matilda blushed whenever she read the explicit directions for the application of those potions.

What did a man like Declan see in Vanessa Arrington, anyway? She was beautiful, yes, but surely a man like Declan would look for more than beauty in his "queen." She wrinkled her nose. If he knew everything she did about the much sought-after Vanessa, he'd likely change his glowing opinion.

Matilda would never tell, though, of course.

Sunday afternoons were usually quiet in her little cottage. It was her day of rest, and no one called on the town witch on Sunday—as if it would be blasphemy to do so. So, when a knock sounded on the door, she jumped in her seat and slammed the book shut on a particularly interesting, if somewhat lascivious, recipe.

Her first thought was—*Declan. He's so impatient, can't he wait one more day?* But the soft chatter of young voices drifted to her before she opened the door, disproving her assumption.

Outside, Hanson and Gretchen stood on either side of a woman Matilda had seen in town once or twice but never met. Plain yet far from ugly, almost as short as Matilda but much more buxom, dressed in a blue calico that had seen a lot of wear but was still attractive, Mrs. Hazelrig, the twins' new stepmother, met Matilda's questioning gaze unflinchingly. She was, Matilda knew in an instant, a strong woman.

And yet she was clearly apprehensive.

"Run! Run!" Gretchen squealed. The girl tried to escape, but her stepmother held her collar, and Hanson's, in a firm grip; one twin securely restrained in each hand. "I told you, she's a witch!"

Matilda merely lifted her eyebrows as she awaited Mrs. Hazelrig's response.

"Gretchen, there are no witches in Mississippi or anywhere else," the woman said sensibly, and then she lifted her eyes to Matilda. "Miss Candy, I must apologize for my stepchildren's behavior. They do tell outrageous stories, on occasion. . . ."

"We don't tell stories," Hanson protested. "At least *I* don't." Gretchen glared at him. "Usually," he added sheepishly.

"I found a half-eaten plate of candy . . ." Mrs. Hazelrig began.

"She's going to cook us in her big oven," Gretchen interrupted. "Run! Run!"

Hanson jumped in. "She made me spit! She . . . she stole my spit!"

Matilda took a deep breath, trying to keep up as the three spoke at once. Finally, she lifted a hand to silence them all. "One moment."

She returned shortly with two large wicker baskets, then handed one to each of the children. "If you will pick the fully blooming red roses from my garden—the red ones only—I'll give you a plate of caramels and marzipan when you're done."

Hanson nodded in acceptance, and Gretchen looked warily up at her stepmother, who released the children almost reluctantly. The twins ran away, rounding the corner and heading toward the flower garden.

Matilda moved back and opened the door wide. "Come in," she said. "I'll make us a cup of tea while the children pick flowers."

Mrs. Hazelrig accepted the invitation and stepped into

the main room, setting a hand to her simply styled brown hair as if to make sure it was not misbehaving. "I must apologize again. Those children tell such tales! Stealing spit. Threatening to cook them! Such nonsense." She was silent for a moment as she looked around the room, taking in everything.

"Just a few days ago they told me you'd taken them into the forest and left them there to starve," Matilda said as she made her way to the small winter kitchen at the back of the cottage. There was not enough room to do her baking here, but there was a small stove, a pantry of food, tea, and Granny's fine china cups.

"Heaven only knows what they've told you, and anyone else who will listen!" Mrs. Hazelrig laid a tired hand on her forehead as Matilda heated water for tea. "They hate me," she added, in a lowered voice that made the statement seem a confidence. "I thought that with time their feelings toward me would change, but . . ."

"They will," Matilda said with assurance. "Gretchen still misses her mother terribly, and Hanson simply follows his sister's lead. Patience, Mrs. Hazelrig."

"Call me Stella," the woman said. "After all, we are neighbors."

"And I'm Matilda." She experienced a moment of warmth. A neighbor. No one had ever made such an overture before. But then, Stella was new to the area and had not heard all the stories. Once she did . . .

"I'm truly at a loss," Stella said softly. "Their mother's been gone four years." There was such despair in the woman's voice, as if she would never know peace again. "What can I do?"

Matilda gave the question some thought as she waited for the water to boil. She mused as she prepared the cups—two of her finest—glancing through the window to see that Gretchen and Hanson were very carefully following her instructions, picking only the fully bloomed red roses and dropping them into their baskets.

45

"You must make your own place in their hearts," Matilda said softly. "And realize that yours will be a new place, not an old one." She flashed Stella her brightest smile. "And I can teach you to make caramels."

Chapter Four

He was a little early arriving at the Candy house, but Declan dismissed his eagerness as a desire to see his plans fulfilled as quickly as possible. Once Vanessa Arrington was his wife, he'd be well on his way to seeing all his dreams come true.

He was not particularly eager to see Matilda Candy again, he told himself as he dismounted before her cottage. Yes, she was an interesting woman, pretty if you liked the type, and a good listener with a great laugh. He might've dreamed about golden braids and bare feet in the past couple of days, or heard a laugh in town and turned to look and see if maybe . . . just maybe . . . it was Matilda he heard. All right, he conceded, she was an attractive woman, but that's not why he had arrived at her cottage well before dark!

She didn't answer his brief knock, but he wasn't surprised. Her big kitchen was out back, and that was where she did much of her work. He wondered what she was making today; hard molasses candy, perhaps?

The smell hit him when he was halfway around the cottage—not candy, not bread, but a tantalizing, feminine scent that teased his senses, a flowery fragrance that wrapped itself around him and made him think of women in long, deep bathtubs. When he rounded the corner he saw Matilda standing before a huge black cauldron with a low fire burning beneath it. She reached into a basket at her feet and came up with a handful of red rose petals. Declan stopped where he was to watch Matilda as she rubbed her palms together and let the petals drift from her hands into the cauldron.

Something unexpected moved in Declan's chest. It was from the fragrance perhaps, or the sight of Matilda standing there surrounded by red rose petals; petals at her feet, raining from her hands. Yet she looked no different from the first time he'd seen her, with her long golden braids and those bare feet, wearing a plain white blouse, sleeves rolled up to her elbows, and a full yellow skirt that danced around her legs. Then again, she did look different, somehow. Prettier. Sexier. He wondered how she'd look immersed in a hot bath of fragrant bath-water, her braids undone and her body bare.

"Rose water," she said without looking over at him as she bent to scoop up another handful. "One of my best-selling products and the base for many of my creams. You're early."

He found himself a little annoyed. Matilda hadn't even looked his way, and he'd been very quiet. She tilted her head as she rubbed the latest batch of rose petals between her palms and let them rain down into the pot. Steam rose off the water in the cauldron, a fragrant mist that seemed to wrap itself around Matilda as she stood over it, the same way the scent had wrapped itself around him.

Maybe she really *was* a witch.

"I can wait," he said, his voice making him sound more short-tempered than he'd intended.

Matilda smiled. She didn't look at him, just smiled as

if she had an amusing secret she would never share. "I heard you arrive," she said softly. "More specifically, I heard your horse."

"Of course," he said. The explanation he had not asked for made perfect sense.

She bent to grab another handful of rose petals, and all Declan's impatience and irritation fled. He didn't care why he liked watching her, he just did. That was enough, for the moment. He took few pleasures for himself; why not this one? The way she worked the red petals in her hands and dropped them into the simmering water was rather pleasing, somehow. There was natural grace in every motion Matilda made, a strangely hypnotic way to her simple task. He leaned against the side of the house, crossed his arms across his chest, and just watched.

If he hadn't already set his course, if he could then allow himself to be led by something besides his head, he could truly enjoy Matilda's company. He wondered if she'd ever had a lover. He wondered what she'd do if he went to her right now and laid her down on a bed of rose petals and . . .

"I imagine you're anxious to get started," she said as red petals floated down from her hands. One wayward petal was caught by the wind and landed on her yellow skirt, clinging there for a moment before drifting to her feet.

"What?" Declan was rudely jerked back to reality. "Oh yes, the potion. Of course I'm anxious. To get started, that is," he added quickly.

"I found quite a lot of information this weekend. More than I'd expected," she said as she continued with her chore.

"Excellent," he muttered, trying to sound completely businesslike.

"Many of the formulas are quite interesting, but . . . difficult for your situation." She gave him a sideways glance.

"Difficult how?" he asked.

She smiled at him as she brushed new petals through her palms and let them drift into the cauldron. "We'll discuss it later. Why did you arrive so early? My goodness, Mr. Harper, isn't there a watch pocket in that fancy suit of yours?"

Declan ignored her question and leaned against the house to watch her as she returned to her task. He was completely and totally entranced. Damn.

"Isn't that the same man who walked home with her last week?" Hanson asked, whispering from his hiding place behind a tall pine.

"Yes," Gretchen hissed. "I didn't think witches had beaus. Oh, he's likely to ruin everything! If he starts hanging around, she'll have less time for making candy."

"Maybe he's not a beau," Hanson said hopefully. "Maybe he's just a friend. Witches can have friends, can't they?"

Gretchen gave her brother what she hoped was a cutting glare to put him in his place. "Can't you see his face, you moron? He's looking at that witch the way Father looked at Stella before he married her." The memory made her frown. They'd gone to another town to buy a horse from a rancher her father had heard about, a task that should've been quick and simple. But no. Her father had taken one look at the rancher's daughter, and everything had changed.

In truth, he *still* looked at his new wife the way the man before them was staring at the witch, but Gretchen chose not to dwell on that fact.

Hanson looked properly horrified. "Witches don't get married, do they?"

"I don't know," Gretchen admitted. "But if she casts a love spell on that man, I'm afraid it's very likely."

A husband wouldn't take kindly to a couple of kids who weren't his own hanging around asking for candy.

Too, there would be another pair of eyes to catch them when they sneaked into her kitchen. And, horrors, what if they got married and moved to *his* house? Oh, that would not be acceptable. Wherever this man lived, it was not close enough.

"She's not making candy today, anyway," Hanson said glumly. "She's making rose water."

"I can see that," Gretchen snapped.

"And we have to get home. Stella said she was making something special tonight."

Gretchen made a derisive noise deep in her throat. Stella was a terrible cook! Her "something special" was usually a pie with a burned crust or underdone bread with runny jam. If her father had to get married again, why couldn't he have married someone who could cook? Why couldn't he have married Matilda Candy?

The stray, unexpected thought caught her by surprise, and yet Gretchen found she couldn't dismiss it immediately. If witches had beaus and got married, if Matilda Candy was going to get married, why couldn't it be to their father? What a wonderful idea! She and Hanson would have all the candy they could eat, then, and when school was in session no one would dare tease them—not with a witch as a stepmother!

The idea was positively brilliant. Of course, first they'd have to find a way to get rid of Stella.

Matilda placed several books on a long table in the main room of her cottage. She hadn't told a lie when she'd told Declan Harper that she'd found the research interesting. The question remained; was any of the material suitable? Would it work?

The man sat in a chair near the table, attentive, as patient as he was capable of being, and unexpectedly attractive. He looked as if he wanted to squirm in his fine suit, but would never dare.

Declan Harper was, very simply, a man. A real, true

51

man. If she looked at him just so, she could almost imagine what it might be like to kiss him. He had a somehow wonderful mouth, full and strong and tempting, and he was built the way she suspected a man was supposed to be built; strong and solid. Perhaps that was why his suits seemed to constrict him unnaturally.

Most of all, she was entranced by his eyes. Oh, she could easily get lost in those dark eyes.

With an absent wave of her hand, she dismissed her inappropriate thoughts about Declan Harper. He had his sights set on Vanessa Arrington, and Matilda herself couldn't possibly be attracted to a man who cared for that vain, vacuous ninny.

"I found several possible love potions," she said, keeping her tone strictly professional. "I divided them into four categories." There was a fifth category, but she would not share that information with Declan Harper. Oils and lotions and the instructions on how to apply them intimately was more advanced than this situation called for, in any case.

She had Declan's full attention. His eyes were practically glued to her!

"The first category calls for plants or drugs with hallucinogenic properties."

"That's not what I'm looking for," he said quickly.

"I'm glad to hear it, because I won't make such a potion for you. The results are unpredictable and dangerous."

He nodded once, silently agreeing with her.

"Then there are a number of supposedly powerful powders in which the main ingredient is the dried testicles of an animal, usually a hare or a fox." She tried hard not to blush, but she felt her cheeks turn warm.

"I think I'll pass on those," Declan said softly, and she almost thought she heard a hint of pained humor in his voice. Almost.

She nodded, relieved.

"I found directions for a number of talismans, some that you could fashion and wear yourself, others that would be given as a gift to your intended to ensure that she returns your affections." She smiled as Declan lifted his eyebrows in disbelief. "But I don't suppose talismans will be effective in this case. Still, I imagine if you want to steal one of her shoes and place it under your bed it wouldn't hurt anything."

"Excuse me?"

"It's supposed to bring a loved one to your bed. Isn't that what you want?" This time she didn't blush; Declan did. And Matilda found it rather charming to watch, however brief.

"I hope the fourth category is more promising than the first three," he said, keeping his voice low and calm.

She opened the book from which she would be working. "These potions contain herbs and flowers, wines and fragrant oils, spices and dried fruits. In the proper combination they look to be quite promising."

"How many promising formulas did you come across?" he asked.

She smiled. "More than a dozen."

"I want the strongest love potion in that book," Declan said intently, pointing at the weathered old tome that lay open on her table.

She felt a rush of disappointment. Why did she constantly look at this man and expect more? It was silly. He was no different from every other man. "You're very determined to have her, aren't you?"

"Damn right I am," he said with conviction. "I've worked long and hard to get where I am, and my plan is almost complete. I don't have time to court the woman I intend to marry. I just want this over and done with."

Again, she looked at him and felt an inexplicable disappointment. What had she expected? More heart? More brains? A hint of a tender soul inside that tough body?

"Is a woman who's not worthy of proper courting worth marrying?"

Declan's jaw clenched and unclenched, and his eyes flashed like dark fire. "If she's the prettiest woman in the county *and* heir to the land that adjoins mine, she is."

Matilda spun around, turning her back on him before he had a chance to see her face and read the expression there. Oh, what a stupid, stupid man! What he really needed was a common-sense potion.

"Come back in two days," she said curtly. "I'll have something ready for you then."

"You don't have anything prepared now?" he asked impatiently. She heard the scrape of his chair across the floor as he rose. Still, she didn't turn to face him; she was not ready.

"No," she said softly. "I don't have anything prepared. You'll have to come back in two days."

She waited to hear him move, waited for the closing of her door; but all was silent for a few long moments. Finally he whispered, "Matilda? Is everything all right?"

Taking a deep breath, she turned to face him. Her lips turned up in a soft smile. She made sure the picture she presented was clear and calm. "Everything is fine. I'm just planning, trying to decide which potion will suit you and Vanessa best."

At that, he bid her a friendly good-bye and left with a smile on his face. When he was gone she slammed the book shut. Long-undisturbed dust tickled her nose, making her sneeze violently. If she'd been given to foul language, she would've cursed Declan Harper heartily as he rode away.

Gretchen looked with dismay at the mess on her plate.

"What is this?" Hanson hissed as he leaned close.

"I'm not quite sure," she answered softly, "but I believe Stella is trying to poison us."

Hanson placed a finger in the brown gooey mess on

54

his plate, and made a winding trail that slowly filled in on itself. "I don't think Stella would poison us. Father would be awfully angry if she did."

"Perhaps not," Gretchen surmised. "Perhaps she wants her own babies and not us, and she's convinced Father that we'll just be in the way."

Stella breezed into the kitchen with a wide smile on her face. "How do you like the caramel?"

Hanson studied his plate with renewed interest. "Caramel? This doesn't look like caramel."

Stella's smile faded. "Well, it didn't firm up the way Matilda said it would. Maybe it'll turn out better next time."

Hanson bravely brought a finger dripping with goo to his lips and shoved it into his mouth, licking his finger clean. He wrinkled his nose. "It tastes burned."

"How can it be burned and not done at the same time?" Gretchen asked, feeling brave and taking a taste of her own. Hanson was correct. There was a distinct undertone of char to the runny mess. She pushed the plate away. Perhaps Stella really was trying to poison them! "I'm not very hungry."

"Me, neither," Hanson said, pushing his own plate away.

Stella looked disappointed as she carried away the plates. "Perhaps the next batch will turn out better."

Gretchen looked over at her brother and grimaced at his expression. Hanson was much too soft for his own good, at times. He still didn't quite understand that their stepmother would do anything, *anything,* to be rid of them. He went to Stella and patted her comfortingly on the arm. "That's okay," he said softly. Then Gretchen was shocked to hear him say, "But if it's all the same to you, I'll take my chances with the witch."

* * *

Declan stood in the Arrington parlor, sipping at a crystal tumbler of Warren Arrington's best whiskey. In his wildest dreams he'd never thought to be here; not like this. A reluctant demon deep inside him waited for his plans to fall apart, for the accusations to begin. *You look familiar. I remember the name Harper. Was your father that white-trash drunk that lived down the road a ways?*

"Cigar?" Arrington offered, opening the humidor on a small end table.

"Thank you," Declan said, pleased to see that Arrington did not buy his cigars from Fox's General Store.

Warren Arrington had never wanted for anything in his life, of that Declan was certain. Born on this plantation, raised here, he'd even managed to survive the war relatively untouched. He was not a tall man, probably standing no more than five-foot-seven, and he was built like a barrel. His hair was silver gray and thinning, his nose was too large for his round face, and yet still he managed to look dignified.

Vanessa, no doubt, had inherited her fine looks from her mother.

They lit cigars and sipped appreciatively at fine whiskey. The denunciations Declan expected never came. His demons faded slowly, and he made himself search inside himself for the patience that was always so difficult for him to find. He knew Arrington well enough to know that the planter had not invited him here tonight to accuse or to entertain. The man wanted something.

"You've done well, for a young man," Arrington said as he took a chair by the window. "How old are you, Harper? Thirty? Thirty-five?"

"Twenty-nine," Declan said, taking the chair to which Arrington gestured.

Arrington raised his eyebrows in mild surprise. "Even younger than I thought. Impressive."

Declan took a long drag on his cigar. There was no need to respond.

"What plans do you have for the old Ashton place?" Arrington asked.

Declan smiled. At last, the real purpose behind the unexpected invitation. "Why, once I get the big house and the servants' quarters in a livable condition, I plan to work the plantation as it should be worked. The cotton market isn't great right now, but I believe it will come back."

Arrington smiled. "I'm glad to hear it. I hate to see good land go to waste." He leaned forward as if sharing a confidence. "Why, some carpetbagger bought the Keenan place over in Turner's Bend and turned that fine old home into a house of ill repute," he drawled. "Then they sold off the land a piece at a time to common farmers. It was scandalous."

"You can rest assured that won't happen to my place," Declan said, holding back a smile.

"Daddy," a sweet, Southern voice called. "I hate to ask, but I must have an advance on my allowance. There's a lovely hat . . ." Vanessa stopped speaking when she saw Declan.

Both men stood quickly, standing straight and tall to greet Vanessa.

"Oh, I'm so sorry, Daddy. I didn't know you had company." She gave Declan a small smile, the corners of her perfect lips turning up, her violet eyes sparkling. "Why, you must think I have terrible manners, to come bursting in on you two this way."

Even now, late in the evening, in the comfort of her own home, she was flawlessly dressed. Her pale green gown was delicate and feminine, unwrinkled and of the finest, most expensive fabric. Her earrings were tasteful pearls. Not a hair was out of place. Her slender neck was graceful, achingly delicate. And oh, what a face.

"Mr. Harper, I don't believe you've met my daughter, Vanessa," Arrington said with apparent pride.

Declan took Vanessa's hand, bending forward in a curt

bow as any fine gentleman would do. Her fingers were long and slender, her flesh creamy smooth. Declan was almost afraid to touch her, she was so very fragile. His lips barely brushed her knuckles. "I have seen Miss Arrington about town, but have never had the pleasure of being properly introduced."

Her father did the honors, introducing them formally. Vanessa gave a small curtsy and a shy smile, and Declan couldn't help but notice, as her foot slipped momentarily from beneath a full skirt, that her shoes matched her gown perfectly. He had the urge to steal one of those pale green slippers and hide it under his bed.

"Oh, Daddy," Vanessa said, lowering her voice as she turned away from Declan and went to her father. "Henry Langford asked me to marry him again. I tried to let him down easy, but I'm afraid he didn't take it well this time. If he comes around, do tell him I'm indisposed and very gently send him away."

"Of course, dear," Arrington promised.

She turned with the grace of a dancer and smiled at Declan. "I'll leave you gentlemen alone," she said softly, her Southern accent refined and honey-sweet. "I won't bore Mr. Harper with my tales of relentless suitors and periwinkle hats."

As Vanessa Arrington left the room, her head high, her face pleasantly set in a serene smile, Declan redoubled his resolve to have her.

In two days he'd have Matilda's love potion. In three days he'd use it.

Chapter Five

Matilda smiled as she placed the stoppered vial on the table before an anxious Declan Harper. A greenish-brown coarse powder with flecks of red caught the candlelight, making the filled vial quite pretty. Even though she did not approve of his plan, she was proud that she'd managed to concoct exactly what he'd been looking for.

"What is it?" Declan whispered from his seat on the opposite side of the table.

"A few common herbs in the right proportions, with just a touch of ground bitter cherries."

He picked up the vial and studied it skeptically. "How can I be certain it will work?"

"You can't be certain, not until you try it," Matilda said, her smile fading.

"How much should I use? How should it be . . . administered?" He lifted dark, questioning eyes to her.

"A pinch should be enough," Matilda said. "You can sprinkle it on her food or drop it into her drink."

"How long after she takes the potion will it take effect?"

"I'm not sure," Matilda said, faltering slightly. "I would think . . . minutes rather than hours."

A suspicious man, Declan removed the cork and sniffed at the contents. "This won't hurt her, will it? Vanessa is a delicate lady. Fragile. How can I be sure there's nothing dangerous in here?"

Matilda sighed, losing her patience with the man. She'd made him exactly what he'd asked for, and all he did was sit there and frown and ask insolent questions.

"Won't you take my word on it?" she asked, more than a little insulted.

"Why should I?" he countered brusquely. "You've never done this before."

No one had ever accused her of incompetence! They called her a witch, they occasionally shunned her in public, but at least they had the decency to respect her skills. "Take it yourself, Mr. Harper," she suggested in a lowered voice. "Surely you won't mind risking your own skin in order to safeguard the life and well-being of the precious, delicate Vanessa Arrington."

He actually seemed to consider the idea, staring at the vial of powder with narrowed eyes. "I'm so much bigger than she is, I don't see how that would be a proper test." Moving slowly, he lifted his head and set his hawk-like gaze unerringly upon her. His dark eyes seemed to pierce her, giving her an unexpected chill. "You're about her size, though."

Matilda shot to her feet. "If you are suggesting that I experiment on myself to see if your potion is safe, you're crazy."

"Where's the risk? You said it was safe."

"It is!" Matilda protested. "But . . . but . . ."

"I'll take it, too," he said calmly. He had visibly relaxed, now that he'd thought of an answer to all his questions.

"I am not going to sit here and take a . . . an aphrodisiac." Her face turned warm. "I will not experiment on myself," she insisted.

Declan was unperturbed. "We know what we're taking, so any influences of the potion we feel will be easily dismissed. Just think of it, Matilda." He held up the vial so that it caught the candlelight again. "If this is effective, you can start a whole new sideline to your business. What do you think a man might pay for a safe elixir that will make his wife want him again? How much might it be worth to a woman to bring a disinterested husband back to her bed? There's nothing harmful here." He locked his eyes to hers. *"Is there?"*

Her fears faded, slowly. It did seem a rather good idea, when he put it that way. Strictly business. And how would she be able to tell people instructions for use if she didn't have any true knowledge?

"I'll get some tea to mix it in," she said, stepping away from the table. "But we both have to drink," she added with a glance over her shoulder. "And we must always keep in mind that no matter what we feel, it isn't real."

"I can control myself, Miss Candy," Declan said with an enigmatic smile. "What about you?"

His arrogance annoyed her, so she scoffed as she stepped into the kitchen. "I am always perfectly in control, Mr. Harper."

Declan couldn't help but grin. It was only fair; Matilda was giving him the kind of smile for which a man could wait a lifetime.

They'd taken the potion half an hour ago, drinking from the same cup of tea and then sitting back to wait. No powerful force had wracked his body, no uncontrollable urges had hit him. Instead, a warm glow had come over him slowly while he sat here with Matilda, as if he'd sipped at fine whiskey and it had seeped into his veins.

She sat in an old, engraved rocking chair, and he sat several feet away in a faded crimson wing chair that matched nothing else in the room. They faced each other directly, but they didn't speak much. Mostly they waited.

The room grew warmer and warmer and Declan began to sweat. With more than a touch of impatience, he stood and shrugged off his jacket, tossing it over a hard-backed chair by the table. He loosened the top button of his shirt before resuming his seat.

There was no doubt in his mind that the potion worked; at this moment, Matilda Candy was more attractive, more appealing than ever. Candlelight made her look soft, feminine, and sexy as hell. Her breasts filled out her plain blouse very nicely, pushing against the simple fabric. Her ankles, peeking out from beneath a red skirt when she rocked, were shapely and delicate. He'd never found a woman's bare feet sexy before, but Matilda's small feet and dainty toes were somehow seductive. With very little effort he could vividly imagine her legs wrapped around him, those ankles resting against his thighs.

He glanced at the curtained doorway to his right. Was that Matilda's bedroom? What kind of bed did she have? Was it hard or soft, narrow or wide? Had any man visited that room before? He set his eyes on her again, not willing to let her see how he was affected by the love potion. *Lust* potion, he amended silently. Isn't that what she'd called it?

She licked her lips. He felt his body react.

"Well, Mr. Harper, what do you think?" she asked softly.

He could certainly never tell her what was on his mind. "I thought you were going to call me Declan."

"But this is business," she said, tilting her chin upward, casting him a powerful glance as she softly, rhythmically rocked. Even in this soft light those green eyes rimmed in darker blue were hypnotic. Seductive. "Mr.

Harper seems more appropriate at the moment, as I ask you a professional question. What do you think of the potion I concocted for you?"

"You first," he said. "Is it working?"

She shrugged her shoulders. "Perhaps. At this particular moment I do find you less irritating than I did earlier."

Perhaps? Less irritating? Not exactly the response for which he was looking. "You don't find yourself the least bit attracted to me?" *Are you aroused, Matilda? Do you ache between your legs for me? Are your breasts heavy, your nipples hard?* "Just a little bit?"

She rocked again, gently. "Perhaps," she said softly. "I never noticed until just a few moments ago what a very nice neck you have."

His eyebrows lifted in dismay and surprise. He sat here, his pecker erect and thinking on its own as he suffered salacious fantasies about Tanglewood's witch, and the only effect the potion had on her was to call attention to his damned *neck*? "My neck," he muttered. "I'm so flattered."

She lifted a delicate hand and gestured gracefully in his direction. The memory of her making rose water assaulted him: the way the fragrant petals had fallen from her hands, the way the steam had wrapped around her body.

"It's a lovely neck," she continued. "Very strong, very nicely shaped. I like the masculinity of it, the width and the muscles and the perfect length." She tilted her head to one side as she continued to study him. "I should like very much to know what it tastes like."

Impossibly, his body reacted more than before; he grew even harder. At this moment, he wanted nothing more than to cross the small room, pick up Matilda, lay her on the floor, and bury himself inside her. Hard. Fast. He wanted to make her scream his name.

Control, he reminded himself. *This is the potion talking.*

"So," she whispered, "is it working for you?"

"Perhaps," he admitted grudgingly.

"You're not sure?"

Well, he couldn't very well tell her that he was painfully aroused, and he sure as hell couldn't tell her about these sexual fantasies. "I find you much less annoying than usual as well," he said calmly. "And I keep wishing you'd take your hair down," he added impetuously. "Unbraid it. Shake it loose."

"That seems a simple enough request," she said as she untied the red ribbon at the tail end of one long braid and began to slowly, *painfully* slowly, unbraid the long, golden strands.

Declan watched, hypnotized. Matilda had capable hands, skillful fingers. He wondered exactly what those fingers could do; he wondered what they'd feel like on his body. She kept her eyes on him as she worked her fingers through her hair, unraveling first one braid and then another. And then, when she was done, she shook her hair out as he had requested. Thick and wavy, it fell about her in a golden cloud. He wanted to run his own fingers through it; he wanted to see it spread across his pillow.

"Job well done, Miss Candy," he said as he forced himself slowly and carefully to his feet. "I'd say you have a successful formula here."

He grabbed his jacket from the back of the chair, and slipped the vial filled with the remaining powder into his pocket. Successful was an understatement; if anything, the potion worked *too* well. At least he knew not to share when he slipped the potion to Vanessa. He wanted her to fall in love with him; he had no intention of making a fool of himself. And certainly not over a woman. *Any* woman. Not the county's most beautiful and sought-after woman, nor a seductive, pixie-like witch with a seductive smile and hypnotic eyes.

"The effects of the potion will wear off. Won't they?" They had to! And preferably soon. He couldn't take much more of this.

Matilda did not come to her feet, but rocked slowly and observed him from her comfortable chair. "Eventually."

"*How* eventually," he snapped, wondering exactly how long he'd fantasize about Matilda.

"A few hours at most, I would guess," she said, apparently unconcerned. "Give Miss Arrington her dose, and work your own magic, Declan." Her smile faded, the happy, seductive light in her eyes dimmed. "Let her know what your neck tastes like, how your lips feel. Let her run her fingers through that thick, dark hair. And then ask her to marry you." Her beautiful mouth worked into a frown, and she sat up straighter and ceased rocking. The spell was apparently fading, for her. "From here on out you're on your own. I can't do everything for you."

"Good night, Matilda," he said, wondering when the effects of the potion would leave him. "And thank you. I have great hopes that your potion will be effective."

As he left, he heard her mutter, "Be careful what you wish for."

Matilda slept deeply and dreamed of Declan. She dreamed that he touched her. She dreamed that she laid her lips on his neck and closed her eyes and tasted to her heart's content.

She woke later than usual; most mornings she was up with the sun. But when she opened her eyes it was fully light outside. Morning sun broke through her window and filled the room with warmth and light.

Disgusted with herself, both for sleeping late and for dreaming about Declan Harper, she threw back her quilt and jumped up. She had baking to do, an extra batch of toffee to make, and rose water to bottle. She didn't have time to lay about indulging in potion-induced dreams.

At least that experiment was over. Declan would sprinkle the powder on Vanessa Arrington's food or in her tea, she'd be overcome by an urge to taste his neck, and they'd likely be married before summer was done. She snorted as she dug through her chest of drawers for a clean blouse and her blue skirt. As far as she was concerned, those two deserved each other.

She attacked her chores with a vengeance, trying to drive away last night's memories and the remnants of her dream. Her bread was rising, the ingredients for the second batch of toffee were laid out on the marble slab in her big kitchen, and a long line of red rose petals were drying in the sun, for the rose-petal jelly she'd make later in the week. With all that done, she found herself in the garden, picking lavender. She'd hang the flowers upside down until they were properly dried and then she'd grind them into a fine powder to be used in a wonderfully scented bath oil. She brought one particularly fragrant bloom to her nose and breathed deeply. And thought of Declan Harper.

The potion she'd made for Declan was more potent than she'd expected. There was nothing extraordinary in the powder she'd prepared, nothing uncommon. So why . . .

"Miss Candy!" A frantic voice cried.

Matilda turned her head to see Gretchen and Hanson come running around the house. She was not concerned by the intensity of the voice that had called her name or the dire expressions on their faces. She fully expected another tale, some sad and outrageous story to wrest sweet bread and candy from her.

All they had to do was ask, perhaps offer to do chores in exchange for sweets, but they seemed to enjoy their fibbing games so very much.

"My goodness," Matilda said, setting her basket of lavender aside. "What's happened?"

Gretchen stopped near the gate, and Hanson jumped onto the lowest rung of the fence that surrounded her garden.

"Our stepmother is trying to poison us," Gretchen said dramatically. Her lower lip trembled.

Matilda smiled and resumed picking lavender. "Stella? Don't be silly. She adores you two."

The twins exchanged a puzzled glance.

"She does not," Hanson said. "She made us the most awful caramels. They were runny *and* burned."

"She wants to get rid of us," Gretchen said forcefully. "Can't you help us? Can't you turn her into a frog or a mushroom or a cat? Something?"

Matilda laughed. "And here I thought all you wanted was candy."

"You have candy?" Hanson asked, his eyes widening in interest. "What kind did you make today?"

"Toffee," she said with a smile.

Hanson licked his lips.

"Miss Candy," Gretchen said, not as easily distracted as her brother. "Have you ever met our father?"

"No, I haven't." She'd seen Seth Hazelrig around town, but he wasn't one of the many who came to her for cures and lotions. He'd never knocked on her door late at night looking for a clandestine exchange.

"He's very handsome," Gretchen said proudly. "And very nice, too. Or at least he was until he married *her*. You should come to the house sometime and meet him. I think you'd like him. I think you'd like him a lot."

Oh, dear. She didn't like the sound of this at all. "That's a lovely invitation, but your father is a married man. It wouldn't be proper. . . ."

"But if you turned Stella into a frog, he wouldn't be," Hanson said brightly. "A man can't be married to a frog. And then you could marry Father and make us caramels and toffee and sweet bread every day of the week." He grinned, pleased with this thought.

The children no doubt thought they were being quite devious, when in fact their nefarious plan was so transparent Matilda had to put forth an effort to keep from smiling widely. She wondered how the twins would react if she could, and did, turn their suffering stepmother into an amphibian.

"I'm afraid I like Stella too much to turn her into a frog," she said calmly. "Besides, the only spell I have for such a transformation only works on the very young. It's particularly successful on small, yellow-haired children."

Hanson's eyes got wide, and Gretchen backed up a step.

"Would you like to try the toffee?" she asked, returning to her task. There was no reply, and when she lifted her head the twins were gone.

It was almost too easy. Declan had arrived at the Arrington house late in the afternoon, bearing a small gift; a bottle of whiskey to replace what he'd consumed in Warren Arrington's parlor a few nights earlier. Being a gentleman, the planter had naturally invited his guest to stay for dinner.

And then Declan had been seated next to Vanessa. How fortuitous. His plan could not be coming together more wonderfully.

It occurred to him that Arrington would probably be pleased to see his daughter marry the neighboring landowner. At least until he discovered who Declan Harper really was; that "white trash son of a drunkard."

Vanessa was beautiful and charming; he'd expected no less of her. Her gown was the palest pink, the pearls around her throat were the perfect compliment to her creamy skin, and her violet eyes were clear and bright.

Perhaps they were not as hypnotic as some he'd seen, but they were quite beautiful.

Vanessa Arrington was a real lady. Soft-spoken, attentive, demure. She was just what he wanted and needed in a wife.

The vial containing the love potion was in the right-hand pocket of his jacket. While Vanessa answered her father's questions about the meals she'd planned for the week—a blatant attempt on Arrington's part to point out what an efficient housekeeper Vanessa was—Declan reached into his pocket and flipped out the cork. He turned the vial up and poured a small amount of powder into his palm.

And while Vanessa gave her father her attention, Declan sprinkled the powder into her soup. The grains sat on top of the thick liquid for a moment, and then dissolved and sank, disappearing from sight.

"Harper," Arrington barked.

Declan lifted his head; that had been too close. If the old man had shifted his attention a few seconds earlier . . . but he hadn't. "Yes, sir?"

"You can spend a fortune on that house of yours," Arrington said brusquely, "but it won't be a home until there's a woman living in it."

Apparently Warren Arrington had decided his new and successful neighbor would make a suitable husband for his beloved daughter. That couldn't hurt, Declan thought. It would even add a touch of irony to the moment when he stood before the old man and told him who he really was.

"That's quite true, sir," Declan said, trying to sound humble. "A woman does make a house a home."

As he waited for Vanessa to consume her soup—and the potion—he wondered if she'd look at him the way Matilda Candy had last night. He wondered if her eyes would devour him, if she'd be tempted to taste him. The memory distracted and aroused him, and shaking the memories and the arousal off was more difficult than it should have been.

Vanessa finally lifted her soup spoon, and Declan caught his breath. He wouldn't have to wonder for long. She finished every drop, taking small, dainty sips from her well-polished, ornate silver spoon.

The soup was followed by a tasty fish and a selection of well-prepared vegetables. Declan ate but he tasted nothing. He tried to carry on a casual conversation with Vanessa throughout the meal. He wanted her attention on him, wanted to see the passion creep into her violet eyes as the potion took hold.

She was a woman. If she felt passion for him she'd think herself in love, and when he asked her to marry him she'd say yes without hesitation. He wouldn't have to suffer poor Henry Langford's fate.

The meal was a leisurely one. A half-hour passed. A quarter-hour more. Declan began to fidget in his chair. Why wasn't it working? Vanessa remained calm, polite, ladylike. There was not so much as a flicker of interest in her cool eyes.

Finally, slices of a delicate white cake were served. Vanessa declared herself much too full to even think of dessert, and then she rose to take her leave. She bid Declan a courteous good night and thanked him for his company, kissed her father on the cheek, and left the room without so much as a single backward glance.

Declan watched the empty doorway where she had not lingered and felt a crushing defeat. It hadn't worked. There had been no fire of passion in Vanessa's eyes, not so much as a flicker of longing. She had not once looked at him as if she wanted to devour him, hadn't one time smiled with promise and yearning. Somehow the powder had lost its potency overnight.

Matilda was just going to have to try again.

Chapter Six

Matilda delivered toffee, spiced nuts, bread, and bottled rose water to Mr. Fox, along with a few jars of rose-petal jelly and three slender bottles of vinegar of roses. She collected the empty basket from last week's delivery, as well as a shipment of spices he'd ordered for her and the few coins difference in this week's transaction. It wasn't much, as the spices were costly.

Mr. Fox was his normal chatty self, talking about the dry weather and the fact that a few of the farmers had discussed the possibility of bringing in a rainmaker—a solution he dismissed as ludicrous.

She'd just begun the walk home when a low, deep voice spoke, much too close to her ear.

"It didn't work."

She started and glanced over her shoulder just as Declan stepped to her side and matched his stride to hers. "What didn't work?" she asked breathlessly.

He looked down at her, annoyance in his narrowed dark gaze, tension in the set of his jaw and his lips. He wore a suit, as always, but the jacket looked as if he'd been squirming all morning, and the top button of his white shirt had already been unbuttoned. "The potion. What else?"

She knew good and well that the potion she'd made was effective. Hadn't she suffered in taking it herself? Hadn't she studied Declan Harper until a strange warmth had almost made her forget herself? "But . . ." she began weakly.

"It didn't work on Vanessa," he clarified. "I'm not criticizing your efforts," he added, the tone of his voice less sharp as they stepped from the covered boardwalk and into the sun. "We know the potion did possess some . . . interesting qualities. For some reason it did not work when I administered it to Vanessa. Perhaps it lost its potency overnight, or perhaps it's effective on some people but not all."

"I'll give you your money back," Matilda said. "I'm so very sorry it didn't work for you." She wasn't sorry at all, she decided. Marriages shouldn't be made with powders and potions, but with love. She frowned at the unexpected thought, glancing past Declan to the tree-lined road that would lead her home. Love brought nothing but heartache and pain to those who suffered from it. There was, perhaps, a momentary bliss, but what followed was always so messy and agonizing.

"I don't want my money back," Declan said sharply. "I want you to try again."

Matilda shook her head. "That's not a good idea. Maybe it's for the best that the potion was ineffective. Maybe it isn't fair to win a wife with a tonic meant to set her heart afire for a short time."

"Fair?" Declan said, a spark of amused incredulity in his voice. "*Life* isn't fair, and I am certainly no tower of integrity."

Matilda couldn't help but smile, in spite of Declan's

apparent seriousness. "Why am I not surprised to hear you say that?"

He cocked his head to look at her and returned the smile. Oh, she liked what a simple grin did to his face, how it made him look warmer. Softer.

"You've found me out," he said softly intimately. "I am a ruthless man who will do whatever is necessary to get what I want."

Matilda's heart did a strange little flip in her chest when he smiled at her this way. Something deep inside fluttered and she found herself, once again, staring at the fascinating lines of his neck. It looked very . . . tempting. She shook off the response, dismissing it as a lingering aftermath of the potion. Heaven knew she still felt the unnatural warmth that concoction had inflicted upon her. And the powder hadn't worked on Vanessa Arrington at all?

"I suppose I can try one more time," she finally conceded. "But no matter what happens, no matter how badly you want something to bring Vanessa to you, I refuse to prepare anything I think might be hallucinogenic, and I will have to draw the line at killing animals for their . . . parts."

"I'm in total agreement," Declan said calmly.

Matilda swung her basket lightly. "I will need a few more days, of course. Come by the cottage Sunday evening, after dark. I'll have something for you then."

She expected him to make a quick escape and head back to town, since their business was concluded, but he didn't. He simply nodded and then glanced into her basket.

"What do you have there?" he asked conversationally.

"Spices," she said, holding the basket up so he could see. "Jamaican ginger, cinnamon, and cloves."

"What will you make with them?" He seemed truly interested.

"Sweet bread and cookies."

"My mother makes the best cinnamon raisin bread," Declan said. "It's really fabulous. Unfortunately," he added with a narrowing of his eyes, "it's the only thing she can cook that's worth eating. When I made some money, the first thing I did was hire her a cook."

"A man who will hire a cook for his mother can't be totally ruthless," Matilda said lightly.

He glanced at her, narrowing his eyes and trying to look harsh and failing miserably. "I was required to eat Sunday dinner at her house every week," he answered. "Trust me, my motives were completely selfish."

She stopped in the middle of the road and turned to face Declan. He stopped as well and stared down at her. There was something undeniably brutal in the set of his jaw and his mouth, something as heartless as he claimed to be. But in those dark eyes she saw something more; she saw his heart.

"Why are you trying so hard to convince me that you're incapable of doing something nice?" she asked.

"Because I'm not nice," he insisted, leaning closer to her, trying, and failing, to appear threatening. "Nice guys don't get anywhere in this world."

"How very miserable you must be, if you really believe that," she said, resuming her journey.

"How very naive you are," he countered as he followed, "if you don't."

She kept expecting him to turn back, to head for town and leave her to finish her walk alone, but he didn't. He talked about his sisters, in an offhand way that made her certain he missed them but would never admit it. He talked about the house he'd built for his mother, and she didn't bother to point out to him that there couldn't possibly be any selfish motives involved in giving such a gift.

She told him how she needed to mend the fence that surrounded her flower garden, and how if it didn't rain soon she'd be hauling water from the spring-fed pond near her cottage to see that her plants survived the summer. She told him about caring for the plants in the greenhouse, and preparing the lotions and powders her customers required of her.

He laughingly asked her if she ever sat down to rest. If she ever read a book or sat by the pond doing nothing or took a nap in the afternoon. She thought about his questions for a moment before shaking her head.

In no time at all, they were at the cottage. Declan seemed surprised, just as he had last week, to find that they'd come so far so quickly.

"I'm going to have to get you on a horse," he muttered.

"I don't think so," she answered with a smile.

She was reluctant to turn her back on him and say good-bye. He seemed just as reluctant to turn and begin the walk toward town.

"It was very nice of you to walk me home," she said softly.

Declan cocked his head and looked at her strangely, his eyes sharp, his lips thinned. He had looked at her this way after taking the potion. This look was less open, less audacious, but still she could see . . . something undiscovered waiting for her. Something new and exciting.

With a long, deep breath, Declan took a single step closer. He was going to kiss her, somehow she knew it. If she were smart she'd turn away before he had the chance to do such a thing, but all her intelligence failed her. She wanted to know what his lips felt like on hers.

Another aftereffect of the potion, she imagined dismissively.

His head tipped slowly toward hers, reluctant and unerring at the same time. Ah, he was no doubt suffering, as she was, from the aftermath of the powerful aphrodisiac they'd consumed. He was likely as confused as she was.

Her confusion fled, and she simply accepted what was

to come. Her heart skipped a beat, she held her breath, her eyes drifted almost closed ... and then with a jerk Declan pulled away from her.

"What the hell?" he snapped, spinning around quickly.

"What is it?" Matilda asked, her voice much too small for the moment, hazy, disappointed.

"Something hit me in the back."

As he spoke, another small projectile flew from the forest, a pebble that barely missed Declan's thigh.

"You'd better get out of here, mister," a familiar voice called from the shelter of the trees. "She's a witch. If you kiss her, she'll turn you into a toad!"

"You little ..." Declan muttered, taking a long step toward the forest. From the trees they heard a squeal, a shout, and the sound of brush being abused as Hanson and Gretchen made their getaway.

"My closest neighbor's children," Matilda explained. "They can be difficult, but I'm sure they meant no harm."

Perhaps they'd meant no harm, but whatever spell had enticed Declan to try to kiss her was broken. She knew it would be foolish to pursue such an inappropriate interest, and from the wary look on his face, so did he.

"Sunday evening," he said as he backed away.

Matilda smiled and nodded and then turned, relieved to retreat into her cottage.

Declan had been uncommonly restless all weekend, so it was no wonder that he arrived at Matilda's house in the woods long before dark. And no mistake. The only way he knew to cure restlessness was to work it off. Good, hard, physical labor was the best way to take his mind off Matilda and her bewitching eyes.

All his life he'd found release in activities that strained his muscles and made him sweat. When something went wrong, he headed for a pile of logs that needed to be split, or his second brother-in-law's wildest horses, or a pile of hay in his first brother-in-law's barn. Anything to make the spinning in his mind stop.

And right now his mind was definitely spinning.

He tethered his horse behind Matilda's greenhouse, in a shady spot where the stallion would be cool and there was plenty of grass on which to graze. And here the horse would be out of sight, should someone drop by. Maybe Matilda was called a witch, maybe she didn't care what others thought of her. But that didn't mean she didn't have a reputation to consider. It wouldn't look right for his horse to be outside her house all afternoon and into the night.

He carried the tools he'd brought with him and headed for the back of the cottage. Without thought, he smiled. He liked this place. It was solid and cozy, substantial and charming. The walls of stone set it apart from the other homes in and around Tanglewood, but something less tangible made it homey.

Maybe it was the way flowers grew so abundantly and brightly around the cottage, or the way the lacy curtains whipped in the breeze. Maybe it was the way the air always smelled of baked bread and rose water and sweets. And maybe, he thought as he caught sight of Matilda in the garden and came to a halt, it was her.

She carefully picked flowers, studying one bloom and then another before either plucking the blossom and depositing it in her small basket or moving on to the next flower. Today she wore a natural linen blouse and a full forest-green skirt. Long braided pigtails, gold in the sun, hung down her back. He couldn't see her feet, but they were most certainly bare.

He'd never known a woman like her; that was an understatement. There were lots of pretty females in the world, and he'd known his share. More than his share, to be honest. Money would do that for a man, he'd found, though Matilda seemed not to care at all for the fortune he'd made. She wasn't the prettiest woman he'd ever

77

met, but there was something about her . . . something as hard to grasp as the charm of this strange cottage. Perhaps they were both enchanted.

Matilda Candy said what was on her mind, she smiled with her heart, captivated him with her eyes. Those brats had said if he kissed her she'd turn him into a toad. And at the moment, that was a chance he was willing to take.

"Where's the break in your fence?" he asked as he stepped toward her.

For the first time since he'd met Matilda, he surprised her. She jumped and spun around, her eyes widening. "You're early," she said accusingly. "Again."

He grinned and held his hammer and a small bag of nails aloft. "I came to fix your fence, ma'am."

She recovered from her shock quickly, and showed him where the fence was damaged.

The white wooden fence that surrounded her garden was high and sturdy. Tall posts stood solidly at each of the four corners. Three slats ran the course of the enclosure, and in many cases a plant growing near the edge twined around and over and through the white strips. In four places, the slats had come loose and fallen. Matilda said they were victims of her boisterous neighbor children, who liked to climb the fence and occasionally jump up and down in excitement or terror.

Declan mended the fence while Matilda returned to her garden and the flowers she picked so carefully. He tried to keep his mind on the chore at hand, but it was a rather easy task to repair the fence, and Matilda was so damned close that there was no way he could put her out of his mind. Hell, he didn't want to put her out of his mind, not yet.

"Surely you have chores to do at the old house you bought," she said sweetly. "Why, last time I saw that place it was practically falling down. Thanks to the Yankees," she added in a lowered voice.

"I've hired several men to see to the repair of the

house," he said, holding a slat in place and positioning a nail. "There's no need for me to get my hands dirty when I'm paying someone else good money to do it for me."

"Why is it that you'll get your hands dirty fixing my fence," she said, finding a sturdy spot a few feet down and climbing up to sit on the fence in question. "But you won't do repairs on your own newly bought home?"

He didn't want to tell her, but the place he'd bought didn't feel like home. Sometimes when he walked through the empty, cavernous rooms, he was certain it never would. "Can't you just say 'thank you' like a normal person?" he asked.

He glanced up to see her smiling brightly, one leg swinging gently to and fro. Her green skirt swayed, and he caught a glimpse of not only a slender ankle, but a small portion of shapely bare calf as well.

"Thank you," she whispered.

He brought the hammer crashing down onto his thumb.

Declan Harper not only fixed her fence, he insisted on chopping wood while she finished picking flowers and then pulled a few pesky weeds from around her beloved roses. Matilda didn't try to stop him; she used a lot of wood in her brick oven, and splitting logs was hard work.

Kneeling on the ground and pulling up weeds by the roots, she kept one eye on Declan. He'd taken off his shirt and hung it over the fence he'd just repaired. When he lifted the ax, muscles bunched and rippled. When he swung down, they did it again, only differently. *My, he is a fine figure of a man,* Matilda thought as she stopped her chore to simply watch for a moment. He tried to pass himself off as a businessman, but it didn't quite work. He was too raw for the staid life of a merchant, too powerful. How could he ever be content sitting around sipping brandy and discussing the price of cotton and the weather? No, he belonged . . . he belonged *here,* chopping wood and mending fences.

"Silly girl," she muttered as she returned her full attention to her chore and yanked up a nasty-looking weed. "He belongs in a fancy house with a dozen servants and that hussy Vanessa Arrington at his side."

She made short work of her weeding, gathered the basket of blooms for the hair pomade she'd make in a couple of days, and made her way to the well. She'd worked up a sweat in the garden, so it was a blessed pleasure to take a cloth and dip it into the bucket of well water, to wipe her face and her throat. She closed her eyes and wiped off the back of her neck, appreciating the feel of the cool cloth on her hot skin. That done, she washed her hands, and then sat on the side of the well to wash the garden soil from her feet.

Vanessa Arrington probably had a hundred pairs of shoes. Kid boots and satin slippers, footwear in every color and fabric imaginable. Matilda wiped a bit of dirt from her ankle. What was wrong with her! She'd never before wished for shoes. She had a sturdy pair of walking boots, and she didn't need shoes for anything else. She was always so grateful to get out of her boots after a trip to town. Vanessa Arrington probably had corns and blisters and ugly, crimped toes. At least, Matilda hoped so.

Matilda suddenly realized that she hadn't heard the crack of splintering wood in a few long moments. She lifted her head and looked to where Declan stood, leaning on the ax the way a fine gentleman might lean on his cane, a huge pile of wood at his side. He took a deep breath and exhaled slowly.

"You might want to clean up before coming inside," she said, noting the way his skin shone with sweat and a few strands of dark hair stuck to his forehead and his neck. "I'll get you a clean cloth."

She used the excuse to escape into the house for a while, to catch her breath and calm her heart and remind herself why Declan Harper had come to her.

By the time she stepped back outside to hand him the small towel, her mind was clear. Well, she thought as she saw him standing by the well waiting for her, clearer than it had been. Declan wanted Vanessa, and he'd paid the local witch well to make sure that he would have her. That sad fact was the sole basis for their relationship.

Why was she so sure there was more than that between them?

"Maybe I should feed you," she said as he dampened the cloth and put it to his sweaty face. "No one's ever chopped wood for me before," she added. "A meal seems like the least I can do."

He raked the damp cloth across the back of his neck. "To be honest, I'm starving. It's been a long time since I spent an entire afternoon doing physical labor." He grinned as if he'd actually enjoyed chopping wood.

With sweat and a smile on his face and mussed dark hair falling over his forehead, he took deep breaths that made his bare chest rise and fall. To Matilda's eyes he looked much more natural in this state than he ever had in a fine suit of clothes. He didn't squirm, he didn't stand so stiff and tall he might've been made of stone. He looked . . . content.

"I worked up quite an appetite," he added.

When he lowered the damp towel to his chest, Matilda spun around and headed for the house. What had come over her? She couldn't very well stand here and watch Declan Harper bathe!

"Dinner won't be fancy, but it'll be ready shortly," she said calmly.

Maybe if she fed Declan well he wouldn't look so hungry, so needy . . . and then maybe she'd be able to dismiss the nagging notion that what he really needed was *her*.

Chapter Seven

When Declan was well-fed, and she'd cleared most of the supper dishes away, Matilda fetched a small tin from the shelf nearest her rocking chair. Her heart skipped a beat as she opened the box and revealed to Declan a dozen small pieces of hard candy.

"No thanks," he said, peering down at the contents. "I don't care for dessert." He patted his flat stomach and smiled. "You fed me too well."

The meal had been simple, but she'd made sure he had plenty to eat: ham, bread, fried potatoes and onions, and greens from her vegetable garden. He'd eaten the way a man was supposed to eat; like he savored every bite and couldn't get enough.

"This isn't dessert," she said softly. "This is your new love potion."

He smiled, apparently taken with the idea of the new form; a golden hard candy shaped like teardrops. "What's in it?"

"Many spices, including the Jamaican ginger I bought

on Friday. Honey. The finest sugar." She cut her eyes up to meet his. "And a secret ingredient." She closed the tin and handed it to him. "It's perfectly safe."

He lifted the lid she'd just closed. "But will it work?"

"You'll have to try it and see," she said. "I'm sure Vanessa will be thrilled when you show up with candy. Sweets for the sweet," she said dryly. "If it doesn't work, you've lost nothing."

He shook his head and reached in to take one sweet between two fingers, to hold the small piece of hard candy up and study it with narrowed eyes. He even turned it this way and that as if looking for imperfections.

"Unacceptable," he finally said in a low voice. "We're going to have to test this one the way we tested the first."

She didn't know whether to be horrified or excited at the prospect. "That's not necessary."

Declan held the candy to her mouth, his long, warm fingers right there against her lips, his hand steady. Matilda reluctantly but obediently parted her lips and allowed him to place the small piece on her tongue. The ginger gave her a jolt, tingling on her tongue as the candy began to melt in her mouth.

"You next," she said, unwilling to go through this torture alone.

Declan waited as she took a piece of the candy between two fingers. She offered the small sweet to him, but instead of taking it from her, he ate the candy right from her hand, closing his lips over her fingers and sucking it into his mouth. His lips barely touched her flesh, but still she shivered.

She saw the surprise in his eyes as the ginger prickled his tongue.

Last time they'd tested a potion, they'd cautiously sat far apart, studying and waiting, approaching the experiment from a purely scientific point of view. That was surely the only proper way to conduct such an experiment; from a distance. Matilda knew she really should

sit in her rocker, remove herself from Declan's imme-
diate presence, and wait for something extraordinary to
happen.

But it was too late. Something extraordinary was already happening. The tingle that had started on her
tongue spread through her body like wildfire. She felt,
so clearly and warmly, the place on her fingers where
Declan's mouth had briefly touched her skin. She still
felt the brush of his fingers against her mouth.

She looked up at him, met his stare. His eyes burned
the way her soul did, with dark fire. Her fingers itched
to reach out and touch his harsh face, to trace the line of
his jaw and the outline of his lips. She wanted to push
back that strand of dark hair that had fallen over his
forehead, then trail her fingers over his face. Much as
she wanted to, she knew she couldn't touch, but she
could stare; and she did. My, he was so handsome.

She should look away, she knew this, and yet she
couldn't force herself to do so. More than that, she didn't
want to. The love potion gave her an excuse to stare
boldly, to think of wicked things best left unthought.

"This one works fast," Declan said softly.

"Yes, it does," Matilda agreed in a whisper. Why deny
what she felt? Why pretend she didn't look at him and
feel something wonderful? Something powerful, and
knee-weakening, and truly magical. Under this spell,
there was no reason to pretend, no reason to hold back.
"You were wonderful today," she said with a smile. "I
watched you, a little," she confessed. "You're very . . .
strong. Very handsome."

"Do you still want to taste my neck?" he asked, his
voice raspy.

"More than ever," she whispered.

She licked her lips. He clenched and unclenched his
fists in a way that proved he wanted to reach out and
touch her the same way she wanted to reach out and
touch him.

He looked slightly pained, and more uncomfortable with every passing heartbeat. "I watched you, too," he admitted. "A little. You're very . . . seductive. Very pretty."

She raised her eyebrows in real surprise. No one but Granny had ever told her she was pretty before, and she knew darn well she wasn't seductive. "My, this *is* a powerful concoction."

"Yes, it is."

She had to tilt her head back to look at Declan, but she boldly did so. Ah, she loved his face, so hard and sweet and sharp at the same time. Hard and sweet and sharp, like the ginger candy that melted on her tongue. At any other time she would've felt compelled to turn her head, to call on her decorum. To blush and lower her eyes. But the potion, and the experimental nature of their taking of it, gave her permission to look her fill.

"It's becoming very difficult," she said, "not to kiss you."

He swallowed. Hard. "I know what you mean."

She felt free to tell him everything. Anything. "It's like a compulsion. No, not a compulsion, but a necessity. Like breathing, or the beating of my heart."

"Maybe we should," he said softly. "Kiss. For the sake of the test, of course."

"Of course," she whispered, very slowly rising up on her toes to bring her mouth closer to his. It wasn't enough to span the distance between them; he had to lower his head slightly to meet her.

It struck Matilda, moments before their lips met, that Declan was looking at her the way he'd looked at his meal earlier; as if he were starving and could never get enough.

Their lips touched, and she closed her eyes. Oh, the sensation was heavenly; warm and soft, thrilling and comforting. When he moved his lips over hers, she quivered to her very bones and her knees wobbled.

She reached up and laid her hand on the side of his head, lightly spearing her fingers through his hair. Her thumb rocked against his jaw, and she felt the stubble there, the roughness of his evening beard. She liked it . . . she liked it very much.

He circled an arm around her and held on tight, as if he knew her knees were about to give out. He was solid, and hot, and the way he kissed her . . . it was as if he were trying to devour her alive. He held her so she could feel his hard body pressed against hers, and the holding was wonderful, as wonderful as the continuing kiss.

Another arm stole around her, and Declan slowly lifted her. Her feet left the floor completely, and he inched her higher and higher until she no longer had to look up and he no longer had to lean down. They were face-to-face, lip to lip. Her arms encircled his neck and she held on tight, in case he should lose his grip and let her fall.

When she felt his tongue on her lower lip, she was so surprised that she gasped. He took the opportunity to slip that tongue into her mouth to tease her own. Heat suffused her body. Liquid heat pooled between her legs and thrummed with every beat of her heart.

She didn't want this kiss to end. Not ever. She rested a hand at the back of Declan's head and held him close, as she copied his bold move and slipped the tip of her tongue into his mouth. He tasted so good, so delicious.

He moaned deep in his throat, and she answered. She was so close to losing control . . . so close. . . .

She slowly pulled her mouth from his. "I'd say it works even better than the first try."

"Maybe it works too well," he whispered, kissing her quickly and briefly, continuing to hold her tight.

She didn't want to say it, she didn't want to be the one to call an end to this moment. But if Declan felt anything like she did, and she suspected that was the case, it was definitely time to stop the kiss.

"Remember," she said softly, saddened by her words.

"What we feel isn't real. It's the aphrodisiac. The candy. What we feel right now is not genuine."

He shook his head slowly and did not put her on her feet. "Damn, it sure enough feels real. As genuine as anything I can remember. I've never wanted anything in my life the way I want you now."

Matilda placed her hands on either side of his head. Declan was a big man, strong and hard, but she felt no fear. He would never hurt her. He would never take more than she offered. "You must put me down, now."

He feathered another kiss across her lips. "But I don't want to," he whispered. "Another kiss like the first one."

"No," she said as his mouth came to hers again. "We've proven that the power of the candy is real. Declan, we have to stop now. You have to go."

He didn't look inclined to obey, though he didn't try to kiss her again. Oh, his eyes, so dark and rich, they spoke to her of much more than another kiss.

"Remember Vanessa," she whispered.

His smile disappeared, and he placed her gently on her feet. He turned from her and raked his hands through his dark, short hair, clearly exasperated and searching for the control he claimed to possess. "Matilda, that potion should come with a warning. I don't think the world is ready for anything like this."

She collected the small box of powerful candies and offered it at the end of an outstretched arm. "If this doesn't work on Vanessa, nothing will."

She stood there with her latest creation on her palm, the aphrodisiac offered to Declan without visible reservation. But in her heart she knew he was right. The world was surely not ready for this. Why didn't he snatch the offering from her hand and go? Instead he looked down at her, staring so hard she could feel the force of his gaze. His hands clenched, unclenched, clenched again, as if he didn't quite know what to do with them.

Finally he took the tin and left by way of the back

door, and before the reverberation of the slamming of that door had faded, Matilda remembered with regret that she still hadn't tasted Declan's neck.

If he waited too long, he'd likely change his mind. Yesterday's kiss, if indeed that's all it was, had stayed with him all night. The memory of Matilda had stayed with him all night as well. Right now it would be insanely easy to sacrifice all his plans and dreams for one night in Matilda Candy's bed.

He'd worked long and hard for this revenge, had dreamed of this day. Matilda had spoken once of purpose. Well, this was his purpose; his reason for living, his one goal in life.

Declan made himself remember the way Warren Arrington had made him feel, the way the man had insulted him, and his sisters, and his mother. The way the townspeople had turned their backs when Brenna Harper had found herself widowed and penniless. He tried to imagine the expressions on their faces when he owned them all and revealed who he really was.

Purposely drawing on the anger that had gotten him through many agonizing nights, Declan prepared himself for what was to come. He needed the anger inside to give him the strength to turn his back on what he wanted in order to take what he needed. Retribution.

He knocked resolutely on the Arringtons' front door. This courtship was an important step in realizing his plan. His plantation, once it was finished, would be the finest for a hundred miles. He'd be married to the most sought-after woman in the county. Respected and accepted, *one of them,* as Matilda said, he'd buy up businesses one by one until there was nothing left.

He waited in the parlor while a maid, one of many, went to inform Vanessa that she had a caller. He waited, and he waited, and he waited. With the small, cool tin box in his hands, he paced the floor. For a few minutes, he sat on the fine green sofa, but a deep restlessness wouldn't allow him to remain still for long, so he paced some more.

It was a good half hour before Vanessa appeared, perfectly coifed and dressed in a pale blue gown with small pearl buttons at the bodice. Pearls also adorned her slender throat and her earlobes. She smiled, and did not apologize for making him wait.

"What a lovely surprise," she said, offering him a seat on the sofa and placing herself beside him. "Did you come to see Daddy? I'm afraid he's gone for the day. Something about a horse in Rankin county that can't wait another day." She gave him a small, genteel, feminine smile.

"Actually, I came to see you," he said calmly. If only he could handle this transaction in a businesslike manner. Courtship was such a waste of time. He offered her the tin, hoping beyond hope that the contents would make short work of his courting days. "I brought you a small gift."

Her smile widened slightly, and her eyes sparkled as she took the small box. "Oh, how very sweet of you. I do love presents," she revealed in a lowered voice. She lifted the lid and looked into the box, and a small bit of the light in her eyes faded. "What is this?"

"Candy," Declan said. "A very wonderful, special candy."

Vanessa very carefully closed the lid. "I'm afraid I don't like sweets much." She returned the box to him. "I love pearls, though, and violets, and rubies. . . ."

He sat there, stunned, as Vanessa listed all the things she liked best. His mother, who had spent her life as a simple farmer's daughter and a poor farmer's wife and then a servant, would be horrified at this lady's lack of decorum. His sisters would laugh out loud.

Once they were married, he'd have to teach this woman something about manners. Couldn't she at least pretend to be pleased? Oh, well, perhaps most rich, pampered ladies were spoiled, to some extent. Perhaps he should not be surprised by her reaction to the simple gift.

She gazed up at him with those violet eyes that were so gentle and radiant. God, what skin she had; so pale and creamy it looked as if it had never seen the sun. He wanted to touch it, to run his fingers over her cheek and see if it felt as soft as it looked.

And at the same time, he was terrified. Vanessa looked like a porcelain doll, not a woman to be touched. She looked as if she would never wrap her arms around a man's neck and kiss him for all she was worth. Sedate pecks on the cheek, perhaps. Delicate fingers offered for a chaste kiss. He saw tremendous beauty in Vanessa Arrington, but he saw no passion. For the first time, he wondered seriously if his plan was, perhaps, flawed.

He dismissed his reservations. Passion was not the hallmark of a lady. Gentility and refinement were what he wanted. Right?

Matilda worked at the long table in the main room, mashing and mixing the pomade ingredients with great vigor. Lavender, rose petals, bay leaves, and cloves filled the bottom of her largest bowl. She seemed to have lots of energy to spare today, lots of anxious, angry energy.

It was well after noon. Had Declan administered the candy aphrodisiac to Vanessa Arrington? What were they doing right now, right this very minute? She viciously worked the dried flowers and the hint of spice with a wooden spoon as she pondered the possibilities.

She was so lost in thought, the knock on her door made her jump. Very few people, but for Hanson and Gretchen, visited her during the daylight hours. And the children never knocked. They crept about and swiped candy and spied on her, but they did not knock at her door.

What if it's Declan? she thought with a leap of her

heart. What if, once again, the potion had proven ineffective?

She left her bowl sitting on the table and went to open the door, and was surprised to see Vanessa Arrington herself standing there. Composed, serene, condescending Vanessa. There was no sign that she might've taken the candy, no flush of her cheeks or restlessness in her eyes. Perhaps tonight . . .

"Miss Arrington," Matilda said, surprise in her voice.

Vanessa didn't look directly at Matilda, but then she never did. Neither did she look directly at Mr. Fox, when Matilda saw her at the general store, or at her servants, like her driver, the still and diligent John Bowers who stood patiently behind her. She treated those around her with open disdain and disregard, and carried herself like a queen.

Declan's queen.

"Miss Candy," Vanessa said, looking to the room beyond. "If you have a moment, I have need of your services once again."

"Of course." Matilda stepped back and Vanessa swept into the room. Matilda gave John Bowers, who was two years older than she, a smile. They'd briefly attended Tanglewood's one-room schoolhouse together. Matilda's stay in that school had been short; she'd quickly grown tired of being taunted and teased because of her grandmother's reputation.

John had not been one of the children to taunt her, though, she remembered kindly. Vanessa probably would have, had she been given the opportunity, but she'd never set foot inside the Tanglewood schoolhouse. Private tutors had taught her, so that she would not have to rub shoulders with the common folk.

John was handsome and, from what Matilda remembered, smart. Why was he still in Tanglewood, a driver and stableman for Warren Arrington? He returned her smile before she closed the door.

"I'm almost out of face cream," Vanessa said. "And I thought I might purchase a bottle of rose water while I'm here."

"Certainly." Matilda collected the requested items, including the latest batch of beauty cream Hanson had spit into. Vanessa had been a regular buyer of the cream for the past three years—since she'd turned twenty.

"Also," Vanessa said in a lowered voice, "that rash on my arms has reappeared. The ointment you suggested last time worked wonderfully, but I'm afraid I'm completely out."

Matilda collected that ointment and placed it with the other purchases. "Anything else?"

A quarter of an hour later, Vanessa was finished. She had too many creams and ointments to carry, so Matilda placed them all in a small basket.

Wouldn't Declan love to know exactly how his queen stayed so beautiful?

Wouldn't Vanessa love to know what Declan had planned for her?

Unfortunately, being the keeper of Tanglewood's secrets meant *keeping* the secrets. Vanessa looked startled when Matilda handed her the heavy basket rather than offering to carry it to the carriage for her.

Matilda opened the door for Vanessa, who immediately handed the basket to her driver. John took the basket as if it weighed nothing, then took Vanessa's hand and assisted her into the carriage. Vanessa never uttered a word or a nod of thanks, she just settled herself in the fine velvet-covered seat and, spine straight as a board, waited for her driver to take her home.

Matilda stood in the doorway and watched the carriage head for the road, then she slammed the door of her little cottage shut with such force the walls trembled.

Chapter Eight

The carriage came to a halt in the shade of a grove of pine and oak trees, and Vanessa waited. Johnny opened the door and offered his hand, and she took it, stepping gracefully from the carriage and onto the ground.

It was pleasantly cool here, with a breeze coming off the water of the pond so near. She loved this place for an afternoon picnic. The trees were ancient and sheltering, the water was somehow calming, and here she was not on public display; there was no one for miles around.

Johnny collected her picnic basket and a thin collection of poetry, as well as a thick blanket he expertly snapped open and spread in the shade. Once again he took her hand, as she gracefully lowered herself to sit on the blanket. He placed the picnic basket and the book at her side.

She lifted her head to look up at him, and she smiled. He was so beautiful—tall and strong, everything a man should be. His thick black hair curled just slightly. He had magnificent blue eyes and dimples that were absolutely adorable, set in a face of even, classic features that belonged on a marble statue of a Greek god.

Vanessa prized beauty above all things; her own and that of everything around her. Her clothes, her jewelry, her home . . . all were things of beauty. She despised all things ugly as much, or more, than she adored things of beauty. They offended her sensibilities.

She patted the space at her side. "Sit with me, Johnny," she commanded. He obeyed, as he always did.

He smiled at her, bringing those dimples into play. Yes, there was nothing on earth as beautiful as the man who had been her lover for the past two years.

Well, almost her lover. When she leaned forward and asked it of him, whispering a husky "Kiss me," he complied. Softly at first and then harder, as if he couldn't get enough of her. She wrapped her arms around his neck and kissed him back with everything she had, plunging her tongue into his mouth, tasting him, teasing him.

Inside, she melted. Her knees felt weak, her heart beat fast, her blood roared. Heavens, she craved this, sometimes. Yearned for the feel of Johnny's mouth on hers.

They kissed for a while, soft and then deep. Easy and then hard. Finally she took her mouth briefly from his. "Unbutton me," she demanded.

His fingers expertly unfastened the tiny pearl buttons down the front of her bodice. He did not accomplish his task too slowly, nor did he rush. By now he knew exactly what she wanted, how she liked it.

"Touch me," she whispered.

Johnny laid the pale blue fabric open and raked his hand across her flesh. His fingers were gentle, teasing, hot, as he explored her breasts lovingly. A low-burning fire flamed inside Vanessa.

He took his mouth from hers to kiss her there, his lips on her chest and then on the swell of her breasts. When he took a nipple deep into his mouth, she held his head tightly against her, wanting more. Sparks shot through her body, the fire grew quickly from her mouth to her breasts to the throbbing insistence between her legs.

Johnny laid her gently on her back and hovered above her, lavishing his attention first on one breast and then on the other. Sucking and nibbling and laving his tongue across her sensitive flesh until she could no longer think straight. She lifted her hips to press herself against the hard ridge of Johnny's manhood. His trousers and her gown came between them, and still the touch excited her beyond words. He raked the length slowly along her, moaning deep in his throat.

"Stop," she commanded in a hoarse whisper. He did. They had all afternoon, and she had no intention of being satisfied so quickly.

She rolled Johnny onto his back and unfastened his trousers as deftly as he'd handled her pearl buttons. The cool breeze blew over her exposed breasts and ruffled Johnny's fine curls as she touched his aroused manhood, closing her fingers around it, stroking until he closed his eyes and groaned. He was a magnificent figure of a man, so large she didn't know how she would ever take him into her body. She would, though. One day.

She climbed on top of him, covering his long body with hers, stroking as she kissed him. "I love the way you feel," she whispered into his mouth, flicking her tongue over his lower lip. She slithered down slowly and tasted his small, flat nipples, much as he had tasted hers. She kissed a trail down his slightly hairy chest, using her tongue, taking her time.

Vanessa knew she could not afford to lose her virginity to a servant, but she and Johnny knew how to take care of each other. She teased him until he was panting, and then she pleasured him with her mouth. Johnny, this beautiful man, was hers, completely and totally. He would do anything for her, would kill for her, die for her. That knowledge excited her as much as the quick response of his body as he climaxed.

She rolled onto her back and Johnny came with her, languidly renewing his attention on her breasts.

"Touch me," she whispered.

Johnny always knew what she wanted, what she demanded of him. He lifted her skirt and teased the inside of her thighs with his fingers while he suckled at her breasts. When his fingers traveled higher to stroke her throbbing center she arched her back and moaned aloud.

There was nothing in her world but sensation. Fabulous, building, heated stimulation. Her body rocked slightly, her breath came heavy. "Johnny," she whispered.

He slithered down her body, and his head disappeared beneath her raised skirt. She let her legs fall open. Her lover kissed her intimately, softly once. Twice. Then he began an attack on her that matched his earlier onslaught at her breasts. He kissed, laved, and sucked, and he thrust his tongue inside her. She cried out softly when he slipped a finger inside her while he pressed his tongue against a most sensitive spot.

"Harder," she whispered, spreading her legs as wide apart as possible and reaching down to clutch his head. "More." Her entire body sang and flamed. She knew nothing, nothing in the world but the feel of Johnny's hands and mouth. He heightened the efforts with his tongue, and slipped yet another finger inside her.

She found release quickly, deeply, and completely, crying out softly and grasping Johnny's head tight against her.

And then she collapsed, satisfied, against the blanket.

Johnny crawled up to lie beside her, resting his beautiful head close to hers. "I love you," he whispered.

Oh, she did wish he wouldn't ruin the moment with such sentimental declarations! "I know," she said, her eyes closed as she savored the deep and complete gratification that made her feel boneless.

He kissed the side of her neck with leisurely passion.

"I want to love you completely," he whispered. "I want to come inside you."

This was a conversation she usually dreaded. She had to go to her marriage bed a virgin. It was expected, even required of someone in her position. There had been a time when what they had was enough for Johnny, but lately he'd begun to voice his desire for more. He wanted everything, and to be honest so did she.

"Soon," she said.

Johnny lifted his head to look down at her. "Soon?"

She smiled widely and rested a hand at his neck. "I've decided who I'll marry."

Johnny frowned. "Not Henry Langford," he muttered. "That ass."

"No, not Henry. Declan Harper," she said sweetly.

"Has he asked?"

"No, but he will," she said confidently. "He came to call on me today," she said. "He brought me candy, can you believe it? I returned the gift, of course, and offered a few more appropriate suggestions."

Her fingers danced languidly and possessively over Johnny's neck and shoulders, a puff of wind ruffling her mussed skirt and his black curls.

"Why him?" he asked.

She placed both hands on his head, bracketing him, holding him. Her fingers threaded through his black curls. "He's rich. He's handsome. He owns the old Ashton place. If I marry him, I won't have to move far away."

She rolled Johnny onto his back and smiled down at him. "And best of all, he doesn't love me. He wants to marry me, but I see no annoying devotion in his eyes. I have a feeling his attentions are spawned by financial considerations more than anything else, and that suits me just fine. Once the wedding night is done, you and I can be lovers always." She smiled wider at the thought.

"I don't think Harper will be demanding. He doesn't

seem the passionate type. He's rather cold, to be honest."
She remembered the way he'd looked at her as he'd offered that obviously cheap tin of candy. "We'll marry,
and soon after he'll put me aside to concentrate all his
energies on his plantation and his other business concerns. That means you and I will have all the time together we want. Long afternoons, entire nights . . ."

Johnny didn't look happy about the plan, but he wasn't
visibly angry, either, as he sometimes was when she
spoke of a proper marriage for herself. "You'll have my
babies," he whispered.

"I know, and they'll be beautiful babies."

He took her head in his large hands and looked deep
into her eyes. She saw such pain in his face, such un-
dying love. "Marry *me*, Vanessa."

"You know I can't. . . ."

"We could leave this place, go out west and make our
own home. I don't want to share you."

"Johnny, don't be silly." She tried not to snap, but this
was a tiresome conversation. "You have no money, and
I couldn't bear to be poor. If I marry Declan Harper, we
can have everything but the same last name."

"And I will get to share you," he mumbled.

"Just a little," she whispered.

He smiled at her, deepening his adorable dimples.
"Maybe one day, before you make the mistake of marrying another man, we'll get caught, and then you'll be
forced to marry me."

She smiled sweetly. "You're such a romantic." In
truth, she knew exactly what she'd do if they were ever
caught in a compromising position. She'd thought of it
many times, usually in her bed late at night when she
could not sleep.

If she and Johnny were ever caught in a compromising
position, she'd yell rape so loud and long everyone in
the county would hear. Johnny would probably hang, and
she would truly hate to see that happen. He was much

too pretty to end up at the end of a rope. But if that was the price she had to pay for her reputation, there was nothing to be done for it.

"Let's eat," she said, reaching past him for the picnic basket. "And then we can make love again." She caught his eye. "Slower this time," she whispered. "Daddy won't be home until late. We have all afternoon."

Johnny smiled and kissed her long and deep. "Vanessa, my love," he whispered. "You're going to be the death of me."

She certainly hoped not, but one could never tell.

The talk about town was all about the drought and the upcoming Founders' Day Celebration. Declan had no patience for either subject.

He should've gone immediately to Matilda's house Monday afternoon, once Vanessa had made it clear she didn't like sweets and provided that long and costly wish list. He should've already sought a new aphrodisiac. But he found himself wondering . . . did he really want to be married to that woman? Vanessa was lovely, but beneath the fine exterior there was only simplicity. No passion. No fire. Just cool beauty.

Instead of going to Matilda's, he'd spent the week shouting and demanding, pushing the workers to finish the house repairs, going over his well-laid plans again and again . . . and occasionally opening the small tin to study its contents and try to *see* the magic that had to be in the amber candy. He'd never forget that kiss. He must also never forget that it hadn't been real.

But here it was Friday, Matilda's day to visit the general store, and he found himself perusing second-rate cigars and waiting. Waiting.

"Good morning, Mr. Fox."

His gut tightened. He'd recognize that voice anywhere.

"Matilda!" Fox's greeting was overly friendly. "What do you have for me today?

"Caramels, sugared pecans, pralines, cinnamon bread, white bread, and lavender soap," she said. "I meant to make more toffee," she said, an apology in her voice, "but I simply ran out of time."

Was she never still? She worked harder than she had to—constantly, from what he'd seen. Why did she never rest?

It was too easy to compare Matilda and Vanessa. Did Vanessa ever do anything productive? He doubted the girl was capable of doing more than looking beautiful and deciding what vegetable to serve with the roast for supper. Matilda had a face that told the whole world what she felt. With her eyes and the wrinkle of her nose and the workings of her mouth, he always knew what she was thinking. Vanessa, on the other hand, always looked the same. Her smiles were not exuberant, she didn't frown or worry, and he never knew what was on her mind. Perhaps nothing. Nothing at all.

His insides were twisted, his mind befuddled. He needed Vanessa to make his plans come together, but he wanted Matilda in his life; in his bed. He'd never wanted anything for himself, he'd never selfishly craved a pleasure, other than his plans of revenge. But he craved Matilda night and day, he dreamed about her, she came to his mind at the oddest times, and the warm thoughts were unlike anything he'd ever known. How could he walk away from Matilda and what he felt? How could he dismiss Vanessa and give up the plans he'd worked so long and hard for?

And then the perfect solution came to him. He didn't have to give up anything; he would have them both.

"Hello, Miss Candy," he said, startling Matilda as he stepped around the shelf and into her line of vision.

"Mr. Harper," she said, her eyes wide. "How nice to see you again."

Yes, he would have them both. It didn't matter that the circumstances would be unconventional. He wanted

Matilda, and he knew he could make her happy. He *would* make her happy.

He smiled, satisfied with the perfectly reasonable solution that had come to him. Vanessa would be his wife, but Matilda would be his lover. Come hell or high water.

Matilda was confused. Vanessa hadn't even taken the second concoction, thanks to an aversion to sweets, and Declan didn't seem to mind at all. In fact, he seemed to be in great spirits this morning.

"So, we'll have to try again," he said in a lowered voice as they walked down the sidewalk. "Sunday evening, perhaps?"

"I suppose," Matilda said, distressed at the possibility of again putting herself through the torture of being alone with Declan Harper and wanting, to distraction, to touch him. It was too much to ask of any woman.

He stayed by her side even after she agreed to try again. Surely he wouldn't walk her all the way home today! What on earth would they have to talk about? They always seemed to find something of interest to discuss, it was true, but after that heart-stopping kiss last week it might be difficult to concentrate on anything so mundane as the weather and his five sisters.

"My horse," he said, coming to a halt outside the closed saloon.

Matilda took a step back. "I'll see you Sunday."

Declan reached out and grabbed her wrist. "Not so fast," he said with a smile. "I'd like you to get acquainted with Smoky."

He gently dragged her a step closer to his gray horse. "I told you . . ."

"Horses don't like you," he finished. "Trust me," he said with a smile. "Smoky will love you."

The horse whimpered softly as they approached, shaking his head in protest. Declan's smile faded, and he cut a sharp glance in her direction, perhaps conceding that she'd told the truth. He did not give up, though. They took a step closer, and the horse snorted loudly and shook his head viciously.

"I told you," Matilda said.

"He probably smells your fear of him," Declan said, refusing to release his hold on her wrist. "Relax."

"It won't do any good," Matilda said. She was afraid. She'd been thrown from a horse once, and that was enough. More than enough.

The horse shied, side-stepping away from her, and Declan caught the reins beneath the animal's chin to hold it in place. He had her in one hand and the horse in the other. "Now," he said softly. "Come here and pat his nose."

"I will not," Matilda said, keeping her voice low so as not to spook the beast any more than it already had been. A knot of fear had settled firmly in her stomach. She hated horses! "What has come over you, Mr. Harper?"

He glanced at her and smiled, and, oh, what a wicked smile it was! Her heart leaped once, and then settled into her chest with a hard thud. She had a sinking feeling that this physical response had nothing to do with fear.

"I want to prove to you that horses are not afraid of you, and therefore you have no need to be afraid of them."

"Everyone should be allowed to be afraid of something," she argued. "Aren't you? There must be something that frightens you."

He leaned closer. "Nothing frightens me," he whispered, his voice low and intimate. "I'm not afraid of the dark, or horses, or the idea of being poor again. I'm not even afraid of witches."

The horse had calmed down considerably, so with a little more coaching Matilda stepped forward and laid her hand on its nose. Sure enough, Smoky didn't shy from her this time. Being so close to the animal, stroking his nose, was easy with Declan still holding her wrist. That small, tenuous connection made her feel safe, somehow. The horse didn't snort or snap, and after a few moments Matilda actually smiled.

"See?" he said with a self-satisfied grin. "He loves you."

Declan released her and the horse, and with a flick of his wrist unhitched Smoky from the post. He stepped into the stirrup and landed in the saddle with the ease and grace of a man who was at home there. Matilda took a step back, ready to resume her walk home.

But it wasn't to be that easy. Declan offered his hand to her. She shook her head. He refused to withdraw that extended hand.

After several moments of silent battle, Matilda ceded. She let Declan take her hand and lift her to sit in front of him. The last time she'd sat on a horse she'd been thrown for her trouble, landing on the ground so hard her breath had been stolen away, and she'd been bruised from head to foot. "When Smoky throws us on the road, don't say I didn't warn you."

Declan turned the horse to the south and the road home, and they left Tanglewood at a slow, leisurely pace. After a few moments the fear faded, and the roar of blood in Matilda's ears subsided so she could hear. Smoky seemed not to be aware that she was sitting on his back.

Declan's arms were loosely but comfortingly draped around her. His limbs did not confine her in any way, but they did support her. He wouldn't let her fall; she knew it.

"Will you be attending the Founders' Day Celebration next week?" he asked, his mouth close to her ear.

Matilda shook her head. "No. At least, I never have in the past. I don't have many true friends, people I socialize with. I think I just make the others uncomfortable."

"That's as silly as your fear of horses," Declan said gruffly.

"I make people uneasy."

"Only the stupid ones."

"No one wants me there," she said, looking to the trees that lined the road home.

Declan was silent for a long time, it seemed. Surely he would accept the fact that she did not fit in, not where social activities were concerned. She'd never been courted, she'd never danced. She'd just make a fool of herself if she went to something so festive and crowded as the Founders' Day Celebration.

"I do," Declan said softly. "I want you there."

Listening to his words, she believed him, and a strange warmth crept through her entire body. Declan wanted her there, and he wasn't afraid to say so out loud. Perhaps he even wanted to dance with her. Never before had she felt truly wanted.

They didn't talk much for the remainder of the ride, but the silence was not awkward, not at all. It was strangely comforting, in fact, as if riding together was natural and right. She saw home too soon.

Declan helped her down before leaving the saddle himself. Mindful of her fear, he was gentle.

"Thank you," she said when he stood before her.

"It was a pleasure as always," he answered. "And this time I get to ride home." When he smiled his entire face changed. Heavens, he was handsome. And the desire to be with him was tempting, she admitted. Much too tempting.

When he leaned down she knew he would kiss her. Maybe it wouldn't be like the kiss they'd shared under the influence of that last aphrodisiac, but it would be wonderful, all the same. She knew it with all her heart and soul.

She closed her eyes as his mouth came near, waiting breathlessly for the kiss he silently promised. Her lips parted slightly as she felt his breath on them. Her eyes flew open when she heard a soft *thwap* and Declan's consequent "ouch."

He was being attacked once again, and she waited, disappointed, for his senses to return. She waited for him to dismiss the kiss as he had the last time they'd stood here and been . . . interrupted. But today he didn't turn toward the woods. His eyes and his attention remained fully on her.

"The kid's got a good arm," he whispered. And then he kissed her. She closed her eyes again and savored the taste and feel of his mouth.

A pinecone whizzed past and hit the house. Another landed squarely on Declan's thigh. More pebbles, one after another, rained around them, some landing in the dirt, some thwacking the stone of her cottage. And still Declan kissed her. Soft and sweet, undemanding and tender. It was the kind of kiss a girl could fall in love to.

Declan pulled away and stood tall, ignoring the projectiles that flew all around and occasionally found their mark. His eyes were so dark she could not read them, not at all.

"Sunday," he said softly. "And I'll be here in time to chop some more wood for you."

"You don't have to . . ."

He ignored her protest and gracefully bounded into Smoky's saddle, easy as you please. Instead of immediately heading for the road, though, he turned the horse toward the forest. Every move languid, he led his mount close to the line of trees and narrowed his eyes. The pebble and pinecone assault ceased.

Matilda wondered if Declan saw the two fair heads barely concealed behind two tall trees, a bit of blue calico and more than a bit of untamed blond curls. When his gaze centered there, she knew he did.

He stared, unflinching, in that direction for a long moment, and then he said one word before riding off.

"Ribbit."

With a wide smile on her face, Matilda entered her cottage to the sounds of two children beating the brush to escape.

Chapter Nine

The last person Matilda expected to be at her door on Saturday morning was Stella Hazelrig. Still, she found it a pleasant surprise; especially when she glanced about and discovered that Stella had come without the twins.

"I understand," Stella said with a small smile, "you've been turning men into frogs."

Matilda laughed and invited Stella in, wondering what had brought the woman to her house. If she were smart, she'd request the herbs for a morning tea that, when taken regularly, would save the world from more Hazelrig children.

"And you," Matilda answered with just as much humor in her voice, "are apparently trying to poison your stepchildren."

"Poison, is it?" Stella asked with a sigh, not at all surprised. "I'm not a wonderful cook, that's true, but I've never tried to purposely poison anyone."

It soon became clear that Stella's visit was purely a social one. Matilda was surprised, but pleased. Apparently Stella thought that since they were neighbors they should be friends as well.

Stella glanced around Matilda's winter kitchen with skeptical eyes. "Your kitchen doesn't look all that different from mine, so why do I have such a terrible time making the recipes you give me?" She cast a comically sharp glance at Matilda. "Is there magic at work here?"

"No," Matilda said with a smile. "I've just had more practice than you."

Stella scoffed. "I tried that recipe for pralines," she said, a hint of frustration in her voice. "And I ended up with one big praline instead of several small ones."

"How did you manage that?"

"I cooked the mixture exactly as you directed, I swear I did." She used her hands as she spoke, mimicking her movements in the process of making the candy. "Then I dropped spoonfuls onto a buttered surface. I waited forever, and they didn't harden up, they just sat there, sticky little lumps of . . . of . . ." She waved one hand in the air. "Well, I don't know what they were, but they were *not* pralines. So I scooped up the little sticky piles, intending to scrape what I could back into the pot and cook it a while longer. I mean, I must've simply not cooked them long enough, right?" She arched her eyebrows.

"That sounds likely . . ." Matilda began.

"But then Gretchen called me upstairs to look at a small tear in her best dress, and we spent a little time on that chore, and when I returned to the kitchen . . ." She spread her hands wide. "I had one big praline."

"It sounds to me as if you lack patience in the kitchen," Matilda said, trying not to smile too widely.

"My father always had a cook," Stella mumbled. "I didn't know it would be so difficult to learn such a simple thing."

Since it seemed that Stella was, in fact, a terrible cook, Matilda gave her a quick lesson in the kitchen. She let Stella help as she made a batch of butterscotch candy and a cherry pie. It had apparently never occurred to Stella to *pit* the cherries before making the filling for a pie.

They laughed, and talked, and all in all it was a very pleasant day, even though Matilda didn't get nearly enough work accomplished. She insisted that Stella take the pie and the candy with her, when the time came for the woman to return home.

"Will you go to the Founders' Day Celebration next week?" Stella asked as she prepared to leave.

Matilda shook her head. "I don't usually go to town, except on Fridays to sell to Mr. Fox."

"You have to go," Stella said. "I still don't know many people in Tanglewood, and I'd feel so much more comfortable if you were there."

Matilda felt she could be honest with this woman. "Even if I were, you wouldn't want to be seen talking to me. You know what they say about me."

"That you're a witch," Stella said bluntly.

Matilda nodded.

Stella looked her up and down critically, but kindly. "Well, you must admit," she said with a sigh, "you do everything you can to encourage them."

"I do not," Matilda said, but her heart skipped a beat. Did she? Did she enjoy her isolation so much that she actually encouraged the rumors? Did she, perversely, nourish the supposition that she was, indeed, a witch?

Stella looked her in the eye. "Attend the festivities next Saturday. Wear a pretty dress and shoes. *Shoes*, Matilda," she stressed. "Unbraid your hair and put it up," she said, waving a somehow disgusted hand in the direction of Matilda's braids. "Make a pie to enter in the pie contest. Dance with all the local men. Smile and flirt and bat your lashes until they're falling at your feet."

Matilda laughed at the absurdity of the suggestion, but Stella simply arched her eyebrows, quite serious.

"I'm not kidding. You're a very attractive woman, and

you shouldn't be hiding out like a hermit." She pinned tenacious eyes on Matilda. "It isn't natural."

Matilda's laughter died. How could she tell Stella, or anyone else, that she didn't have a pretty dress, that her only shoes were a pair of battered old boots, and that she didn't have a clue how to put her hair up properly? She'd never danced, and she'd never stoop to batting her lashes at a man like a . . . like a Vanessa Arrington.

But somehow Stella read the dismay on her face, and *knew*. "I have an old dress or two that might fit you, pretty things I've outgrown lately. It's trying to make all that candy, I suspect," she muttered. She looked at Matilda's feet and stuck out one of her own. "My feet are too much larger than yours for any of my shoes to be of any service, though. They'd fall right off your feet."

"Stella," Matilda protested. "Really, there's no need to . . ."

"I'll come by early on Saturday and help you fix your hair. It's so thick and such a lovely color, I can't wait to give it a try."

"But we can't . . ."

Stella lifted a hand to still Matilda's protest. "It's the least I can do. If I can pass this pie off as my own cooking, Seth will fall in love with me all over again and those kids might quit accusing me of trying to kill them with my dreadful cooking."

Only one thought kept Matilda from completely and sternly refusing Stella's offer.

Declan Harper.

On Sunday afternoon, Declan arrived at Matilda's cottage even earlier than he had the week before. He reasoned that a woman living alone might have a number of chores, besides chopping wood, that a man should be doing for her.

Since he'd decided to make her his mistress, his mind was calmer, easier. He always needed to have a plan of

110

some sort, a goal, an objective. A purpose to everything he did. Now he had a new plan, a more exciting objective. Actually, it was the old plan, revised. He'd simply added Matilda Candy to the list of all he intended to have. Perhaps not tonight, perhaps not even next week, but eventually, and soon, she would be his.

He caught her in the garden again, but this time she was pouring a bucket of water onto the dry ground near the roots of her flesh-colored roses. Her back was to him, her wonderfully shaped back beneath a plain white blouse, her tiny waist accentuated by the waistband of a blue and green calico skirt.

"We all need rain," he said as he approached the garden.

She faced him, not exactly surprised to see him, as she had been last week. Her cheeks were flushed, pink and shining. "That's the truth," she said, picking up two empty buckets and exiting the garden by way of the open gate.

"I have a surprise for you," he said. "A gift."

Matilda stopped outside the garden and placed the buckets on the ground. She stood there, more fetching than any woman had a right to be, and gave him a tired, tolerant smile.

"You don't look exactly delighted to hear that I've planned a surprise for you," he said tersely, annoyed by her less-than-wild reaction.

"I'm afraid I know you too well, Mr. Harper. Can I help it that I find myself wary of gifts from a man unwisely named for an Irish saint?"

She breathed too deeply; he could see she was uncommonly fatigued.

Declan dismissed Matilda's less-than-thrilled reaction to the news that he'd brought her a gift. "How many trips have you made from the pond to the garden?" he asked with a frown.

"Four," she said. "And I need to make four more."

111

With that she picked up her buckets and turned her back
on him, heading around the house and for the pond.

"Wait," he commanded.

Wearily, she turned to face him. "I do not have time
to play games with you, Declan."

"This is no game."

She set the buckets down and left them there, walking
slowly to him. *Dammit,* he thought, *she should not be
hauling water like a common laborer!* The very idea angered him, actually made a muscle in his right cheek
twitch.

"All right," she said as she came near. "Where is this
supposed gift?"

He took her hand and led her toward the greenhouse,
and when they were near to the corner he ordered her to
close her eyes. She did, without hesitation, a faint smile
creeping across her face. He led her around the corner,
placed her in front of him, and rested his hands on her
shoulders.

"All right," he said softly. "Open your eyes."

She did, and when she saw the two horses tied up in
the small grassy area, she groaned aloud. "Oh, you
didn't," she said softly. "Declan, I don't *want* a horse! I
don't like to ride, I have no way to take care of such an
animal, I don't even know how to take proper care of a
horse."

He led her to the black mare he'd ridden all the way
to Jackson to buy for her. "This is Shadow. She's small,
she's gentle, and she's yours."

"I can't possibly . . ."

"I'll board Shadow in my stables, and you can ride her
whenever you like. You've helped me so much, Matilda.
You've talked to me, you've fed me, you've fulfilled my
strangest requests." He didn't want to mention what he'd
asked of her specifically, not at the moment. Right now
he wanted to focus on the two of them, without Vanessa
in the equation. "The saddle is yours as well."

"I can't accept such a gift," Matilda said softly.

Declan sighed tiredly, frustrated. He'd been so sure Matilda would be delighted with the mare, that she would at least be a little bit pleased. So far, he was not doing well in the courting arena. Vanessa had returned his candy and given him a list of more appropriate, and more expensive, gifts, and now Matilda was turning him down as well. Women! He wondered what kind of list she'd give him.

"It's too much," she continued. When she turned to look up at him, her eyes filled with tears. "But it's the nicest, most wonderful gift anyone has ever given me, and I thank you, even if I must refuse."

He didn't know how to deal with a woman's tears. You'd think that growing up with an emotional Irish mother and five sisters would've prepared him for a moment like this, but he was completely and totally taken aback.

"She's yours," he said gruffly. "Whether you accept her or not. I'll take care of her, I'll board her, but Shadow is your mare, Matilda," He gave her a smile, hoping it would dry her tears. "But first you have to learn to ride her."

That did the trick. Her tears dried. "Alone? By myself? Oh, no. I can't. I can't possibly. Besides, I have work to do." With that she stepped past him, heading for her damn pails.

He passed her easily. "You'll not carry any more water today," he said.

"But we haven't had rain in weeks, and my roses . . ."

"I'll water your damn roses," he said, scooping the buckets up without slowing his step. "And anything else you tell me needs watering."

"But Declan . . ."

"And when everything has been well watered, you're going to get into Shadow's saddle."

She didn't leave him alone, but followed silently as he

113

rounded the cottage, climbed the small hill, and descended to the spring-fed pond below.

"But Declan," she finally said, as he dipped a pail into the water. "I can't ride, and I can't allow you to come here and do my chores for me. It just isn't right."

He carried the full buckets, sloshing water with each step, to where she stood. For a little thing, she had a lot of energy, a lot of power. It radiated from her like heat off a baking stone, or the aroma from one of her roses. No wonder people thought she was a witch; she was definitely no ordinary woman.

"Sit down," he said softly. "Stare out over the water and do nothing for a few minutes."

"Do *nothing?*" she asked. "I can't . . ."

"Sit," Declan interrupted. "It's a beautiful day. Enjoy it," he ordered.

"I can't . . ." she began again.

He laid his eyes on her face, felt a jolt deep inside that could only be sexual. "Sit," he whispered.

She did.

Matilda glared at Declan. It wasn't enough that he had hauled her water and chopped her wood, he now insisted that she come face-to-face with Shadow, the mare who was bound to hate her as much as every other horse did.

Declan held the reins beneath the mare's chin, and kept a clamp on Matilda's arm. She and Shadow were face-to-face. The mare snorted at Matilda, blowing hot horse breath into her face.

"See? She hates me."

Declan smiled. "That's her way of saying hello. Blow gently in her face," he said. "Say hello back."

Matilda did as Declan requested, certain that the horse would revolt and trample them both to death. But Shadow just snorted softly and shook her head.

In spite of herself, Matilda relaxed. How could she stare into those big, brown eyes and be afraid?

114

"Come here," Declan ordered impatiently, pulling her to his side and forcing her against the mare's shoulder. "Give her a hug."

"A hug?" she protested. "How do you give a horse a hug?"

"Just snuggle against her shoulder," Declan said patiently. "Pat her, lay your head against her, let her feel you."

All had gone well so far, so Matilda obeyed. She'd never smelled a horse before, not really, and she found it wasn't an altogether unpleasant odor. Shadow's coat was silky and dark as night, truly beautiful.

As she stroked the inky-black mare, Shadow turned her head and seemed to try to hug her back.

Declan pulled her further away from Shadow's head. "Now, into the saddle with you."

"I can't," she protested. "I'm not ready. I'm not absolutely positive that she likes me . . ."

She got no further. Declan put his hands around her waist and lifted her, placing her squarely in the saddle. For a split second she was dizzy, disoriented, close to panic. She had no control, here on the horse's back. The mare might run, or toss her rider onto the ground. Her skirt was full and allowed for freedom of movement, but, straddling the animal, her ankles and calves were exposed. Still, at the moment, modesty was the least of her concerns.

Matilda remembered the last time she'd sat on a horse's back. She'd been twelve. The horse had thrown her off moments after her rear end had hit the saddle. She'd flown through the air and landed hard.

But this horse didn't bolt, or rear back, or try to throw her. Shadow remained perfectly calm, even though Matilda was not.

Declan led the mare in an easy walk. They walked in and out of the shade, not heading anywhere at all, but simply allowing Matilda and the mare to get a feel for each other.

"Why are you doing this?" she asked.

"Because I figure if I just tossed you in the saddle, told you to hold on, and hit Shadow on the rump you'd never forgive me."

"Well, that's the truth." Matilda laughed at the mental picture. She had a feeling handling her dread that way would've come more naturally to Declan. "But it doesn't answer my question. Why are you so determined to see that I get over my fear of horses?"

"Because fear is a weakness," he said logically. "And you are an extraordinary woman with no room in her life for weakness." He said the words as if he meant them, as if he spoke from the heart.

Matilda was afraid she was developing an all-new weakness. For Declan. Oh, no good could come of this. She really should remind herself of why he'd come to her in the first place. But when he helped her from the mare, his hands firm on her waist again as he declared they'd done enough for one afternoon, she knew it was true. If she had a weakness at all, it was for this man.

She fed him again. This Sunday she was prepared, and the meal was not something she simply threw together at the last minute. There was a pot roast, rolls with honey-butter, beans and squash from her garden, and a cherry pie for dessert. Declan ate well, as she imagined he always did. A man of his size surely required a lot of feeding. But he not only ate well, he enjoyed every bite. She knew it, and was glad. She got so little opportunity to watch other people eat what she prepared. Mr. Fox swore her breads and sweets were popular and all sold by Saturday afternoon, but except for Hanson and Gretchen she'd never seen a person roll their eyes in delight, or smile as a particular taste pleased their tongue, or close their eyes and savor something particularly tasty.

When dinner was done, and it was almost dark outside,

Matilda fetched the latest potion from a shelf in the main room. Declan sat in his usual chair, calm, satisfied after his big meal, and apparently in no hurry to take possession of her latest effort.

"This," she said as she walked to him, placing herself boldly before him, "is something a little different. The first powder apparently lost its potency overnight, or else was not effective in Vanessa's blood. The second she never ingested, since she does not like sweets." An abnormal trait, Matilda was sure. "So I thought we might try this."

She lifted the cork stopper from the small, green glass bottle. "This oil," she said, sniffing lightly at the opening, "smells lovely in the bottle, but is perfectly safe. Place one drop on the skin, however, and the scent changes. It becomes an aphrodisiac of the highest order, a stimulating scent that should work immediately."

She stoppered the bottle and handed it to Declan. "Dab a bit of this on your neck before you go to see Vanessa next, and I believe you will be pleased with the result."

Something in her heart shriveled. Vanessa Arrington! What did a man like Declan see in her? It was a mystery, as were all things relating to love.

Declan removed the stopper and brought the bottle to his nose for a long sniff. "It does smell nice," he conceded. "But how can I be sure it will work?" He lifted his dark eyes to her and raised his eyebrows.

Heaven above, she could not stand another test. She could not bear to torture herself with wanting what she could not have. "Since there is no possibility of danger to Vanessa with this method, I see no reason to conduct another of your experiments. If it doesn't work, simply return it, and I will try again."

"I want to know," he said, barely touching his finger to the opening and tilting the bottle so that the oil touched his finger, bringing that fingertip to his neck, just beneath the ear.

117

This wasn't fair, Matilda thought with a touch of panic. She already liked Declan Harper too much; she did not want or need any stimulant to make her affection grow to more than it was, to make her fancy a man she could never, ever have. She closed her eyes as the faint, intoxicating scent drifted to her, spicy and musky. She could not keep it out, could not deny the way it made her feel . . . the way she already felt.

"Here," Declan said softly. "It hardly seems fair for you to have all the fun."

Fun, she thought hysterically. He thought this anguish was fun?

He touched an oiled fingertip to her throat, raking the slick finger slowly from beneath her chin to the top of her blouse, going no further. It was too late; she wanted him to go further. She wanted him to touch her breast with that finger, to put his strong hands around her waist again. She wanted another kiss, and more. So much more.

The knowledge that she was under the power of the oil gave her the strength to tell him what she wanted; some of it, anyway.

"I do wish you would kiss me," she whispered.

He did so without hesitation, bending his head and taking her mouth with an almost savage molding of his lips to hers. There was nothing gentle in this kiss, no trepidation, no hint of uncertainty. He forced her lips apart and flicked his tongue into her mouth, danced it there, stoked the fire that had been smoldering deep inside her since the first time they'd kissed.

She didn't have to ask him to touch her breast; he did so all on his own, first brushing the nipple with his fingers and then laying the palm of his hand over her, brushing cotton and flesh with a rhythm that matched the kiss.

Her knees began to wobble, to quiver. Standing was too much of an effort. She held on to Declan, and then, after a few moments more of kissing and touching, he laid her on the floor.

Declan's long body hovered close above hers, touched her hard in some places and soft in others. A lock of dark hair fell across his forehead, and she pushed it back, slowly, tenderly, taking her fingers from his hair as he kissed her again.

Knowing she should protest, knowing these feelings weren't *real,* Matilda uttered not a sound. From here the kiss was different, deeper. Better. Declan held his strong body over hers, and she felt and savored his heat and his weight, the smell of him, the way his body skimmed hers.

With her arms around him and her hands on his back, she held on as they kissed, and kissed, and then kissed some more. With every passing heartbeat she was more lost, more out of her head with delirium.

Declan moaned low in his throat and took his mouth from hers. He shifted slightly, and she felt the length and hardness of his arousal pressing against her. She should be scared; she should be terrified.

But Declan had told her, without the influence of the potion, that she was an extraordinary woman who should be afraid of nothing. Perhaps he was right. She should have no fear. She turned her head and kissed him on the neck, barely touching her lips to his flesh at first, flicking her tongue out to taste him at last, finally clamping down and sucking against his skin. One leg cocked up on its own, so that he rested more comfortably between her thighs.

"I want you," Declan whispered hoarsely.

"I know."

"I want to make love to you all night long and into the morning and then all day."

She smiled and closed her eyes.

"I know."

"And I will, Matilda," he whispered. "I will make love to you."

"I know," she breathed softly, reveling in the feel of his body, touching him lightly and possessively. "But not tonight," she finished reluctantly. "Not with any love potion stirring your blood. I want to know, when the time comes, that you truly want me."

"I do," he whispered. "I do want you."

She raked her fingers through his hair and held his head so she could look at him. By the light of a few burning candles only half of his face was illuminated well. She could see, though, that he desired her, that it was difficult for him to call a halt to what might have been a terrible mistake for both of them.

At that moment, Matilda wanted Delcan Harper more than she'd ever wanted anything in her life. She wanted him so badly she was willing to do anything, even fight Vanessa Arrington for him.

"I've decided to go to the Founders' Day Celebration next week," she whispered, not yet ready to let him go as she knew she must. "I hear there may be dancing. Will you dance with me?"

"Yes."

"Will you kiss me?" she asked with a gentle smile.

He grinned back. "If the opportunity arises," he whispered, "I will most certainly kiss you."

Before he removed himself from her, she kissed his neck, tasting it one last time. She closed her eyes as her lips very lightly brushed the base of his throat. Goodness, she'd had no idea a man could taste so good.

As her lips drifted away, Declan helped her from the floor. They rose slowly, almost as if they were in a daze. When they were on their feet, Declan released her so quickly her head gave a quick spin. He quickly gathered his small green glass bottle and, with his back to her, said a gruff good night.

When he was gone, she settled into her chair and rocked gently with a smile on her face. She glowed from the inside out, warm and tingly still, from all the kissing.

The latest potion, the fragrant oil, was quite possibly the most powerful aphrodisiac yet.

A few moments later, her smile faded. Would Declan still want her when the effects of the oil wore off? Would she still want him with such urgency her heart beat too fast, and it seemed there was nothing in the world but the two of them and this small room? This afternoon, long before she'd taken the oil from the shelf, she'd felt something for him, something she couldn't name. Something warm and new, something she tried to push back inside where it belonged. And just a few days ago he'd kissed her, without any potion between them; no powder, no wicked candy, no stimulating oil.

Ah, yes, the scent of the oil was powerful. Would he dare to wear it for Vanessa Arrington? Surely not. Surely he would not kiss her to distraction and talk about making love, and then turn around and wear the fragrance for another woman.

She wished, with all her heart, that she could be sure, and she resolved, again, to fight for what she wanted.

Chapter Ten

Declan viewed it as an experiment of sorts, dabbing on a touch of the oil before calling on Vanessa Monday evening. He was still amazed by the way in which the oil had affected Matilda, the way her reserve had melted away. He was just as amazed by the way he himself had almost lost control. From the moment he'd touched the oil to her skin, he'd been half-crazy with wanting her.

He did intend to have Matilda, but he had to be careful not to give too much of himself to her. In a contrary sort of way, he was glad she'd called a halt to their heated response to the last aphrodisiac she'd concocted. When he made love to Matilda, he would be in control. There would be nothing hazy or unclear; he wanted to savor every moment, every touch, every new sensation. And he would be sure that she truly wanted him and was not lost in the clutches of some artificial essence or potion.

Funny, but he had no such reservations about Vanessa. He would do whatever he had to in order to make her his wife. He didn't care why she agreed to the match, only that he got what he wanted.

"Declan," Vanessa said sweetly as she came floating into the parlor. This time she'd only kept him waiting twenty minutes. Her dress was of the palest lavender, and her hair and her skin were immaculate. Perfect. Striking.

"I brought you a gift," he said. "Something more suitable, I hope." He offered her the posy of violets, and she came to take them from his hand. A perfect smile crossed her perfect face, and she fluttered her lashes at him and whispered a breathy and feminine thank-you. What man would not want her as his wife?

Still, she seemed unaffected by the oil he wore. No flash of passion darkened her violet eyes, no quiver of her lips suggested that she was affected by the fragrance. He leaned closer to her, to make sure she got a good whiff, but she simply buried her nose in the small bouquet of flowers.

The scent of the flowers no doubt had a negating effect on the scent of the oil. Just his luck.

Oddly enough, he found he didn't care. Sooner or later he'd find something that would bring Vanessa to him. Sooner or later. He no longer felt the need to rush his revenge, he no longer felt compelled to accomplish his goal as quickly as possible. His desire for Matilda had dulled his need for vengeance.

Vanessa led him to the plush green sofa, where she sat and then instructed him to sit beside her.

"I'm so looking forward to the festivities Saturday," she said breathlessly. "Music and games and dancing. It's always so exciting. I do so love to dance." She fluttered her eyelashes at him. "Why, when I'm dancing, I feel like I'm flying, like I might just float right up off the ground."

Declan had no interest, at the moment, in Vanessa's love for dancing, but he was rather interested in the way she leaned closer and closer to him as she spoke in low, intimate tones. Maybe, in some small way, the fragrance was beginning to work. "Really?" he said softly.

She smiled and cocked her head to one side. "Really."

There was no one else in the parlor at the moment. He could steal a quick kiss, surely, a quick peck on the lips to see what might stir in him, and in Vanessa.

The kiss happened very quickly. He laid his lips over her pursed, tightly closed mouth, and she closed her eyes for the short duration. She held her breath and did not move, but to pucker her lips. He waited for some reaction, some indication that Vanessa enjoyed the kiss, but he waited in vain. All in all it was rather like kissing Smoky, only Smoky was warmer.

As she pulled away with an unaffected smile on her beautiful face, Vanessa said, "I'll save a dance for you Saturday."

"Wonderful," he said softly, and without enthusiasm, wondering if it would be unforgivably rude to swipe his hand quickly across his mouth. He refrained.

She leaned a bit closer and took a deep breath. Her nose wrinkled and her lips pursed again. "What on earth are you wearing?"

"A new cologne. Do you like it?"

She wriggled her nose slightly, in obvious distaste. "No. It smells rather nasty, like a barn and a kitchen all rolled into one. Do me a favor, Declan," she pleaded like a small, whining child. "Do not wear that cologne again when you are with me."

"Don't worry," he said softly. "I won't."

Tuesday was laundry day, and Matilda used a long-handled paddle made of pine to stir her dirty clothes in the hot water in the black cauldron. Steam rose off the water and bathed her, making her face and neck sweat. It was hard work, but then she felt like she needed a little hard work this morning. She'd been thinking about Declan too much lately, and those thoughts had her body and her mind agitated. She worked the dirty clothes in the water more vigorously than usual.

She didn't know how long the man had been standing there, but she lifted her head and, through the steam, saw a wiry figure with his hat in his hand.

"Hello," she said, leaving the paddle behind and stepping to the side so she could see her visitor. "I'm sorry, I didn't see you standing there. Can I help you?"

Without the steam between them, she saw that he was a young man, surely no more than eighteen, and he was much too thin. He shook his head and watched her warily, clearly uneasy to be in the presence of the Tanglewood witch. Finding her over the cauldron probably hadn't helped her image any, but what was she to do?

"Mr. Harper sent me," he said, his voice low. "I'm to chop wood and haul water and do anything else you ask me to do." He swallowed hard and went ghostly pale. "That's what he said. Anything you ask me to do."

"I'm sure Mr. Harper's intentions were good, but I really don't need any help. You can tell him I sent you home."

The thin young man shook his head. "I can't do that. He said if I let you send me back I'd be fired. I need my job, Miss Candy."

Matilda sighed. It was so like Declan to think of everything, and to make arrangements to get his way. She couldn't dismiss this young man without costing him his badly needed job.

"If you're going to chop my wood, you'll have to call me Matilda," she said sweetly. "And your name is . . . ?"

"Robert," he said, looking very much like a fatally doomed man. "Robert Webster."

"Well, Robert, I have to return to my laundry." She nodded to the shed. "You'll find everything you need over there."

"Laundry," he said, obviously relieved as he placed

his hat atop mouse-brown hair that hung just a little bit too long, and headed, one cautious eye remaining on Matilda, to the shed.

Since Robert was obviously nervous about working in the presence of a witch, Matilda went back to her work and left him alone to his. Soon she became accustomed to the steady *thwack* and crack of lumber being struck and split. She continued with her chore, and thought about Declan. Robert's forced assistance was a gift, she supposed, like the mare. If Declan had his heart set on Vanessa, why did he waste so much time and energy on her?

Cynically, she suspected his heart had nothing to do with his interest in her.

As it was Tuesday, laundry day and not candy or bread-making day, she was surprised to see Hanson and Gretchen peek around the corner of her cottage. She understood a moment later when Stella appeared, a large parcel in her hands.

"Good morning," Stella said brightly. "I've brought something for you."

They left Robert to his chores and Hanson and Gretchen skulking around the big kitchen looking for sweets they would not find, and carried the parcel inside.

"I brought two dresses," Stella said before the door had closed securely behind them. "One blue, and one peach. I think either of them will look lovely on you." She laid the parcel on the long table in the main room and untied the string. The brown paper fell open to reveal the neatly folded dresses, peach and pale blue silk looking ludicrous against the rough wood of her table.

"I don't know," Matilda began skeptically. "They're beautiful, but . . ."

"You'll need shoes," Stella interrupted. "Mr. Fox keeps a few pairs in stock, perhaps he'll have something you can purchase. It's too bad there's no time to order a pair. I have a lovely catalog at home."

She wondered what Declan would think of her in one of the lovely silk gowns, wearing shoes on her feet and sporting a painstakingly arranged coiffure. How could she ever compete with someone like Vanessa Arrington?

"Perhaps I'll visit Mr. Fox tomorrow and see what he has. Otherwise, I'll simply have to polish my boots and wear them."

Stella wrinkled her nose in obvious distaste. "Oh, I do hope he has something suitable! Boots! How will you possibly dance with grace and lure all those men in your walking boots?"

Matilda grinned widely. She'd likely not dance with grace unless the shoes she purchased were enchanted, and the only man she cared to lure was Declan Harper.

Stella did not stay long, but as she left, she said she'd be by Saturday morning to help Matilda style her hair. Then, she said in a voice that held no room for argument, they'd all ride to town together in the Hazelrig buckboard.

Declan impatiently awaited Robert's return. The young man had not been happy about his assignment, but the promise of a much-needed bonus had encouraged him. It was almost dark before Robert returned to the plantation house.

"Did you get a lot accomplished?"

Robert, who had apparently not seen Declan standing in the shadows of the deep porch, snapped up his head as he dismounted. He narrowed his eyes, searching, until Declan stepped into the fading light.

"Yes. I chopped wood and hauled water, mostly, and this afternoon I suggested to Matilda that we build a wooden trench from the spring to her garden, something high at the water's edge and tilting down to the garden. That way she could water the garden whenever she wanted without carrying those heavy buckets." The young man smiled widely at his own suggestion, his mood a far cry from the frightened boy who'd left here hours ago.

And he called her Matilda, already, Declan noted. "That sounds like a fine idea," he said calmly.

Robert placed a dirty boot on the front-porch steps. "She's not what I expected," he said in a lowered voice. "All the talk about her, it can't be true. She's too sweet and pretty to be a witch, and she made me the best lunch I've had in . . . in forever."

Young Robert was obviously smitten, Declan realized with dismay. He should not be surprised. Who could weather Matilda's smile and not be smitten? "You'll go to her cottage three times a week," he said in a calm, businesslike tone of voice. "I don't want her hauling water or cutting wood, and I feel sure there are other chores you could do for her, as well."

"I'll be happy to, Mr. Harper. When I finish with the everyday chores, I can set about building that trench for her."

"Excellent," Declan said as he turned away and headed for the cavernous plantation house he grudgingly called home.

"Has he asked yet?" Johnny whispered in the dark, his voice less than warm.

Vanessa sighed. Sometimes she wished Johnny loved her less, that he only wanted what she did: the fabulous physical element of their relationship. "Not yet," she whispered.

They'd met in the guest house many times in the past two years, in the afternoon or at night when they should be sleeping. Right now her father thought she was sound asleep in her canopied bed, rather than half naked in the guest house bed with Johnny lying beside her.

"You said soon," he said, raking his hand down her body in a familiar way. "*Soon.* Why do you torture me like this, Vanessa? I've waited, and waited, and I've tried to be patient and give you what you want and need. I've given you everything you've ever asked for." She could hear the growing frustration in his voice. "If only I could convince you to marry me."

"Johnny . . ."

"But you won't, I know that. If all I can have is a part of you, I'll take it. But dammit Vanessa, I've waited long enough."

She came up and rolled over him, letting her hair fall over his chest and neck. "I feel like we've waited forever," she whispered.

"So do I," he groaned.

Vanessa trailed her fingers over Johnny's face, tracing the lines of his jaw and his lips. Even in the tiny bit of moonlight that broke through the window, he was uncommonly beautiful. And he was right. They had waited long enough.

"Maybe I can speed things along." She kissed his cheek, then his neck, then his bare chest. "Maybe I can get Mr. Harper to propose marriage this weekend." She wanted Johnny so bad it hurt, but she would not sacrifice her virginity to just any man. "I can push for a quick wedding, make him think I can't wait to be his wife." She grinned and reached down to touch Johnny's erect flesh, to stroke its length with teasing fingers. "On my wedding night," she whispered, "I'll leave his bed and come to this one."

Johnny groaned, and his arousal grew.

"I'll expect you to be waiting."

Mr. Fox was obviously surprised to see her. His eyes widened and his eyebrows arched as Matilda walked into the general store on a Wednesday afternoon. The sweets she'd prepared that morning were in danger of being pilfered, but she knew Hanson and Gretchen wouldn't take too much. They never did.

"Good afternoon, Matilda," Mr. Fox said suspiciously. He touched a hand to his dark hair, dark hair aided by a special cream made with walnut juice, administered regularly to cover his premature gray strands. "What can I do for you this fine day?"

She was suddenly embarrassed, and her toes unconsciously wiggled in her boots. "Shoes," she said, her chin high. "I'd like to purchase a pair of shoes."

Mr. Fox smiled and led her to the back of the store, where a shelf accommodated several pairs of boots and shoes. They were plain and fancy, large and small. "What size?" he asked.

Matilda stuck out one boot-encased foot and looked down at it, trying to remember. Mr. Fox looked down as well. He reached knowingly for a pair of plain black leather shoes.

"Try these on," he suggested.

Matilda sat down and removed her boots, and slipped on the black shoes. They were unadorned, square toed, and a bit too large for her feet. Looking at them, she found them not much more suitable for dancing and enticing than her boots.

Perhaps this was a silly plan, perhaps she was as vacuous as Vanessa Arrington for even thinking of trying to lure Declan Harper with a dress that was not her own and something as inconsequential as a pair of shoes.

She slipped the black shoes off, certain that she was a fool for coming here. She'd wasted half a day in pursuit of something completely inconsequential. A pair of shoes! Granny would surely be disappointed. She could not make herself into someone she was not, and she should not even try.

But when she looked up and spied a bronze-colored heel peeking out from a shelf high on the wall, a spark of something like hope lit her heart. Maybe she had not wasted half a day, after all.

"What about those?"

Mr. Fox reached up and snagged the bronze shoes, and as soon as Matilda saw them she knew these shoes were meant for dancing and flirting. The heel was almost an inch high, and a matching bow adorned the pointy-toed shoes. They caught the light and positively sparkled.

She found herself immediately and senselessly in love with a pair of shoes.

"I ordered these for Miss Arrington," Mr. Fox said with a grimace, "but when they arrived she took one look at them and said she'd changed her mind."

Matilda couldn't imagine anyone, not even Vanessa Arrington, refusing such a beautiful pair of shoes. "Do you think they'll fit me?"

Mr. Fox offered Matilda the shoes, which she very carefully slipped onto her stockinged feet. She stood and put her weight on them, took a few tentative steps to test the feel of them on her feet. "They're very comfortable." She felt light as air, as if she could dance after all. She gave a little twirl right there in the general store. When she looked up, Mr. Fox smiled.

"I believe those shoes were made for you." He leaned toward her and lowered his voice. "I can offer you a special deal."

She could imagine, too well, dancing with Declan Harper in these shoes, she could imagine they would catch the light, sunlight or moonlight or candlelight, as her feet flickered from beneath a silk skirt that twirled around her legs. She'd never had such dreams before; she'd never before wanted to be beautiful.

She did now.

"I'll take them."

As Mr. Fox wrapped her new shoes in brown paper, he smiled contentedly. "If all my customers were as agreeable as you, Miss Matilda, I'd truly love my profession."

"You don't?" She'd always found Charles Fox to be a perfectly agreeable man who enjoyed his business. He *seemed* happy, at least.

He glanced around the store to see if anyone else was

listening. "This is a good business, and most days I'm perfectly happy with my life. But I sometimes wish I could make something, the way you do. Something lasting, something beautiful."

"Would you like me to teach you to make candy?" she teased.

His eyes widened, and he grinned. "Now there's something that doesn't last long." His smile faded, his eyes sparkled. "Actually, I would love to be a carpenter." His eyes lit up, softened, and glowed. "I should like to build furniture that would last a hundred years or more, things of beauty and usefulness."

"Then why don't you?"

She shrugged his shoulders as if it didn't matter. "Tanglewood needs this store, and it is a profitable business." He nodded briefly. "Besides, Mrs. Fox would be quite peeved with me if I gave up my profession to dabble in carpentry."

"Perhaps you could hire someone to help you about the store," she suggested, "and dabble in carpentry in your spare time. Why, I would dearly love a new cupboard for my kitchen."

"Would you?" his eyes lit up again.

"And perhaps a new bookcase. I'm quite outgrowing the ones I have."

"Really?"

"I would certainly be willing to pay well for something of quality and beauty." She took her shoes from a wide-eyed Charles Fox.

"That's not a bad idea," he said softly. "Someone to help out around the place. Miss Matilda," he added as she turned to leave, "you are a treasure."

She clutched the bronze shoes as if *they* were a treasure, a discovery to be protected and cherished. If they were magic shoes, perhaps she'd even find herself able to dance.

Chapter Eleven

Matilda frowned as she studied her reflection in the mirror. Why had she been so foolish as to think she could become someone she was not?

Stella's dress hung on her, the difference in their shapes made obvious by the baggy fabric in the bosom and the hem that trailed on the floor. The ruffles were too large and overpowering, the bows ridiculous and somehow all positioned awkwardly. No matter how beautiful the gowns looked on Stella, or even spread across the bed, it was obvious that they were *not* beautiful on Matilda.

Why had she waited until Friday evening to try them on? Perhaps if she'd seen the faults on Tuesday or Wednesday she might've altered one of the gowns. She'd gotten so caught up in making extra sweets for Mr. Fox, delivering them this morning, looking in vain for Declan while she was in town, she hadn't had time to even think about her garments. If only she'd thought of this earlier. If only . . .

Who was she kidding? She was not a good enough seamstress to remake a fancy gown in a matter of days! Even in a matter of weeks, given the amount of time she had to devote to such a project. She looked down and stuck one foot out, admiring the bronze shoe that adorned it. Well, at least her feet looked good.

She removed the blue gown and tossed it onto the bed, where it landed atop the peach one. For a few minutes she paced the small room in her chemise, white stockings, and bronze shoes.

As she paced her anxiety faded, the pressure to be beautiful and charming and alluring for the Founders' Day Celebration was gone.

It would be best if she stayed home, as she'd originally planned, if she gave up her silly dreams of Declan Harper. She was now and always would be Tanglewood's witch, no matter what she did, no matter how many pretty dresses she wore.

Yes, this was the easy way out. The gowns didn't suit her, she had nothing to wear, she would simply have to stay home. But something inside her didn't want to give up, not yet, not so easily. Her eyes fell on her grandmother's cedar chest, where a few old belongings were stored. She hadn't looked in that chest for years, and she tried to remember what was there: a few pieces of jewelry, an elaborate wedding dress, her father's baby clothes. Was there another dress or two there as well? Gowns so hopelessly out of date as to be ridiculous?

Matilda dropped to her knees and opened the chest carefully. There was probably nothing here suitable to wear to the Founders' Day Celebration, nothing pretty enough to dance and flirt in, but since she had no other options but her usual plain clothing, she felt like she should at least look. She was not going to give up so easily, no matter how tempting the idea was at the moment.

There was a white Bible on top, a baby's quilt and a

few tiny clothes, and the yellowed wedding dress. She moved them all aside, lifting the wedding gown carefully and setting it on the floor. Beneath the silk, lacy dress was a small box containing the few pieces of jewelry her grandmother had owned: a cameo and an opal ring, a silver pin shaped like a bird, and a pair of dangly opal earrings. Matilda set them aside and looked at the dresses on the bottom of the chest.

There were two gowns here, dresses she had never seen her grandmother wear. There had been a time, she knew, when her granny had tried to fit in, to be a proper wife. The wedding gown attested to that; it was elaborate and elegant. The gowns at the bottom of the chest were simpler, one the palest buttery yellow and the other a soft minty green. She pulled the yellow one out and spread it across the floor.

Yes, it was years out of fashion, but there was still something enchanting about the gown. High waisted and more narrow in the skirt than was fashionable, it had a quaint quality to it. A fine lace overlay adorned the bodice and the sleeves, but other than that, the dress was plain. Elegantly plain, in Matilda's opinion. She fingered the fabric, finding it in excellent shape.

These gowns were more to her liking than Stella's fancy silk dresses. But would Declan like them as well? She pulled the yellow bodice up and laid it over her torso, covering her legs with the skirt, lifting a sleeve with one hand, and holding the scooped neckline in place to see if it might be too low cut. It might not be fashionable or fancy, but she liked the way the gown looked and felt, and she liked the fact that this dress had once been worn by her grandmother. At the moment, she felt like Granny was with her, in this very room, telling her not to be afraid.

A small smile crossed Matilda's face. She couldn't worry about what Declan would think about her choice of clothing. If he was half the man she thought he was, he'd see the woman inside the dress, not the trappings of silk and ruffles.

But was she, once again, hoping for too much from him?

It hadn't been easy to stay away from Matilda all week, but it was for the best, he knew. If he went after her like a panting dog he'd scare her off and never make her his mistress. Best to take this seduction slow and easy.

Today would be tricky, at best. His relationship with Matilda would have to be discreet, something just for the two of them; especially after he married Vanessa. He could not ignore Matilda today, but neither could he indicate to those watching that he was courting her. Perhaps he should not have asked her to attend the celebration, but the idea of dancing with her was too tempting.

He had been one of the first to arrive, but then there was nothing to keep him at home, in that vast old plantation house with room after empty room. His lack of affection for his new home didn't concern him. After all, it was just a house, a too-empty building. Once he was married it would be a warmer place. Vanessa would see to that. That was, after all, a wife's duty.

One by one, on horseback, wagon, and on foot, people began to arrive. Boring speeches by town leaders were to be held at a stand at the north end of the main street, and games had been set up for the children. There were pies lined up on a table by the church, the early entries in the pie contest, and the café had set up a table to sell fried pies and little cakes. People laughed and talked in voices just a touch too loud.

The festive air was dampened somewhat by talk about the lack of rain. The drought had not yet reached a disastrous level. If it rained good and hard in the next couple of weeks, the farmers and the wells would be fine. But if it didn't rain soon, Tanglewood was looking at an economic crisis that would last for months, maybe even years.

Declan stood restlessly in the shadows of the board-walk. His eyes kept drifting uneasily toward the south-ward road, looking for Matilda. He imagined she'd arrive in her usual calico skirt and white blouse and pigtails, carrying a basket with a pie for the contest and more sweets for Mr. Fox. She'd say she'd only come to town to deliver the sweets, but he'd convince her to stay, if need be.

A rough wagon came into view from that road, a man and two women on the seat, two familiar fair heads in the wagon bed behind. It took him a long moment before he realized that one of the women on the seat was Matilda.

Her hair was not in pigtails, it had been styled elegantly atop her head. A few waving tendrils floated to her shoulders. Her dress was a very pale yellow, and the neckline was low enough to offer a view of skin she did not normally reveal, but not so low as to be scandalous. The wagon came to a stop, the driver set the brake, and then the man disembarked to assist the ladies. His wife, a handsome woman in bright pink whom Declan had seen once in the general store, left the wagon first, and then the man assisted Matilda from the wagon.

Declan stepped behind a wide post, hiding and watching, not quite ready to reveal himself. Matilda looked like a fairy stepping from the pages of a book, a woman not of this earth. She looked as if she might fly away at the drop of a hat. Her dress was not elaborate, like many of the others that graced the street today, it was not bright or ostentatious or fashionably eye-catching. But it was lovely and somehow suited her. No frills, no flounces, that was Matilda Candy.

He thought about going to her immediately and telling her how exquisite she looked today, but thought better of it. Like it or not, he could not spend the entire day

Linda Jones

following Matilda around, mooning over her, making his desires obvious to her and everyone else in Tanglewood.

At least she would not be lonely. The woman she traveled with stayed close as they walked toward the festivities, and the twins were at their heels. Since Matilda had expressed reservations about coming to this event, though, he really should spend some time with her, make her feel as if she belonged here as much as anyone else. It would not do for her to feel alone, not today when she looked so damn beautiful.

Really should spend time with her? Who was he kidding? How could he possibly stay away?

She whispered to her friend, then lifted her head and trained her eyes down the street. Looking for him, perhaps? He made himself smaller behind the post. A moment to compose himself, that's all he needed.

Matilda searched the crowds, her eyes narrowed, and then she smiled so widely her entire face lit up. She stepped away from her friend quickly, lifting her skirt slightly to make her step less impeded. She was almost directly in front of him, just a few feet away, when she spoke.

"Ezra," she said, her smile widening as she quickened her step. "My goodness, I had no idea you'd be here!"

Declan turned his head slowly to see a man who hurried down the middle of the street toward Matilda. He had longish brown hair and stepped quickly in her direction. He was a man some women might possibly find handsome, if they went for the boyish, slender, pretty-faced type. Declan looked beyond the young man for an older gent, a gray-haired merchant who asked Matilda to marry him when he came to town. He continued searching until the long-haired pretty boy threw his arms around Matilda and lifted her off her feet.

"Look at you!" he said, laughing as he twirled her around. "You're downright gorgeous."

She was laughing with him when he set her on her feet. "And I have shoes," she said, lifting her skirt to show off a pair of feminine, burnished shoes on dainty feet.

"If I'd known you'd developed a liking for shoes," the man said with a wink as he took her hand, "I would've brought you a hundred pairs."

This was Ezra Cotter? The merchant who regularly asked Matilda to be his wife, the one she jokingly said might father her twelve children? Impossible. Inconceivable. Unthinkable.

Discretion be damned. Declan stepped from behind the post that had concealed him to that point and headed straight for Matilda with a scowl on his face.

She should've attended all the past Founders' Day Celebrations, Matilda thought as she lifted her head to listen to the mayor talk about the way Tanglewood had prospered in the past thirty years. The speech was rather dull, but she pretended to pay attention. Her mind was definitely elsewhere.

Declan stood on her right, arms crossed over his chest, a hint of a frown on his face. Ezra stood at her left, an amused smile flitting now and then across his wide mouth, as if he were on the verge of laughing out loud. Both men had behaved in a proprietary manner since they'd met on the street and grudgingly shaken hands. Neither of them seemed inclined to leave her side.

While it was nice to have her good friend Ezra on one side and the man she loved on the other, there was a less enjoyable aspect to this trip. She hadn't been here an hour yet, and already she could see the division she caused among the other celebrants. Those she knew well, Mr. Fox, Stella, Ezra, and Declan, and a few others, treated her with kindness and openly expressed friendship.

But there were others who were not so glad to see her

here. The minister, the man who ran the saloon, Henry Langford, and his pals Reggie and Wendell—they all glared at her with open hostility. A few mothers steered their children away from her as she walked down the street, as if to come too close to the witch would be disastrous. Even Seth Hazelrig occasionally glanced at her with apparent suspicion.

Ezra leaned slightly to the side. "You really are gorgeous, Matty," he whispered. "Let's sneak away from this dull as ditch-water mayor and get married."

She grinned at his preposterous jest. "Today? Why, I haven't a proper gown," she said jokingly. She cut her eyes up to him. Ezra was a very handsome man, with honey-colored hair he wore too long. He stood almost six feet tall, and was thinner than Declan but not what one would call skinny. His best feature was his gray eyes; they were constantly laughing.

What she liked best about Ezra was that he didn't care that people called her a witch. Nor did he ask her if the rumors were true. He'd once said she could cast a spell on him anytime, then he'd winked at her and changed the subject.

Of course, she did not take his flirting seriously. It was his nature to tease, to have fun with everyone he met. He probably had a dozen girls in Mississippi that he regularly asked to marry him. It was amazing to her that not one of them had yet said yes.

"At the very least," he said in a lowered voice, "let's slip away from your chaperon and have a little fun." He waggled his eyebrows and grinned.

Declan leaned across her to whisper to Ezra. "Do you mind? Some of us are trying to listen to the mayor." He narrowed his eyes. "And I am *not* Matilda's chaperon."

Ezra shrugged his shoulders and seemingly returned his attention to the mayor. Declan, obviously proud of himself for silencing Ezra, straightened his spine and lifted his chin.

140

Ezra placed his hand casually at the small of Matilda's back. The move was so unexpected she jumped a little. He didn't remove his hand, even when Declan glared at him so hard Matilda could almost feel the heat.

Matilda looked down at the toes of her bronze shoes and stifled a smile. She, who had never really had a suitor, was caught in the middle of two males posturing for her attention. She should be horrified and embarrassed, but to be honest she enjoyed the attention.

Declan took her arm and very gently pulled her away from Ezra and through the mass of people. "I feel the need for some lemonade," he said as they wound their way to the back of the crowd. "Are you thirsty?"

"A little," she confessed.

From directly behind her, Ezra added a cheery, "Me, too! A glass of lemonade sounds grand right about now."

Declan glanced over his shoulder and scowled.

Vanessa purposely arrived late, planning her entrance carefully. She'd step from the carriage, her hand in Johnny's, and all heads would turn in her direction. All the *men's* heads, that is. It barely mattered what the women noticed or thought.

Declan would come directly to her, of course. She would maintain her cool exterior, but she would bestow upon him an encouraging smile or two. She might even lay her hand on his arm, while he looked at her lovingly. Perhaps he would be encouraged enough to propose marriage this afternoon, or this evening as they danced.

She would have to dance with others, of course, but she imagined Declan would watch her with sad eyes as she turned about the dance floor on the arms of other men. Perhaps his jealousy would spur that proposal of marriage.

The carriage came to a halt, and she smoothed the skirt of her periwinkle gown and touched a hand to her perfectly arranged hair. She pinched her cheeks for color, and straightened her back so her bosom was shown to its full advantage. When Johnny opened the door, she rose gracefully from her seat and took his offered hand. Before she left the carriage, she gave him a wickedly promising smile. By the time she stepped into the sunlight her face was perfectly expressionless.

She opened the parasol that matched her gown and allowed her eyes to adjust to the bright light. Declan would be easy to find even in this crowd; he was so tall and masculine, so charismatic. Perhaps she would not find herself completely adverse to sharing his bed, once they were married. Two adoring lovers would surely be more wonderful than one.

She did see Declan, but he was not watching her arrival as she'd assumed he would. In fact, no one was watching her but Henry Langford and those two moronic friends of his.

Declan had his back to her, as he and another handsome man hovered over something . . . or someone.

"It looks as if your intended's interests lie elsewhere today," Johnny whispered.

"Shut up," she hissed. "And don't speak to me in public! Someone might see you."

Johnny remained by the carriage while Vanessa walked toward Declan Harper, her gaze and her step unerring. Whatever claimed his attention so completely, he would forget the moment she smiled at him.

She was tempted to frown when she saw a head of blond hair just beyond Declan's shoulder, the back of a fair head and a scrap of plain yellow fabric. Good God, no one looked good in yellow! The other man who hovered over the woman laughed at something she said and lifted a glass of lemonade to his lips. Declan gave the man a cutting glare.

He should've seen her by now, should've sensed her presence and turned about to see her walking so elegantly toward him. But no, she had to stop and call his name.

"Declan?"

He spun about, obviously surprised to hear her voice. The other man turned his head as well. And the woman turned slowly around.

The witch! Matilda Candy was smiling when she turned, but that smile quickly faded. Ah, the woman was smart enough to know when she was outclassed. The witch was no competition for Vanessa, not where a man was involved.

"Good afternoon," Vanessa said. "I hope I'm not interrupting."

"Matilda was just telling us about her neighbor's children," Declan said. "They're . . . quite a handful."

Vanessa hoped with all her heart that she herself was barren. She hated children. Brats, every one of them. She forced herself to smile. "Why, I'm sure they're adorable."

The other man laughed, and the witch took that opportunity to introduce him. Ezra Cotter was quite attractive, in spite of his unfashionably long hair, but he was a merchant, for goodness' sake! Ah well, Miss Candy could have the merchant. Johnny and Declan would be enough for her.

As soon as the introductions were done, Ezra returned his attentions, his absolute adoration, to the witch. Unfortunately, so did Declan. He seemed, in fact, loath to leave Matilda's side.

Vanessa stepped into the circle. "Miss Candy, that is a very . . . interesting dress. Wherever did you find it?" Surely such a rag had been found, not purchased.

The witch smiled. "It belonged to my grandmother."

"A hand-me-down," Vanessa said with a weak smile. "I've heard of such things."

"I think it's a lovely dress," Ezra said enthusiastically. "As beautiful and unique as the woman who's wearing it."

Declan agreed, though without quite as much enthusiasm.

Vanessa lowered her head to take a deep breath and calm herself, and that's when she saw the shoes. *Her* shoes.

When she'd gotten a good look at the bronze shoes Mr. Fox had ordered for her, she'd decided they were not quite right, but she certainly hadn't expected that the witch would buy them. They were *her* shoes!

Vanessa lifted her eyes and looked squarely at the girl. She smiled sweetly and leaned just slightly toward Declan, laying a possessive hand on his arm. So the witch thought she could take her man *and* her shoes.

This meant war.

Chapter Twelve

She was so glad Stella had convinced her to come! Matilda wore what she knew had to be a silly smile on her face, as the judges looked over the entries in the pie contest. A long table was laden with pies of all kinds, her own cherry pastry among them.

Declan had left her side a while ago, at Vanessa's whimpering insistence. The Arrington girl had dragged him away to meet someone she deemed important, and he'd never made it back. He did, however, Matilda noticed, keep a close eye on her and Ezra. Every time she looked up, she caught Declan watching her.

After examining the pies to determine their aesthetic appeal, the three judges took their forks and began the real test; they set about tasting each and every one. Matilda found she was actually nervous about how her own entry would fare. She didn't expect she would win, but she did want her cherry pie to be well received. She wanted at least one of the judges to roll his eyes in ecstasy when he tasted it.

That wasn't too much to ask, was it? Especially when Mr. Fox claimed her baking was always so well received by his customers.

"You might've put that cherry pie aside for me," Ezra whispered, leaning just a little bit too close.

"How was I to know you would be here?" she answered in her own lowered voice. "Goodness, I never know when you're going to show up, so how can I possibly be prepared?"

Matilda held her breath as the first judge came to her pie, fork raised above the perfect crust. In a movement made without conscious thought, she nervously laid her hand on Ezra's arm. The judge was poised to dig out a small bite of the dessert when Vanessa Arrington whispered in a horribly loud voice,

"I don't think I could make myself eat a pie made by a witch."

The crowd hushed, and the judge stopped with the pie not quite to his mouth. Oh, no wonder Vanessa had asked, as they looked over the table earlier, which pie was Matilda's. The girl had planned all along to humiliate her.

The judge lowered his fork and blushed, his eyes raising to search the crowd for Matilda. When he found her and held her gaze, she was horrified to see a touch of fear there.

No one moved for a long moment. All was silent, and all eyes were turned to her. Matilda wanted to disappear; she wanted to drop through the earth and never come up again. She let her hand fall from Ezra's arm as he muttered a low curse and scowled. Ezra never scowled, and he never cursed.

Matilda wondered, with a touch of panic in her heart, how she could escape, how she could make this horrid moment go away. She scanned the crowd quickly, her eyes finding familiar faces that were angry and afraid and ashamed. And then her eyes landed on an incensed Declan and a deceptively innocent wide-eyed Vanessa.

Most of all, she did not want Declan to see her humiliated this way.

Declan abruptly left Vanessa's side to stride to the long table of pies. He scooped up a clean fork from the end of the table, and then, without hesitation, dug out a forkful of her cherry pie and popped it into his mouth. "Fabulous," he said, glaring at the cowardly judge.

Ezra patted her comfortingly on the shoulder and then worked his way through the crowd to do the same, to take up a fork and taste her entry. Bless him, he rolled his eyes in delight.

Robert then joined them, his spine straight as he made this gesture for her. He grinned as he took a big bite, and then he winked at her. To her amazement, John Bowers, Vanessa's driver, joined them for a taste of his own, and so did Charles Fox.

Tears clouded Matilda's eyes, not because she had been embarrassed, but because she apparently had friends who would stand up for her in front of all these people.

Declan glared at the judges. "Have we made our point?" he asked softly, but loud enough for everyone to hear.

The judge looked sheepish as at last he took a bite, and then smiled as he took another.

The second judge shoved him aside. "Leave some for us. How are we to determine which pie is best if there's none of this one left?"

People in the crowd laughed; some of them, anyway. Vanessa's expression was unnaturally calm, but her cheeks had turned beet-red. There were a few in the crowd who remained solemn, who turned censuring eyes on Matilda. Henry Langford and his two friends, redheaded Reggie and portly Wendell, watched her suspiciously and whispered to one another.

Then Declan caught her eye, and Matilda no longer cared about Vanessa or the others who condemned her.

She wanted to laugh out loud, to run to him and throw her arms around his neck. She wanted, more than anything, to shout "I love you!" at the top of her lungs.

But for now a smile would have to do.

Why had he been so afraid Matilda would be lonely without him today? Dusk had cast the town in a soft half-light, and the dancing had begun. Hell fire, everyone wanted to dance with Matilda. That idiot Ezra Cotter, Mr. Fox, Robert, even Vanessa's driver. She'd not been neglected for a moment.

And she loved it, didn't she? She smiled widely and danced with an artless grace, laughing as her partners instructed her on the steps. Even her mistakes were charming!

He looked down at Vanessa, an accomplished dancer, who was prattling on about something or another. He had chastised her earlier for her comment about Matilda's pie, and she'd met the admonishment with a charming naiveté, swearing that she didn't mean anything by it, and after all Matilda *was* a witch. And what did it matter now, since she'd won the contest, and why anyone would want a blue ribbon for something so mundane as making a pie she would never know.

It had taken all Declan's powers of restraint to keep from shouting the woman down for her frivolous thoughtlessness.

When the music ended, and Henry Langford arrived to ask for the next dance, Declan gratefully handed Vanessa over and turned to make his way back to Matilda. He barely beat out Ezra Cotter, who had already danced with her twice.

"This one's mine," Declan said, never taking his eyes from Matilda's beaming face.

He was glad the next dance was a waltz, so he could hold Matilda and not have to pass her around.

"I am so very glad you asked me to come here today."

"I can see that," he grumbled.

"I can't remember when I've ever had so much fun." She stepped on his toes, then laughed lightly as she resumed her step. "Sorry."

It was the first time all day he'd had her to himself. He held her in his arms and twirled her around while she smiled up at him, and the cross words that flew out of his mouth were, *"That's* Ezra Cotter?"

Her grin widened. "Yes."

"I thought he was an old man."

"Did I say he was an old man?"

"No." He spun her toward the edge of the crowd. "You said there was an age difference."

"He's two years younger than I am," she said innocently.

"I just assumed," Declan began awkwardly. "I mean I guessed . . ." He sighed, unable and unwilling to explain. "You've seriously considered marrying him?"

Matilda's smile faded. "Ezra is a good friend. I like him very much." Her voice remained low. "I imagine there are worse fates than marrying a friend."

He looked down at her and sighed. She was much too spirited to marry a man she only liked. She needed passion, heat, love. In that moment, Declan wished with all his heart and soul that he could be the man to give Matilda everything she wanted. Everything she needed and deserved.

"I never did get a chance to thank you," she said softly.

"For what?"

"For walking up there and tasting my pie. For letting the town know that you're not afraid of me."

"I wasn't the only one," he said modestly.

"You were the first," she whispered. "And I thank you with all my heart."

The waltz ended, but he didn't let her go. They'd moved beyond the knot of dancers, and it took just a few steps to move her into the alley between the general store and the dressmaker's shop. In the fading light, they were well hidden here.

"Thank me properly," he whispered as he lowered his mouth to hers.

It was dangerous, to steal a kiss here and now, but he felt the need to claim her, to put his mark on her, to taste her lips and feel her body lean against his. The kiss was brief, soft, and undemanding, achingly sweet. She closed her eyes and melted against him; the tender touch was so familiarly intimate he wanted to stay there all night.

She pulled away and opened her eyes, reaching out to straighten his collar. "I don't think that last mixture is entirely out of my blood," she whispered.

"I know what you mean," he whispered. Something of the aphrodisiacs he'd taken must be lingering, too. What he felt for her could not be real. It was too powerful—potent enough to make him question his plans to marry Vanessa and become the respectable gentleman. He tried to forcibly remind himself of why he was here in Tanglewood, what had taken him to Matilda Candy's cottage.

He had plans, big plans. One day *he'd* be the one giving Founders' Day speeches.

Right now none of that mattered. "Have you ever kissed Ezra Cotter?" He hated to ask, but he had to know.

Matilda shook her head and laid a gentle hand on his face. "No," she whispered. "You're the only man I've ever kissed."

A flood of relief washed through him. "Let's keep it that way, shall we?" And then he stole another kiss.

She was exhausted, but it was a good, warm, wonderful exhaustion. When had she ever had so much fun?

"Wanna dance?" Wendell Trent, one of Henry Langford's cohorts, cornered her, rocking back and forth on his heels and grinning widely. He was not yet thirty, but he was losing his hair at the temples and had the rounded stomach of a much older man. As he awaited her answer, he belched.

"No, thank you," she said, smiling and doing her best to be polite. "I'm afraid my feet are killing me. I'm not used to all this dancing."

He did not take her refusal well. "You've danced with damn near every other man in town," he growled. "There something wrong with me, witch?"

Her smile faded; she saw no more reason to try to be polite to this man. Vanessa had cornered Declan, and Ezra was dancing with the preacher's daughter. Neither of them were watching her at the moment, so she would have to handle Wendell on her own.

"Perhaps I don't care to dance with a man who likes to hit his wife," she said in a lowered voice. How many nights had she opened the door to find Sally Trent standing there, searching for a lotion to make the cuts and bruises on her body heal faster?

Wendell's eyes narrowed. "Sal ain't even around no more. She went to live with her sister in Mobile."

"Smart woman," Matilda said. "I just wish she'd gotten smart a little sooner." She bit back the words *before she married you*. Wendell was already close to losing his temper. There was no need to goad him further.

Ezra was headed her way again, and Wendell apparently saw that they were about to be interrupted. He slunk away, casting a narrow-eyed glance over his shoulder as he rejoined his friends.

Less than half an hour later the music ended for the night. The energy that had filled the town all throughout the day began to fade. People yawned, small children slept against a father or mother's shoulder. The laughter dimmed as the light in the sky did.

Many in the crowd were saying their good-byes when a creaking, colorful wagon made its way down Main Street as if the time of arrival had been planned.

Matilda was not the only one who stopped to watch the slow progress of the creaking conveyance. Everyone soon knew who the traveler was; the words *Raleigh Cox, Rainmaker,* were painted in a faded red across the front and sides of the wagon.

The mood of the crowd changed. For today they'd put their worries aside, but rain was needed badly, and soon. Welcoming a rainmaker into their midst would be a desperate move, but the farmers here were desperate men. They were looking at ruination.

Raleigh Cox, a tall, scarecrow-thin man with long, stringy pale hair, leaped from the wagon and strode toward the waiting crowd. When he stepped into the light, a few women gasped.

He was, perhaps, the ugliest man Matilda had ever seen. There was nothing symmetrical about his face, not a single beautiful feature. One eye was set higher than the other, and it wandered aimlessly, a lazy eye. His nose was long and crooked, his mouth thin, his chin sloped. His plain clothing hung on him, and when he lifted one hand to gesture to the crowd, she saw that his hands were unnaturally long and pale. The fingers looked almost like those of a skeleton.

"I understand you folks need rain," he said.

He might look ugly, but his voice was beautiful, sonorous and rich, commanding. With those words, he commanded the crowd. Some even held their breath as they waited for the rainmaker to continue.

"I can bring it," Cox said confidently. "And I see no reason to waste your time or mine with niceties. I'll need two weeks, a place to stay, food to eat, and care for my horse. I'll also need two hundred dollars."

"Two hundred dollars!" Henry Langford shouted from the center of the crowd. "That's outrageous." Wendell and Reggie nodded their agreement. "How about one hundred?"

152

Cox looked to the cloudless sky. "Sir, this is a two-hundred-dollar job. Take it or leave it."

People put their heads together and whispered, casting suspicious glances at the rainmaker as they muttered. Voices rose and fell. The rainmaker stood calmly and silently by as a budding spark of new excitement wove slowly through the crowd.

There was little doubt that the men of the town would take their chances with Raleigh Cox. Desperate men would try just about anything.

She hated the smell of the room by the stables where Johnny slept, but this could not wait. After saying good night to her father and making her way to bed, Vanessa had waited to hear his own bedroom door close, and then she'd sneaked silently down the stairs, her anger growing with every step.

Johnny was not asleep. He was lying on his cot, still dressed, with a single lamp burning low at his side.

"How could you?" she said as she stepped into his tiny room.

He sat up, then stood, surprised to see her. "How could I what?"

She slapped him across the chest. "You danced with her! You ate her damn pie!" She hit him again with the flat of her hand. "She's a witch, and you smiled at her and treated her like . . . like she was a regular person!"

He smiled at her and she hit him again. "Are you jealous?"

"Of a witch? Don't be ridiculous."

Johnny put his arm around her. "I wasn't the only one who treated Matilda like she was a real person. I noticed your intended has taken quite a liking to her."

He was enjoying this too much! "Declan was just being kind, I'm sure."

"Was he being kind when he pulled her into an alley for a quick kiss?"

Her blood boiled. "He didn't," she seethed.

"He did. I saw them."

She closed her eyes. Nothing was going as she'd planned. Nothing!

She should simply dismiss Declan Harper and move on to someone else, but he was so damned convenient! Henry adored her too much, he would likely keep her under lock and key if she married him. Gordon Smith, who'd proposed just last month, lived in the next county, and would certainly not take kindly to her bringing her father's stableman along when they married. Every suitor presented some kind of similar problem.

Declan was perfect. He owned the land right next door, and he didn't worship her; she'd have all the time for Johnny she wanted.

Although, she did wish Declan would show *some* interest. He should be panting after her the way the others did. He should be flattered that she bestowed her attentions upon him. For a brief moment Vanessa doubted herself. Had she lost her beauty? Of course not. Her charm? Never. What was wrong? Declan Harper should be falling at her feet by now, begging to marry her.

She pushed back the panic that threatened to rise up. "You still love me," she crooned. "Don't you, Johnny?"

He hesitated. "Of course I do, Vanessa, but I wish you wouldn't be so . . ."

"So what?" she asked, dropping slowly and gracefully to her knees before him and unfastening his trousers.

"Sometimes you're downright mean."

"I know what I want, and I make it happen." She finished the task at hand, unfastening each and every button, then clasped Johnny's bottom with her hands and hugged him against her, gently, so as not to wrinkle her gown. "Is that a bad thing?" she whispered. "If I were a man, you'd say I was determined, but since I'm a woman, you say I'm mean." She placed her chin against Johnny's unfastened trousers and looked up at him, making her eyes wide, pouting just a little then licking her lower lip.

"I don't understand you, sometimes," he said softly.

"But you love me," she said, certain of the answer.

"Yes."

"You'll do anything for me? Anything I ask?" She rubbed her cheek against the ridge in his trousers, felt him grow even harder.

"Yes," he moaned. "Anything."

She slipped her hands into his trousers and pushed them slowly to the floor. Johnny might not understand her, but she understood him quite well.

But then, men were so terribly simple to understand.

Chapter Thirteen

Matilda spent the morning bottling rose water and oils and counting out jars of cream for Ezra to take to his store in Jackson. He'd want a few bottles of rose of vinegar, too, as well as rose honey and jelly.

After yesterday's excursion, Matilda was filled with energy and a new excitement that made it hard for her to keep her mind on the task at hand. The night had been wonderful, magical, a day to remember always. Surely Declan would not marry Vanessa now!

Before the Founders' Day Celebration had ended, she'd invited Ezra to Sunday dinner. He arrived right on time, just before noon, a smile on his face and a bouquet of clumsily gathered wildflowers in his hand.

"Hello, beautiful." His smile was wide and familiar, the twinkle in his eyes charming. "I'm starving," he said.

She placed the wildflowers in a tall, narrow vase and put them on the table. Her books and tools had been cleared away, and two places had been set.

Ezra sat in the rocking chair as she carried food from

the kitchen to the table. As he watched her, his smile faded, and his eyes became deadly serious. She'd never seen him look so somber before, but she was afraid to ask why his mood had changed so drastically.

When she called him to the table he came quickly, moving the plate she'd set across the table from her own place and putting it beside her, taking the seat at her left and making himself comfortable as he filled his plate.

"So," he said as he speared a piece of beef. "Are you serious about this Harper fellow?"

Her heart skipped a beat. "Serious?"

Ezra pinned his eyes to her. "Are you in love with him?"

She lowered her eyes and played with her peas. "I don't know. I think so."

He sighed long and loud, giving the simple exhalation an overly dramatic flair. "If he breaks your heart, I shall have to kill him."

She lifted her eyes and gave in to a small smile. "That's very gallant of you, I suppose."

"Of course, you could always forget that dark, brooding hulk of a man and move to Jackson and marry me."

"You're too young for me," Matilda said.

Ezra shook his head. "Yesterday you didn't have a proper wedding dress, and today I'm too young. I fear you are simply offering me one excuse after another. Ah, if you loved me the way you love that Harper fellow I'd have you out of here and married by midnight."

"I'm sure your father and your brothers would be less than thrilled if you came home with a witch as your bride." Her tone was light; the look Ezra shot to her was not.

"Is that why you always say no? Because you're afraid of what my family will think?"

"I always say no because you're not serious. Really, Ezra, you probably propose marriage to a dozen girls a week."

He set his fork aside and pushed his plate away. "Only you," he said seriously. "I guess I've been hoping that one day you'll change your mind and say yes."

Matilda placed her hand over his. "You're such a good friend," she began.

"But you don't love me," he finished for her.

She shook her head.

Ezra was not one to brood. He placed his hand over hers, sandwiching her hand between his, and gave her a wink. "If things don't work out with that Harper fellow, you let me know. If he breaks your heart, I'll mend it. After I kill him, of course."

"Of course." She leaned forward. "You're a wonderful friend," she whispered as she laid her lips on his cheek. He responded by placing an arm around her and hugging her as close as possible, considering that he sat on one chair and she sat on another.

The front door flew open, banging against the wall as if a powerful gust of wind had flung it inward. The sound of the door slapping the wall was so sharp that she and Ezra both jumped as they turned to look that way.

Declan crossed his arms over his chest and glared at them both. "How cozy."

When he'd seen Matilda and Cotter through the window, he'd become instantly enraged. She said they were friends, but they looked much too friendly for his liking.

"Don't you know how to knock?" Matilda asked, as if she were the injured party.

All of a sudden Declan felt like a fool; he'd come storming into Matilda's house like a jealous lover on a rampage. No wonder Cotter looked like he was having a hard time containing a laugh.

Maybe Matilda saw his vexation. She saved him from finding the words to apologize. "Are you hungry?" she rose from her seat. "There's plenty. Let me set another plate."

He felt like he should get out of here and leave the two *friends* alone, but he didn't care for the gleam in Cotter's eyes, the almost-smirk on the shopkeeper's pretty face. He took the seat on the other side of Matilda and glared at her guest.

While Matilda was fetching a plate and silverware, Cotter's smile died and his gaze hardened. "Hurt her, and you'll have to answer to me," he said softly.

"I'm terrified," Declan sneered.

"You should be."

Cotter's silly grin returned as Matilda did, and the conversation abruptly turned to mundane things: the drought and the Founders' Day Celebration and the rainmaker who had arrived on the heels of last night's dance. Cotter teased Matilda about stepping on his toes as she learned to dance, and when she asked, he told her about his brothers and sisters—the extensive Cotter family who all resided in and around Jackson. It was so clear these two were close, that they had confided in each other over the years, and Declan remembered Matilda's words: *There are worse fates than marrying a friend.*

And suddenly he was more jealous than he'd been when he'd looked through the window and seen the two of them holding hands and smiling at each other.

Matilda insisted that Ezra take a small basket of sweets and bread and cheese on his trip, as he loaded his wagon with the oils and pomades he'd purchased for his store. He looked over her shoulder, probably to make sure that Declan was watching, and then he scooped her up for a long hug that hoisted her feet from the ground.

"Remember what I said," he whispered. "If he breaks your heart, he's a dead man."

She did love Ezra a little, at that moment. Not the way she loved Declan, of course, but it warmed her heart to know he cared.

"You're a rare prize," she whispered back.

"Not prize enough for the prettiest gal in three counties, apparently," he said as he set her on her feet.

Her first thought was *Vanessa?*, and then she realized he was talking about her. "You're a shameless flirt."

"Guilty." Ezra climbed into the wagon and winked at her, then nodded his head at Harper before setting the horses in motion.

She waved until she could no longer see the wagon, and then she turned to face Declan.

The sun shone brightly on his face, but Declan glowered at her. He had no right to look angry. Especially since, as far as she knew, he still planned to marry that mean-spirited, rash-ridden Vanessa Arrington.

"I came to see if you needed any wood chopped," he said tersely.

"Good heavens, no. Robert has me quite well supplied for the time being." She kept her voice calm, giving away none of her hopes or fears where Declan Harper was concerned. Goodness knows she had plenty of both. "He did repairs to the greenhouse, too," she said. "And he's started building an ingenious trench from the pond to the garden. As long as the underground water supply doesn't dry up I should be—"

"I think Robert's a little sweet on you," Declan interrupted, crossing his arms over his chest.

"I think he's just relieved that I'm not the evil crone he expected me to be."

"It's more than that," Declan whispered, his apparent irritation fading. "Did you cast a spell on him, too?"

"What do you mean, *too*? Who else have I supposedly cast a spell on?"

He hesitated before answering softly. "Me."

She turned away from him before he could see her smile. "Come to the pond and see what Robert's building. Why, I'll never have to carry water again."

She walked over the small hill, not turning to see that Declan followed. She could hear his footsteps and ob-

Thrill to the most sensual, adventure-filled Romances on the market today...

FROM 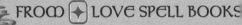 LOVE SPELL BOOKS

As a home subscriber to the Love Spell Romance Book Club, you'll enjoy the best in today's BRAND-NEW Time Travel, Futuristic, Legendary Lovers, Perfect Heroes and other genre romance fiction. For five years, Love Spell has brought you the award-winning, high-quality authors you know and love to read. Each Love Spell romance will sweep you away to a world of high adventure...and intimate romance. Discover for yourself all the passion and excitement millions of readers thrill to each and every month.

Save $5.00 Each Time You Buy!

Every other month, the Love Spell Romance Book Club brings you four brand-new titles from Love Spell Books. EACH PACKAGE WILL SAVE YOU AT LEAST $5.00 FROM THE BOOK-STORE PRICE! And you'll never miss a new title with our convenient home delivery service.

Here's how we do it: Each package will carry a FREE 10-DAY EXAMINATION privilege. At the end of that time, if you decide to keep your books, simply pay the low invoice price of $17.96, no shipping or handling charges added. HOME DELIVERY IS ALWAYS FREE. With today's top romance novels selling for $5.99 and higher, our price SAVES YOU AT LEAST $5.00 with each shipment.

AND YOUR FIRST TWO-BOOK SHIP-MENT IS TOTALLY FREE!

IT'S A BARGAIN YOU CAN'T BEAT! A SUPER $11.48 Value!

Love Spell 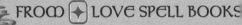 A Division of Dorchester Publishing Co., Inc.

GET YOUR 2 FREE BOOKS NOW—AN $11.48 VALUE!

*Mail the Free Book
Certificate Today!*

*Free Books
Certificate*

YES! I want to subscribe to the Love Spell Romance Book Club. Please send me my 2 FREE BOOKS. Then every other month I'll receive the four newest Love Spell selections to Preview FREE for 10 days. If I decide to keep them, I will pay the Special Member's Only discounted price of just $4.49 each, a total of $17.96. This is a SAVINGS of at least $5.00 off the bookstore price. There is no shipping, handling, or other charges. There is no minimum number of books I must buy and I may cancel the program at any time. In any case, the 2 FREE BOOKS are mine to keep—A BIG $11.48 Value!

Offer valid only in the U.S.A.

Name_____

Address_____

City_____

State _____ Zip _____

Telephone_____

Signature _____

If under 18, Parent or Guardian must sign. Terms, prices and conditions subject to change. Subscription subject to acceptance. Leisure Books reserves the right to reject any order or cancel any subscription.

A
$11.48
VALUE

Get Two Books Totally
FREE —
An $11.48 Value!

PLEASE RUSH
MY TWO FREE
BOOKS TO ME
RIGHT AWAY!

Love Spell Romance Book Club
P.O. Box 6613
Edison, NJ 08818-6613

AFFIX
STAMP
HERE

scene muttering clearly enough to know he was directly behind her.

"See?" she said, gesturing to the work in progress. "These stilts support the trench so it's at the highest point here. All I have to do is dip water from the pond, pour it in here, and it's downhill all the way to the garden. Robert's going to lead the trough around that way," she said, pointing to her right, "so we won't have problems with the hill."

She turned around to see that Declan studied the work with some appreciation. "It's not a bad idea."

"It's a wonderful idea."

Declan continued to look as if he'd eaten something bitter. "Perhaps."

"What's your problem today?" she asked, finally becoming annoyed with his petulance. "You are certainly in a foul mood."

"I don't have a problem, and I am *not* in a foul mood." He couldn't look at her as he delivered this obvious lie. "I just wish you wouldn't make such a fool of yourself with that Cotter fellow."

She laughed out loud, surprising Declan.

"What's so funny?"

"He calls you *that Harper fellow*."

Declan wrinkled his nose. "Does he?"

She could not, for the life of her, understand why someone like Declan would ever be insecure enough to be jealous, but he obviously was. Did he love her? Just a little? And if he did, was it real love, or were his feelings false side effects of the love potions she'd made for him?

Since she'd met Declan, she'd often thought that he looked like a man who wanted to be aristocratic but fell short, who tried to be refined but could not. Standing before her, glaring down with an unnatural heat in his dark eyes, he conjured images of his ancestors—semi-civilized Celtic warriors raring to charge into battle.

161

He did not run but walked slowly toward Matilda, joining her at the bank of the pond with a few long strides. "I don't want to argue with you," he said softly. "Not about Cotter, not about anything."

"Good," she whispered.

"It's just . . ." he towered over her, looking down with narrowed eyes. "I want you all to myself."

"Ezra is just a friend," she said, wrapping her arms around Declan's neck and leaning into him. "A dear friend, at times the only person in my life who didn't either fear or hate me."

"I can't believe that," he said, shaking his head. "There's nothing about you that isn't good."

"You always know the right thing to say."

She kissed him, softly, gently. They came together with the ease of two lovers who had been together for years. There was no awkwardness in the way his arms went around her, no uneasy shifting. They just fell together in a perfect embrace. Even though she stood on the edge of the bank, her feet slanting downward toward the water, she felt no fear. Declan held her.

"I want you in my life," he whispered. "Forever, Matilda. Never in my twenty-nine years have I wanted anything or anyone *forever,* but I can't imagine my life from this day forward without you in it."

They were sweet, heartfelt words of permanence and commitment, and she could tell that he was sincere. She could also tell that the admission pained him a little.

"I'm not going anywhere," she whispered.

She heard a shout, the pounding of little feet breaking from the forest.

"What's this?" Hanson shouted.

She couldn't see the twins yet, but they were close, and they'd spotted the water trough Robert was building.

"I don't know. Slow down!" Gretchen demanded.

Hanson came flying over the hill, a smile on his face, his pale hair dancing as he ran at full speed toward the water channel. His face was red with the effort of running, and his long, thin legs pumped tirelessly.

His smile faded as he saw Matilda and Declan. He tried to stop, or at least he appeared to try as he flew down the hill. He had three choices: He could run into the water trough or he could run into the water or he could run into Declan.

He chose to run into Declan, hitting forcefully with a whoosh of air and an exclamation.

Declan tottered, holding on to Matilda as she fell back and toward the pond. He surely could've let her go and righted himself while she fell backwards into the water, but he didn't. He held on and started to pull her back. They were almost stable when Gretchen arrived on her brother's heels, giving Declan what Matilda was sure was a well-planned shove.

The pond water she landed in was tepid. Declan landed almost on top of her with a loud splash. She went under for just a moment, water in her ears and her eyes and up her nose, soaking her skirt and blouse and hair. She broke the surface sputtering and laughing, and Declan came up cursing at the top of his lungs.

When he was finished, he wiped the water from his face and looked up at the kids. "You brats!" he bellowed. "You did that on purpose!"

Hanson looked properly chastised, but Gretchen wore a small, not-quite-innocent smile. "We did not," she said primly. "It's not our fault that y'all are so very clumsy." With that the twins turned and ran.

Matilda laughed again, and Declan turned to her, obviously furious.

"What's so funny?" he snapped, pushing his wet hair back with both hands.

She covered her mouth in an effort to still her hysteria, but it didn't work. Eventually Declan's anger faded, and he grinned at her. Water ran in rivulets down his hard face.

"We must look pretty funny."

She nodded.

He grabbed her arm and pulled her close; she moved slowly through the water until her wet chest rested against his. She could feel his body heat beneath the wet shirt, and the sensation was strangely intoxicating. She reached up and wiped a drop of water from his cheek, taking her time and reveling in the feel of her fingers against his wet skin.

"Forever is a long time," she whispered, resuming their conversation where they'd left off before the Hazelrig twins had dumped them both in the pond.

Declan shook his head in a kind of wonder. "Not nearly long enough for everything I want from you."

Matilda Candy had never depended on anyone in her life. She'd been stronger and more sensible than her mother. Even as a small child she'd known that to be true. She'd loved and learned from her grandmother, but she'd always known that Granny would not be there forever. Except for Ezra and Stella she had no real friends, and in her heart she tried very hard not to depend on their friendship too much. She should not depend on anyone, she knew.

But at the moment she felt like she needed Declan Harper. She needed to be his forever, to look at his face every day, to hold him like this on good days and bad. She felt like she could never, never get close enough to him. Even if she were able to crawl inside his skin and live there, she would not be close enough.

The thought terrified her. To need someone so much surely made one vulnerable, weak. Defenseless. But the same thought warmed her to her soul.

"I love you," she whispered.

Declan answered by kissing her deeply, then lifting her from her feet and carrying her from the pond. She rested her head against his shoulder and tried her best to get inside his skin, to slip inside his warrior's soul.

She kissed his wet neck and buried her nose against the place where neck turned to shoulder, lost in the warmth of his skin and the taste of him on her lips. Her body throbbed, ached, and hungered for more. For everything.

Today there was no love potion at work here, no oil or powder or candy, no ancient aphrodisiac. This wondrous feeling of need and love was generated artlessly by the two of them. It was real and good and true.

"I love you," she whispered again. Declan forcefully kicked open her door for the second time that day.

Chapter Fourteen

He didn't want to put her down. They were both soaked to the skin, hair dripping, water running onto her floor, and still he did not want to put Matilda down. She smelled fresh and clean and sexy. She was warm and light, and he could feel her heartbeat, as if it beat inside him.

No matter what it took, he would keep her. He would never let her go.

She kissed his neck and burrowed against him, her wet blouse sticking to his soaked shirt. Then she stopped, lifting her head so she could look into his face. He saw, in that instant, that she meant what she'd said. She *loved* him. He didn't know what he felt for her, only that it was powerful and good. And overwhelming.

"Would you put me down?" she asked. "I'd like to try something."

He reluctantly put her on her feet, giving her one last kiss before she stepped away.

"Sit down," she said, backing into the kitchen. "I have something for you to take."

He shook his head and began to follow her. "Not another potion. Matilda, I don't need . . ."

She lifted her hand to stop him. "Do you trust me?"

"Completely." It was the truth, one that scared him a little. He'd never trusted anyone so completely.

"Then sit."

He did as she asked, and watched her disappear into her small kitchen. She was soaked to the skin, barefoot, and her hair had once again been plaited into childish pigtails. And still she was the sexiest sight he'd ever seen. He didn't need any lust potion. If he were any readier, he might ignite.

She returned minutes later, a cup and spoon in her hands. She sat on his knee and spooned up a small portion of her latest concoction.

"I really don't . . ." he began.

"A small taste," she whispered.

After the last time, he'd assumed she would want this coming together without any aphrodisiac in their blood, without any aid churning their emotions to a fevered pitch. Hadn't she insisted? And yet right now she looked almost eager for him to take the spoonful of liquid she offered. He opened his mouth and she spooned the sweet liquid onto his tongue.

And then she watched.

"What about you?" he asked, taking the spoon from her and dipping it into the syrupy potion. "Just a taste?"

Matilda opened her mouth and allowed him to dribble a small amount onto her tongue. Just a few honeyed drops. Her mouth closed slowly, then she took the cup and spoon from him and set them on the table.

"Now do what we did before," she whispered. "The first time. Just look at me, and let me look at you."

He'd never thought simply watching a woman could

be so arousing, until he'd met Matilda. How often was a man allowed to look his fill, to stare unabashed, to watch and allow his fantasies to run wild? Perched on his wet knee, she began to undo her braids, to slowly loosen the wet strands and run her fingers through the dampened, golden hair. Her eyes—witch's eyes, he'd always known—sparkled and danced. For him.

His heart leapt; he grew harder. He stared at her and imagined what she'd look like lying beneath him, what she'd feel like when her bare skin pressed against his. Impossibly he wanted her more than he had minutes ago. He burned for her.

"It's strong stuff, Matilda," he said hoarsely as he watched her shake out her hair.

"As strong as what we took before, do you think?"

"Stronger," he whispered. "I've never in my life wanted anything the way I want you now." He reached out and gently touched her: her neck, her hair, her breasts through the wet linen. She shivered. "I can feel it in my blood, burning and building with every heartbeat." She touched him, her fingers in his hair and on his shoulder. "This has got to be the strongest potion yet," he whispered.

Matilda smiled and leaned forward to kiss him on the mouth, not once but a dozen fleeting times. She laughed, then pressed her chest to his. "It does seem to be quite effective."

He wondered at her mirth, and why she'd insisted on testing this potion now. Did she need it? Did she think he needed it? He looked into her strange and beautiful eyes and felt a jolt he could not explain.

"I had to be sure," she whispered, taking his face in her hands. "I had to know . . ." she kissed him again. "Declan, what we just took was sugar water. Plain, ordinary sugar water. There is no love potion, there was never any magic about any of the things we took. All this time it's been us. Just us. We thought those things I made were real, so we allowed ourselves to look and crave and speak without restraint. That's all it was." She kissed him again, deeper this time. "I'm so glad it's just us," she whispered against his mouth.

Relief made her light-headed, dizzy, and breathless. All this time it hadn't been herbs and spices making her heart beat fast and her blood boil. It had been Declan all along.

He stood, lifting her in his arms as he rose from the chair. "Just us," he said, amazed.

"Yes."

He pushed past the calico curtain that separated her bedroom from the main room, placing her on her feet by the bed. The light was dimmer here, with the curtains at the single window pulled shut, but still she could see Declan's face and the passion in his dark eyes quite well. She wanted to see everything.

He unbuttoned her wet blouse, moving slowly even though he was obviously as anxious as she was for them to lie together. She could see the need in his eyes, feel it in his every touch. She didn't hurry him, even though her body trembled and her knees shook. This was a moment to be savored.

When her blouse was unbuttoned, Declan, slipped his hand inside the wet fabric to touch her breast. His hand was warm and tender against flesh still cool and damp, his fingers teased her nipple and traced the rise of her breasts. She closed her eyes and thought about nothing but the feel of his hands on her flesh. He touched her gently, and yet she felt it everywhere; in her heart and her weak knees and most especially in the throbbing rhythm between her legs.

He removed the blouse and dropped it to the floor, and pulled her against him for a deep kiss. His tongue teased hers as he held her tight.

When he released her, she reached out to unfasten the buttons of his damp shirt. He stood very still while she flicked one button after another through her fingers. When she'd unfastened them all, she spread the cotton in her hands and leaned forward to kiss his chest, to lay her mouth against flesh warm and hard and lightly sprinkled with dark hair. While she kissed him there she pulled his shirt from his waistband and pushed it up, raking her hands along his sides as she lifted it slowly up and over his head. It landed on the floor next to her blouse.

He unfastened the button at her waist, and the next and the next, and with a gentle push the skirt fell to the floor, pooling at her feet. She was vulnerable, standing before him in nothing more than her damp drawers, but she wasn't afraid, not of Declan. It didn't matter how big he was, how commanding, how determined; he would never hurt her.

She kicked her skirt away and laid her hand on his trousers. The damp fabric made working the buttons there more difficult, but she managed to unfasten them all without running into unbearable difficulties. She shucked the trousers down slowly. Declan kicked off his boots, one at a time, and stepped out of the trousers.

They stood facing each other, each wearing nothing more than flimsy, wet undergarments.

"I can't believe that what I feel right now is real," Declan whispered, pulling her close.

Matilda's eyes drifted shut, and she melted against his chest. "I know," she whispered. Knowing that what she felt was genuine was more amazing to her than the possibility that a true love potion might exist.

While she leaned against Declan, he slipped the fingers of one hand into the waistband of her drawers as he unfastened the tapes with the other. He pushed them down and she stood against him absolutely naked. Exposed. Wanting. Could a woman offer anything more to a man than this? He held her heart and her body in his hands, she was his wholly, without question or regret.

He removed his own underwear and laid her on the bed, covering her body with his. "Your skin is still a little cold," he whispered, running his hands over her skin to warm her. He brushed his hands over her arms and her sides and her thighs, and she felt the heat grow, warming her from the inside out.

"So is yours." She raked her hands down his back, skating her palms over the muscles, feeling him grow warm as she did.

She felt, also, the erection that pressed against her thigh. In the past weeks she'd learned as much from reading the books that contained recipes for love potions and erotic oils as she had from her grandmother, who thought that no woman should be ignorant of anything, not even the intimate ways of a man and a woman. Hearing and reading about intimacy had not prepared Matilda for the way she felt, for the power and the sheer beauty of the sensation of Declan's body against hers.

Matilda knew what was to come, and she wanted it. She wanted Declan inside her.

Her hand skimmed boldly to his hips and rested there as Declan kissed her, slanting his head as if he could deepen the kiss this way, touching her as he held her mouth open with his lips and flicked his tongue against hers.

She slipped her hands between their bodies to touch him, raking her tentative fingers along his length, wondering how she could possibly take it into her body and yet knowing that it would be wonderful and right to have him there. He moaned as she wrapped her fingers around him.

There was no longer anything cold in the bed. The skin, hers and his, that met along the length of their bodies was warm. The wetness between her legs was warm, too. Hot even.

Declan reached down and spread her legs, then raked

his hands slowly along the insides of her thighs. His fingers barely touched her flesh.

"I've never felt anything so soft in all my life," he whispered as he stroked her, teasing the tender skin of her inner thigh with long, patient fingers. Matilda quivered so hard she was quite sure the entire bed shook.

Declan's fingers moved higher to touch her intimately, and she arched off the bed and moaned, the response instinctive and powerful. He kissed her, caught the moan in his own mouth as he did and, in an unexpected move, slipped a finger inside her. She gasped and trembled as he began moving that finger—in and out, in and out, in a motion that promised what was to come. She rocked against him, unable to help herself, unable to think of anything but the way her body sang.

He took his hand from her, then grazed her body with his as he positioned himself so that he rested between her spread legs. The tip of his erection barely touched her; a quiver shook her body as he pressed forward.

Her body stretched, changed to accept him. There was pressure and even pain as her body expanded to accommodate their joining, but she felt not an instant of trepidation. He rocked above her, in and out, not with great force but with tenderness and ease.

When he broke through her maidenhead, there was a moment of pain that made her gasp and arch her back, but the pain was quickly over, and Declan pushed deeper into her body. He made love to her, kissing, whispering, stroking, and they fell into a natural rhythm, a dance of sorts that wiped away everything but intense physical sensation and a depth of emotion she had never before imagined.

She found herself swaying against him, meeting his increasingly vigorous thrusts with surges of her own as her body took over. Eyes closed, heart pounding, she lost herself in the act of loving Declan and allowing him to love her.

Her climax hit her with such force she cried out softly and seized Declan tight as unexpected tremors wracked her from the inside out. Intense pleasure seeped through her body, her spasming inner muscles wringing everything from Declan. He moaned and drove deep inside her one last time, finding his own release.

She could not breathe, could not move, as Declan drifted down to cover her.

A sigh escaped her lips, as her breath returned. Her body trembled and ached, and yet she felt good. Wonderful. Remarkably fine. Declan remained inside her, a part of her, and she felt as if she'd succeeded in crawling beneath his skin. This was what it felt like to be a part of another person, to truly be one.

"Oh, my," she whispered into his ear. "I didn't quite expect that."

He lifted his head and looked down at her, brushing a damp strand of hair away from her face. "What did you expect?"

She smiled. "Something rather like a kiss, I suppose. A meeting, a moment of pleasantness. I never expected to be shaken to my very bones."

He smiled and kissed her lightly. "You are an amazing woman, and I will never let you go," he whispered.

"I'm glad to hear it." She draped her arms around his neck. She thought of telling Declan again that she loved him, but since he had not yet said the words to her, she held them back. Maybe he wasn't ready to admit that what they had found was love.

Matilda experienced a moment of suspicion, a shiver of apprehension. She knew of no true stories of love that had worked out well, and very few fictional ones. In the end there was always pain and death and heartache. But for once she thought—no, she *knew*—that there could be happy endings for true lovers. At the moment she felt too good to consider anything else.

He woke knowing exactly where he was and what had happened in Matilda's bed. There was not so much as a split second of disorientation or doubt. A deep peace filled him, a satisfaction he was unaccustomed to, making him feel strangely content.

Matilda was not sleeping beside him, though she had been a while back when he'd opened his eyes briefly to study her. He couldn't have been asleep more than two hours or so; it was still bright outside. The summer days were long.

His shirt, trousers, and underwear had been hung across a couple of chairs by the window, where they caught the diffused sunlight streaming through the curtains. They were not quite dry, so he wrapped Matilda's quilt around his waist and went in search of her.

She wasn't hard to find in the small cottage. Almost immediately after stepping from the bedroom he saw her in the kitchen, her attention resolutely on her worktable and a sticky mass she shaped and stretched and kneaded. She was so intent in her work she didn't hear or see him, so he took the opportunity to study her.

She'd donned new, dry clothes—a white blouse with a narrow band of lace at the collar, and a blue skirt. Her hair was loose and waving down her back in soft, silky waves. Her feet were bare.

Why did he feel this way about this woman? Why, of all people, was he obsessed with Matilda Candy? She was pretty, yes, open and honest and innocent, but there were other women in the world with those qualities. None of them did *this* to him.

Knowing that what he felt was not aided by any witch's brew confused him more than it should have. He hadn't known such strong feelings were possible, not for him. Matilda had said this was real, that it was purely them. She'd even said it was love. And right now, he didn't want to argue with her.

"What is that?" he asked, stepping into the kitchen.

She cocked her head slightly to look at him and smile, seductive and innocent at the same time. "It's a surprise."

He watched her fingers work through the gooey mass, stretching and kneading. The mass was slowly changing in texture, growing more opaque and firmer. But her hands were definitely occupied.

Holding the quilt at his waist with one hand, he stepped behind Matilda, nosed her hair aside, and laid his mouth on her neck. She giggled in response and tried to move away, but her task at the worktable kept her in place. He laid his free hand on her hip and sucked on her neck.

"Declan!" she said with gentle laughter.

"Matilda," he whispered, moving his attentions to the other side of her neck.

"My hands are full at the moment."

He loosened his hold on the quilt and let it fall to the floor, reaching around her to caress her breasts. "So are mine."

His arousal pressed against her backside, and she quit laughing. Her hands still moved urgently in the mass of goo, but she leaned against him and sighed deeply as he cupped her breasts in his hands and gently flicked his thumbs over the nipples that hardened at his touch.

"This is so unfair," she whispered.

"Did I ever claim to be a fair man?"

She shook her head.

He kneaded her breasts in rhythm with the movement of her hands in the sticky mess on the table and kissed her neck, sucking and licking and tasting her. "Do you want me to stop?"

She shook her head again.

He unfastened her blouse and slipped his hand inside to touch her. She wore nothing beneath—no chemise or underthing to impede him. He teased her with his fingers and wondered if she wore anything beneath her blue skirt.

Lifting the skirt revealed that she had nothing on below. He stroked her hip and her bottom, reveling in the feel of her soft skin, pressing his arousal against her.

He wanted her again, here and now, with an urgency that overwhelmed him. His hand slipped around her and lower, to touch her where she was already wet for him. She quivered and melted at his touch, moaning and spreading her legs slightly. She continued to knead the mass on her worktable, but with less enthusiasm. The movements of her hands were lazy, distracted. Finally they stopped entirely.

He spun her around and kissed her. She held her hands away from him, but leaned forward and closed her eyes and wrapped her arms around him.

He lowered her to the floor, and when she lay beneath him, he parted her unbuttoned blouse and greedily took a hard nipple into his mouth. She moaned as he suckled her, opening her legs in invitation and scooting down and against him.

He moved the blue calico of her skirt up and aside and parted her thighs wide. Dammit, she wasn't the only one trembling as if she couldn't wait another second for him to be inside her; he was shaking like a leaf, quaking deep down.

Pushing forward, he buried himself inside her. She gasped, and arched up and against him and rested her warm hands against his back. This time he was not afraid of hurting Matilda; he came together with her fast and hard, surging into her again and again with relentless passion.

The climax came quickly for them both, intense and unrelenting. He felt her milking him as she cried out, taking everything he had to give and more.

Matilda was his. In this moment, he claimed her, he

cherished her, he would fight for her. In all his life, he had never felt this close, this completely intimate, with another person. Not his family, not the women that came and went. He was strangely content, and he was terrified. He was tempted to tell her all this, that she had changed his life, that he was scared to death of what came next. That he loved her.

Matilda hooked one leg around him and began to laugh. He lifted his head to look down at her, and she just laughed harder. He was not about to tell a laughing woman that he loved her!

"What's so funny?"

"We're stuck," she said, and then she burst out laughing again.

He smiled and moved within her. "Not exactly *stuck,* darlin',"

She tugged on her hands at his back, hands that had not moved since she'd grabbed him. He felt the strange sensation of something against his back, something that was not flesh.

"What do you have all over your hands?" he asked, a hint of disquiet forming within him.

"Hard molasses candy," she said, laughing again. "I was making it as a surprise for you, but it was taking forever to harden up." She pulled at her hands again; they did not come loose. "I think the candy finally set."

"So we're stuck here," he said, settling in comfortably on Matilda's kitchen floor.

"No, we're just stuck together."

He didn't argue and she didn't tug at her hands again. They lay on the kitchen floor, joined, stuck, and perfectly happy. He laid his forehead against hers and dismissed his earlier worries.

Yes, this complicated matters. No, he didn't know what would happen next. He only knew there were many worse places to be stuck than to Matilda Candy.

"I love you," he whispered.

The confession didn't hurt nearly as much as he'd expected it would, and the expression on Matilda's face made up for everything else; the indecision, the complications . . . Nothing could touch what they had.

Chapter Fifteen

It was Wednesday—candy day. Gretchen crept through the woods with her brother right behind her.

"I wonder what she made today," he whispered.

Gretchen sniffed at the air. They were close to the break in the trees that would reveal the witch's cottage, but still she smelled nothing tantalizing. "I can't tell yet. I don't smell anything at all, not even bread." She narrowed her eyes and forged onward. Something wasn't right. She sniffed at a wrongness in the air that didn't smell of cinnamon or sugar or roasted nuts.

From the shelter of the trees, they peeked into the cleared ground around the witch's cottage. All was quiet, but for the two horses that had been hitched outside her front door. One was a very pretty, very small black horse, the other belonged to Mr. Harper, the man she'd pushed into the pond. She hadn't pushed him on purpose, not really, but he wasn't likely to believe her if she said so.

Running at full speed, they burst from the forest and headed for the shade at the side of the house. Gretchen listened for sounds of movement in the large separate kitchen where the witch worked her sweet magic, but heard nothing. She peered around the corner and looked across the courtyard and through the kitchen window, and saw nothing. The place appeared to be deserted.

But there were *two* horses here!

She flattened her back against the wall and turned to Hanson. "Go take a good look through the kitchen window and see if there's any candy cooling there."

"You," he whispered, as spooked by the unnaturalness of the quiet as she was.

She narrowed her eyes and glared at him. "Do you want me to tell Stella what you did with your beef last night?" The woman would find the tough bit of meat eventually, but Hanson didn't want to face their stepmother's ire any sooner than he had to.

He frowned and stepped away from the wall. "I couldn't eat it," he mumbled, "and the buffet was right there."

"When she finds it in the linen drawer and figures out what happened, you'll be in big trouble." She lowered her voice. "But if you do as I ask, this afternoon I'll distract her while you retrieve the beef and toss it out. Then she'll never know." There was likely to be a stain on the linens the beef had touched . . . but then again maybe not. There had been *no* juice in that tough, dry roast.

"All right, then," Hanson said, rubbing his hands together in preparation.

He ran, quickly and silently, through the courtyard, past the black cauldron, past the garden gate, to put his head through the kitchen window to look quickly around. Mere seconds later he was at Gretchen's side once again, breathless and red-faced.

"There's nothing," he whispered. "The kitchen is cold and the counters are clean. *Nothing!*"

Gretchen held her breath. What could keep the witch

from making candy on Wednesday, as she always did? She laid her hand against the stone wall at her back. Maybe the witch was in trouble. Maybe she was still in her bed, unable to wake up. Ill or hurt or dead. *Like my mother*, Gretchen thought before shaking the disturbing remembrance aside.

They heard the front door open, and flattened themselves against the wall.

"But I don't need to learn to ride," the witch said in a soft, amiable, very healthy voice.

"Yes, you do."

Gretchen recognized that voice. Declan Harper. The man she'd pushed into the pond, who'd made such a scene of eating the witch's pie at the Founders' Day Celebration, who'd said *ribbit* once after he'd made the mistake of allowing the witch to kiss him.

"But, Declan . . ." Matilda began, and then she squealed. It wasn't a scary sound, but was very much like the way Gretchen herself squealed when her father lifted her from the ground and spun her around.

"That's not so bad, is it?"

"Horses don't like me," the witch said in a small voice.

"Shadow loves you," Mr. Harper said softly. "I love you."

Hanson looked at Gretchen and screwed up his face, sticking out his tongue in an almost comical gesture.

"I love you, too," the witch said. "I'll try to learn to ride, but only because it seems to be important to you."

All was quiet for a moment; they were probably kissing. How disgusting. Hanson stuck out his tongue again, and this time he grabbed his throat as if he were trying to choke himself and rolled his eyes way up in his head. He remained perfectly silent.

"A nice and easy ride to town," Mr. Harper said.

"I have so much work to do," the witch protested.

"If Fox doesn't get his caramels this week, the world won't come to an end."

"I know, I know."

The horses left at a slow and easy pace, heading for the road and away from Gretchen and Hanson. For a long moment after they were gone, the children stood there quietly.

"No candy this week," Hanson muttered.

"Maybe no candy ever again." Gretchen slapped her hand against the wall. "What if they get married and move away? What if she spends all her days with him and decides she doesn't have time to make candy anymore?"

It was a small thing, the candy they stole from the witch. But it was also the only fun they had these days. Her mother was gone, and her father was busy with his farm and his new wife. If she and Hanson drifted apart, if they didn't have these excursions to plan and execute, she'd lose her brother, too. They *would* grow apart, the way brothers and sisters did. Father hadn't seen his sister in more than two years!

"We have to stop this," she muttered.

"Stop what?"

She glared at her brother. "We have to make sure the witch and Mr. Harper don't get married, we have to make sure things return to normal here."

Please, please. Things weren't normal anywhere else these days.

"How?" Hanson asked.

Gretchen shook her head. "I don't know, but I'll think of something."

Declan was at the plantation house this morning, overseeing the rebuilding of a large side porch and the attached dining room. Robert had arrived bright and early, less than half an hour after Declan had departed Matilda's cottage, to continue working on the trench.

The walk to town was pleasant. Overly warm and long as always, but Matilda's mind was occupied with thoughts of Declan, so she minded neither the heat nor the length of the walk. Her basket was light this Friday. Last night she'd found time to make a couple of quick batches of caramels and one batch of cinnamon-roasted nuts, but that was all she'd had time for.

Love was not terribly horrific after all. She and Declan would be different from the other lovers of which she had known: they would defy tradition and be happy forever. She knew it in her heart. She wanted that eternal happiness with every fiber of her body.

"Good morning, Mr. Fox," she said brightly as she entered his store.

He had a wide smile for her. "Matilda!" His smile faded when she set her basket on the counter and he looked at the contents. "What happened?"

"I've been rather busy this week," she explained. "I'll bring lots of extras next week, I promise."

His smile came back. "Well, we're all allowed a lazy week now and again. Make me some toffee next week, and I'll forgive you."

He brought out the empty basket from the last week and set it on the counter, but Matilda was already heading for the back of the store. "I'd like to look at your shoes again," she said. "The bronze ones are lovely, but much too nice for every day." She'd found she had an odd liking for shoes, and her old boots were no longer sufficient for her needs. "A new pair of boots, perhaps, and a pair of plain leather shoes."

The prospect of a sale wiped away Mr. Fox's disappointment at her small delivery. "I have some lovely boots, and a pair of kid shoes that will feel so comfortable on your feet, you'll think you're barefooted."

Since Mr. Fox had never visited her at her home, he had no way of knowing that she spent most of her days barefoot. "Comfortable would be nice."

Matilda quickly decided on a pair of lace-up boots that would be perfect for walking, once they were broken in, and a soft, slim pair of black leather shoes. Who would have thought that purchasing footwear could be so much fun?

She placed her purchase in the basket to carry home, and again promised Mr. Fox more candies in next week's delivery.

Before she reached the door, two customers tried to enter at once: Vanessa Arrington with her nose in the air and her gaze unerringly forward, and the rainmaker Raleigh Cox, who tried to cut in front of Vanessa so he would not have to slow his stride on her account. They didn't exactly jostle each other, but there was a moment of struggle for dominance in the doorway.

Vanessa, apparently deciding quickly that she was not going to win, graciously stepped back and allowed Cox to enter before her. She narrowed her eyes and glared at his back, regained her composure, and whispered something no one could hear. Matilda suspected it was vile.

As Cox passed Matilda, not even looking at her as he passed, he muttered something vile himself. The only words she could make out were, "Spoiled harridan."

"Any luck?" Mr. Fox asked the rainmaker, a hint of anticipation in his voice.

"Not yet," Cox answered absently, walking through the store and handling the merchandise, picking up one thing and then another, looking this way and that and then putting it down again.

Fox quite deftly slipped the basket of candies beneath the counter, almost as if he were hiding it.

"Mr. Fox, have the gloves I ordered arrived?" Vanessa asked as she stepped briskly forward.

"Yes," he said, smiling again. "And if I may say so, they're quite lovely."

From across the room, Cox shouted. "Are these all the cigars you have?"

"Yes, sir," Fox answered.

"My gloves?" Vanessa pressed.

Matilda made her way to the doorway, hiding her smile. Poor Mr. Fox! He had two difficult customers, it seemed. No wonder he sometimes dreamed of becoming a carpenter.

"Miss Candy," Vanessa called, "would you mind waiting? I need a moment of your time."

"Of course." She stepped back inside and watched as Raleigh Cox took what he wanted, berated the storekeeper, and left without paying. All the while he and Vanessa vied for Mr. Fox's full attention.

Once Cox was gone, Vanessa inspected her gloves and accepted them, though she was disappointed in the color. It was not exactly what she'd expected.

On the boardwalk, Vanessa handed her purchase to a waiting John Bowers, who smiled at Matilda and said hello, then received a cutting glare from his employer's daughter for his trouble.

"Wait here," Vanessa snapped, lifting her chin and glaring at John. "I won't be long."

They walked a ways down the boardwalk, and Vanessa came to a sudden halt in front of what had once been a barber shop. It had been closed up for months, now, so no one was close at hand.

"I don't know you very well," Vanessa said softly, "but you have been a friend to me."

"I have?"

Vanessa flashed a charming smile. "With your beauty creams and sweet waters and oils, why I consider you to be a very special acquaintance."

Of course. All of Vanessa's friends surely provided some sort of service. "That's very sweet of you to say," Matilda said, confused.

Vanessa sighed. "More than that, you are a woman, and we ladies must stick together when times are difficult."

Matilda felt a shimmer of warning pass through her body, as if a summer storm brewed there. What on earth did Vanessa want? She surely wanted something.

"I suppose that's true."

Vanessa leaned close to Matilda and lowered her voice. "I couldn't help but notice how friendly you were with Declan Harper at last weekend's festivities."

Declan. Matilda's mouth went dry.

"He's a friend," she managed to say calmly.

Vanessa smiled coyly. Her eyes glittered, hard and unforgiving. But only for a moment.

"Men like Declan Harper don't have women *friends*, dear."

"You're wrong," Matilda protested weakly.

"He's rich, he's handsome, he's powerful," Vanessa continued with confidence. "Declan can have any woman he wants. Why do you think he wastes his time on a witch?"

Heat rose in Matilda's cheeks, and more than anything she wanted to turn and run home as fast as she could. "What are you trying to say?"

"I just want to warn you that if Declan is being friendly, it's likely because he expects something of you, something he could never get from a *lady*. Until after the wedding, of course," she added. Surprisingly, there was no anger or obvious malice in her voice. "Men have powerful physical needs," she said in a lowered voice. "I suppose they must take care of those needs in some way, but I do so hate to see a woman taken in by a man."

All her doubts and fears came rushing back. What if Vanessa were right? She shook the doubts aside. "Your . . . concern is kind, but . . ."

"Besides," Vanessa interrupted, her eyes hardening. "I've rather taken a liking to Declan Harper myself. You do know you don't have a chance if I decide I want to marry him?"

"Have you?" Matilda asked softly. "Have you decided to marry Declan?"

The smile that spread across Vanessa's face was smug

and somehow sinister. "Yes, I believe I have. I haven't told him yet, of course. Why would a man ever respect a woman who falls at his feet and grovels for him? Goodness, how humiliating that would be." Vanessa glanced back to where her coachman waited for her. "I just wanted to warn you that if you've set your sights on Declan, you're going to be disappointed. Men like Declan Harper don't marry witches with braids and bare feet. They marry women they can be proud of. Like me." With that, she turned away and walked calmly to her carriage.

Something inside Matilda began to throb, to physically, sharply hurt. She pushed the ache deep, knowing in her heart that Vanessa was wrong.

But no matter how hard she tried to make it go away, the pain didn't quite disappear.

Matilda was in the big kitchen making bread when he arrived, and Declan smiled the moment he looked through the window and saw her standing there. She was oblivious to his presence, so he watched her a moment, enjoying the view.

Coming to this place at the end of the day felt so much like coming home it warmed his heart and made him forget why he'd returned to Tanglewood. Coming home to Matilda every night made everything better. It was so unexpected.

Robert was long gone. In fact, Declan had timed his arrival to come after the handyman's departure. He didn't want to damage Matilda's already tenuous reputation by making their relationship public. She deserved better.

"This place smells so good," he said as he stepped into the kitchen. Matilda stood before the brick oven, taking out a loaf of perfectly browned bread on her long spatula.

"There's nothing like the aroma of fresh-baked bread," she said, not turning to look at him.

"Actually, I was talking about you." After she set the

bread down, he slipped his arms around her waist and held her tight, smelling her neck and her hair. "I missed you today."

"Did you?" She turned in his arms to face him, to look up with wide, anxious eyes.

"What's wrong?"

She hesitated before answering, as if she considered keeping whatever bothered her to herself. It didn't take her long to decide to answer his question.

"I saw Vanessa Arrington in town today." Her mouth, usually so quick to smile, worked into a small frown. "Are you still . . . you've never said . . . she's what you wanted . . ."

"Are you asking me if I still plan to ask Vanessa Arrington to be my wife?"

"Yes," she breathed, as if afraid to speak aloud.

He had considered, for a while, continuing with his plans: Vanessa as his wife, Matilda as his lover. The situation was not unheard of, even in this day and age. One woman for social standing and money, another for love. Kings and princes and men of great power had been doing it for hundreds of years.

But being with Matilda made him dismiss such notions. He couldn't imagine marrying a woman like Vanessa Arrington; he couldn't imagine taking another woman as his wife. Matilda had teased him, early on, about making himself King of Tanglewood. He didn't want to be king anymore.

"No," he said.

"You hesitated," she said in an accusing voice.

"I was shocked that you would ask such a question. It took me a moment to gather my wits about me after such a shock." He smiled as he said this, lifted his eyebrows in mock dismay.

He saw relief wash through Matilda's eyes. "You don't want her anymore?" she asked.

Declan shook his head. "I just want you."

When she rose up on her toes and kissed him, he could almost taste her relief. Heaven above, he *did* want Matilda. He held her tight and pressed his arousal against her, deepened the kiss and cupped his hands on her bottom. He could take her here and now, on the floor, against the wall, and it wouldn't be the first time he'd been so anxious to bury himself inside her that he couldn't make himself endure the long trip to her bed.

But not this time. He'd had a long day and so had she. He wanted to burrow beneath a quilt with her, in her soft bed, in the near dark, and he wanted to stay there for a while. He wanted every stitch of clothing, his and hers, discarded. He wanted to lose himself in her. It was so easy to do just that when her body came to his.

After the past week, he should be tired of Matilda; he should at least not be aroused every time she kissed him, or touched him, or smiled at him. If he truly believed she was a witch, he'd think himself enchanted.

They left her bread cooling on the long counter and headed for the house, hand in hand at first, until Declan tired of Matilda's short steps. He impatiently but tenderly swung her into his arms and she laughed. God, he loved the way she laughed.

"I made something special for you this morning," she whispered as he kicked the back door closed behind them.

"I'm not hungry."

"It's not food." She reached into the deep pocket of her apron and withdrew one of her small, green glass vials. Declan didn't slow down, but headed straight to the bedroom. "Am I supposed to drink that?"

Matilda shook her head. "No. This is one of the other recipes I found when I was looking for your love potion."

"Another perfume?" Heaven above, he didn't need anything to make him want Matilda more than he already did.

"Not exactly." She placed the vial on her bedside table, and moving slowly, without displaying the urgency they both felt, they began to undress each other. Buttons, tapes, sashes, they all cooperated and came undone easily. Matilda gave him a sweet and wicked smile, and her eyes . . . her eyes told him that she wanted him. That she loved him. "This ointment is for a man and a woman who are already lovers," she said as she shed the last of her clothing.

When he pulled her down to the bed, she reached out to grab her vial from the table and bring it with her as she fell into his arms. "It will make you want me more," she teased, her smile bright.

"Impossible."

"It will make you my willing love slave."

"I am already your willing love slave," he said, only slightly impatient.

Resting against him, her breasts pressed to his chest, she uncapped the vial and dribbled a single drop of the concoction onto his skin. Thick and oily, it shimmied across his chest in a thick, languid ribbon. With gentle fingertips, she worked the fragrant potion into his flesh.

"What is that, exactly?" he asked as the warmth of the oil and her fingers seeped deep beneath his skin.

"Oil of roses," she whispered, "lavender. A few of my best spices."

She raised up slowly, straddling him as she dropped a few beads of the oil onto his chest. When she offered the vial to Declan, he took it, and with both hands free she began to massage his skin, spreading the oil with the palms of her hands, with gentle fingers, her eyes on the striking picture of her pale hands against his chest.

The heat rushed through his entire body, from the places Matilda touched outward, as if a fire grew there and she stoked it. Her fingers brushed against his nipples, massaged the flesh above his heart, explored and teased and tortured.

"Well, what do you know?" he whispered. "It works.

Whatever you wish, madam, it is yours. *I* am yours."

She grinned as her hands slipped down, over his ribs, over his sides to his hips.

He did not close his eyes to savor the intense sensation, but kept his eyes open so he could watch Matilda's face. Such wonder grew there, such tenderness and passion. The mere sight of her was a more powerful aphrodisiac than anything she could ever manufacture.

Gripping the vial tightly, he watched her, wondered at her. Matilda was a small woman, delicate, petite, and he was never so struck by that fact as he was when she touched him, when he could see her small hands against his rough flesh, when he could compare her dainty stature to his own length and breadth. Yes, she was tiny, but she was also strong. There was so much strength in her hands, in her deceptively soft body. Most of all, there was strength in her spirit.

She lowered herself slowly, kissed him as her oiled hands dipped lower to rake across his thighs, pressed against his slick chest and raked her breasts over his oiled skin. And all the while she kissed him, her hands moved against his thighs, her thumbs tender, too tender, against the sensitive flesh of his inner thighs. She shifted, moving like a cat against him, and ran the palm of one sleek hand up the length of his arousal. Slowly, firmly, and only once.

With a growl he quickly rolled Matilda over so that he towered above her. Her answer was a smile, as her eyes drifted closed and she leaned her head back, offering her neck to him. He kissed her there, lingering until she purred, then raised up and dribbled a few drops of the oil onto her chest. She was already slick, from brushing her chest against his, and the oil beaded and ran slowly down the globes of her breasts.

He stopped the progress with his fingers, and she reached out to take the green glass vial from him and place it on the bedside table.

Her flesh was soft and slick in his hands. The tantalizing odor of the oil wafted up to greet his nose, but he knew the roses and lavender and spices had little, if any, effect on his desire. It was touching her that drove him wild; it was the feel of her breasts in his hands, her flesh against his, her soft thighs opening beneath him. It was knowing that she loved him, that he loved her.

He ran his hands, so large and rough-looking against her soft, pale skin, down to her belly. His hands moved in circles, gently rubbing and dipping ever lower. Her skin flushed pink, from her face to her thighs, and her smile gradually faded. Her lips parted, her head tilted back, and he felt a deep, telling tremble with the hands that continued to massage her.

Moving slowly, he raked his slick hands down the length of her thighs, down skin so satiny and creamy pale, he never ceased to be amazed. He brought those hands back up just as slowly, taking his time in arousing her before he touched her intimately and dipped his head down to take one oiled nipple into his mouth. Matilda wrapped her arms around his neck and held him tight, as she wrapped her legs around his and drew him close. He brought his mouth to hers as he guided himself inside her, moving slowly, even though he was impatient. Easily, even though she urged him not to be easy with her. He moved above and within her, her chest and legs slick against his, her lips tasting faintly of the trace of oil he had carried there from her breast.

He had never lost himself so completely, so deeply, as he did when he was with Matilda. He had never been so sure that this was his place, that this was where he belonged. It was more than physical, more than the primal impulse that brought them to this moment.

His movements quickened and so did hers. He buried himself deep, and she rose to meet him. She arched up off the bed, into him, with a soft cry and a shudder. He felt her trembling around him, squeezing him with rhythmic spasms and coming apart in his arms.

And he gave himself over to his own completion, thrusting deep inside her one more time and coming apart himself. Unraveling. Losing every part of himself, but for this joining, which was as spiritual as it was physical.

Depleted, he eased his body down to cover Matilda's. She sighed, a long, satisfied exhalation of breath, and threaded her fingers through his hair.

"I never did get to rub your back," she said, sliding a palm down his side in a languid, lazy caress. "I intended to massage every inch of your body with that oil."

"Next time," he said, his voice just as low and breathless as hers was.

"Next time," she whispered.

He moved against a sated Matilda, his glistening chest sliding against hers, as he raised his head to look down at her.

"How did I ever get along without you?"

She smiled, as if he were making a lighthearted joke, and raked an almost limp hand down his chest. "I don't know how you managed."

"Neither do I."

She continued to smile, and then she kissed him, light and sweet, tasting slightly of her special oil. "Lucky for you, you have me now."

He lowered himself and closed his eyes. "Lucky for me."

Chapter Sixteen

Matilda had all but chased Declan off, since Stella and Gretchen Hazelrig would be spending the day with her; learning to cook, she said. He hated to leave her, but at the same time he was glad she had found herself a friend in Stella.

As always, Tanglewood was a bustling place on Saturday. There was not the excitement of the Founders' Day Celebration today, but the normal Saturday flurry was lively. Shoppers from near and far visited the general store and the dressmakers and a multitude of other specialized shops. Children ran in the streets, shouting and playing as their parents did the weekend chores.

Declan glanced at the busy saloon, thinking of his earlier plans to buy the place. Restoring the plantation house, the labor and materials, was more expensive than he'd planned. He still had a healthy sum of cash, but much of his fortune was tied up in the house he hated, the land he was not yet working. Buying the saloon would have to wait.

The delay did not distress him, as it would have a few weeks ago. He no longer had the urge to take over as much of Tanglewood as possible, to own its inhabitants. His need for revenge seemed less urgent, was no longer the center of his life. Matilda had changed everything, including his dream of making everyone in this small town pay. He could see, now, that there were good people here as well as bad. Yes, he looked at everything differently these days.

A crowd had gathered around the rainmaker. Cox had the men he'd assembled form a large circle around him. Farmers made up the circle, mostly, desperate men on the verge of losing everything. It was too late to make the season a good one, and a few more weeks of dry weather would mean ruination for many of the smaller farmers.

Henry Langford, Vanessa's rejected suitor, was one of the more vocal participants. His cronies, the freckled, red-haired Reggie Brewster, who worked a farm with his father, and potbellied Wendell Trent, who worked a small farm alone and looked as if he wanted to strangle the rainmaker, nodded and agreed loudly with everything Henry said.

When Cox called out in his booming voice and pointed to the heavens, the farmers looked up expectantly, even the angry Wendell. When he began to dance and chant in another language—some kind of Indian dialect, Declan suspected—a few of the farmers closed their eyes and prayed.

"Pathetic, isn't it?"

Declan turned to face a disapproving Warren Arrington. Even if he had given up on marrying Vanessa, he needed to remain cordial with his neighbor. He would never like the man; the past was too painful. But if he were to build anything here in Tanglewood—with Matilda—he needed to keep up appearances.

"They're scared," Declan said.

Arrington snorted. "Scared enough to hire a con man to take what little money they have left. Yesterday afternoon he made a bunch of those halfwits follow him to the edge of town and dance around an oak tree shouting some nonsense at the top of their lungs. You mark my words, one day that Cox fellow will disappear in the dead of night, taking his two hundred dollars and a belly full of Tanglewood food with him. And there will still be drought."

Surely Arrington's plantation was suffering as well. "What about your place, sir?"

"It won't be a good year, that's for sure, but I've saved all my life for the difficult times that come to us all. Next year will be better."

There wouldn't be a next year for a lot of the farmers who'd put their faith in Raleigh Cox.

Arrington turned his back on the spectacle. "Revolting display," he muttered. The farmers dismissed, he cocked his head and smiled at Declan with narrowed eyes. "I'm here to play poker with an old friend who has come to town. Linden Durant is his name, and he used to live hereabouts."

The name was not familiar, but even if it had been, Declan would not have worried. No one had yet made the connection between his past and the wealthy planter he'd become. "Sounds interesting."

"The mayor, the doctor, and the sheriff will be there," Arrington said with a tight smile. "Everyone in this town who's worth knowing. Care to join us?"

The idea of spending more time with this hard-hearted, crass *gentleman* was not exactly appealing. Declan still hated Warren Arrington and everything he stood for; he still dreamed of the day the old man would get his comeuppance. But the idea of playing cards with "everyone in this town worth knowing" was tempting, and since he was at loose ends and loved to play poker, and was quite good at it . . . "Why not?"

* * *

The session had gone fairly well, considering that neither Stella nor Gretchen would ever be great cooks. Gretchen had no patience for mundane matters, and Stella tried but simply did not have the gift. Matilda decided to stick to the simpler recipes. What choice did she have?

Declan came home in a terrible mood, scowling and muttering beneath his breath, tossing his hat onto the table with more force than was necessary. He jerked off his jacket and tossed it aside, unbuttoning the top button of his shirt as if he could barely breathe. Tonight he definitely looked more warrior than gentleman.

He sat in the wing chair in the main room and stretched out his long legs, eyes narrowed and body tense.

"My goodness." She sat in his lap and pushed a strand of stubborn dark hair off his forehead. "What's the matter?"

"I lost," he said softly. "I actually *lost.*"

"You lost what?" She snuggled comfortably into his lap, sure that nothing was bad enough to make him stay in this dark mood.

"Money, that's what I lost. I lost at poker. A friend of Arrington's is in town for the week, and they were playing a friendly game with a few other men from town. They met this afternoon in the hotel, in Durant's room." His eyes narrowed. "I think he cheated."

"Did he win everything?"

"No. Actually, everyone won but me. Even when I had hands I knew couldn't be beaten . . ."

She kissed Declan to silence his complaints. "Everyone has an unlucky day now and then."

"Not me," he grumbled.

"Are you now destitute?"

He almost smiled. "No, of course not."

She flicked open one button and then another, then lowered her head to kiss his throat while her hand rested

197

against the bare skin over his heart. "I'm so sorry you had a bad day," she whispered between kisses. "My goodness, you do taste good for an unlucky man."

She felt him relax, his body seeming to unfold in her hands. He unbuttoned her blouse and did a little tasting of his own, taking her nipple into his mouth and sucking deep. There was no urgency to their actions, just a warm, gentle boldness that did not need to be hurried.

There was something extraordinary about the feel of his skin against hers; she would never tire of it. When his shirt and her blouse had been unbuttoned as far as possible, she pressed her chest against his and kissed him, deep and slow.

"I remember," she whispered, "sitting across the room and watching you sit in this chair. The more I looked, the more tempted I was to cross the room and sit right here in your lap." She ran her fingers through his hair and trailed them down his neck. "But I didn't dare move. I just sat there and wondered what your neck would taste like, and you asked me to take down my hair."

"I remember that night, myself," he breathed, lifting a hand to run it through her loosened hair.

"I thought it was a potion that made me want you, but it was just you. You and me, Declan. Nothing false, nothing concocted."

"I know."

He slipped his hand beneath her skirt, the move familiar. His hand on her thigh felt so perfect, so right. He spread her thighs and touched her intimately; a jolt of pleasure rippled through her body.

"No drawers?"

"I planned to seduce you when you got home."

He grinned, and every hint of unhappiness left his handsome face. "Did you, now?"

"I did." She reached between their bodies to unfasten his trousers. She no longer had to keep her eyes on the buttons; she could feel her way around the task quite effectively. He touched and teased her with his fingers while she opened his trousers and freed his erection, stroking slowly and firmly. "How am I doing?"

His answer was a moan she caught in her mouth, through parted lips.

As they kissed, she shifted until she was straddling him, a knee on either side, one arm around his neck. She lifted her hips and guided him to her, then into her, sinking down to take him inside her.

She took her mouth from his to watch his face as she rose and fell slowly, lifting her hips and then lowering herself gradually until he was deeper inside her than he'd ever been before. She held his gaze as she lifted up until he almost left her, then floated down to join them completely again.

He held her tight, moved his mouth to her breast, and suckled her while she swayed gently against and away from him. She closed her eyes as the sensations grew almost too strong for her to bear. She moved faster, harder, and Declan moved with her, taking her hips in his hands as she dropped down and he pushed up.

Completion crackled though her, shattered her body into a million pieces and forced her to cry out. She felt Declan's release, the stiffening of his body, the eruption inside her, the low cry of his own. She moved once more, a slow, ending motion before she melted against him and laid her head on his shoulder.

"I love you so much," she whispered. For a long moment they remained there, unmoving, joined, entangled.

His hand tangled in her hair. "I love you, too."

They didn't move, but remained entwined and satisfied, caught in a long, peaceful silence. Rays of the afternoon sun drifted through the window and warmed them.

She had never known complete peace, until meeting Declan. She had never even imagined she could feel this way. He did love her; she could hear the truth in his voice when he told her. He told her every day.

"So," she finally whispered, moving slightly against him. "How do you feel now?"

Declan didn't hesitate. "Like the luckiest man alive."

Vanessa was impatient. She did not like the fidgety unpleasantness that came with impatience. Usually when she wanted something, she got it immediately.

She had plans to meet Johnny in the guest house after supper, but until she was married she couldn't do everything she wanted; she couldn't know what it was like to have him inside her. Oh, the very thought made her quake, right here at the supper table.

"Daddy," she said, glancing at him over a bowl of stew. "You haven't invited Declan Harper to dinner in a while. Don't you think we should ask him to Sunday dinner tomorrow?"

Her father gave her a sharp glare. "No, I do not. Mr. Harper will likely be a guest here next week, for a meeting of gentlemen, and while he is in the house I do not want to see you in attendance. Make yourself scarce, you hear me?"

But Daddy *liked* Declan. Didn't he? "I don't understand."

Her father gave her one of his loving, patronizing smiles. He did adore her, she knew that, and he thought he knew her. But in his eyes, she would forever be his little girl, a child who needed to be coddled and protected. "Declan Harper is not for you, young lady. He is not who he appears to be."

This sounded like a complication she did not need! "What do you mean by that, Daddy? Who is he?"

Her father shook his head. His white face hardened. Oh, she knew that look. It was rare and ruthless and nothing good ever came of it.

"Years ago there was a family living on the outskirts of town, on the farm Seth Hazelrig works now," he snapped. "The woman was Irish, never did learn to speak proper American English. She spit out a baby every year or so, like the brood mare she was. The man was a miserable drunk who didn't mind making babies but couldn't see to keeping them properly fed and clothed." He screwed up his face in distaste. "Damn white trash."

"What does that have to do with Declan?"

Her father set his eyes on her, hard and unflinching. "Declan Harper was one of the brats that Irish whore spat out."

Vanessa's eyes widened in real surprise. "And you knew this all along?"

Her father shook his head and waved a dismissive hand. "No, not at first. Good heavens, for a while I even thought he might make you a suitable husband." He shook his head in horror. "I kept thinking that he looked familiar, though, and with good reason. Damn trash looks just like his no-good daddy. I got curious and asked around and finally made the connection." He snorted and reached for his whiskey. "No matter how much money he makes, beneath it all he's still common trash."

Vanessa experienced a moment of real, true disappointment. Well, so much for her scheme to wed Declan and take Johnny as her lover. She certainly could not marry white trash! What would her children be like? She shuddered. How close she'd come to making a horrid mistake!

"How unfortunate," she said calmly. "But if that's the case, why are you inviting Mr. Harper to the house next week? Are you going to confront him?"

Her father smiled coldly and shook his head. "Oh, no. I'm not going to confront that lying, deceitful son of a drunkard, not yet. I have plans for him, just as he no doubt had plans for Tanglewood. I will confront Harper, but not until I'm finished with him and he's left with nothing."

"Nothing?" she asked, almost feeling sorry for Harper. "Absolutely nothing."

Declan was at the plantation house again this morning, and Matilda busied herself cleaning around the house. She dusted and rearranged and swept, a smile on her face as she went about her everyday chores.

The old books with the recipes for love potions and aphrodisiacs were stacked on a low, crowded shelf. Since she did not need them anymore, she pulled a chair to the bookcase and returned them to their proper place on the top shelf.

As she made sure they were firmly seated, she spotted another book, a slim, ancient volume that had been hidden among the larger tomes.

Intrigued, she slipped the book from its hiding place and sat at the table. This was surely the oldest of all. The pages were yellow and cracking, the spine in danger of crumbling. She turned the first few pages carefully, looking with interest to see what was written on the yellowed pages.

The third recipe in the book was for a love potion.

A new sheet of folded paper had been left there; for her, she knew. She unfolded it and read her grandmother's note.

By now you surely know that the other love potions in my library had no power that were not supplied solely by the ones who consumed them. Matilda smiled. She knew quite well. *But this recipe is real and powerful. The one foolish or unlucky enough to ingest this concoction will love the first person of the opposite sex he or she sees. The love conjured will be physical and emotional, and impossible to resist. Take care.*

A real love potion. Matilda read over the complex recipe and further warnings in the book, her interest piqued. If such a formula existed, it was surely powerful and magical . . . dangerous and best left untested.

Into the Woods

What she felt could not be conjured by a potion, what she and Declan had found was real and natural, not called upon in desperation.

Matilda ran her fingers over the note. She loved her granny, so dearly, but this note was proof that the sweet old woman had not truly seen the future. There would never be a need in her life for a love potion, real or not. She would never be tempted to concoct artificial affections when the real emotions were so powerful and beautiful.

Matilda smiled and closed the ancient book gently. She didn't need this recipe anymore, thank goodness. She dusted the spine and stood on the chair to return the decaying book to its proper place.

Chapter Seventeen

He could not believe it was happening again. Over cigars and whiskey, sitting in a leather chair in Warren Arrington's study, Declan lost several hundred dollars. The game was played with the same group as before: Sheriff Marston, Mayor Saunders, old Doc Daly, Arrington, and his friend Linden Durant. Everyone won. Everyone but Declan.

Daly had been in Tanglewood all those years ago, and so had Saunders. They were both in their sixties, tall and thin and gray. Marston was new, and if not for Declan, he would be the youngest at the table. He had a harshness about him that the older men did not possess.

It didn't seem to matter who had been here years ago and who had not; no one remembered anyone so insignificant as a drunken farmer's son.

Declan did his best not to let his growing panic show. He didn't want to let these men know that losing money made him sweat.

A young woman in a plain calico dress and a white

apron slipped quietly into the room. She moved like a mouse; quiet, stealthy, trying not to gain anyone's attention as she gathered dirty glasses and a few plates. She was thin as a rail, bony and shapeless. Her face might have been pretty, but for the long, prominent nose and the frizzy curls that had a tendency to fall across her gaunt cheeks.

"Lettie Mae," Arrington snapped, and the woman jumped, then scurried to the table. There was a wart on that long nose, Declan noticed.

"Yes, sir?"

Arrington did not bother to look up. "Is there any of that white cake left?"

"Yes, sir."

"Pack some up for Doc Daly," Arrington ordered. "His wife has a liking for white cake."

"Yes, sir."

Lettie Mae scurried away, looking as if she were grateful to escape the room, and Arrington.

"Lettie Mae does make excellent white cake," Doc Daly said as he perused his cards.

"Yes," Arrington said absently. "Too bad she's dumb as a fence post and ugly as sin. If she wasn't such an excellent cook I'd send her packing. Trash," he mumbled beneath his breath. "What do you expect?"

Hand after terrible hand passed through Declan's fingers. Whenever he got a decent deal, someone else had better cards to beat him out. When he bluffed, someone always called it.

"Maybe I should give up gambling," he said with a smile as he folded. He would not allow these men, the fine leaders of Tanglewood, to see that the idea of losing his hard-earned money was crushing him. He'd been poor most of his life. He knew what it was like to be hungry and not know where his next meal was coming from, to not have a roof over his head even on a stormy night. He could not, would not, be put in that position again.

"You're just having a bad run, son," Arrington said as he tossed a silver coin into the pot. "You can't walk away from a friendly game."

He shook his head, thinking of Matilda waiting at home. The thought soothed him, bad run or no bad run. "A man has to know when to call it quits." He would walk away with his pockets much lighter, but he wouldn't let these men see that losing a few dollars bothered him. He had his pride, and any one of them would protest that it was, after all, just money.

Easy enough to say if you didn't know what it was like not to have any.

"Another night," he said, stepping away from the table.

"Wednesday evening?" Arrington asked absently as he studied his cards. "Maybe your luck will change."

His luck at the tables had always been so good, until now. A chance to win back some of what he'd lost was too tempting to refuse. "Eight o'clock again?"

Arrington smiled, but he did not lift his eyes. "Eight o'clock."

Declan left to the sounds of laughter, cards shuffling, and coins *pinging* on the table. Mingled, they were sounds he usually enjoyed. Tonight they reminded him that he was a fool.

He had almost reached the wide front doors when a soft, feminine voice stopped him.

"Declan Harper, as I live and breathe."

He turned to see Vanessa heading toward him, a perfect smile on her face, a lilt to her walk and in her soft voice. Her gown of pale pink danced about her like a fluffy, pastel cloud.

"Vanessa, how are you?" he asked, just to be polite.

She was upon him when she answered. "Lonely." She pouted, a facial gesture so lovely she had surely practiced it before a mirror. "After we danced and visited at the Founders' Day Celebration, I expected you to call on me again. Why haven't you? Did I do something wrong?" She turned searching violet eyes up to him.

"Of course not, I've just been busy. Very busy, with remodeling the plantation and all."

She smiled seductively. "Then you are forgiven."

No one could say that Vanessa Arrington wasn't beautiful. She was the very picture of Southern womanhood, sweet and feminine and vulnerable. Artists painted faces like hers to preserve for posterity, lovestruck fools groveled and pleaded for smiles like the one she cast his way. Throughout history, men had killed and died for women like this one.

And at the moment Declan could not understand why. There was nothing behind those perfect violet eyes, no real laughter in her smile. She was beautiful the way a painting or a sunset might be. Nice to look at, but it sure as hell wouldn't keep you warm at night.

He bowed politely and bid her good night.

"I thought you said you couldn't marry him," Johnny said tiresomely.

"I can't, but that doesn't mean I'm going to step back and let that . . . that witch succeed in taking a man from me." She did not like to lose, something Johnny should know by now.

The windows of the guest house were open, allowing a warm breeze to wash over their bodies. They were completely naked, a dangerous pleasure but one she looked forward to. She liked the feel of Johnny's fine body against hers, and she kept him well satisfied so he was not too sorely tempted to take elsewhere what he could not get from her.

"You should leave them alone," he whispered. "They haven't done anything to hurt you."

She liked Johnny as a lover, and would like him even

more when she was married and properly deflowered, but his morals were annoying, at times. She'd practically thrown herself at Declan earlier, and he'd looked at her as if he couldn't wait to get away! What did Johnny expect of her? That she'd allow such an insult to go unpunished?

"I have my pride," she explained. "I can't allow a barefoot hag in braids to steal Declan Harper from me, even if I don't want him anymore. How demoralizing."

"Maybe he loves her and doesn't care that she's a barefoot hag in braids," Johnny said as he rolled over her, spreading her thighs with his knee as they turned. "Maybe you should leave them the hell alone."

She felt Johnny's growing erection brush against her inner thigh, and trembled from the inside out. Rocking up, he barely grazed her wet entrance. He'd never touched her this way before. It was dangerous and exciting, thrilling to her very bones.

"Johnny, what are you doing?" She reached up and threaded her fingers through his hair.

"Nothing," he whispered, rocking just slightly against her, teasing her mercilessly. "I know my boundaries, Vanessa."

"You're very close to going over those boundaries, Johnny, my dear."

Vanessa wanted, more than anything, to make the small move that would finally bring Johnny inside her, to grasp his hips and pull him into her, but she didn't. She fought the urge and tried to close her legs, but that was impossible.

"But I won't go past them," Johnny whispered. "You've made it very clear that I'm not good enough to be your husband, to take a husband's privileges." A touch of anger colored his soft voice. "Sometimes I think you're more of a witch than Matilda Candy will ever be."

She grinned, enjoying the feel of him and the exciting

. nature of the situation, reveling in the danger and the sensations that jolted through her body. Her pleasure didn't last long enough. Johnny abruptly rolled off her, left the bed, and scooped his clothes from the floor. He stepped quickly into his trousers and headed for the door with the remainder of his clothes in his hands.

"Get back here," she ordered sharply. She pushed herself into a languid sitting position, arching her back to present the most seductive possible picture; breasts thrust upward, legs slightly spread. She licked her lips hungrily. "I'm not finished with you."

"Maybe I'm finished with you," Johnny said, leaving the room without so much as a glance back.

Her head on Declan's shoulder as they lay in bed, Matilda stared up at the ceiling. He had loved her when he'd come home, then he'd held her quietly for a while. They were both silent, but neither of them had fallen asleep. A palpable tension filled the air, a tension she was anxious to dissolve.

"You'll never guess what I found today."

"What's that?" His voice was low. Still disturbed over losing at poker again, he was not his usual self. He had only scowled at her when she'd told him, with a smile, that if losing was going to upset him so, perhaps he should not play.

"A recipe for a genuine love potion," she whispered. "At least, Granny's note said it was real, and the recipe is quite unusual. There's even an incantation to be said over the brew, three times, and it's not the kind of potion you can throw together in an afternoon. It has to steep for two days and two nights."

"Do you really think it would work?" He sounded only slightly interested.

"I guess we'll never know," Matilda whispered. She raised up and smiled down at Declan. A hint of moonlight broke through the curtains to show her lover's face.

"There were many cautions, some my grandmother's, some printed in the book itself and others scribbled in the margins in different hands."

He laid a hand on her cheek, a loving, almost unconscious gesture. "What cautions?"

She shifted slightly in the bed, bringing her body closer to Declan's and staring down into his dark eyes. "There were warnings, printed in the book and written in the margins, about misusing the potion's power or taking too much of the liquid or using it for personal gain. But the last sentence said it best." She leaned over him in the dark so that her shadow fell across his face and whispered. "Love is not the end, it's the beginning."

In spite of his foul mood, he smiled. "The beginning, huh?"

She nodded. "Think about it. Some people think falling in love is the ultimate goal. Others, like me before I met you, think it's a terrible end. But falling in love is neither. It's a bright turn in the road, a sharing of hearts and bodies, a new beginning."

"I never believed in love," Declan whispered. "Not really. It was a pretty word for sex, an excuse to bind yourself to another human being so you didn't have to live alone, a fantasy to satisfy women."

"Sounds very cynical," she said, gifting him with a brief kiss.

"I'm a very cynical man," he breathed against her lips.

"You *were* a very cynical man," she amended. "But that's not so anymore."

"I guess it's not."

She settled against him and drifted toward sleep. A new beginning. The prospect sounded so bright and good, so full of wonderful possibilities.

This Wednesday the air was sweet with the smell of cinnamon and roasting nuts, caramelized sugar and something fruity. Cherries, perhaps.

"See?" Hanson said. "She hasn't stopped making candy."

"I still think we need to make sure that she stays unmarried. Mr. Harper could ruin everything for us," Gretchen insisted.

They ran toward the side of the cottage, their eyes on the courtyard and the big kitchen beyond. Through the window they could see that the witch was hard at work there. Her hair was in pigtails again, and sweat from the overly warm kitchen dampened her face.

"Hello," Hanson called loudly, giving them away long before they reached the kitchen.

The witch looked out the window, smiled, and wiped her face with the tail end of her white apron. "I haven't seen you two in ages," she said, looking almost as if she were glad to see them.

Gretchen searched the courtyard, the area around the greenhouse, and then turned her gaze to the house. "Is *he* here?"

"Mr. Harper?"

Gretchen nodded.

Matilda left the window and walked out the kitchen door into the sunlight. "No, he's not here today."

Gretchen lifted her chin defiantly. "Is he still angry because I *accidentally* pushed him into the pond?"

The witch smiled. "Of course not. Mr. Harper is not one to hold a grudge over a simple mistake."

Gretchen found herself wrinkling her nose. She didn't quite believe that Mr. Harper wasn't still angry. Besides, what was important was that he not come here at all anymore. "Do you like him?"

"Yes, I do," the witch said warmly, a sparkle in her eyes. "Very much."

Gretchen took a deep breath. "Well, he likes *lots* of women, from what I see about town."

"Is that a fact?" Apparently the witch was not convinced.

Linda Jones

"I see him kissing women all the time," she said, her face and voice completely calm.

"Which women?" Matilda asked.

Gretchen had not been expecting that question. The witch was supposed to be angry, she was supposed to turn Declan Harper into a toad or at the very least tell him not to come around kissing her anymore! "Ummm, there was the preacher's daughter, Sarah," she said after a moment's hesitation, trying to think of all the women she usually saw about town. "And the doctor's wife, Mrs. Daly. And Mrs. Fox, and Lily Peterson the dressmaker, and Vanessa Arrington."

The witch continued to smile. "Sarah Wilkes is no more than fifteen, and Mrs. Daly is sixty-five if she's a day. My goodness, Mr. Harper isn't very discriminating, is he?"

Hanson saved his sister from making an even bigger fool of herself by asking, in his usual excited voice, what kinds of candy the witch had made today.

When she'd allowed them to taste a little of everything, the witch led them down to the pond to show off her new watering trough. She carried a bucket with her, and at the edge of the pond she used that bucket to scoop up water and lift it up to pour it into the mouth of the trough. She did it again, and they watched the water flow down the channel. It would empty itself, the witch said, in her garden.

"My father says if it doesn't rain soon we won't have anything left," Gretchen said, watching the water run. "He said the farm will be worthless, that it will dry up and blow away." She didn't like to admit how much that possibility scared her, but her heart lurched, an extra thump jolting in her chest.

The witch laid a hand on her shoulder. "There's time for rain," she said softly. "The situation isn't dire just yet."

"Your pond looks fine, a lot better than our well."

Which in itself was suspicious, Gretchen thought. The witch was in no danger of being without water.

"It's fed by an underground spring," Matilda said. "We'd have to go a very long while without rain for this pond to dry up. Water's heavy to carry, but if you'd like to carry some home to drink, you're welcome."

If only she'd known sooner that witches had beaus! They could've introduced Matilda Candy to their father months ago, long before he'd met Stella. They would have water, and candy, and all the pies they could eat. Matilda might be a witch, but she was a very nice witch, most of the time. She gave them sweets, and never yelled at them even when they swiped candy and she caught them red-handed. She even offered to share her water.

As they headed back to the house, Gretchen almost felt guilty for lying about Mr. Harper kissing all the women in Tanglewood.

Almost.

Chapter Eighteen

Declan felt better already. He'd lost a few hands in the beginning, but he was winning now. His luck had changed. Arrington, Durant, the mayor, the sheriff, and the doctor were not so cordial tonight; they'd all lost some of their money.

They'd only lost money they'd won from Declan in the previous card games, so he didn't feel guilty about winning it back.

"How is the remodeling coming along?" Arrington asked as he tossed a coin into the pot.

"Slower and more expensive than I'd expected," Declan said, his eyes on the cards in his hand. "It's coming along, though. The house itself should be in good shape by the end of the year and a real showplace by spring."

"You have big plans for the place, do you?"

"Yep."

The pot grew, as each man raised. Declan remained expressionless as he looked at his hand: four jacks and a deuce. Four jacks! This could be the hand to win back everything he'd lost.

Doc Daly dropped out first, declaring the game too rich for his blood. Mayor Saunders folded next, then Sheriff Marston reluctantly tossed his cards down. Linden Durant studied his hand intently, stroked his thick mustache, glanced at Declan and then at Arrington with narrowed eyes, and quietly folded.

Declan found it somehow poetic that the field had been reduced to no one but him and Warren Arrington. In the back of his mind, he even wondered if this would be revenge enough, if he could win a good bit of Arrington's money and then tell him who he was. He didn't have to marry the man's daughter, didn't have to take over the whole town. He just wanted the man to respect him and all he'd accomplished.

That would be enough.

Arrington raised the bet considerably, so much so that Marston whistled under his breath and the doctor muttered an obscene word that could be heard well in the thick silence of Arrington's study. Mayor Saunders took a long drink of his whiskey, and Durant leaned back and watched intently.

Declan called and raised again, betting everything he had on the table.

Arrington smiled. "I think you're bluffing, Harper." He left the table and went to his desk, unlocked a drawer, and came up with a thick wad of bank notes he tossed into the mountain of coins and bills on the table.

Declan's smile faded. "I don't have any more cash with me tonight. Will you take an IOU?"

Arrington lit a cigar and leaned back in his chair. "How do I know you've got the cash to make an IOU good?"

"You have my word."

Arrington looked suddenly ancient, old and wrinkled

and sunken-eyed. "Not good enough, unless you want to make the IOU for that plantation of yours."

Declan almost tossed his cards facedown into the table. Everything he had was tied up in that place! If he lost it, he'd have nothing. He glanced at the four jacks and reconsidered. Arrington thought he was bluffing, that he was just waiting for the old fool to fold so he could take the pot.

"My place is worth a lot more than what you have there," he said, nodding at the pot.

"I'll throw in the parcel of land by the lake and the old cabin that's there."

That particular parcel adjoined Matilda's place. Hell, he'd make her a gift of it.

They each drew up markers that were witnessed and signed by the mayor and the sheriff. Doc Daly just shook his head, and Durant seemed to be having a good old time watching the proceedings.

When the markers had been added to the pile in the center of the table, Declan fanned his cards and laid them down. Mayor Saunders exclaimed loudly, and Doc Daly muttered an obscenity and fanned himself with one of his own discarded cards.

Marston laughed. "I've never seen four jacks played before. Impressive!" He grinned and clapped Declan on the back.

Arrington smiled and laid his own cards on the table. Four kings.

Declan's heart stopped. He couldn't breathe, and he couldn't make his heart start beating again. His legs went numb, his hands balled into fists. "Impossible," he whispered. What had he done?

"I guess your luck didn't change after all, did it, Harper?" Arrington said as he raked in his winnings.

No one wanted to continue. The sheriff clapped Declan on the back again, in consolation this time, and the doctor and the mayor muttered their condolences. Declan sat numbly in his chair while the men from town left. They took Arrington's gambling friend Durant with them.

Arrington sat across the table from Declan and leaned slightly forward. There was a sick satisfaction in his eyes. "What's the matter, Harper? Can't move?" he asked softly. "Can't make yourself leave the table where you lost everything to me?"

Declan's heart had started beating again, thumping too hard in his chest.

"Now that you're no longer a property owner in this county," Arrington said smugly, "I suggest you leave town the way your mama left," he whispered. "With your tail between your legs and nothing in your pocket."

"You knew?" Declan asked calmly. He should have been angry, horrified, but at this point, nothing surprised him.

"It took me a while, but you look just like that good-for-nothing drunk your mama married." His evident satisfaction faded quickly. "You're a fool just like Brenna. You don't know when to quit, you don't know when to give up."

There was more to Arrington's hatred than a dislike of a poor, drunken farmer, Declan saw in the fury that flashed in the old man's eyes.

"What did she do to you?"

Arrington scowled. "She chose to marry that sot when I could have given her anything she wanted: a fine home, the best clothes, servants. She preferred toiling on a farm with that drunkard and spitting out baby after baby after baby."

Nothing was the way it was supposed to be; not the game, not this conversation he'd imagined for years. "You asked her to marry you?"

"God, no!" Arrington exclaimed, horrified. "I couldn't possibly have married a woman like her. She was unrefined, she came from a poor family. Hell, she couldn't

217

even manage to lose that damned accent." He smirked. "But she was a beautiful woman," he whispered.

Everything fell together for Declan. "She refused to be your mistress," he whispered.

"Said she was too good for me," Arrington seethed. "She should have been honored!"

Declan looked at the scattered cards on the table, and everything suddenly made sense in a way that made him feel physically ill. He'd been duped. Arrington had known the truth all along, and had been making his own plans.

"The game was rigged, wasn't it? You brought Durant in just to break me."

"Of course not," Arrington said indignantly, a wide smile stealing away his bitter memories. "That would be illegal and immoral. And of course if you decide to propose such charges you might remember who sat at the table with you. I feel quite sure the others will swear that there was no cheating at my table."

Declan stood slowly. "I could kill you right now," he said softly. "I could strangle you with my bare hands."

"I should expect no less from a barbarian like yourself," Arrington said, "which is why I asked a few of my friends to stand behind me this evening. Just in case such a situation should arise, of course," he added.

An armed man appeared in the doorway from the entry hall, another in the door that connected the study to the parlor.

"So I suggest you run along, little Harper. Run like your mother. Become a drunkard like your father." He smiled. "How could you have ever expected to make anything decent of yourself?"

For a moment, he tried to decide if he had time to strangle Arrington before one of the goons got off a shot.

And then a better route of revenge occurred to him. His anger faded, a little. He no longer saw red.

"You have everything," Declan said as he walked to-

ward the doorway. "You won everything I worked all
my life for, and I have no one to blame but myself."

"That's right, Harper," Arrington called as Declan
made his way to the door. "Run."

Declan had already decided he was not going to run;
he was going to fight.

Vanessa sneaked into the room by the stables, sure that
Johnny was ready to forgive her by now. He loved her,
so he couldn't stay mad at her for long!

Johnny was not in his room, though. She frowned. It
was late. He should be sleeping!

She walked from the stables to the guest house. Maybe
he was there, hoping she'd come to him. Her step was
light on the grass, her way clear by the light of a full
moon. She passed in and out of the shade of the majestic
trees along the way, her eyes on the white cottage ahead.
The window of the bedroom was open, she saw. The
night breeze made the curtain dance in and out of
the opening, like a ghost trying to escape but tied to the
house. That meant someone was there, since the house
was kept closed up when not in use. Who else could
possibly be there but Johnny, bemoaning what he'd lost
and hoping for her return?

As soon as she'd exacted suitable revenge on the
witch, she'd find a proper husband and make Johnny her
proper lover. She could hardly wait, but of course she
had no choice.

She crept quietly into the guest house, planning to surprise Johnny. He would be happy to know he was forgiven. So happy he would do anything she asked.

From the hallway, she saw a form on the bed, long
and male and indistinct. The quilt was pulled all the way
up over his head. Perhaps he was asleep, because he
didn't move at all. He didn't so much as turn his head
her way.

She crept into the room and to the side of the bed.

Johnny continued to sleep beneath the fat quilt, his back to her as he breathed deep and even.

With a smile, Vanessa sat on the side of the bed and laid her hand on his shoulder. "Wake up," she whispered. "You knew I would come here tonight, didn't you?"

He stirred slightly, but did not turn to face her. She lay down beside him, her chest against his back, her hand encircling his waist until it rested against his stomach.

Her hand dipped lower, searching for the sure sign that he was aroused, even though he played at being distant. His body could not lie to her.

"I forgive you," she said softly, feeling quite magnanimous. "Let me show you how much I forgive you." She finally found a small bulge and laid her hand over it, surprised that her touch elicited no response.

He moved, rolling slowly onto his back, pushing down the quilt. Her first clue that something was wrong was the shock of moonlight on pale hair that stood up like straw. When that moonlight illuminated the ugliest face she had ever seen, she rolled from the bed and squealed.

"I did not expect such hospitality," Raleigh Cox said in a pleasant voice as he sat up, "when your father offered me the use of his guest house."

He looked like a scarecrow sitting up in bed; thin arms like sticks, hair like straw, and a face uglier than any she had ever seen, even on a scarecrow. "I . . . I . . . there's been a mistake," she gasped.

He grinned and leaned against the headboard. "Pity. Who's Johnny?"

"None of your business," she snapped, panicked. This horrid creature knew her secret! If he told . . . she calmed herself. No one would believe him. Raleigh Cox was a con man, a drifter. If he dared to tell what he'd seen and heard tonight, no one would believe him. Who would believe anything from such a repulsive mouth?

"I won't tell," he said, stretching out to his full length. "We all have secrets."

For some reason, she believed him. It made perfect sense. What would he have to gain by ruining her reputation? "I suppose that's true. What's *your* secret, Mr. Cox?"

He grinned. She wished he hadn't. "I have too many secrets to tell, Miss Arrington. Since we have shared a bed, don't you think we should be on a first-name basis?"

She almost laughed at him. Did he think they were going to be friends? "I don't know that it's wise for us to be too familiar, Mr. Cox."

"Perhaps not."

She should run, now, escape from her embarrassment and try to find Johnny. But she was bored, and since Johnny was not in his room and not here, she didn't know where to look next. "My father thinks you're a con man."

"Then why did he offer me the use of his guest house when I complained about the hotel?"

"Because he thinks it's funny to see you make fools of the farmers. He thinks they're all imbeciles."

Cox smiled again, and Vanessa almost shuddered. "It always rains eventually, Miss Arrington," he said, emphasizing the proper use of her name. "If I'm around when it finally falls, I take the credit. If rain takes too long to come, I disappear in the night."

"I suspected as much."

"Now you know my secret and I know yours," he whispered. "We're even."

Vanessa hardly considered them even. Anyone with half a brain knew Cox was a con man. No one else knew she liked to indulge in decadent pleasures with a servant.

"How much longer will you be here?" she asked, wondering how much time it would be before he was far away, and she could breathe easy again.

"A few days," Cox said. "The farmers are already getting restless." He sat up straighter and smiled. "Maybe if you don't have any luck finding your Johnny, you can

221

come back here and let me keep you company."

She laughed out loud. Laughing was rude, and unwise, but she could not help herself. The thought of allowing a man this hideously ugly to touch her was ludicrous.

Cox's grin faded quickly, and Vanessa's laughter finally died.

"I'm sorry," she said. "But the very idea . . ."

"Of allowing a monster to touch you," he interrupted, "is laughable."

"You're not a monster," she said. "You're just not very pretty. I like pretty men."

Cox laid down, pulled the quilt to his chin, and turned his back to her. "Maybe one day you'll find out that in the dark, all men are very much the same. And all women," he added in a softer voice.

He should've been home hours ago! Matilda paced in the main room. A single lamp burned, casting eerie shadows all around. Her heart wouldn't be still, wouldn't beat regularly as it should. Something had happened to Declan; she knew it. He'd been thrown from his horse and broken his neck, set upon by robbers on the deserted road. Set upon by Vanessa in the Arrington house. Which scenario was worst?

She made herself sit, but she couldn't relax. Her hands clenched in her lap, and her heart kept beating too fast. Declan should've been home hours ago!

A new fear intruded. What if, in spite of all he'd said, he didn't think of this place as home? What if he'd gone to his plantation house and was presently sound asleep in his bed while she fretted?

She breathed a sigh of relief when she heard slow hoofbeats outside her cottage, closing her eyes as she took her first deep breath in quite a while. He had come home, after all.

The door opened and Declan stepped inside, his clothes disheveled, his jacket discarded. He still wore his vest, but it and the buttons of his shirt had been unfastened. Matilda knew the moment she saw his face that something was wrong. He was pale, his features tight and rugged. He looked as if he'd aged ten years since he'd left a few hours ago.

"What's wrong?"

He lifted his eyes at her question, as if he was surprised to see her sitting there. "I thought you'd be asleep."

She shook her head. "I was too worried to sleep."

Declan paced as she had moments earlier. "I rode out to the house for a while, then walked through town while everyone else was asleep, then headed here. I stopped a few times to walk, to think."

She rose and went to him, but he turned so that she faced his broad, tense back. "What happened?"

He spun around to face her, but kept his distance. "I lost everything," he whispered, as if to say such a thing aloud was too awful to consider. "Everything, Matilda."

"All the money you took with you?" she asked.

"Everything I own but the saloons and general stores my family is operating out West." He anxiously raked his fingers through already mussed hair, and it seemed his hand trembled, just a little. "I lost the plantation, Matilda. I let that son of a bitch sucker me in."

She reached out and again he turned his back on her and stepped away. Her outstretched hand fell on nothing but the air where he'd been standing a moment earlier.

"You can start again," she said softly.

His back to her, he shook his head slowly. "Arrington knew who I was. He's known almost from the beginning. He set me up and took everything I've worked for, and I'm going to get him for what he's done."

"Of course you are," Matilda said in a soothing voice. "You'll get your place back."

He spun to face her again, and the expression on his face was terrifying. His jaw was hard, his mouth thin, his dark eyes devoid of the warmth she was accustomed to seeing there. She had never seen him so harsh, so hopeless. Or so determined.

"I don't want that damn plantation," he seethed. "It's not enough anymore. I want Arrington to suffer. I want him to pay."

"Declan, I don't—"

"He took everything from me: my land, my money, my vengeance." Declan looked as if he were about to explode, as if it took all his concentration and energy to keep from falling apart. "I'm going to hurt him, Matilda, and the only way to do that is to take the one thing in the world he cares about."

Knowing where he was going with this, she began to shake her head long before he finished by whispering the damnable words, "His daughter."

"You're not thinking clearly tonight," Matilda said, trying to remain calm. But that was impossible. Her heart beat too hard, her mouth was too dry. "In the morning . . ."

"No."

"In the morning things will look different."

He shook his head and reached out to touch her at last, laying his hands on her cheeks and gazing into her eyes. His hands trembled; his touch was distant, hesitant. The tips of his fingers were cold as he brushed them over her face. He looked so lost, so desperate, and she wanted nothing more than to take away his pain. "I have nothing to offer you," he whispered desolately. "Nothing."

Since coming home, he'd done his best not to look at her too hard, too long, always turning away when she sensed some softness in his heart or in his conviction. She saw a hint of that now, a weakness for her and what they had, and he did not turn away from her this time. That alone gave her hope.

"All I want is your heart. It's all I need," she said quietly. Love was enough for her, and it should be enough for him, too. He did love her. She knew it as surely as she knew that the sky was blue and the summer was hot. But as she looked at him, she realized that something as simple as love wasn't enough for Declan; it would never be enough.

When he responded, his voice was low and held no room for indecision. "Dammit Matilda, I can't go back."

He'd said once that he wasn't afraid of anything—not witches, not the dark, not of being poor again. It was, perhaps, the only time he'd ever lied to her, and he probably didn't even realize it. She reached out to touch his cheek, much as he continued to touch hers. Her hands trembled, as his did, but she pushed away her fear and called upon the only thing she had to hold Declan to her. Her love for him. If she could reach the deepest, warmest part of him, if she could make him realize that what they had was all that mattered, this night would end as it should: with Declan in her bed and her arms. "What we have is worth more than a thousand plantations."

Her heart broke when he shook his head. "If I walk away from this now, I'll be less of a man. Arrington defeated me in a hell of a lot more than a game of cards. If I stop now, if I let him win, I might as well run like he told me to." His eyes grew distant, too cold for such a warm brown. "But I'll take his daughter, his only child," he said gruffly, determined. "I'll marry her and make her love me and he'll have no choice but to welcome the white trash son of a drunkard into his family with open arms. I'll make his life hell."

He did not drop his hands, but moved them to her neck where they rested, cool and large and possessive.

"You can't mean it," Matilda whispered.

"This doesn't mean I don't want you," Declan breathed softly. He was at war with himself; she could see the battle in his eyes. "More than anything, I want you in my life. Being with you, loving you, was the happiest time of my life. This cottage has become more

225

of a home to me than any house I ever lived in." His words gave her hope. What man could walk away from something so precious? A woman who loved him, a home.

"I'm so damn tempted to ask you to be my mistress forever, to keep this place here for me so I'll have a home to come to. To keep your bed warm for only me."

"Declan—"

"But I won't," he interrupted, his voice cracking. "As much as I need you, as much as I need *this*, I can't offer you less than everything. It wouldn't be fair. You deserve better."

What little hope she had died quickly. Declan hadn't forgotten that he loved her, he had simply decided his revenge was more valuable. More important than anything they ever had or would have together.

"This is good-bye," she whispered in horror, knowing now why he'd taken so long to make his way from the Arrington plantation to her cottage. He didn't like this parting any more than she did, but he'd made his decision.

"Yes," he whispered, leaning down and laying his forehead against hers.

She closed her eyes as red-hot rage welled up inside her.

"You're willing to throw away everything we have for revenge?"

"I have no choice."

"You have a thousand choices," she said, her voice gradually rising from the low whisper they'd fallen into. "You choose this over me and then tell me you have no other option?" She could not remember anger every hurting this way, gnawing at her insides and making her quiver. "Face it, Declan, you never intended to marry me. Deep inside I knew it all along." Oh, she was such a fool! "I'm not a fine lady who can enhance your image when you make yourself King of Tanglewood. I'm a woman with a reputation, a witch, and I can only hurt your chances of getting everything you want."

"That's not true," he said as she shook him off and backed away.

"Then why did you never ask me to marry you?" It was rage that kept her on her feet. Heaven help her, without this anger she would dissolve, would literally fall apart. "Why did you only kiss and hold me when there were no prying eyes to see? You liked what we had, but not enough to embarrass yourself by declaring your affections in public."

"I was going to ask you . . ." he began.

She shook her head. If she listened to him, if she let herself believe that what he said made any sense at all, she was lost. "No. If you'd throw me away for this precious retaliation, you never loved me. If you prefer a life of misery with a woman you care nothing for, you never loved me." Everything she'd wanted to believe was false. Maybe Vanessa was right, and he'd just been using her all along, telling her what she wanted to hear.

Declan raked his fingers through his hair in clear exasperation. "I've worked all my life for this!" he shouted. "All my life! I can't allow Arrington to swipe it out from under my feet when I'm so close. I can't slink away and die when I have him right here." He thrust out his hand, palm up. That hand no longer trembled, she noticed, but was steady as a rock.

Matilda looked at Declan and realized that she didn't know him at all. Had he only used her, telling her he loved her so she'd sleep with him? Had he taken his comfort here while he planned his life and revenge with Vanessa Arrington?

"Get out," she whispered.

"Matilda . . ."

"Get out!"

He stood by the front door and looked at her as if *he*

were hurt, as if *his* heart was breaking. "Did you really love me, Matilda?"

I still do! "Yes." Her heart clenched, her throat closed so she could barely breathe.

"Then do me one last favor."

Surely he would not ask it of her. Surely even he . . .

"Make the potion for me," he whispered. "The ancient recipe you found in your grandmother's book. It's the only chance I have to do what I must do."

How could he ask that of her now? After everything they had been through, after all the nights he'd slept in her bed and told her he loved her. She felt like she was melting on the spot, growing smaller and smaller. Anger was no longer enough to keep her on her feet. It was no longer enough to hold her together. Soon she would melt through the floor and disappear. Perhaps then the pain would stop.

"I told you it's dangerous. Much too powerful to trifle with." She stared at Declan, wondering if she'd ever really known him, wondering what he would do if she broke down and threw herself at his feet and begged him to stay. She lifted her chin defiantly. No matter what happened, she would not beg, she would not grovel. She might have nothing else, but she did have her pride. "If you give the potion to Vanessa, you'll be with her forever. She won't let you go, not even when you realize what a horrible mistake you've made."

"I don't care."

Of course he didn't care. That was the problem, wasn't it? He didn't care for her, he didn't even care for himself. There was nothing in his life but hate and revenge, and his precious schemes.

She hardened her breaking heart. "Then you might as well drink it yourself," she whispered. "When the time comes and she drinks, you'd better take some of the potion yourself so you can fool yourself into thinking that you love Vanessa when you make her your wife."

"Never," he whispered hoarsely.

"Why not?"

He shook his head but did not answer her question.

She wanted her anger to grow until it consumed her. Pure rage couldn't possibly hurt more than this. She wanted to hate Declan, she wanted to put him out of her mind and her heart forever. But she couldn't. Like it or not, her love was stronger than rage and pain and sorrow. Her love for Declan wouldn't die tonight. Maybe it would always be with her, a curse she had brought upon herself.

"Saturday, not before noon," she said. "The potion will be ready for you then."

"Thank you."

She shook her head, softly and violently. Tears filled her eyes, and she lowered her head so he could not see. She would not sob in front of Declan. "Don't thank me for this," she whispered. She heard the door open and close, and in the echo of Declan's departure she whispered to an empty room. "Don't you dare thank me."

Chapter Nineteen

He couldn't sleep, so Declan rode Smoky slowly down the rutted road to the Hazelrig place. It had been the Harper place, long ago, the home he and his mother and his sisters had ridden away from not knowing what the West would hold for them. At the time, he was sure wherever they went would be better than here.

The anger inside him was mingled with sadness over what he was giving up, but the anger was stronger than his regret. He would give up *everything* to make Arrington pay. Even Matilda.

Matilda. She could marry Ezra now, maybe move to Jackson where she wouldn't have to worry about running into him at the general store or the next Founders' Day Celebration. They'd have fair-haired babies and once Matilda had forgotten this love affair, she and her husband would laugh a lot, make a home, sell rose water and candy to the people of Jackson.

She was right; there were worse fates than marrying a friend. Declan fought the urge to turn Smoky around and fly him back to the cottage in the woods. The thought of Matilda married to Ezra or anyone else made him ill. No matter what had happened, no matter what was to come, she was his in a way no other woman would ever be.

His heart clenched, his eyes burned and watered in the night wind. He did not want to give her up, but what choice did he have? He certainly wouldn't offer Matilda what Arrington had offered Brenna Harper years ago, he would not tell the woman he loved that she was good enough to bed but not good enough to marry.

But it hurt. Giving up Matilda hurt more than he'd imagined it could.

The only thought that soothed him as he rode slowly toward town in the gray light of approaching dawn was that before he was finished, Arrington was going to hurt even worse.

Matilda didn't bother trying to sleep, but fetched the slender volume from the top shelf and opened it to the proper page. She ignored the warnings and gathered the necessary ingredients and a large glass bowl, to start.

She should not be surprised by this turn of events, should she? All along she'd known that love would bring only heartache, that her love for Declan would somehow end badly. Perhaps somewhere on the shelf at her back there was an *un*-love potion, something to make her stop caring about a man who would sacrifice everything, even love, for revenge. A concoction to stop the pain of her breaking heart.

She sniffled, but refused to break down and cry. Declan had come to her, in the beginning, for this love potion. He'd intended all along to make the gentle lady Vanessa Arrington his wife. A witch might make a proper lover, for a while, but one would not make a suitable wife. Wouldn't people talk?

Anger dried her tears, and she carefully measured the

first ingredient as the sun came up, drizzling it into a green glass bowl. She whispered the required words as she sprinkled the next ingredient, a spice she had just enough of for this one potion, over the first.

As she mixed together and whispered the incantation, something rather frightening happened: The mixture, the perfectly common ingredients, sparkled strangely in the first rays of morning sunlight that shot through her window. A thick, swirling mist formed in the bottom of the bowl, momentarily obscuring the glittering potion. When the cloud dissipated, the liquid in the bottom of the bowl looked perfectly ordinary again.

But something out of the ordinary had just happened, and Matilda knew it. She wondered if this was her gift: the making of love potions. With the right words and a few commonplace ingredients, she could bring love to the world; she could bring love to anyone.

Well, to anyone but herself.

Vanessa was fit to be tied. She could not remember the last time she'd been so angry. She did her best to hide her anger as she looked over the newly arrived notions at Fox's general store, but she barely saw the colorful satin ribbons that slipped through her fingers.

Johnny was gone. He'd packed his clothes and moved out, going to work for another planter who lived outside Tanglewood. The place was not as large as her father's, the pay surely less.

She refused to admit to herself that the pounding of her heart and the way her breath came strangely might be panic. She did not need John Bowers. There were other beautiful men in the world, men who would be glad to fall at her feet and worship her and do anything she asked of them. Anything!

Try as she might, at the moment she could not think of another man who could take Johnny's place.

Vanessa held her head high. There was no need for her to go on alone, without a man in her life. Perhaps she should make Declan Harper her lover. He no longer represented suitable marriage material, but he was quite handsome, and rugged, and he absolutely reeked of masculinity. Yes, he might very well do, and given his current state of affairs, he would likely fall at her feet if she suggested that she might bestow upon him a pleasurable favor or two.

But she still missed Johnny, and she blamed Matilda Candy for the loss. The witch had surely cast a spell on Johnny, just as she had on those other men who'd come to her defense at the Founders' Day Celebration. Yes, it was certainly a witch's spell that made Johnny walk away from what they had. It certainly wasn't only because he didn't think she should pay Matilda Candy back for stealing her man and her shoes.

Suddenly Vanessa wanted those bronze shoes more than anything in the world.

"Mr. Fox," she said, making her way to the front counter. "A while back you ordered a pair of shoes for me. They were bronze, and when they came in I decided they were not the right color for the ensemble I had in mind."

The man grimaced. "I remember."

She gave him her sweetest smile. "Well, I've changed my mind. There is another outfit those shoes would be just perfect for. I can't imagine why I didn't think of it at the time."

"I'm sorry, Miss Vanessa, but I sold those shoes to someone else."

She lifted her eyebrows, putting on a surprised expression that included wide eyes most men found irresistible. "Did you? Well, surely you can ask the customer who bought them to return those shoes. You can explain that you made a mistake."

Fox shook his head. "I'm afraid I can't do that."

"Of course you can."

"I'd be happy to order you another pair, but . . ." He pulled against his shirt collar just slightly. "I would ask that you pay a portion of the cost in advance. Those shoes were right expensive, and . . ."

"Why, Mr. Fox," Vanessa interrupted. "I'm shocked. My daddy is one of your best customers."

"Yes, yes he is," Fox conceded, sighing. "I'm sorry. I'll be happy to order those shoes for you."

She smiled. "Yes, do that." *And choke on them,* she thought as she stared at the shopkeeper. He'd never see a dime for those shoes. It would be fitting repayment for selling the last pair to the witch!

Vanessa stepped onto the boardwalk and opened her parasol. Damnation it was hot! Dry and shimmery hot. Her new driver, an old man her father had pulled from the stables for this new duty, stood by the carriage, waiting. Let him wait; she was in no hurry to head home.

She was walking toward the dressmakers, intending to order something new and expensive to cheer herself up, when she saw the knot of farmers gathered around the rainmaker. Her old suitor, Henry, was there with his two moronic friends.

No one seemed happy, and the raised voices that reached her contained words like *swindler* and *cheat*. She came upon the group just in time to hear Wendell Trent remind Cox that in two days his two weeks would be up.

"Excuse me, gentlemen," Vanessa said sweetly. Her voice was low, but everyone heard her, and they stepped dutifully aside to let her pass. She did not pass, though, instead taking a couple of steps until she stood in the center of their knot. Henry laid his adoring eyes on her, and he was not alone. The admiring glances bolstered her flagging self-confidence.

"It does seem a shame that you have not been able to bring us rain, Mr. Cox." She looked up at the ugly man and batted her eyelashes. "I was so hoping you would be successful."

"There's still time," he said, and Vanessa wondered how it was that such a hideous man had such a lovely voice. "I'm sensing some sort of interference. As I was telling these gentlemen, as soon as I locate the problem and eliminate it, the rain will come."

"I'm sure you're right," she said sweetly.

Cox would not be in Tanglewood much longer, she suspected. Just as well. She'd turned her back on him and resumed her easy pace toward the dressmaker's, when a brilliant idea stopped her.

"Interference," she said softly as she spun around to face the men who scowled at the rainmaker. She even flashed a quick smile at Henry and gaily twirled her parasol. "Mr. Cox, is it possible that a *witch* might interfere with your efforts?"

The crowd became silent, as the farmers considered this possibility.

"That's entirely possible," Cox said. "Is there a witch in the area?"

She smiled. "Oh, yes. Matilda Candy is her name, and she lives just south of town. She is a sweet girl, and I'm sure she would never purposely bring on a drought, but then again, you never know." Vanessa waved her fingers dismissively. "Just a silly idea I had."

She turned away once again, a satisfied smile on her face as she walked away. This time the angry words that drifted to her ears were *witch* and *spell* and *magic*.

Matilda made her usual Friday-morning trip to town, her basket loaded down with sweets and breads, pomades and a few bottles of rose water, rose-hip marmalade and rose honey. There was no spring in her step, no joy in this weekly chore.

She couldn't even muster a smile for Mr. Fox when

he exclaimed over the candies and the marmalade in the heavy basket.

And when she left the store and found Declan waiting on the boardwalk, her heart nearly stopped beating. He had not bothered with one of his fine suits today; he wore a simple white shirt and denims and a pair of scuffed western-style boots. The clothing suited him more than the citified outfits he used to constantly wear. Still, she didn't like it. The simple attire made him look as if he'd somehow given up.

No, the surrender was not in something so simple as the clothes he wore. The defeat was in his eyes.

"I wanted to see you," he said, joining her as she tried to walk away.

"Your potion will be ready tomorrow," she said without looking at him. "There's no need for us to talk until then."

He ignored her and fell into step at her side. "I'm staying at the boardinghouse," he said. "And I've wired my sister Angela to send me a bank draft."

"I'm sure you'll get by just fine," she said sharply.

Declan didn't answer, but he didn't leave her, either. He stayed beside her as she began the long walk down the road that led to her home.

"I'm boarding Shadow at the livery in town," he said after a few awkward moments of silence. "I know you don't have any way to care for her . . ."

"Perhaps you should sell her." Matilda interrupted. "Or make a gift of her to Vanessa."

She wanted to scream at Declan, to tell him that he was throwing away something precious for his vengeance, but she didn't. She couldn't speak to him, she didn't even want to look at him. And yet he would not go away.

She loved him still, would probably always love him. That was the true curse of love, wasn't it? That it worked itself in so deep it was impossible to displace, that it

236

became a part of you whether you wanted it or not.

"Shadow is yours," he said softly. "I won't take her back, and I won't give her to someone else."

"Vanessa," Matilda said, spitting out the name. "Can't you even say your intended's name aloud? Vanessa. Not *someone else,* not *her.* Vanessa." Every time she spoke the name, her heart hurt.

Declan nervously raked his hands through his hair. "I don't want to talk about her, about . . . about Vanessa; I just want to make sure you're all right."

All right? Was he insane? "I'm fine," she said, her voice weak and certainly unconvincing.

"I never wanted to hurt you."

Hurt was too easy a word for what she felt, too small and ordinary. She picked up the pace, hurrying toward home, anxious to escape from Declan before she said something incredibly stupid. Like *I love you, don't do this.*

He wasn't dissuaded, and continued at her side.

"Go away, Mr. Harper," she said without looking at him. "I can find my own way home."

"I just want to make sure you get home safely, that's all."

"I've been making this walk on my own for years; I don't need an escort now."

Declan didn't argue. He simply fell into step beside her, as he had so often since returning to Tanglewood; his long stride shortened to accommodate her so that they walked in a kind of harmony.

The walk into the woods seemed longer than usual, the air hotter, the road endless. How could he stand this? How could *she?* Having him so close was pure torture. Matilda comforted herself with the knowledge that once she was home, Declan would leave her alone. And after she saw him to hand over the love potion tomorrow, he would be out of her life forever.

Unless even after he married Vanessa he took to meeting her in town on Fridays and escorting her home. What torture that would be. To see him this way, to talk awkwardly and maybe even pretend to be friends, would be more painful than she could imagine.

It was too early to pretend, too soon. The hurt was too fresh, the wounds too raw. They had nothing to say today, so they walked in silence. The heat was stifling, the sun unbearably hot. Matilda felt like her heart had crawled into her throat and meant to stay there.

At last her cottage came into view; she had never been so happy to see home.

"Home safe and sound," she said, trying, and failing, to sound indifferent. "I'll see you tomorrow. Not before noon, Mr. Harper. I am following the directions diligently, and the love potion won't be ready until then."

"Noon," he said, and then he reached out and grabbed her arm, just as she was about to make a safe escape.

She looked up into his dark eyes. He held her too close, reminding her of all they'd had and would never have again. It was as if he was trying to make sure her broken heart was fatal.

"I kissed you here once, after another long walk from town," he whispered, trailing his free hand along the curve of her cheek.

"Did you?" she asked, trembling. "I don't remember."

"I do." He released his grip on her and wrapped his arm around her.

To break and run would reveal her feelings too clearly, wouldn't it? To cry out that he was torturing her would show Declan how he was hurting her. She didn't want him to know, didn't want him to think her pathetic.

"It was just a kiss," she whispered. "The world is full of kisses."

"Then one more won't hurt." He leaned down, dipping his head toward hers. "Kiss me good-bye, Matilda. We owe each other that. One long, sweet, good-bye kiss."

Matilda wanted to fight, but couldn't. She wanted to

tell Declan no. More than anything, she wanted him to know that this one last kiss *would* hurt. Too much.

But she said nothing. She closed her eyes as his mouth touched hers. In an instant, she was submerged in love and longing and pain. Those feelings and more washed over and through her like a rolling wave of heat.

Surely a good-bye kiss shouldn't turn so deep and passionate, so full of yearning pain that her entire body throbbed.

I love you. The words were on the lips he devoured. *Don't leave me.* Her heart begged. *Don't let this be good-bye.*

The kiss ended abruptly, as Declan took his mouth from hers. He held her, still, pulling her head to his shoulder and breathing in her ear.

How could she make herself despise Declan when he obviously hated this parting as much as she did? How could she let him go?

In the end she didn't have to; he dropped his arms and turned to stalk away from her without a word.

From her hiding place in the woods, Gretchen sighed deeply. She had hoped that since she hadn't seen Mr. Harper around the Candy place for a couple of days that the romance had ended on its own. Clearly that was not the case.

"Have you come up with a plan yet?" Hanson asked, his voice low as the witch entered her house.

"Not yet. I told her he'd been kissing other women, but she didn't believe me. I should have known better. She's a witch, after all. She *knows* things."

"Maybe we should tell Mr. Harper that she's been kissing other men," Hanson said. "He's not a witch, so he won't know it's a lie."

She wondered if such news would enrage the man so much that he'd call an end to their romance. Perhaps, but she suspected it might not be enough.

"You'd think a man would be wary of falling in love with a witch," she muttered.

"He does know she's a witch, doesn't he?" Hanson asked.

"Of course," Gretchen snapped. "Everyone knows."

"Yeah, but not everyone believes it's true. Stella doesn't believe in witches at all."

Gretchen made her way to the path she and her brother had made through the woods. "We could convince him," she said, "that Matilda Candy is a real witch, that she's dangerous. We can tell him that she casts spells by moonlight and that maybe she's even cast a spell on *him*."

Hanson followed her toward home. "That might work."

Gretchen smiled. Yes, it just might.

Chapter Twenty

He hadn't slept well in three nights, and knowing he'd see Matilda in a few hours—perhaps for the last time—made Declan's whole body ache. He'd tried to remain in his small room at the boardinghouse, but ever since he'd awakened, well before dawn, he'd felt as if the walls were closing in on him. So he walked the streets with restless anger.

Saturday morning in Tanglewood always bustled, but on this morning Declan found he had no tolerance for the people who laughed and shopped and pushed their way through the crowds as if nothing had changed. A few spoke to him, but he barely answered. He walked on as if he hadn't heard, trying to look like he was going somewhere with purpose, but in reality moving on aimlessly. Lost.

He was outside the saloon when the Hazelrig twins placed themselves in his path and refused to move out of his way. He couldn't move to the side, as a group of farmers had cornered the rainmaker demanding their money back as well as repayment for the past two weeks of food and lodging.

"Hello, Mr. Harper," Gretchen, the brat who had pushed him into Matilda's pond, said.

"Hello." He did his best to move around the little girl, but as he did the little boy stepped practically under his feet.

"Where are you going?" the kid asked.

"Don't you two have somewhere you're supposed to be?"

"No," Gretchen answered, apparently missing the broad hint in his question. "Our stepmother is in the general store, and Father is at the blacksmith's. They told us not to wander far, though."

"Yes, well . . ." Declan began, trying to make his way around the children.

"Did you know that Matilda Candy is a witch?" Hanson asked loudly. "A *real* one."

Declan was no longer trying to escape. He felt it was his duty to defend Matilda from the ridiculous charge. "That's nonsense."

"No, it's true," Gretchen said. "We've seen her cast spells over her black cauldron, calling out the dark spirits." She lifted her arms slowly and arched pale eyebrows.

"You've seen no such thing," Declan said, aware that the nearby farmers had stopped their discussion to listen.

"We have, too," Hanson said. "You just don't see it because she cast a spell on you. That's scary, isn't it?" he asked, wide-eyed and excited. "That she cast a spell on you? She could turn you into a frog if she wanted to. She told me so one day when I spit into one of her magic potions."

"Matilda Candy is a lovely young woman who can make candy and bread and a hundred other useful goods." He tried to keep his voice calm. "The idea that she's a witch is absolutely ridiculous."

Gretchen leaned close and whispered loudly. "Is it? She's never denied that she's a witch like her grandmother. She doesn't care who knows, because she knows that if somebody makes trouble for her . . ." the little girl snapped her fingers, "they're a slimy toad, just like that."

Hanson nodded wisely and patted Declan consolingly on the arm. "I'd be real careful if I were you."

Declan finally made his way around the children, shaking his head as he went. Ridiculous! The people of Tanglewood had nothing to fear from Matilda. Nothing at all. She was good and sweet and wouldn't hurt a fly.

And in a couple of hours Matilda was going to make his dreams come true, just as her grandmother had promised. Too bad she could no longer be a part of that dream.

The potion had been carefully mixed with elderberry wine and poured into a fine-cut glass decanter. Only the best for Declan Harper, Matilda thought sourly as she stared at the way the sunlight, touching the bottle that sat near her window, made its contents sparkle.

A love potion. The very idea chilled her more than any bump in the night or bad dream or imagined monster. The crimson liquid looked harmless enough, was beautiful, even, the way it caught the light and seemed to hold on to it, but surely no good would come of something intended to manufacture love.

If any man but Declan had asked her to concoct such a powerful potion, she would've refused. But she would do anything for the man she loved, even this.

He arrived right on time, and she was ready for him. Sitting in her rocking chair with her hair in pigtails, feet bare, she was Tanglewood's witch again. Nothing more, not to Declan, not to anyone.

She waited a moment after his knock to call him inside. She used that moment to steel herself for what was to come.

Preparing herself to face Declan had been a waste of

time. She couldn't be strong where he was concerned, couldn't pretend she didn't still love him. He looked so tired, so bone-weary, that she wanted nothing more than to rise to her feet, go to him, and give whatever comfort she could.

But she remained in her seat, by sheer force of will. Taking her eyes from Declan, she pointed to the table by the window, where the love potion mixed with wine caught the sun like a rare ruby.

"There's what you came for, Mr. Harper." She couldn't steel herself to look him in the eye. "I hope it brings you all the happiness you expect."

With his back to her, he stood over the table staring down at the potion. He was apparently reluctant to lay his hands on the decanter; those hands flexed and then formed easy fists that hung at his sides.

"According to the book I found this recipe in, the potion will be almost immediately effective, and the effects are somewhat permanent."

"Somewhat?"

She took a deep breath. "After a while the love the recipient of the potion experiences will sometimes fade, moving in and out like the tide. There will be moments of clarity during which your beloved will wonder why she ever fell in love with you, and then, sometime later, she will love you madly once again. I would think that to be a rather unpleasant sensation, myself," she added softly.

Declan finally reached out and touched the bottle, but he did not lift it. She wished, with all her heart, that he would take the bottle in his hands and smash it against the floor. She wished he would come to his senses.

"How much?" he whispered. "How much should I give her?"

"How much do you want her to love you?" Matilda snapped. "The more she drinks the more besotted she'll be. Be sure to save some for yourself," she added in a subdued voice.

He shook his head slowly.

"How will you endure a lifetime married to someone you don't love?" she whispered. "Perhaps you can convince yourself you love Vanessa, just a little, in order to do what must be done. You can both drink. Make arrangements to be alone at the time, and I'm sure she'll succumb to your charms." Her voice shook, but only slightly. "Compromise her, love her, and the wedding you so desire will take place. Very quickly, I would imagine. Vanessa Arrington is not the kind of woman you bed unless you intend to marry her."

Declan finally turned to face her. He looked every bit as miserable as she felt, deep inside. "Don't say that," he whispered hoarsely. "You're worth a thousand Vanessas; you're a better woman than she will ever be. I didn't use you, Matilda. I loved you."

"Not enough," she muttered.

He took a step forward, but stopped when she lifted her hand, palm outward, to silently tell Declan that she did not want him to come any closer.

"I wish there was another way," he said, looking as if he meant it.

"If you wished it hard enough, you would find another way."

He spun around, took the decanter in one impatient hand, and stormed from the cottage.

After he had gone, after she'd listened to his horse's hoofbeats fade away, Matilda cried.

Vanessa walked toward the small knot of farmers as if she were headed somewhere else, as if she had not deliberately chosen this direction. She'd already heard, from Mrs. Daly, that the farmers had decided to grant Mr. Cox a full-time escort, in case he should decide to run with their two hundred dollars. Wendell Trent and

Reggie Brewster had been assigned the task of making sure the rainmaker didn't disappear in the night.

She found the entire situation to be rather entertaining. As she approached, she saw that Cox was actually sweating; an unfortunate state that did nothing to improve his already dismal appearance. She almost turned away when she saw that Henry was one of the men surrounding Cox, but decided to continue for the greater good. Once she was finished, no one in town would have time for that witch Matilda Candy. They'd all hate her.

"Good afternoon, gentlemen," she said. "How are you all this fine day?"

Henry turned longing eyes to her, and the others looked at her as if she were daft. They wouldn't consider it a fine day until there was rain.

Cox narrowed one eye as he stared at her. She could see the panic in it.

"Any luck manufacturing rain?" She peered out from under the boardwalk to a pure, blue, cloudless sky. "I guess not." She smiled widely. "Must be the witch."

Henry quickly agreed with her. "Did you hear those kids this morning? They've seen her do things." He shuddered. "Terrible things. They've even seen her turn a man into a toad."

Reggie Brewster recalled hearing that same conversation, nodding his red head enthusiastically as he confirmed what Henry had heard.

"Matilda Candy," Wendell Trent said with narrowed, angry eyes, apparently liking the direction the conversation had taken. "That interfering witch is the one keeping the rain away. If we get rid of her, we'll have rain again for sure!"

"Yeah!" someone else agreed enthusiastically.

If we get rid of her. Oh, it was delicious. "How do you . . . get rid of a witch?" Vanessa asked, lowering her voice.

Many of the farmers expressed their opinions, keeping

their voices low and their heads together. An aging farmer suggested that they unite and run her out of the county. Someone else said she should be stoned, another suggested stringing her up, and even another suggested drowning her in her own pond. As they tossed ideas back and forth, some of the farmers became downright excited. Including Henry. Still, none of their suggestions were quite what Vanessa was looking for.

It was she who said, "They burn witches to get rid of them, don't they? In the old days they used to burn them so they wouldn't come back." She leaned in and laid a hand on Henry's arm. "We don't want her to come back, do we?"

There was a soft chorus of "no" from the farmers, but Raleigh Cox remained silent. Vanessa lifted her eyes to him. "Do you think that would break the curse and bring rain, Mr. Cox?" What could he say? If he had a choice of burning a witch or finding himself at the end of a rope, which would he choose?

"Perhaps," he finally answered, his oddly spaced eyes glaring down at her. The one lazy eye waggled, and she shuddered and looked away.

The older man who'd suggested running Matilda out of the county took a step back. "I don't know. Can't we just . . . talk to her?"

It was Henry who answered. "Talk to a witch? What good would that do?"

One by one, the men who were uncomfortable with this plan moved away. They were too cowardly to participate, but they were desperate enough for rain that they wouldn't try to stop what might happen.

Eventually there were five left, Vanessa, Raleigh Cox, Henry, Reggie, and Wendell. Four men would be plenty to see that Matilda burned, Vanessa was sure. But still she wondered—was any one of the four men surrounding her man enough to see the chore through? Or would they

Linda Jones

chicken out when faced with the task of setting a passably pretty woman afire?

She knew how to make sure they wouldn't. As long as *one* of them persisted, as long as *one* of them led the undertaking, the others would follow.

"Henry," she said, taking her old beau's arm and pulling him aside. "I don't think I'll rest easy until I know she's dead. She'll know we've been plotting against her, and who knows what kind of retribution she might seek, should she survive." She gave the man her most vulnerable look, wide-eyed and pouty-lipped. "Why, the very idea terrifies me."

Vanessa knew Henry well, knew his strengths and his weaknesses. He did have a powerful weakness for her. "If you would do this for me, I would be forever in your debt." She licked her lips. "I would be grateful, and once this is done I will repay you any way you ask." She tried to give the simple words meaning. "*Any way,* Henry."

He looked like he was about to dissolve and seep through the boardwalk. "I'd do anything for you, Vanessa, anything you ask."

"You're such a sweetheart," she said, leaning forward to give him a peck on the cheek.

"There is one problem," Cox piped up, drawing her attention, and Henry's, back to the group.

"What's that?" Reggie asked.

"Him." Cox nodded down the street, and all heads turned to watch Declan dismount in front of the boardinghouse at the end of the street. He held a bottle in his hand—a whiskey bottle perhaps—as he headed inside.

"Yeah, he seemed kinda sweet on that witch at the Founders' Day dance," Wendell said angrily.

"She's likely cast a spell over him," Vanessa suggested, and the others quickly agreed. "I can handle Declan," she said softly. Her father had ridden to Jackson to see about a horse. He'd probably stay over to play a game of cards and not return until tomorrow, as always.

248

She'd have the house to herself. "I'll keep him occupied while y'all do what has to be done."

Vanessa wanted, very badly, to watch Matilda Candy get her comeuppance, to actually see her burn. To her way of thinking, it was fitting punishment for all of the so-called witch's interference. Unfortunately it looked as if she would not be able to attend the festivities.

She'd just have to satisfy herself by toying with Declan Harper while the woman who had bewitched him burned.

Chapter Twenty-one

Declan sat on the edge of the bed in his tiny room in the boardinghouse, the decanter of wine in his hands. The sun went down, and still he held the wine. *Wine, hell. Call it what it is,* he thought angrily. *The love potion.*

When it was too dark to see, he lit the bedside lamp and set the potion beside it. There was an evil beauty to the liquid in the bottle, a riveting, entrancing, sinful beauty.

Everything he wanted could be had with the proper use of the potion in that bottle: revenge, security, the life he'd always craved. Money, position . . . revenge. He always came back to revenge again.

But he would have to take his vengeance without Matilda, he'd have to give up the only woman he'd ever love. She was right; it would be easier if he joined Vanessa in taking the potion, if he fooled himself into thinking that he could not only bear but enjoy a lifetime with a beautiful, vapid woman like Vanessa Arrington. He wouldn't take even a sip of the potion, though, no matter how easy it might make the days and years to come. He'd rather suffer the pain of loving Matilda and not having her than to wipe her out of his heart completely.

Thinking about Matilda hurt too much, so he concentrated on his revised plan. He would have to find a time to be alone with Vanessa, a time when her father was not around. One afternoon, perhaps, when he caught a glimpse of Arrington in town alone. A quick trip to the Arrington plantation, a glass of wine, or two, and the deed would be done.

He wasn't expecting anyone, so the knock on the door surprised him. He was even more surprised when he saw one of Arrington's young servants standing there with a folded sheet of paper in his hand.

"Miss Vanessa asked me to deliver this to you," the kid said, handing over the paper. The boy was young and not too bright, most likely unable to read. Why would Vanessa send a note this way?

> *Dear Declan,*
> *I am distressed to learn of my father's inexcusable behavior and would like to make amends. He is out for the evening. Perhaps we should take this opportunity to discuss this unfortunate situation.*
> *Yours,*
> *Vanessa*

How timely, how interesting. How odd that she should choose this, of all evenings, to ask him to call.

Before he could change his mind, he scooped up the decanter of wine and left the room.

Matilda loosened her braids and brushed out the wavy strands, thinking of Declan as she performed the mindless task. Had he used the potion yet? Were he and Vanessa, at this very moment . . .

251

She shook her head vigorously. Why did she torture herself this way?

She wasn't surprised by the knock at the door. It was after dark, a time when people came to her for cures and advice. At the moment she felt no anticipation, just sadness. She didn't want to face anyone tonight.

Throwing open the door, she found not one but four men standing there—the rainmaker, Henry Langford, Reggie Brewster, and a smiling Wendell Trent. Henry held a gun trained on her as he and his accomplices forced their way into her cottage.

"Tie her up, Reggie." The farmer, rope in hand, moved forward to do as Henry ordered. Within seconds she was bound tightly.

"What if she tries to put a spell on me?" Reggie asked as he tied the last knot.

"I'm pretty sure she needs her hands free to cast spells," Henry said knowingly.

"What are you doing?" Matilda asked as Reggie forced her to her knees.

Wendell stepped forward and leaned down to boldly place his face close to hers. "Think you can keep away the rain, do you? Think you can just keep on interfering in other people's lives?" he whispered hoarsely. "Well, we'll see about that."

"Wendell," Henry snapped with authority. "You plant that stake good and firm in the clearing out front."

"Stake?" Matilda said, her voice barely working. She cast a sharp glance at the rainmaker, who stood back and allowed the other men to do their wicked business. He knew this was wrong; she could see that truth in his face, in the way he stood anxiously to the side. The others were ignorant, but he *knew*.

"Tell them," she pleaded. "Tell them that this is wrong."

He looked slightly dismayed, but said nothing to stop what was happening.

Wendell threw open the door. From her place, on her knees in the middle of the room, she saw the stake tied to one of the horses out front. It was six feet long, at least, the width of a pine tree, and sharpened at one end.

"Reggie, give him a hand," Henry ordered.

"Why don't we just tie her to the hitching post out front and get this over with," Reggie moaned. "Or just tie her up in here and set the cottage on fire. It'll take forever to get that stake planted."

Henry grabbed Matilda by the hair, forced her to her feet and dragged her into the night. The rainmaker followed. Reggie was already taking the stake down from his horse. Wendell lent a hand, since the length of wood was quite heavy.

"Vanessa wants this done right," Henry said, gesturing to the clearing before him.

"Vanessa?" Matilda whispered. She'd always thought the woman vain and selfish and useless, but evil? Only someone truly evil would have a part in this.

Henry turned his face to her and smiled, even as he continued to hold her by the hair. "She's entertaining your beau at the moment, to make certain we have time to complete this task properly. Once you're gone, burned and dead forever, then it'll rain." He cast a glance to the rainmaker. "Right, Cox?"

Cox hesitated only momentarily before whispering, "Right."

Gretchen ran, faster than she'd ever run before. Hanson was ahead of her, for once, his legs pumping as he flew down the path.

She couldn't believe what she'd seen and heard. They were going to burn the witch!

Hanson threw open the door to their house and together they fell inside, breathless, frightened, shaking.

"What on earth?" Stella asked as she came to her feet,

253

setting her mending aside. "I thought you two were in bed."

"It's . . . it's . . ." Hanson said, unable to catch his breath.

"Come quick!" Gretchen said breathlessly. "They're going to burn the witch!"

Stella glowered at her. "I have told you a hundred times. There are no witches . . ."

"Miss Matilda!" Gretchen shouted. "They're going to burn Miss Matilda because they think she's the reason it's not raining!" She looked desperately around the room. "Where's Father?"

"He's gone to see Mr. Herrin about getting a job at the mill, just until things improve around here. When he gets home he will be distressed to hear that y'all are still making up your outrageous stories."

Gretchen went very still. "You don't believe us," she whispered.

"There are no witches," Stella said sensibly. "And there are certainly no witch burnings. I don't know what possessed y'all to sneak out of the house and then come back here with this preposterous tale, but . . ."

Hanson looked at Gretchen, his eyes wide and frantic. Perhaps he suspected, as she did, that this was all their fault. She'd seen the farmers listening this morning, as she'd told Mr. Harper about Miss Matilda's powers.

"We need Mr. Harper," Hanson said, and then he turned and ran.

Gretchen was right behind him. They both ignored their stepmother's shouts to come back.

Matilda could do nothing but watch as the men dug a hole in the ground and planted the stake. The dry earth was hard, so they carried buckets of water from the pond to soften it.

She'd never cared that people thought her a witch, had more often than not found it amusing, but then she'd never suspected that anyone would resort to this.

Vanessa was keeping Declan occupied, and he'd probably given her the potion by now. While she burned, they would likely be kissing, laughing, whispering of matrimonial plans. Declan was going to seduce the woman he wanted as his wife, a woman who knew full well what was about to happen here.

Matilda wondered if Declan would take a sip of the potion himself, for courage. She wondered if he would be making love to Vanessa while she herself burned.

Reggie and Wendell stopped their work, wiping at their brows and drinking from the bucket they'd carried from the pond. *Her* bucket, *her* pond.

Wendell walked toward her, grinning with unabashed meanness all the way. "I need to rest a few minutes," he said breathlessly. "Henry, why don't you do a little of the grunt work and let me hang on to the witch for a few minutes."

Henry didn't think much of the idea. He argued briefly, but when Wendell insisted, he grumbled and tossed Matilda roughly away so that she fell against Wendell's potbelly.

Wendell caught her with fingers that grasped her arms so tight tears came to her eyes. He didn't seem inclined to let her go or loosen his grip.

"I always did think you were mighty pretty," he whispered, his sweaty face pressed against hers. "And you wouldn't have nothin' to do with me. Wouldn't even dance with me at the Founders' Day Celebration." His eyes narrowed. "You think you're too good for me, is that it? Well, before you burn, maybe I'll give you a taste of what you missed by not being nice to me when you had the chance."

One of his large hands held her bound wrists, the other reached out to grope at her breasts.

"Before you burn," Wendell whispered, "I'll show you what it's like to have a real man. Seems a shame for you

255

to die without knowing what you missed."

Matilda looked down, struggling ineffectively against Wendell's clumsy fondling. He'd hit her next, the way he'd hit his wife, and then he'd . . . she didn't want to think about what he had planned for her. He was so much stronger than she, what could she do to stop him? Her heart beat so fast, she was afraid it would burst, her mouth was so dry she could barely make herself speak.

Declan had told her she should never be afraid. He'd told her a remarkable woman should have no fear. In that moment she vowed that she would not end her life this way.

"Let go of me," she whispered.

"I'm not through with you," he muttered. "I don't think Henry or either of the others would mind if I stole off with you for a few minutes." His grip on her wrist tightened and with the other hand he reached around to grasp her backside and pull her up against him.

Maybe Wendell was stronger than she was, but he was not smarter. He was dim and mean and simple and always had been.

She lifted her face boldly and looked him square in the eyes. *No fear.* "Tell me, Wendell," she whispered. "What do you think happens to a man who forces himself upon a witch?" There was no dread in her voice, only calm assurance. "What do you think you might find beneath the covers when you wake in the morning? A shriveled, blackened, lump of coal nestled between your legs where your privates used to be? Or perhaps you'll wake in the middle of the night to find a fire blazing there. A hot, charring, cooking . . ."

"That's enough," he said hoarsely, a light of real fear flashing in his eyes as he released her.

She didn't think twice, but took the opportunity to run. Her hands were bound but her legs were not, and she ran toward the woods. She could hide there, if only she could reach the forest in time.

"Hey!" Wendell shouted.

She ran past the rainmaker, but he didn't even try to stop her.

Henry fired one shot into the air and then he shouted. "Cox, if you don't stop her, we'll damn well burn *you* at the stake!"

The rainmaker cursed, but took off after her. His legs were so long, she knew she had little chance—yet still she ran. She had almost reached the complete blackness of the forest, safety, when he caught her from behind, and they both fell to the ground.

"Let me go!" she shouted into the ground. He pressed her into the dirt, heaving as he breathed heavily. "You know I'm not the cause of the drought. Tell them!"

Cox lifted himself up but kept a firm grip on her bound wrists. He dragged her up and spun her around. The others had already begun to gather kindling to place at the base of the stake.

"I'm sorry," Cox whispered as he shoved her into Henry's hands.

Vanessa had met Declan at the door herself, telling him that she'd given the servants the night off. The domestic staff would be close by, in their quarters, Vanessa told him, but their visit would be uninterrupted. They would not be disturbed.

Perfect, Declan thought as she escorted him to the parlor. Absolutely perfect.

Vanessa had gone all out this evening, wearing a white gown flocked with lavender flowers and wearing the requisite pearls at her throat and ears. Her cheeks were pink, her lips lush. And she left him absolutely cold.

"You brought wine," she said, taking the decanter from him and placing it on the table at the end of the green sofa. "How sweet."

"It's elderberry wine," he said. "Nothing special."

She sat on the sofa and patted the seat beside her.

"Come sit with me and let's talk," she said, batting her eyelashes. "I heard what Daddy did to you, and I'm just mortified. Why, I'd do anything to make it up to you, Declan, just *anything*."

Yes, he couldn't ask for a more perfect opportunity than this one. Vanessa was here and agreeable, and Arrington was out for the evening. All he had to do was offer her the wine, and he was set. Done. On his way to getting everything he wanted, everything he'd planned so long and hard for.

"I do hate it that you have nothing, now. I did so hope that there could be more for you and I," Vanessa said sweetly. "I can't marry a penniless man of poor stock," she said with a wave of her hand, and then she looked squarely at him. "No offense intended."

"None taken," he said softly.

"But I do hope that you and I can be friends, Declan. Good, *good* friends." She puckered her lips and leaned toward him. Her gown was low cut, so low cut the pale globes of her breasts were practically thrust toward him.

He had no desire to kiss her; his fingers did not itch to touch her offered breasts.

"How about some wine?" he asked, rising from the sofa and leaving Vanessa hanging there, leaning forward.

Her eyes snapped open and she said, as if nothing had happened, "That would be lovely."

He knew his way around the Arrington parlor. Glasses were kept near Warren Arrington's stash of whiskey. Declan grabbed two of them, set one down, lifted it again. Finally, he banged the second glass, rim-down, onto the bar with decisiveness. Dammit, he would not ingest anything that would take Matilda from him.

Declan poured Vanessa a small glass of the wine, watching all the while the way the potion caught the lamplight, the way it seemed to sparkle and swirl, dancing in the glass as if eager to be set free to do its work. He handed the glass to Vanessa.

She took the offered wine with pale, slender fingers. "Why, thank you, Declan."

Declan held his breath as she raised the glass to her lips.

"You know," she said, bringing the glass down before taking a sip. "I think Daddy is being completely unreasonable about the whole situation. He didn't have to take everything from you. That's just so cruel." She shook her head and lifted the glass to her lips again.

Lamplight shone on the ruby-red potion, making it twinkle seductively. Everything he needed was in that glass, everything he wanted. Everything he'd always dreamed of.

Everything but the woman he loved. Reaching out with a lurch and a snap he jostled the glass before Vanessa could drink. The contents spilled onto her white dress, staining the bodice.

"You clumsy oaf!" she shouted, coming to her feet. "This gown is ruined, do you hear me? Ruined!" For the first time, he saw something genuine in her eyes. He saw petty anger, selfish rage.

"I'm sorry," he said, reaching for what remained of the love potion. "I never should've come here."

Her anger vanished as quickly as it had come, and she reached out to touch his arm. "No, don't go. I'm sorry I lost my temper. It's just that I did so want to look nice for you tonight." She smiled, took his hand, and placed it over her breast. "And see what you've done," she whispered. She took a deep breath, her breasts rising and falling beneath his hand.

"I shouldn't be here," Declan said, anxious to get to Matilda and tell her what a mistake he'd almost made. He would beg her to take him back, if necessary. He would do whatever he had to do.

"Don't you want to hold me, Declan?" Vanessa whispered. "I'm an untouched lady," she said batting her eyelashes. "A virgin who will go to her marriage bed intact.

But that doesn't mean I don't want you to touch me, or that I can't touch you."

Untouched? He seriously doubted it. In the past Vanessa had always seemed passionless, cold, but at the moment she looked at him like she wanted to eat him alive. She licked her lips, making sure he saw her flickering tongue, as she laid her hand on the flat of his stomach and inched it downward.

He backed up quickly. "Vanessa, this is not right." He only wanted to take the love potion and escape. He'd pour the wine onto the road and make Matilda love him again the right way. The only way.

Another flash of anger sparked in her eyes. "It's gracious of you to show such respect for me, Declan, very gentlemanly, in fact, but what I want from you right now is . . ."

The front door opened with a bang, and frantic footsteps sounded in the entryway.

Vanessa muttered, "Damnation!"

Declan backed gratefully away from her, and turned to see Gretchen in the doorway.

"He's here!" she shouted, and a moment later her brother, who had been searching other downstairs rooms, joined her. "Come quick," she said. "They're going to burn the . . . they're going to burn Miss Matilda!" She was red-faced, shaking, and breathing heavily.

"What?" Declan set the decanter aside and walked to the doorway.

"Pay no mind to them," Vanessa said sharply. "Everyone knows this child tells nothing but lies."

That was true, and yet . . . He looked down at the children. "Calm down and tell me what happened."

They told him everything, ignoring Vanessa's interruptions. Declan went cold as he heard what they'd seen, or what they'd claimed to see.

"Get out of here, you brats, and take your lies with you," Vanessa snapped.

Gretchen pointed an accusing finger at Vanessa. "She knows all about it! I heard one of them say that Vanessa wanted it done right, that she was supposed to keep you here so you'd be out of the way!"

It all came together with sickening clarity: the note, the dismissed servants, the apology, and the attempts at seduction he'd endured since coming into this house tonight.

Declan turned to face Vanessa. How had he ever thought her beautiful? There was no beauty on her face, none in her heart.

"If Matilda dies, I will come back here and kill you with my bare hands," he promised.

She didn't try to declare herself innocent, not this time. "You wouldn't dare," she said haughtily, and then she glanced at the mantel clock and smiled. "Besides, I fear you're already too late to save the witch, Mr. Harper."

Declan ran from the house. The children were right behind him, and he ordered them to go straight home.

With his head down, Declan and Smoky flew toward Matilda's house. "I'm not too late," he whispered aloud. "I can't be."

And in the far distance, thunder rolled.

Chapter Twenty-two

Matilda lifted her face as Henry set a match to the kindling at her feet. She didn't want to see the fire flicker, she did not want these men to see her cry. "Declan," she whispered.

Henry, Reggie, and Wendell stared at the kindling and the logs—wood Declan and Robert had split for her—surrounding the stake they'd lashed Matilda to, their faces excited, expectant, demon-like. She didn't have to look down to see that the fire had started. She heard the crackle, felt the heat.

The rainmaker backed away, inching toward the horses. Matilda set her eyes on him and stared hard. He might've stopped this, had he wanted to. He knew she was no witch, just as she knew he was no rainmaker.

Henry saw her staring and snapped his head around to discover what had claimed her attention. "Get back here, Cox," he ordered, waving his pistol in that direction. Cox sighed and complied.

Reggie had a sudden, and much too late, flash of conscience. "Maybe we should cut her down. I mean, what if we burn her and it still don't rain? What if she casts some spell before she dies, and it'll never rain again?"

"Shut up," Henry snapped. "Don't turn coward on me now."

"I'm not a coward," Reggie protested. "I just think we should be sure."

Now he wanted to be sure? Matilda laid her eyes on the farmer, and he shivered and took a step back.

She felt the growing heat of the spreading fire now, and made herself look down. The flames grew rapidly, inching inward from the outer edge of the circle of kindling and logs they'd surrounded her with.

This was no way to die, lashed to a stake and burned alive, a sacrifice to the stupid fears of brainless, ignorant men. She'd lived a good life, she'd never done anyone harm. A few days ago, she'd had everything a woman could ask for: love, new friends, a safe home. Now it was all gone, and as the flames grew, so did Matilda's anger.

"Declan!" she screamed at the top of her lungs.

Matilda reached deep inside herself and found something heretofore unknown. A strength, a force, a power. That potent power had been hidden behind a stone wall of her own making, a shield that had protected her from the truth for years. A few of those stones crumbled.

She lifted her head to the skies, looking far beyond her cabin. "Declan!" In the distance lightning streaked across the sky as she screamed. Faint thunder rumbled. The men around her did not hear, not yet. They were too excited by their own actions, too proud of themselves.

With another flash of anger, the dam inside her shivered and crumbled some more. Something new and tangible grew inside, a force as real and strong and unstoppable as the underground spring that fed her pond.

"Declan!" She wanted him to hear her, to save her, but she knew he would not. He was with Vanessa, work-

263

ing a magic she had conjured for him. A magic that would bring him his long-awaited vengeance. He wasn't coming, not now, not ever. She was as alone as she had ever been, more lonely, since she now knew what it was like to be a part of something more.

A stiff breeze came out of nowhere, and Matilda lifted her face to welcome the force of the wind that pressed her clothes to her body and pushed her hair back and away from her face. The wind was an ally, she knew, perhaps even a part of her. It gave her strength.

Her heart swelled, her mind cleared. She would not die wishing for what she had lost; she was stronger than that, even now. She took a deep breath, taking in the strong gust that was, somehow, linked to the power hidden inside her.

There was rain in the wind; she could smell it.

The flames flickered higher, and Matilda looked down at Henry and smiled. His eyes widened in fear, and he took a step back, as if she had all the power here, as if he wanted to run from her.

"You want rain?" she shouted to be heard above the wind. "I'll give you rain!"

She lifted her face and bid the storm to come. The shield inside her crumbled away, and she called on her gift, the power of her ancestors, the force that made her, truly and irrevocably, a witch.

A few drops fell, sizzling on the fire that grew hotter and hotter, startling the men who had bound her to the stake. "I'll make it rain," she shouted, "and it will never stop, do you hear me. Never!" She thought of Declan and Vanessa, and her rage grew as she screamed his name again. Lightning cracked over her cottage, thunder made the men before her jump.

"What will become of your farms, do you think, when the rains come endlessly? They'll become bogs of useless mud, then ponds, then rivers," she promised. "You'll never see the sun again."

Matilda wanted, more than anything, to scare these men before she died. She wanted them to carry this moment to their graves. Tied to this stake, she was trapped. But she was not powerless. They would survive this night, but she wanted to make sure they never slept well again. She had to give them something they would never forget. *Snow in the middle of summer,* Granny had said.

Cold, she thought, concentrating. *Ice. Snow.*

Snowflakes fell. A few, at first, and then more. Tanglewood had only seen snow once in the ten years she'd been here, a January dusting years back that had delighted everyone. This was not a friendly dusting of soft flakes, but a blast of icy precipitation that pelted the men who had come to her home to burn her.

The horses hitched near the cottage reared back and snorted, fighting their reins. Reggie dropped to his knees and prayed.

Too late.

"You will never be warm again!" she screamed. "Winter will follow you wherever you go. You will die with ice in your veins, longing for the warmth of the sun. You will carry winter in your heart forever. Forever," she reiterated in a hoarse whisper. The snow fell softer, now, gentle flakes drifting around them all.

The flames grew, but they did not touch her. Reggie stumbled to his feet. He and a trembling Wendell, who did not look so threatening at the moment, headed for the horses. The rainmaker stared at her, slack-jawed and trembling.

"Get back here!" Henry shouted to his friends. "We have to make sure she's dead."

"You make sure!" Reggie shouted. "I'm headin' for California, and I'm not stoppin' till this horse gives out."

"I'm goin' with him," Wendell yelled. "Goddamn, I never figured on this."

"Do you think it's *easy* to kill a witch?" Matilda shouted, and she smiled at the men one last time, knowing they would carry the memory of this moment to their dying day. "Did you think you wouldn't have to *pay?*"

The flames grew taller, closer, hotter. They danced toward her skirt and scorched her feet. *Declan.* She whispered the name this time instead of screaming into the night. She was angry and wounded, her soul was enraged. But she didn't want to die, not tonight, not like this.

Rain, she thought, closing her eyes and picturing a deluge. She could see it in her mind, clear and so real she could almost feel the drops. Water falling in sheets from the sky, soaking the ground, dousing the fire.

The snowflakes stopped falling, and the rain began again. Drops sizzled in the flames at her feet. Lightning flashed above her head; thunder deafened her. But the fire had grown too large, too hot, too powerful. She couldn't make it rain hard enough. Dammit, she was going to burn.

"Declan!" she screamed, and suddenly he was there.

The sight stopped his heart. Matilda latched to a stake, wind pushing her hair away from her face, flames licking at her feet as she screamed his name.

Declan jumped from his horse and ran toward Matilda. Henry Langford stood as close to the fire as was safe, staring up at her. A gun hung from his right hand. The rainmaker, Raleigh Cox, stood just behind Henry, motionless and staring, as if he'd been entranced.

"Cut her down!" Declan shouted as he reached them. "Jesus Christ, cut her down!" There were sharp knives in the kitchen, but he was afraid it would take too long to run inside and find what he needed. He couldn't leave Matilda here alone.

Raleigh Cox reached into the top of his boot and pulled out a pearl-handled knife with a long, thin blade. He said nothing as he offered it to Declan.

Declan took the knife and ran into the fire, kicking the

flaming logs closest to Matilda aside. The rain had dampened the fire's force, but it continued to flicker and occasionally flame up, coming dangerously close to Matilda's skirt.

She set her eyes on him. "You came," she said. Her eyes were glassy, her face ghostly white. "I didn't think you would."

He began to cut the ropes that bound her while flames licked at their feet.

"Stop that!" Henry ordered, raising the weapon he held. "Dammit, you stop that right now!"

Declan ignored the hysterical order. "Are you all right?" he asked, cutting through one rope after another.

"I made it rain," she whispered, no inflection in her voice.

She was delirious. "Of course you did," he said in his most soothing voice. Dammit, how many ropes did these simpletons think it took to contain one small woman?

"Really, I did. I made it snow, too." When her arms were free, she held her hands before her and studied the chafed skin. "Granny was right. I really am a witch."

"Don't talk nonsense. . . ."

Henry fired a warning shot over their heads as Declan cut the last of the ropes away, then the man took aim at them; at Matilda, actually. Declan didn't think, he just placed his body in front of hers as Henry pulled the trigger again.

He felt the impact into his shoulder, a spreading pain, a sticky dampness that seeped down his back.

"Declan?" Matilda whispered behind him.

He went light-headed, weak in the knees, but he made sure he stayed on his feet and between her and Henry. Shielding her. He tried to wrap his body around hers to protect her from every angle. Nothing else mattered. Nothing.

"Declan?" she whispered his name again. He tried to hold her tighter, but his strength was failing him already.

Matilda lifted her head and screamed, and all of a sudden the rain fell harder. It fell in sheets, in buckets, drenching them all and obscuring their vision. The fire sputtered and went out. Lightning lit the night and thunder cracked so hard, he was momentarily deafened.

And he knew then that Matilda was telling the truth. She'd brought the rain with a vengeance.

Behind him horses neighed, Henry shouted and cried aloud. Raleigh Cox cursed. Moments later the muffled sound of hooves on the road rose and fell.

"They're gone," Matilda said. "Let's get inside and let me take a look at you."

"Son of a bitch shot me," he murmured, his voice too soft to be heard above the falling rain.

"I know," Matilda said. He could barely hear her.

He did not think the wound was fatal, but then bullet wounds were strange things. You never knew what might happen. Infection. Blood loss. Hell, his heart might just stop.

"I love you," he shouted to be heard above the storm. He wanted to say more, but his strength was rapidly failing. He wanted to tell her that he couldn't imagine his life without her in it, that he hadn't allowed Vanessa to take the potion, that . . . *the potion*.

Outside, thunder crashed and lightning lit the night sky. The violent weather matched Vanessa's black mood as she paced in the parlor.

Her plans never went awry. Never! The servants had all been dismissed for the evening, laying way for Declan Harper to be thoroughly enraptured and captivated by her charms. He might've even taken the first steps toward taking Johnny's place.

But Declan was gone, those Hazelrig brats had ruined everything, and to top it off, her gown was stained with wine, and she had no one to help her undress.

When she heard the knock on the front door, she was

certain it was Declan. He'd come back to her!

But when she threw the door open a less-than-attractive sight awaited her. Raleigh Cox, soaked to the skin, stood beneath the overhang. A streak of lightning illuminated the sky behind him.

"It all went wrong," he said, stepping into the foyer without waiting for an invitation; not that she would've issued one.

Vanessa slammed the door behind him. He turned to face her, and in candlelight Cox was even uglier than usual. Wet clothing clung to bony flesh. Soaked, thin hair stuck to his scalp and neck. In this light his pale eyebrows and eyelashes disappeared completely.

"What went wrong?" she snapped.

"Everything." He ran a bony hand through his hair, causing the damp strands to stand straight up in one place. "Wendell got . . . carried away. He attempted to molest the Candy woman. And Langford was determined to actually burn her."

"That *was* the plan," Vanessa seethed. "Wasn't it?"

Cox shook his head. "Maybe it was your plan, but it was never mine. I just wanted to make those farmers think I would really burn the witch to make it rain. I thought maybe I could slip away while they were occupied planting the stake, but they kept too close an eye on me. I couldn't escape." He narrowed his eyes and nervously shrugged one shoulder as he remembered. "I figured if I disappeared they'd know what was up and let the woman go. But as time went by, and I knew I wasn't going to get away, I kept wondering what was going to happen when they burned her and the rain didn't come."

"It's raining cats and dogs," Vanessa said, her hands balling into tight fists.

Cox lifted his head and looked her square in the eye. With the one wandering eye it was hard to tell, but she was pretty sure he was looking right at her. "She made it rain," he whispered. "The witch, she did it."

"Don't be ridiculous. Matilda Candy is not really a witch."

Cox shook his head. "She is. They tied her to the stake and laid the dried brush and logs around her, and when that Henry fellow set a flame to the brush she lifted her face to the night sky, screamed Harper's name, and the storm moved in. Fast."

"Coincidence," Vanessa muttered.

Cox shook his head again. "She brought the rain. For a few minutes she actually made it *snow*. I saw it happen."

Vanessa was less concerned by any proof that Matilda Candy really was a witch than by the annoyance that yet another plan had gone wrong. "Where is Harper now?" she asked. With the witch, she assumed. Damn Matilda!

"Henry shot him when he tried to protect the witch. I don't know how bad it is," he said with a touch of regret.

Serves him right! Vanessa thought. If Declan had stayed here, as he should have, he never would've been wounded.

"Where is Henry?" At least *he* hadn't lost his nerve!

"Dead," Cox whispered.

"The witch or Declan?" she asked, curious but not disturbed.

Cox swallowed hard. "We were riding back to town, and he was hit by lightning. Blew him right off his horse and killed him on the spot. Trent and Brewster said they were going to keep riding out of town and not stop until they hit California." He nodded his ugly head. "I think I should do the same." He hugged his long arms to himself and shivered. "It's cold in here. Are you cold?"

"Cowards, all of you," Vanessa said with a stomp of her foot, ignoring Cox's discomfort. "Matilda Candy is just one tiny woman, and four supposedly capable men can't manage to get rid of her! It appears she truly is in league with the devil."

A calmness came over Cox, and he sneered. "If anyone in Tanglewood is in league with the devil, it's you,
Miss Arrington. You have a black soul, a withered heart.
You didn't set this up so the rain would come, you
planned to have the witch burn because she angered you
in some way." He leaned closer to her. "Maybe you do
have a pretty face, but on the inside you're every bit as
ugly as I am on the outside."

Vanessa lifted her chin haughtily. No one had ever
spoken to her so rudely before! This had been a horrid
evening, and she would not stand here and abide such
insults from this hideous man. "Get out of my house, Mr.
Cox."

At that moment, a crack of thunder rattled the house.
Cox jumped. "Not yet. I don't intend to end up fried to
a crisp like Henry. Besides, I need a drink to warm me
up."

She would not waste a drop of her father's fine whiskey on this man. Still, perhaps he'd enjoy the cheap wine
Declan had brought over.

She led him into the parlor, where the bottle and two
glasses sat on a small table. After what she'd been
through tonight, she needed something bracing, herself.
She poured two full glasses and handed one to the so-
called rainmaker.

"What is this?" Cox asked as he sniffed at his glass.

"Elderberry wine," Vanessa said as she lifted her own
glass to her lips. The wine was sweet, common, but
rather tasty. And rather pretty, she conceded. It sparkled
and twinkled like a finely cut gem.

She drained her glass and so did Raleigh Cox.

Chapter Twenty-three

Declan lay, facedown, on the long table in Matilda's main room. Four lamps burned, lighting her way as she cut the wet, bloody shirt from his body.

Outside the storm continued, lashing the house with heavy rain, thunder, and lightning close and far. Matilda felt the storm inside her, too, as if it raged deep in her heart.

She'd found her gift, and as Granny has predicted, it had come when she needed it. But as she looked down at Declan's wounded body, she knew her so-called gift was worthless. She'd trade it in a heartbeat for the healing power another ancestor had possessed.

The bullet had entered his shoulder, and there was no exit wound. She would have to get the bullet out and stop the bleeding. She didn't have time to think about anything else.

She packed the wound to staunch the bleeding while she gathered her supplies: alcohol for sterilizing, a sharp knife, a pair of long tweezers, needle and thread, and more bandages. Once she had what she needed, she stood over Declan and held her breath as she removed the bandage.

"I can do this," she whispered.

"I know you can," he answered, his voice low and watery.

She'd thought he'd passed out, and almost wished she'd been right. She did not want to hurt Declan, but she was about to do just that.

"It doesn't look very deep," she said, trying to sound optimistic. Henry apparently hadn't wielded a powerful weapon; if he had, the bullet would've gone straight through, or else it would have buried itself even deeper in Declan's body. She shuddered at the thought.

"Matilda," Declan said, raising his hand to stop her as she leaned over him with the knife in her hand. "I have to tell you. . . ."

"Later," she interrupted. She didn't want to know what had happened tonight, didn't want to know how Vanessa had reacted upon taking the love potion.

"Now," he insisted.

She would not wait any longer, she would not stand here and watch Declan bleed to death. "Well, you'll just have to talk while I take out this bullet. I'm not going to stand here while you clear your conscience because you think I can't save you."

"Tonight," he whispered, "Vanessa sent for me, I . . ."

She held her breath and made a small cut so she could work the tweezers into the wound. Declan sucked in his breath, muttered a curse, and passed out.

"Just as well," Matilda said. "I don't think we want to discuss Vanessa while I have a knife to your back."

Vanessa no longer felt distressed by the evening's events. A strange serenity settled over her. A wondrous heat filled her, from the inside out. Raleigh Cox had calmed down himself, and sat in the wing chair by the window with his long legs stretched before him and his eyes closed. As she stared at him, he opened those eyes and set them on her. And smiled.

Raleigh didn't look so ugly when he smiled, even though his teeth were yellow and crooked and his lips were so thin they were almost nonexistent. There was something charming about his face at the moment, something very attractive. She smiled back.

"Would you care for more wine?" she asked, rising slowly and carrying the decanter to him. He lifted his empty glass, and she refilled it. As he carried the glass to his lips, she took a long swig straight from the decanter. This really was *very* good elderberry wine.

"What happened to your dress?" Raleigh asked, reaching up to boldly lay his long fingers over the stain on her bodice. The tips of his fingers touched her nipple, sending a spark of desire shooting through her body. She shuddered in response and closed her eyes.

"It's wine," she said weakly. "I spilled it."

He took the decanter from her and set it aside before pulling her onto his wet lap. Without a moment's hesitation he laid his wide mouth over the wine stain and sucked the nipple and the stained fabric into his mouth. Her knees went weak. She moaned aloud and closed her eyes.

She had always loved the way Johnny made her feel when he touched her, the excitement, the wickedness, the ultimate pleasure. But she had never spun out of control the way she did as Raleigh sucked and nibbled at her covered breast. Her hands shook to touch him, her insides quaked.

"You really should get out of these damp clothes," she said breathlessly, tearing at the buttons of Raleigh's shirt, pushing the wet fabric off his shoulders. "Why, it's no wonder that you're feeling a chill." She touched his skin eagerly, caressing his narrow shoulders, his hairless chest, his protruding ribs. He felt a little clammy, and indeed cold, but every breath she took made her want him more.

Her gown was low cut, as she'd planned to tease that fool Declan Harper to distraction. She was glad she'd chosen this gown for the evening, because right now, perched in Raleigh's lap and growing more excited with every passing heartbeat, all she had to do to free herself was tug the material a few inches lower. She heard a stitch or two pop, but paid no mind as the rainmaker's lips closed over her bare nipple and he sucked gently.

She melted against him, held his head, and guided him against her as he took her into his beautiful mouth. The caresses he lavished on her were exciting and satisfying— for a while. Soon she wanted more.

"Harder," she demanded. "Use your tongue and your teeth." He did.

She ran her fingers through his soggy hair, clasped his head and held him tightly to her breast. "That's right," she said, closing her eyes and reveling in the demand of his hungry mouth on her breast. She rocked against him. "Deeper," she whispered. "Don't be gentle with me, my love." He wasn't.

When Raleigh slowly took his mouth from her, she grasped his face in her hands and tilted his head back so she could lower her head and kiss his tempting lips. There was such power in his kiss, such wonderful promise. His mouth was wet, soft, irresistible. As she thrust her tongue deep into his mouth, she knew this was the man she'd waited for all her life, the man she was destined to be with.

"Make love to me," she whispered when she pulled her lips from his. "I want you to be my first. My first true lover, the first and only man to be inside me."

"What about that Johnny?" he whispered, distrust in his eyes.

She shook her head swiftly. "I . . . I did kiss him, on occasion," she explained, keeping her account simple.

Raleigh didn't need the details of her relationship with Johnny. "But I never allowed him to take a husband's liberties." She caught his eyes with hers and gave him her most seductive gaze. "I was saving that privilege for you."

Raleigh grinned and tossed up her skirt, reaching beneath the petticoats in an attempt to remove her drawers. He had a little difficulty accomplishing the task, as his cold hands shook with eagerness and need, but he did, finally, manage to loosen her tapes. His breathing was as labored as hers, and she could feel the thudding of his heart in his chest.

Raleigh stood, bringing her with him and guiding her to the sofa that sat in the middle of the parlor. With a wide grin, he spun her about and bent her over the back of the sofa so that she found her face against green brocade and had to come up on her toes to maintain her balance. He pitched up her skirt, and without ceremony yanked her drawers down so they pooled around her ankles. He caressed her bottom with cool, shaking hands.

"You have such smooth, white buttocks," he said, wonder in his voice as he stroked her bare backside. "I never saw the like." He stroked and caressed her bare bottom with strangely cool hands, stoking the fire inside Vanessa.

She trembled inside, quivering with need, impatient to have this man, her love, inside her. "Now, Raleigh," she demanded, spreading her legs as wide as she could manage. "Now!"

She waited anxiously, as Raleigh came up behind her and placed his body close to hers. "Don't you worry, sweetheart," he whispered gently. "I've been told I have a little willy, so this won't hurt you too much." He nestled himself against her. "Won't take but a minute," he added in a soothing, soft voice.

With a bumbling nudge and an awkward poke, Raleigh Cox put an end to the virginity Vanessa had guarded for so long. Without ceremony or fanfare it was over. Gone. There wasn't much pain, not much at all, as he plowed inside her. Vanessa hugged the sofa, closed her eyes, and waited for more.

"Again," she whispered huskily. "More." She prepared herself for ecstasy.

Raleigh withdrew almost completely and then thrust into her once more. Yes, that was more like it, she felt the beginnings of ecstasy, the promise of something wonderful. "Again," she whispered. "Harder." Without so much as another nudge, he pumped his seed into her, writhing and moaning as he grasped her hips and pulled her against him. And then he withdrew and backed away, leaving her hunched over the sofa with her drawers down around her ankles.

Confused and dismayed, supremely disappointed, Vanessa righted herself and turned to face Raleigh . . . and saw Johnny standing in the doorway.

She smiled. He didn't.

She didn't let Johnny's obvious repugnance bother her. No matter what quarrel had made him leave, he loved her, he always had. And he, she knew, did not have a *little willy*. He was young, and vigorous, and he had the stamina to put an end to the burning need inside her. He would finish what Raleigh had started.

"Johnny," she whispered, stepping forward. The step was a small one, since the drawers around her ankles impeded her. Cool air on her breast reminded her that the nipple Raleigh had suckled was still exposed. She righted the bodice quickly. "This is not what it seems to be." Out of the corner of her eye she saw Raleigh fasten his trousers and pull at his ripped shirt. He was dazed, smiling, paying no attention at all to her conversation.

Johnny stepped back into the hallway. "I heard what happened at Matilda's place tonight. Wendell and Reggie stopped by the saloon on their way out of town and told the most outrageous story. They said you planned the whole thing. Tell me it's not true." His blue eyes looked sad, angry, distant.

"She didn't die, so what difference does it make?" Vanessa said impatiently. She lowered her gaze to rest below his belt line and licked her lips. She glanced behind her to see that Raleigh sat in his chair, eyes closed. He looked like he was about to doze off, if he hadn't already. The dear man.

Johnny shook his head. "I can't believe I ever thought I loved you," he whispered. "I don't know you at all."

She gave him her most seductive smile. The smile that always drove him wild. "You still love me," she said softly. "You know you do." It was the one constant in her life. Johnny loved her; he would do anything for her.

He shook his head. "No. I don't love you anymore."

She didn't believe him. He had always loved her! She glanced at Raleigh to make sure he wasn't listening. He was not asleep, but sat in his chair with a stunned expression on his face as he fiddled absently with the shirt she'd ripped. She took a few small steps closer to Johnny, her normally graceful step hampered by the linen around her ankles.

Maybe she did love Raleigh, but at the moment she needed more. "I want you, Johnny," she whispered. "Make love to me."

If anything, the man who had always loved her looked more repulsed than before. "Good-bye, Vanessa," he said, and then he turned his back on her and walked away.

"But, Johnny . . ." she began. He didn't answer or even turn to look at her. He stalked to the front door and walked boldly into the storm. How dare he dismiss her like this! How dare he refuse her!

She sighed and wrinkled her nose, dismissing her former lover. She didn't love Johnny, she never had, but she would miss him.

Disappointed, she turned about to see Raleigh standing

before the sofa, two glasses of wine in his hands and a satisfied smile on his face. She forgot all about Johnny as she studied the majesty of Raleigh's tall, thin frame, the intensity of his pale eyes. Something in her heart lurched as she looked at him. This was love, real, true love as she'd never hoped to feel it.

It was a shock to realize that she'd do anything for this man. Anything! Her body throbbed in time with her heart as she kicked her drawers aside and joined him.

Matilda sat in a chair that had been pulled close to the table so she could see Declan's face. She'd removed the bullet, cleaned the wound, stitched the gaping hole shut, and bandaged it with some of Granny's favorite salve to prevent infection.

But still Declan didn't wake. She couldn't possibly move him to the bed by herself, and no matter what had happened here tonight, no one would be coming to help. The storm was too vicious, and once Henry and Wendell and Reggie and the rainmaker spread their tales and everyone knew their worst suspicions about Matilda Candy were true, she'd have no friends left who'd want to help, anyway.

At that thought, a crack of thunder shook the cottage. Still Declan didn't open his eyes.

She reached out and touched his cheek. There was no fever, not yet, but fever was likely later in the night, perhaps tomorrow. A little fever was all right, it would fight infection, but too much would be as hurtful as the bullet that had torn into his flesh.

"You came," she whispered, leaving her hand on his cheek. "I didn't think you would, I didn't dare even hope." Now that her work was done, she could admit how scared she'd been. She could not even imagine the kind of hate that Henry and the others had to possess. They would have gladly burned her alive tonight, with no regrets. They'd watched and proceeded with interest, but no misgivings. She didn't understand, she didn't *want* to understand.

She remembered screaming Declan's name, watching the storm move in, realizing that she was the one who'd brought the rain.

"Where will I go?" she whispered, expecting no answer. "I can't stay here, not now. Everyone will know what I am. Those who were suspicious before will be terrified of me. The few friends I managed to make won't want to have anything to do with me. And one night, more men like Henry will knock on my door and they'll try to kill me again. Maybe they'll succeed next time."

Where would she go? She didn't know, couldn't make plans right now. But she did know she couldn't stay here.

Declan slowly opened his eyes. She could see the puzzlement there, as he remembered all that had happened.

"How do you feel?" she whispered.

"I don't know," he mumbled, then his eyebrows scrunched together. "It hurts."

"When you can move, I want to get you to bed," Matilda said softly. "You need to sleep."

"I need to talk to you," he said hoarsely.

"Sleep first. Can you move?"

She used all her strength to support Declan as he left the table. He put his arm around her and leaned into her, and they walked, inching their way one slow step at a time toward the bedroom. Declan did not try to talk as they walked; she suspected it took every ounce of strength he had to remain on his feet. If he fell, she would not be able to catch him. He was too big, too heavy.

They reached the bed without incident, and Declan climbed in and laid, once again, on his stomach. He was unconscious before she could get the quilt over him.

"But you don't understand," Vanessa cooed as she set her empty glass aside and perched on Raleigh's knee, squirming gently. "I still want you. I still *need* you."

"Maybe tomorrow," he said, sleepy and satisfied.

Tomorrow? Not likely. "Now," she said reaching down to touch the limp bulge in his trousers. "You had your pleasure, now I want mine."

He smiled and speared his fingers through her hair, pulling her to him for a quick kiss that did not last nearly long enough to suit her. "My sweet, innocent Vanessa," he whispered. Oh, his voice was wonderful. Masculine, hypnotic, seductive. "Women don't enjoy intimate relations the way men do, especially not ladies like you. Female climax during the sex act is a myth."

She knew that wasn't true, but how could she tell him so without telling him details about her relationship with Johnny? She'd told him that they had only kissed, and he apparently believed that to be true. If she told him more, if she told him to do to her what Johnny had . . .

Maybe he wouldn't care about the past. Could she take that chance? At the moment she was terrified, *terrified,* that she might lose Raleigh. Life would not be worth living without him. "But Raleigh . . ."

"Darling." He laid his hand lovingly on her cheek. That hand was oddly cold, still. "I've been having relations with women for nigh onto twenty years. I've been with more than a hundred gals, and I've never seen it happen." He smiled. "Trust me. I know more about the intimate goings on between men and women than you do."

Judging by their quick encounter, she doubted that. And still, this was the man she wanted. She gave Johnny a brief second thought, but dismissed him without a qualm. That was over. She had Raleigh, now.

She expertly flicked open the buttons of his trousers and slipped her hand inside to find what she so desired. Yes, he did have a rather small male member, but as she stroked, he began to grow. A little. Men adored her, they gave her what she wanted. Always. Raleigh would be no different.

"I can feel an extraordinary sensation growing inside me, Raleigh," she whispered, biting lightly on his ear. "I'm almost there, I'm on the edge of something powerful and wondrous."

She took Raleigh's hand and very gently, as if she were shy, placed it between her spread legs. "Touch me," she commanded. "Stroke me where I burn for you." He did nothing. "If you'd like, you can kiss me there," she whispered.

"Oh, Vanessa, I couldn't ever . . ." Raleigh sputtered, but he did grow harder in her hand.

"Yes, you can."

His hand lay motionless between her legs, when what she longed for was a masterful stroke that would bring her to completion. He seemed not to know what to do with what he held in his hands. No matter. His manhood grew with every passing heartbeat, as she stroked and plucked and teased. Soon she would have what she wanted.

"Make love to me again, Raleigh," she commanded, tossing her annoying skirt up and whipping one leg around so she straddled him, bringing his arousal closer to the aching need that burned deeper and harder than she'd ever imagined it could. Stroking to make him grow. "I love you. I want you inside me again. And again. And again."

Raleigh's eyes rolled back in his head. His lips quivered and a touch of saliva dribbled down his chin. Vanessa continued to stroke, since he was not yet completely hard. She'd touched Johnny this way a thousand times. This was *not* what an aroused man was supposed to feel like. But Raleigh twitched, and grew, and hardened. As she stroked, she had great hopes that soon . . . soon . . . yes, *now*.

Without warning, Raleigh spent himself outside her body, dripping spittle from his lips and bucking beneath her before she had a chance to guide his arousal into her eager body. Just as she was about to scream in frustration, someone screamed for her.

"Vanessa!"

She glanced over her shoulder. "Daddy?"

Chapter Twenty-four

Declan opened his eyes at the sound of a clap of nearby thunder. Almost at the same instant a flash of lightning lit the night sky and the room in which he rested.

Matilda sat on the floor at his bedside, her face lifted to watch him. In the twinkling of white light that streaked through the room, she looked ghostly.

"You're awake," she whispered as the room returned to near darkness. A single lamp, on the floor beside Matilda, burned low.

His eyelids were heavy, his body warm. "Not for long, I'm afraid."

"Sleep," she whispered. "You need your rest."

"Not yet," he breathed.

Matilda came up on her knees, placing her face close to his. She still wore wet clothes, her hair hung in damp, waving strands around her face, and there were streaks of blood, his he imagined, on her blouse. He remembered how he'd found her tonight, and his heart damn near stopped.

"I couldn't do it," he said, reaching out to touch her face.

"There's no need to talk now," she insisted. "Rest tonight. Tomorrow we'll talk."

He tried to shake his head and found he could not. "Now, Matilda. Tonight, when I sat across from Vanessa Arrington and watched her lift that potion to her lips, I suddenly realized that nothing in the world, not even the revenge I've dreamed of all my life, is worth the sacrifice I was willing to make."

"You decided too late," she whispered.

Again he tried to shake his head and couldn't. "No. I knocked the glass out of her hand before she could drink. I was coming here for you even before the twins burst in and told me what was happening."

"You were?"

He was able to nod gently.

Tears filled her eyes. He had never seen her cry before; she was so strong, so damned tough.

Maybe not so tough, after all. "It doesn't matter," she said, tears in her voice. "Granny was right. I'm a witch, Declan. I made it rain."

"Doesn't matter," he said weakly.

"Doesn't matter?" she snapped, her voice soft and angry. "I can't stay here. I can't get married, I can't fall in love, I can't have children. . . ."

"Why not?"

"Because I'm a freak," she whispered. "I can make it snow in July, I can bring on storms that will wash Tanglewood away, thunder that shakes the strongest house." Her voice cracked. "I will never be normal, I will never have an ordinary life."

"Normal is highly overrated," Declan said, trying to keep the tone of his strained voice light. "Ordinary is boring."

She didn't argue with him, but she didn't agree, either. "Get to sleep."

285

"Do you still love me, Matilda?" Declan asked as he closed his eyes. He had to know if he'd ruined everything, if he'd come to his senses too late.

She hesitated, and then laid her hand on his cheek. "I can't. I want to, Declan, I really do. But I can't love you or anyone else."

He would be crushed, if he didn't hear the hurt and the lie in her voice. She did love him, still. Somehow everything was going to be all right. He fell asleep with her hand on his cheek.

Vanessa and Raleigh were married in the Arrington parlor that very night, as outside the storm raged around them. Vanessa wore her white gown with the wine stain and Raleigh's saliva over one breast. She distantly noticed the stain and the way her skirt hung askew and the way her hair fell in disarray around her face. Her drawers remained on the floor nearby where she'd kicked them a while ago.

Raleigh wore a torn shirt and trousers that had been ripped at the seams as she'd reached impatiently inside them to arouse him. His hair had dried in long, stringy wisps that touched his narrow shoulders. He was oddly beautiful. All throughout the ceremony he seemed chilled, shivering without warning on occasion and leaning into her to steal her warmth.

Neither of them minded the wicked storm that shook the house, any more than they minded the impromptu wedding performed by a waterlogged minister while Warren Arrington glared at them with pure hatred in his eyes. Once the ceremony was over, Vanessa's father kicked her out of the house, ordering her never to return. She took none of her personal belongings with her, didn't even think to take what little was left of the elderberry wine Declan had provided. She didn't mind that she had left her home with nothing; she had Raleigh, and she loved him madly.

They spent their wedding night in the back of his wagon, a few miles down the road where the storm was not so fierce. The wagon leaked; their marriage bed consisted of wet, scratchy wool blankets. The only light was the occasional flash of lightning, creeping through the many cracks in the wagon.

With water dripping all around them, they sat on damp blankets, kissing and touching and whispering sweet words. A new and stronger surge of love shot through Vanessa as she held her husband.

Raleigh said he was too cold to undress completely, but he did free himself when she requested a proper marriage bedding of him. Whispering that he was ever mindful of her comfort, he was quick and to the point. Their first time together as man and wife was over too quickly—again. He fell asleep beside her, satisfied and exhausted, shivering with a chill he should not have on a night as warm as this one.

Vanessa curled against her husband and tried to be satisfied. Love would be enough, wouldn't it? She didn't need anything so common as physical pleasure, she didn't have to reach the heights of ecstasy Johnny had introduced her to in order to be truly happy.

Raleigh snored in her ear and twitched in his sleep, and no matter where Vanessa positioned herself rainwater dripped onto some part of her body. No she didn't need fulfillment to be happy, but her insides did quake so.

She would teach Raleigh how to pleasure her, she decided. She would tutor him until he was the consummate lover. Eventually she fell into a fitful sleep.

Just before dawn, she cried out her new husband's name in her sleep.

By midmorning of the day following the coming of the storm, the thunder and lightning ceased. By midafternoon the drenching turned into a steady rain that fell constantly but not with blinding force.

Matilda stared out her bedroom window, curtain lifted in her hand. From here she could see the stake, which had fallen in the night thanks to a softening of the ground and the stream of water that ran over the base. Most of the kindling had burned away, but a few charred logs had planted themselves firmly in the mud along the stream, reminders that last night had been real. Not a nightmare, but an indisputable fact.

"Come away from there," Declan muttered hoarsely.

She dropped the curtain and turned around. He slept on his stomach, still, but had his face turned toward her. "I thought you were asleep."

"I was." He grimaced.

"You're hurting," she whispered.

"A little." He shifted and tried to work himself into a sitting position.

"Don't move. I have a tea that will ease the pain." She placed her hand on his arm as she commanded him to stay.

He grabbed her wrist and held her there. "I don't want any damned tea that will numb my pain or my mind. We have too much to talk about."

"We have nothing to talk about," she whispered. When he looked at her this way she remembered why she loved him. The rain pattering on the roof reminded her why she couldn't love him, not anymore.

"Did you really make it rain?" he asked. "I remember last night, looking at you and being so sure you did, but now . . ."

"By the light of day it seems impossible, doesn't it?" she whispered. Declan was a no-nonsense man; he would convince himself, if it suited his purposes, that he'd imagined everything he'd seen last night.

This time when he tried to sit up, she helped him, adding her strength to his, holding on to him as he held on to her. When he was positioned against the headboard, his weight on his good shoulder and his legs stretched to the end of the bed, she left him there and returned to the window. She parted the curtains and looked out at the rain that fell straight and steady, soaking the ground and feeding the streams that crossed her yard, and doubtless the roads and the farms and the town of Tanglewood, as well.

She closed her eyes and reached inside herself and found that place she'd discovered last night, in her anger and desperation. It was a dark place, and she was afraid to go there. But she did, because she knew Declan too well. There was no other way.

She thought *cold* until she felt it to her bones. She pictured ice until she shivered with the chill. The cold was a part of her, the way the storm was a part of her. She whispered *snow* and opened her eyes to see the rain outside her window turn to soft white flakes.

And then she stepped aside, the curtain held back to offer Declan a wide view. "You cannot argue with this," she whispered.

From his reclining position on the bed, he stared at the July snow. She waited for the fear that would surely come to his handsome face, the tension that told her he was afraid of her, as they all surely would be. But he only lifted his eyebrows in surprise and leaned slightly forward, narrowing his eyes.

"I'll be damned," he muttered.

It took concentration to maintain the abnormal snow, and as Matilda watched Declan, the snow turned to rain again.

He laid his eyes on her as she let the curtain fall closed. "Your gift," he whispered. "It appears your grandmother was right."

"A gift," she said softly. "How can you call this a gift? Making potions and salves and teas is one thing, but controlling the weather? I don't want to be a freak, Declan."

"You're not a freak," he insisted angrily.

He might say that now, but she knew that if she tried to pretend nothing had changed, one day she'd wake up and find him looking at her the way Henry had last night, when he'd realized what she could do. What a mistake he'd made in loving her.

"I'll get you that tea," she said, turning to leave the room.

Declan stopped her at the door. "Speaking of teas and potions," he said, not quite casually. "I'm afraid I ran out of the Arrington house last night and left your love potion sitting on an end table in the parlor. I didn't even think to grab it."

"I doubt anyone in the Arrington household would lower themselves to drink elderberry wine by choice," she said softly. "I'm sure it's too common. Odds are it's still sitting there, untouched."

"And if it's not?"

"Do you think I care what happens to Vanessa Arrington?" Matilda snapped. Her heart lurched, in spite of her protests. "When the rain stops, I'll go there and see if I can get it back."

"When will the rain stop, Matilda?" Declan asked.

Her eyes filled with tears as she answered. "I don't know."

He couldn't have asked for a better doctor. A mild fever came and went, Matilda forced tea and broth on him, changed his bandage frequently, and he grew stronger every day.

This afternoon he sat with her at the long table, eating a more substantial soup than she'd allowed him to have in the past three days.

The rain continued, but it had lessened to a drizzle. Still, three days of a steady drizzle brought a substantial amount of rain. Puddles filled the land around Matilda's cottage, rivulets ran through her garden; the sun never peeked through.

Matilda was determined to leave this place as soon as Declan was recovered. She wanted to go on her own before she was run out of town, before someone else showed up with a stake and a box of matches.

She started when someone knocked on the door, her head snapping up and her eyes widening.

"I'll get it," he said, standing slowly.

"No." She laid a hand on his shoulder and forced him gently back into his seat. "I'm not going to be afraid forever, I'm not going to panic every time someone knocks on my door." She looked down at him with big, vulnerable, strangely beautiful eyes. "I can't, can I?"

He shook his head. "I'm here, remember," he said softly. Matilda actually smiled. It was a weak attempt, but the first he'd seen in quite a while.

Stella Hazelrig blew into the room as soon as Matilda opened the door, drops flying off her yellow oilskin as she pushed back the hood.

"Are you all right?" Stella asked, laying a hand on Matilda's arm. "Good heavens." She removed her wet oilskin and hung it on the coat hook by the door. "I would have been here sooner, but Seth refused to let me leave the house until the rain stopped. I finally convinced him it had slowed enough to be safe. I took the children's path through the woods. Mercy, I couldn't wait another minute to talk to you."

Stella's mood had been nothing but friendly, but Declan could see that Matilda expected the worst to come.

"I'm so sorry I didn't believe the children when they came to me and told me what was happening." The always-sensible Stella teared up. "I just couldn't believe anyone would . . ." She turned to Declan. "I'm so glad they found you in time."

She reached out and gave Matilda a hug, a move that

so startled Matilda, she jumped and stiffened before placing her arms around Stella and squeezing back. They didn't part quickly, but stayed there for a long moment. Finally Matilda let out a sob and allowed herself to cry.

Declan was a little jealous that Matilda let her friend comfort her in a way she wouldn't allow him to. It was as if she didn't completely trust him anymore, as if there was something between them that kept them apart. He wanted to be everything to her—friend, lover, husband. If only she'd let him.

Matilda and Stella both cried, bawling openly as they held on to each other. Declan looked down at his soup, feeling like an intruder in a private moment. The tears did not last long, and when they were done the girls parted and amazingly enough they both smiled. Matilda fetched a couple of handkerchiefs from a drawer and handed one to her friend.

Stella sat in the rocking chair and wiped her eyes. "Matilda, the most outrageous stories are circulating. They're saying *you* made it rain." She shook out her handkerchief. "Isn't that ridiculous?"

"No," Matilda answered without hesitation. "It's the truth."

Stella lifted her face, giving Matilda an expression of sheer disbelief. "How is that possible?"

Matilda shrugged her shoulders and turned around so she would not have to face her friend. "I'm a witch, like my grandmother before me and all the other female ancestors in that branch of my family tree. I just didn't know what my particular gift was until . . . until I needed it. And now I have to leave. It was bad enough when a few vague suspicions surrounded me, but this . . . this is different."

Stella opened her mouth to argue, then snapped it shut and pursed her lips thoughtfully. She looked at Declan, and at Matilda, and at the floor. Finally she said, "Who will believe such a thing is possible? Who will listen to those tales? Declan is the only one who was here that night who's still around."

"Where are they?" Matilda asked, her voice low.

"Reggie Brewster and Wendell Trent left town that night," Stella scoffed. "And good riddance, I say. Two good-for-nothings, that's what they are. Henry Langford was struck by lightning," she said matter-of-factly. "I consider that to be justice, myself," she said without sympathy for the dead man.

Matilda went pale. "I killed him."

"You did not!" Stella and Declan said at the same time.

"I did," she insisted. "Not on purpose, but I certainly *did* kill him. I brought the storm, and he was struck by lightning." She laid her eyes on Declan. "He shot you, and I was so angry. Maybe deep inside I wished him dead," she whispered, "and my storm killed him."

"Nonsense," Stella said. "I cast my vote for the Lord's justice, and will not be swayed."

"What about the rainmaker?" Declan asked, anxious to change the subject. "He was here, too."

Stella, wide eyed, leaned forward in her chair. "This is the most delicious part of the story," she said in a lowered voice. "Warren Arrington got home during the storm to find his daughter, that uppity Vanessa, in a . . ." she blushed, "Shall we say a compromising position? With the rainmaker. That ugly man! Can you believe it? Arrington sent a servant to fetch the preacher in the rain, and made sure Vanessa and the rainmaker were married then and there." She leaned back in some kind of triumph. "And then he kicked them out."

Matilda caught and held Declan's gaze. They both knew what had happened. The love potion.

"So you see, you have nothing to worry about. The tales Reggie and Wendell told before they left town were dismissed as hogwash as soon as everyone found out what they'd been a part of. They're all so sorry, Matilda."

"But it's true," Matilda whispered. "I brought the rain. I made it snow."

No-nonsense Stella laid her eyes on Matilda. "I don't believe you'd lie, so I must accept what you tell me. You really made it rain?"

Matilda nodded.

"Can you make it stop? The town's not flooded yet, but the roads are all but impassable and a few farms are about ready to start floating."

Matilda sat in the wing chair. He saw the energy leave her, as if a gust of wind had blown it away. "I don't know how," she whispered. "I don't know if I can make it stop or not."

"Have you tried?" Stella asked.

Matilda laid her eyes on Declan, apologizing, grieving, scared. "For the past two days," she whispered.

Chapter Twenty-five

It had been raining a full week; at least, it would be a full week in two hours or so. The rain still fell, an endless drizzle, and most of the land around the cottage was covered in puddles that grew together until her yard looked like a lake, or another spring-fed pond.

Declan was well enough to leave the cottage. He pretended that he was not, but he couldn't fool her. He stayed out of guilt, she knew, afraid that if he left she'd immediately disappear. He wasn't quite ready to say good-bye. Neither was she, to be honest.

She'd tried to make the rain stop, she really had, but nothing seemed to work. She tried to think and feel dry, and picture the sun, and she tried to feel the warmth inside her the way she'd felt the storm. Nothing worked. She suspected that until her heart stopped crying, the rain would continue.

And she didn't know if her heart would ever stop.

"Get away from the window," Declan muttered.

She turned as he rose from his chair, illuminated by

the small fire he'd started to warm the room. A fire should not be necessary, not in the first days of August, but the lack of sun for a week had seemed to sap the warmth from everything.

"Why can't I make it stop?" she whispered.

"It'll stop, eventually." He didn't seem concerned, but he *had* to be. Of course, he didn't know what she'd screamed at her attackers the night they'd tried to burn her at the stake; he didn't know that she'd screamed in anger that the rain would never stop.

"I don't want to be a witch," she whispered, fighting down the panic. "I know this doesn't make any sense to you, but when I thought it wasn't true I didn't mind what people believed. When I thought I had no powers and never would, the rumors didn't bother me. They were just . . . silly rumors. Now that I know it's true, I'm terrified."

Declan crossed the room and turned her about so she could no longer look out the window at the ceaseless rain. "Witch is just a name," he said, his hands on her shoulders. "You have a gift, a power no one understands. If you feel you must mark yourself with a title to explain away your gift, why not call yourself an enchantress, or a healer. Or a rainmaker."

"I just want to be a woman," she said softly.

Declan smiled at her, that heart-grabbing grin that warmed her from the inside out and made her think maybe she could love him, no matter what.

"Matilda Candy, you are a woman first and foremost. Never doubt that for a moment."

He kissed her, wrapping his arms around her so she couldn't move away, trapping her warmly in his embrace and kissing her so softly and sweetly she felt as if she were melting.

In that moment she forgot that she was a witch and a rainmaker, and let herself be the woman she wanted to be. She allowed herself to love Declan, for now.

They undressed each other without hurry, lingering over long kisses and stopping on occasion to let their hands roam over newly exposed flesh. It had been so long—a hundred years surely—since they'd touched each other intimately; it seemed as if they were making love for the first time. She wanted to savor every passing second.

Declan lay down on the rug in front of the dying fire, drawing her down with him. Completely unclothed they lay there face-to-face, her leg cocked over his, his hands roaming over her flesh as if he'd never touched her before.

With her face against his neck she whispered *I love you*, so softly he could surely not hear her. She couldn't keep him, so she couldn't make that confession. Not now, not ever. But they could have tonight; they would always have tonight.

Declan rolled onto his back and tugged her along, guiding her with patient hands until she rested on his chest. She straddled him so that his arousal touched her intimately, setting off a shower of sparks inside her.

He rocked up, barely entering her. She pushed down, forcing him deeper inside her, closing her eyes to savor the way their bodies fit together.

They made love slowly, relishing every moment, every long, easy stroke. She leaned forward and kissed him deeply, and still her hips moved against his in a rhythm that was timeless and primal, as love and lust mingled into one delicious bundle.

Deep inside, she grew warm, wonderfully, delightfully warm. There were no worries here, no regrets. Her heart was full, her body—and soul—had found its mate, and nothing else mattered. Nothing.

As the need grew, their pace increased. She closed her eyes and allowed herself to feel, just *feel*. Every plunge took Declan deeper inside her than before, every stroke carried her closer to completion.

She cried out when her release hit her, shaking her from the inside out, shattering her into a million pieces. Declan found his own on the ebbing waves of hers, pumping his seed into her as she milked him with trembling muscles.

Depleted, happy for the moment, she dissolved atop him, sinking down, lying on his chest and taking a deep breath. Her heart pounded, her body trembled. She did not think she would ever move from this spot. She certainly didn't want to.

Declan's hand settled in her hair, threaded in the tangled strands. "Marry me," he whispered. It wasn't a question, it was a command.

"I can't."

"Don't say you don't love me."

She shook her head but said nothing.

"We belong together."

She lifted her head and looked down at him. In the firelight, his eyes were warmer than usual, deeper and more tempting. But she knew who she was, and she knew full well what she could not have.

"No," she whispered. "You're done with Tanglewood, Declan. You have no more reason to stay here. Arrington knows who you are, and you will never, ever be king."

She saw the anger in his eyes, the hurt. "Maybe I don't want to be king."

"That's all you want," she argued. "It's why you're here. I knew it the first time I saw you. If it doesn't happen in Tanglewood, you will make it happen somewhere else."

He laid his hand on her cheek. "With you."

She shook her head. "No. I will never marry, I will never have children, I will never be the kind of woman you need as your wife." Arguing with him made her angry all over again.

"What if there's already a baby?" he whispered. "What if we made one just now?"

"We didn't," she answered lowly, knowing he would hate her when she told him what she'd done. "I've been taking a special tea to prevent such an occurrence."

That news angered him. She saw the pain and rage in his eyes and the set of his jaw. "Since when?"

"Since the morning after the first time we tested a love potion that wasn't really a love potion. I knew you and I would, eventually . . . maybe I just hoped," she whispered. "In any case, I thought it wise to be cautious, since I knew there was no future for us." She'd known all along that Declan was a bright and wonderful gift she could not keep, hadn't she? She'd fooled herself into thinking otherwise, now and again. Too many times, to be honest. "I knew you wouldn't stay," she whispered. "No matter what you said, no matter what I wanted, I always knew we wouldn't end up together."

"So this is it, huh?" he asked angrily, a trace of grief in his voice. "What we had was just . . . temporary, and now we're finished."

She nodded.

He closed his eyes, but a moment later they flew open. "Do you hear that?"

"What?" All she heard was the crackle of the fire, Declan breathing, her heart pounding.

"The rain's stopped."

She stood slowly and went to the window. Moonlight shone on still puddles. "You're right." A few clouds danced across the sky, but already they were breaking apart, drifting away.

She turned as Declan was standing, the task made only slightly difficult by his healing injury. "You can leave in the morning."

He pinned his eyes on her. "I can, can I?"

"It would be for the best. I know the roads will be a mess, but Stella said they found your horse the morning after the storm began. It's a quick walk through the woods to their place, and from there you should be able

299

to make it back to town. Or wherever you're headed."

"You have this all thought out," he muttered beneath his breath.

I've thought of nothing else. "I suppose I do."

"You have everything figured out, so nice and tidy," he snapped. "Are you leaving?"

She shook her head. "Not right away, at least. I'll see how things go. Stella seems to think no one believes the stories about me bringing the rain. I'm not sure I believe that, but if I can stay here for a while longer, I will." She looked around the room. "I have so many things here. I'd hate to leave them behind, if I have another choice."

"So you don't want to leave your *things* behind, but you don't mind tossing me out on my ear," Declan snapped, reaching for his clothes. "Fine, Matilda. I think I know when I'm not wanted."

Not wanted? Heaven help her, she wanted Declan most of all. She watched him dress in his trousers and the shirt she'd washed and mended as best she could. He even gathered his shoes and socks from the other room and sat down in the wing chair to put them on.

He was leaving. Now. "You can wait until morning."

"Why? We're done, right? Why the hell should I stick around and torture myself."

"You'll get lost," she argued weakly.

He laughed at her, but there was no humor in that harsh laughter. "I used to live on the Hazelrig property, remember? There's moonlight to light the path, muddy as it might be."

She gathered her own clothes, feeling suddenly vulnerable and very *naked.*

"Have Doc Daly take out your stitches in a couple of days. Or another doctor," she added quickly, "if you're not in Tanglewood."

Declan didn't answer, but left the cottage with a slam of the door. He didn't even say good-bye.

*   *   *

Vanessa and Raleigh traveled and lived in his wagon. It rained often in the three weeks following their marriage, dampening their bed, but Vanessa didn't mind. The wagon didn't ride smoothly; it jerked and lurched and bounced its way down the road. Vanessa didn't mind.

Every night for those three weeks Raleigh performed his husbandly duties in the back of the wagon with the same ineptitude and brevity and awkwardness he had called upon on the night he'd taken her virginity. She *did* mind, but not very much. She loved him dearly, and she was sure that with a little patience and time he would learn to pleasure her.

She tried to teach him, she tried to *direct* him, but he was oddly resistant to her simplest request.

He often seemed to be cold, the chills usually coming at night and most often when it was raining outside their leaky home. When the chills came, he buried himself beneath every blanket they owned, and still he shivered. Sometimes Vanessa touched him and felt the unnatural chill, as if she'd married an icicle.

Three weeks to the day after they left Tanglewood, they each suffered a moment of painful clarity. Vanessa opened her eyes one morning to discover that she slept next to an ugly, odious, despicable man who had no real skills or ambitions and was probably the worst lover in the Western hemisphere.

Raleigh's moment came an hour or so later, as they rode down the bumpy road. He found himself married to a shrew who could not manage to keep her mouth shut for longer than it took her to take a deep breath, a woman he would never be able to satisfy.

Vanessa was tempted to beg a ride home and throw herself at her father's feet and beg his forgiveness. After the past three weeks dressed in the same raggedy, stained dress, living in a wagon for God's sake, she was not too good for a little begging.

Raleigh was tempted to dump his shrew of a wife by the side of the road, but he didn't. She was his responsibility now, like it or not. By noon Vanessa felt a hint of love again, a shadow of the passion that had driven her to Raleigh on a bad, stormy night, and she forgot why she'd been so morose all morning. Raleigh felt a swelling tide of love before suppertime, and forgot why he'd ever been unhappy with his beautiful bride. He made up for his hurtful words in the back of the wagon after they'd shared a plate of beans. He loved and wanted her so much, all he had to do was look at her to be ready. One quick thrust inside her and he spent his seed.

He told Vanessa he loved her and tried to go to sleep, hoping that in the years to come they would not have bad days like this one, days when the love seemed to disappear like fog in the sun. When, just as he was drifting off, Vanessa punched him in the shoulder and uttered a filthy curse, he knew his hope was most likely in vain.

They did not know it yet, but by that time Vanessa was already carrying Raleigh's child, the first of nine she would bear him in the years to come.

They would all look just like their father.

Two weeks of sunshine and mild, windless nights repaired the landscape in and around Tanglewood. The farmland that had not been washed away by the storm survived, and some of the crops thrived. The rain had come just in time.

Matilda learned all this from Stella, who dropped by the cottage at least twice a week. Matilda had no desire to leave her cottage, not just yet. She was afraid, still, to look into the faces of the residents of Tanglewood, afraid that Stella was wrong, and they knew she really was a witch. And hated her.

She continued to make bread and candies and beauty supplies for Mr. Fox, but she did not deliver them herself. For a price—coins and candy—Gretchen and Hanson de-

livered two baskets full for her, on Friday as usual. The
twins had been especially obliging lately.

They had confessed to Matilda their part in that terrible
day, but she had forgiven them. She could not forget that
they had saved her life, and she knew she would never
be able to repay them.

They no longer called her witch, at least not where she
could hear.

Warren Arrington had apparently developed a sudden
passion for his cook, Lettie Mae Pickles. He'd pursued
her for a full week, courted her unrelentingly, Stella said.
Last she'd heard Lettie Mae had finally consented to be
his wife, and her five brothers—pig farmers from just
outside Jackson—moved into the big Arrington house,
bringing their wives and children, and a few favorite
pigs, with them. They had already turned the place upside down.

She was glad that Arrington had gotten his comeuppance, even though it had not come in the way Declan
had hoped.

Matilda had not asked about Declan, did not dare, but
Stella had informed her that he continued to reside at the
boardinghouse. There was no reason for him to stay, unless he had more plans for Arrington. Surely he would
soon realize that there was nothing more he could do,
and he'd move on. Eventually.

What had she given up in her fear? Afraid of what the
future might hold, she'd practically kicked Declan, her
only chance for a normal life, out of her house. Maybe
it had been a mistake, the worst of her life, but she would
never know for sure. Declan was too proud to come back,
begging her to change her mind, and she was too afraid
of what he'd say to walk to Tanglewood and confront
him.

Besides, a man as ambitious as Declan Harper didn't
need a witch as his wife, he needed a lady. Someone he
could be proud of. All they'd ever had was a secret sex-

ual relationship. He probably thanked his lucky stars every day that she'd refused his impulsive marriage proposal.

So why was he still in Tanglewood?

Gretchen and Hanson arrived right on time, bright and early on this Friday morning.

"What did you make this week?" Hanson asked brightly.

"Toffee, caramels, spiced nuts, dried orange peels, and hard molasses candy," Matilda said, checking the contents of the two baskets on the long table.

Hanson nodded his head in approval. "That's a lot."

She didn't want to explain to the child that she could not bear to sit still, that as long as she kept her hands busy she had less time to brood. "Well, Mr. Fox has been asking me for months to increase the stock. Besides," she laid a hand in Hanson's hair. "I have to make extra to keep you in good supply."

Gretchen stood by the door. "You look very pretty today," she said.

"Thank you."

"Your hair is very pretty, down instead of in pigtails. I wish my hair was wavy like that and not so curly," she added.

"Your hair is perfect," Matilda said with a smile. "Many a woman works hard and long to fashion curls like yours upon her head."

Gretchen actually blushed. Goodness, in a few years she would be a lovely young woman. "That's what Mother says."

They had finally taken to calling Stella "Mother." All would be well in their house in no time, Matilda was certain. Especially once the fall session of school began.

Matilda handed the children their baskets and opened the door. They stepped outside, but before they could proceed, Gretchen spun around, a patently false expression of surprise on her face. "What's this?"

Matilda stepped into the sunlight and turned her eyes toward the road. Shadow, the mare Declan had given her, was tied to the hitching post. Yellow silk ribbons had been woven into her mane, along with a few white flowers. Beyond the mare there were a few red rose petals, arranged in a line on the ground and leading toward the road to town, a trail of some sort. Matilda walked to the mare and laid her hand on Shadow's shoulder. From here she could see that the trail of red rose petals continued down the road.

"I think you're supposed to follow the trail," Gretchen whispered.

"Do you?"

"Yes!" Hanson said.

Only Declan would have left this trail. Who knew where it led, what would be waiting at the other end?

She sent the children on, and they ran toward town. When they had disappeared down the path of rose petals, she went inside her cottage and closed the door.

Declan was waiting at the other end of that trail, she was sure of it.

There was no reason for her to follow the trail of rose petals, no reason to seek out Declan. There was nothing left between them. Right? He needed to move on, and so did she. Right? Maybe he simply wanted to say good-bye.

It took her no more than a few minutes to decide to follow the trail and see what Declan had waiting at the end. He was her weakness, and to see him one more time . . .

She was not going to meet him in this brown skirt and old homespun blouse! She fetched her yellow skirt, which was wide enough for riding without exposing her legs, and a white blouse with lace around the collar and sleeves.

And shoes! She went to the chest for her bronze shoes,

305

but to her dismay there was only one where the pair should've been. The other was lost. Gone. There was no time to look for it now. She grabbed her new black shoes and decided they would do.

She mounted Shadow with great care, and guided the mare down the road, her eyes on the trail of roses. Perhaps around the bend they would lead her into the woods, and Declan would be waiting there for one last kiss.

She knew she shouldn't be excited at the prospect of seeing Declan again, but she couldn't help herself. No matter what had happened—what was yet to happen— she did love him. She was afraid, she was shaken to her bones with fear, but the love remained.

The trail of rose petals changed from red to peach, and they continued on the road. They did not turn toward the woods or vary in any way. The trail was straight and certain, and it led her unerringly into town. The peach petals ended, and yellow took their place. She could see Tanglewood ahead, as the trail of rose petals turned to white.

On the main street, the rose petals were replaced by wildflowers of every color, whole flowers and different shaped petals in yellow, pink, lavender, and white. Matilda lifted her head, and there ahead, in the middle of the street, stood Declan Harper in his finest suit. A circle of red rose petals in the street surrounded him.

He stood on the street like he owned it, tall and proud, commanding and composed. Today he did not squirm in his suit, but seemed quite comfortable with himself.

Most everyone in Tanglewood stood on the boardwalk and watched as she continued at a slow pace toward Declan. They watched as if they waited anxiously for . . . for something spectacular. She was afraid to look anyone in the eye. Her heart was in her throat, beating much too hard.

She dismounted in the middle of the street, and Hanson hurried forward to take Shadow from her. She smiled down at him. "What is this? You knew, didn't you?"

He just smiled and led Shadow away.

She walked toward Declan, hesitating only briefly before joining him in the circle. "What on earth have you done?" she whispered, not wanting everyone watching to hear.

"Matilda Candy, a woman like you deserves to be courted, but I am not a patient man."

"Declan . . ."

He brought his hands from behind his back. Red roses were offered in one hand, a familiar tin containing ginger candy in the other. "Being impatient, I decided to do it all at once. Flowers, candy . . ." he met her gaze. "Anything you want."

When she did not take the offered items, he placed them on the ground at her feet. "You accused me of some terrible things, the night I left," he whispered, leaning close so only she could hear.

"Declan," she pleaded hoarsely, "we can't have this discussion *here*."

He was not dissuaded. "It hurt to hear those words, but some of your accusations were too close to the truth. You were right, Matilda. I hid you, like a guilty pleasure I didn't want to share. You were the secret of my heart, my sanctuary in a world I couldn't control. I cherished you, but I did not want to share you or what I felt with anyone.

"When you told me you were taking a tea to keep you from having my baby, I was furious. It was my pride, I guess," he said sheepishly. "I felt rejected, and I took my heartache out on you. About halfway to the Hazelrig place I realized what I'd done." He reached out and touched her face. "So I asked everyone to be here today to watch me do this. No more hiding, Matilda."

He knelt before her and took her hand in his.

"Get up," she whispered.

He smiled at her and shook his head. "No. I'm going

to ask you to marry me, and I'm going to do it right."
He raised his voice. It was as if he wanted everyone in
town to hear, to see.

"Declan," she breathed.

"Matilda Candy, I love you. I'm asking in front of all
these people. Will you marry me?"

She opened her mouth to refuse, but he continued, not
giving her the chance.

"I must warn you, before you answer, that I don't have
much to offer. I foolishly lost almost everything gambling, a vice I have since given up," he added.

"I'm glad to hear it."

"I did once own a number of general stores and saloons out west, but I have recently made gifts of them
to my sisters and their husbands."

"Declan! You gave away everything you worked so
hard for?"

"All but two saloons, which I sold. I used the proceeds
from those sales to buy this." He lifted his free hand and
pointed to Fox's General Store, which now sported a new
sign. Harper's General Store. "That's all I have," he said.
"I've been living in the room upstairs for the last week."
He leaned forward and lowered his voice. "Where one
bronze shoe rests under my bed. I figured it couldn't
hurt."

"How did you . . . you haven't been . . ."

"The Hazelrig twins have been quite helpful," he
added in a low voice.

His face became deadly serious, and his grip on her
hand tightened. "You told me once that love is not the
end, it's the beginning."

"I did," she whispered.

"You were right. I'm starting over, Matilda. Come
with me. Let this be our beginning."

She looked down at him and smiled. This was more
than she could've hoped for, everything she wanted.

"How can I refuse an offer like that one?" She did not

pull him to his feet, but dropped to her knees and threw her arms around his neck. "Yes," she breathed into his ear. "I love you so much."

Someone on the boardwalk shouted out his approval, and soon others chimed in.

Matilda pulled back slightly so she could see Declan's face. "Your daughters will be witches," she whispered.

He grinned at her as if he wasn't at all bothered by the fact. "Your sons will be stubborn."

"I don't doubt that."

They rose to their feet and, arm in arm, headed for Harper's General Store. "A shopkeeper," she said.

"For now," Declan answered. "As soon as this place is running well and making money, I might buy the saloon. It's a disgrace."

She was not surprised. "The saloon."

"And this town needs proper lodging for visitors. That boardinghouse is not sufficient, and the hotel is in worse shape than the saloon. When the first two businesses are up and running, I might look into building a decent hotel."

"A hotel."

He led her into the general store. "I might run for mayor, one day," he said absently. "I've always been interested in politics."

"King of Tanglewood," she said, teasing him as he gathered her against him for a kiss.

"Did I ever tell you," he whispered, his lips almost touching hers, "that your grandmother told me I would one day return to Tanglewood and claim everything I wanted, that here I would make all my dreams come true?"

"Did she, now?"

He lifted her so that she dangled before him, lip to lip. "Matilda, my love," he whispered. "That day is today."

Gretchen and Hanson crept into the store. Gretchen

held the red roses they'd left in the street, Hanson held the tin of ginger candies.

"I thought you might want these," Gretchen said sheepishly as Declan placed Matilda on her feet.

"And these," Hanson said, offering the tin of candy, then looking down to study it carefully. And hungrily. "Though I imagine you have more than enough candy," he said, his fingers just beginning to close over the tin.

Matilda reached down and took the flowers and the tin. The flowers, the most beautiful roses she had ever seen, she held against her chest. The tin she slipped into Declan's pocket.

"Just in case," she said with a wide smile as he raised questioning eyebrows at her. "Just in case."

Cinderfella

Linda Jones

The daughter of a Kansas cattle tycoon, Charmaine Haley is given a royal welcome on her return from Boston: a masquerade. But the spirited beauty is aware of her father's matchmaking schemes, and she feels sure there will be no shoe-ins for her affection. At the dance, Charmaine is swept off her feet by a masked stranger, but suddenly she finds herself in a compromising position that has her father on a manhunt with a shotgun and the only clue the stranger left— one black boot.

___52275-6 $5.99 US/$6.99 CAN

Dorchester Publishing Co., Inc.
P.O. Box 6640
Wayne, PA 19087-8640

Please add $1.75 for shipping and handling for the first book and $.50 for each book thereafter. NY, NYC, and PA residents, please add appropriate sales tax. No cash, stamps, or C.O.D.s. All orders shipped within 6 weeks via postal service book rate. Canadian orders require $2.00 extra postage and must be paid in U.S. dollars through a U.S. banking facility.

Name_____
Address_____
City_____ State_____ Zip_____
I have enclosed $_____ in payment for the checked book(s).
Payment <u>must</u> accompany all orders. ❏ Please send a free catalog.
     CHECK OUT OUR WEBSITE! www.dorchesterpub.com

Jackie & The Giant

LINDA JONES

It isn't a castle, but Cloudmont is close: The enormous estate houses everything Jacqueline Beresford needs to quit her life of crime. But climbing up to the window, Jackie gets a shock. The gorgeous giant of an owner is awake—and he is a greater treasure than she ever imagined. It hardly surprises Rory Donovan that the beautiful burglar is not what she claims, but capturing the feisty felon offers an excellent opportunity. He was searching for a governess for his son, and against all logic, he feels Jackie is perfect for the role—and for many others. But he knows that she broke into his home to rob him of his wealth—for what reason did she steal his heart?

____52333-7 $5.99 US/$6.99 CAN

Dorchester Publishing Co., Inc.
P.O. Box 6640
Wayne, PA 19087-8640

Please add $1.75 for shipping and handling for the first book and $.50 for each book thereafter. NY, NYC, and PA residents, please add appropriate sales tax. No cash, stamps, or C.O.D.s. All orders shipped within 6 weeks via postal service book rate. Canadian orders require $2.00 extra postage and must be paid in U.S. dollars through a U.S. banking facility.

Name_____
Address_____
City_____State_____Zip_____
I have enclosed $_____ in payment for the checked book(s).
Payment <u>must</u> accompany all orders. ❑ Please send a free catalog.
CHECK OUT OUR WEBSITE! www.dorchesterpub.com

One Day, My Prince

Linda Jones

Joe White is the most dangerous and best-looking gun-fighter in town, which makes him powerful enemies who bushwhack him and leave him for dead.

But Joe is saved. And though his woes dwarf those of his rescuers, the answer to their problems mirror the solution to his own. The seven newly orphaned Shorter sisters are in danger of being separated, and only a prissy schoolmarm named Sarah Prince can save them. And while the Shorters know that the bewitching Sarah is just what the wounded marshal is looking for, *he* doesn't know it yet. Miss Prince's kiss will open Joe's eyes to love—and one taste of forbidden fruit will keep them open forever.

___52388-4 $5.99 US/$6.99 CAN

The Wild Swans

KATE HOLMES

King Richard has had it with frivolous females filling his ears with their foolishness. Yet for all his castles and dragon-slaying, he still needs a wife. Preferably one who won't plague him with womanly whining. One who knows when to shut up. So why not lay claim to the sweetly saucy—and utterly silent—wench he encounters in an enchanted forest?

Princess Arianne has had it with meddling males making her life miserable. When her twelve brothers anger an ogre, *she* is the one stuck spinning nettles into shirts to save them from eternal servitude as swans. And she has to complete the task in total silence! To make matters worse, along comes chatty King Richard, wanting to bed her, wanting to wed her. Rugged Richard makes her virginal knees weak. But could even a king know a woman's mind—without her speaking it?

___52383-3 $5.99 US/$6.99 CAN

Dorchester Publishing Co., Inc.
P.O. Box 6640
Wayne, PA 19087-8640

Please add $1.75 for shipping and handling for the first book and $.50 for each book thereafter. NY, NYC, and PA residents, please add appropriate sales tax. No cash, stamps, or C.O.D.s. All orders shipped within 6 weeks via postal service book rate. Canadian orders require $2.00 extra postage and must be paid in U.S. dollars through a U.S. banking facility.

Name_____
Address_____
City_____ State_____ Zip_____
I have enclosed $ _____ in payment for the checked book(s).
Payment <u>must</u> accompany all orders. ❑ Please send a free catalog.

The Snow Queen

ANNE AVERY

When Boston-bred Hetty Malone arrives at the Colorado Springs train station, she is full of hope that she will soon marry her childhood sweetheart and live happily ever after. Yet life amid the ice-capped Rockies has changed Michael Ryan. No longer the hot-blooded suitor Hetty remembers, the young doctor has grown as cold and distant as the snowy mountain peaks. Determined to revive Michael's passionate longing, Hetty quickly realizes that no modern medicine can cure what ails him. But in the enchanted splendor of her new home, she dares to administer the only remedy that might melt his frozen heart: a dose of good old-fashioned loving.

_52151-2 $5.99 US/$6.99 CAN

THE FOREVER BRIDE **Evelyn Rogers**

"Evelyn Rogers delivers great entertainment!"
—*Romantic Times*

It is only a fairy tale, but to Megan Butler *The Forever Bride* is the most beautiful story she's ever read. That is why she insists on going to Scotland to get married in the very church where the heroine of the legend was wed to her true love. The violet-eyed advertising executive never expects the words of the story to transport her over two hundred years into the past, exchanging vows not with her fiancé, but with strapping Robert Cameron, laird of Thistledown Castle. After convincing Robert that she is not the unknown woman he's been contracted to marry, Meagan sets off with the charming brute in search of the real bride and her dowry. But the longer they pursue the elusive girl, the less Meagan wants to find her. For with the slightest touch Robert awakens her deepest desires, and she discovers the true meaning of passion. But is it all a passing fancy—or has she truly become the forever bride?

_4177-4 $5.50 US/$6.50 CAN

The Seduction of Roxanne
Linda Jones

Roxanne Robinette has decided to marry, and Calvin Newberry—the sheriff's new deputy—has a face to die for. True, he isn't the sheriff: It was Cyrus Bergeron whose nose for justice and lightning-fast draw earned the tin star after he returned from the War Between the States, a conflict that scarred more than just the country. Still, with his quick wit and his smoldering eyes, Cyrus seems an unfair comparison. And it is Calvin who writes the letters she receives, isn't it? Those passion-filled missives leave her aching with desire long into the torrid Texas nights. Whoever penned those notes seduces her as thoroughly as with a kiss, and it is to that man she'll give her heart.

___52357-4 $5.99 US/$6.99 CAN

Dorchester Publishing Co., Inc.
P.O. Box 6640
Wayne, PA 19087-8640

Please add $1.75 for shipping and handling for the first book and $.50 for each book thereafter. NY, NYC, and PA residents, please add appropriate sales tax. No cash, stamps, or C.O.D.s. All orders shipped within 6 weeks via postal service book rate. Canadian orders require $2.00 extra postage and must be paid in U.S. dollars through a U.S. banking facility.

Name_____
Address_____
City_____ State_____ Zip_____
I have enclosed $_____ in payment for the checked book(s).
Payment <u>must</u> accompany all orders. ❏ Please send a free catalog.
      CHECK OUT OUR WEBSITE! www.dorchesterpub.com

The Indigo Blade

Linda Jones

Penelope Seton has heard the stories of the Indigo Blade, so when an ex-suitor asks her to help betray and capture the infamous rogue, she has to admit that she is intrigued. Her new husband, Maximillian Broderick, is handsome and rich, but the man who once made her blood race has become an apathetic popinjay after the wedding. Still, something lurks behind Max's languid smile, and she swears she sees glimpses of the passionate husband he seemed to be. Soon Penelope is involved in a game that threatens to claim her husband, her head, and her heart. But she finds herself wondering, if her love is to be the prize, who will win it—her husband or the Indigo Blade.

Linda Jones
On A Wicked Wind

Hurled into the Caribbean and swept back in time, Sabrina Steele finds herself abruptly aroused in the arms of the dashing pirate captain Antonio Rafael de Zamora. There, on his tropical island, Rafael teaches her to crest the waves of passion and sail the seas of ecstasy. But the handsome rogue has a tortured past, and in order to consummate a love that called her through time, the headstrong beauty seeks to uncover the pirate's true buried treasure—his heart.

___52251-9 $5.99 US/$6.99 CAN

Dorchester Publishing Co., Inc.
P.O. Box 6640
Wayne, PA 19087-8640

Please add $1.75 for shipping and handling for the first book and $.50 for each book thereafter. NY, NYC, and PA residents, please add appropriate sales tax. No cash, stamps, or C.O.D.s. All orders shipped within 6 weeks via postal service book rate. Canadian orders require $2.00 extra postage and must be paid in U.S. dollars through a U.S. banking facility.

Name_____
Address_____
City_____State_____Zip_____
I have enclosed $_____ in payment for the checked book(s).
Payment <u>must</u> accompany all orders. ❑ Please send a free catalog.